BOOK SOLD
NO LO   ER R.H.P.L.
PROPERTY

Self-Determined Stories

AMERICAN INDIAN STUDIES SERIES
Gordon Henry, *Series Editor*

EDITORIAL BOARD

Jill Doerfler   P. Jane Hafen   Margaret Noodin
Heid E. Erdrich   Matthew L. M. Fletcher   Kyle Powys Whyte

Bawaajimo: A Dialect of Dreams in Anishinaabe Language and Literature, Margaret Noodin | 978-1-61186-105-1

Centering Anishinaabeg Studies: Understanding the World through Stories, edited by Jill Doerfler, Niigaanwewidam James Sinclair, and Heidi Kiiwetinepinesiik Stark | 978-1-61186-067-2

Curator of Ephemera at the New Museum for Archaic Media, Heid E. Erdrich | 978-1-61186-246-1

Document of Expectations, Devon Abbott Mihesuah | 978-1-61186-011-5

Dragonfly Dance, Denise K. Lajimodiere | 978-0-87013-982-6

Facing the Future: The Indian Child Welfare Act at 30, edited by Matthew L. M. Fletcher, Wenona T. Singel, and Kathryn E. Fort | 978-0-87013-860-7

Follow the Blackbirds, Gwen Nell Westerman | 978-1-61186-092-4

Gambling on Authenticity: Gaming, the Noble Savage, and the Not-So-New Indian, edited by Becca Gercken and Julie Pelletier | 978-1-61186-256-0

Indian Country: Telling a Story in a Digital Age, Victoria L. LaPoe and Benjamin Rex LaPoe II | 978-1-61186-226-3

The Indian Who Bombed Berlin and Other Stories, Ralph Salisbury | 978-0-87013-847-8

Masculindians: Conversations about Indigenous Manhood, edited by Sam McKegney | 978-1-61186-129-7

Mediating Indianness, edited by Cathy Covell Waegner | 978-1-61186-151-8

The Murder of Joe White: Ojibwe Leadership and Colonialism in Wisconsin, Erik M. Redix | 978-1-61186-145-7

National Monuments, Heid E. Erdrich | 978-0-87013-848-5

Ogimawkwe Mitigwaki (Queen of the Woods), Simon Pokagon | 978-0-87013-987-1

Ottawa Stories from the Springs: Anishinaabe dibaadjimowinan wodi gaa binjibaamigak wodi mookodjiwong e zhinikaadek, translated and edited by Howard Webkamigad | 978-1-61186-137-2

Plain of Jars and Other Stories, Geary Hobson | 978-0-87013-998-7

Redoubted, R. Vincent Moniz, Jr. | 978-1-61186-282-9

Sacred Wilderness, Susan Power | 978-1-61186-111-2

Seeing Red—Hollywood's Pixeled Skins: American Indians and Film, edited by LeAnne Howe, Harvey Markowitz, and Denise K. Cummings | 978-1-61186-081-8

Self-Determined Stories: The Indigenous Reinvention of Young Adult Literature, Mandy Suhr-Sytsma | 978-1-61186-298-0

Shedding Skins: Four Sioux Poets, edited by Adrian C. Louis | 978-0-87013-823-2

Sounding Thunder: The Stories of Francis Pegahmagabow, Brian D. McInnes | 978-1-61186-225-6

Stories for a Lost Child, Carter Meland | 978-1-61186-244-7

Stories through Theories/Theories through Stories: North American Indian Writing, Storytelling, and Critique, edited by Gordon D. Henry Jr., Nieves Pascual Soler, and Silvia Martinez-Falquina | 978-0-87013-841-6

That Guy Wolf Dancing, Elizabeth Cook-Lynn | 978-1-61186-138-9

Those Who Belong: Identity, Family, Blood, and Citizenship among the White Earth Anishinaabeg, Jill Doerfler | 978-1-61186-169-3

Visualities: Perspectives on Contemporary American Indian Film and Art, edited by Denise K. Cummings | 978-0-87013-999-4

Writing Home: Indigenous Narratives of Resistance, Michael D. Wilson | 978-0-87013-818-8

Self-Determined Stories: The Indigenous Reinvention of Young Adult Literature

Mandy Suhr-Sytsma

Michigan State University Press | *East Lansing*

Copyright © 2019 by Mandy Suhr-Sytsma

♾ The paper used in this publication meets the minimum requirements of ANSI/NISO Z39.48-1992 (R 1997) (Permanence of Paper).

Michigan State University Press
East Lansing, Michigan 48823-5245

Printed and bound in the United States of America.

28 27 26 25 24 23 22 21 20 19   1 2 3 4 5 6 7 8 9 10

LIBRARY OF CONGRESS CATALOGING-IN-PUBLICATION DATA
Names: Suhr-Sytsma, Mandy, author.
Title: Self-determined stories: the indigenous reinvention of young adult literature / Mandy Suhr-Sytsma.
Other titles: American Indian studies series.
Description: East Lansing : Michigan State University Press, [2018]
| Series: American indian studies series | Includes bibliographical references.
Identifiers: LCCN 2017055651 | ISBN 9781611862980 (pbk. : alk. paper)
| ISBN 9781609175788 (pdf) | ISBN 9781628953428 (epub) | ISBN 9781628963427 (kindle)
Subjects: LCSH: American literature—Indian authors—History and criticism.
| Canadian literature—Indian authors—History and criticism.
| Young adult literature, American—History and criticism.
| Young adult literature, Canadian—History and criticism. | Indians in literature.
Classification: LCC PS153.I52 S84 2018 | DDC 810.9/897—dc23
LC record available at https://lccn.loc.gov/2017055651

Book design by Charlie Sharp, Sharp Des!gns, East Lansing, Michigan
Cover design by Erin Kirk New
Cover art is *Waabananang* ©2014 by Elizabeth LaPensée
(www.elizabethlapensee.com) and is used courtesy of the artist. All rights reserved.

Michigan State University Press is a member of the Green Press Initiative and is committed to developing and encouraging ecologically responsible publishing practices. For more information about the Green Press Initiative and the use of recycled paper in book publishing, please visit *www.greenpressinitiative.org*.

Visit Michigan State University Press at *www.msupress.org*

RICHMOND HILL PUBLIC LIBRARY
32972001229055 RG
Self-determined stories : the Indigenous
Dec. 05, 2018

Dedicated in loving memory to
Shirley Jeanne McQueen (1954–2016).
You always liked a good story, Mom.

Contents

Acknowledgments

Thanks are due first to the Creator, and then to my University of Connecticut (UConn) advisor Robert (Bob) Tilton and Julie Loehr at MSU Press. Bob shepherded the initial research out of which this book grew; I am deeply grateful for his guidance and enduring faith in the project and in me. Julie convinced me that MSU was the right place for the book. It is a better book thanks to the hours she spent advising me in writing, over the phone, and at one of my favorite places: her conference book table.

At UConn Kate Capshaw, Cathy Schlund-Vials, and Theodore Van Alst provided smart guidance. Tom Deans and Barb Gurr never failed to support and inspire. Countless other UConn faculty mentors, administrators, graduate student peers, and undergrads in my courses helped shape the scholar I am today. Down in New Haven, my conversations with Alyssa Mt. Pleasant and the Yale Group for the Study of Native America impacted my work in ways that still reverberate.

I developed this book amidst a nurturing community of colleagues and students at Emory University. I am particularly grateful for professional and personal support from Deepika Bahri, Michael Elliott, Dave Fisher, Alexis Hackney, Walter Kalaidjian, Dawn Peterson, Ben Reiss, Pamela Scully, Joonna Trapp, and Craig Womack. Allison Adams at the Emory Center for Faculty Development and Excellence (CFDE) organized two writing groups that provided a room, a timer, and camaraderie conducive to turning out pages even at the busiest times of year. Allison also facilitated the CFDE Scholarly Writing and Publishing Fund grant that enabled me to hire an experienced editor to assist with book revisions. That editor, Katie Van Heest, chipped away the clutter, clarifying the heart of this project for me and for my readers.

I thank Gordon Henry for taking me on as an author in this series and for his supportive presence at the Native American Literature Symposium (NALS) over the many years I have been participating. That symposium has drawn me into a community that I cherish for its deep generosity as much as for its intellectual and ethical rigor. I will not attempt to list here the many NALS folks whose insights have contributed to this work, but I am deeply thankful to them and to Gwen Westerman for her tireless commitment to NALS and to all of us there.

I owe much to two anonymous readers of the book manuscript whose thorough comments informed my revision at the global and local level. Feedback from Chadwick Allen and two reviewers of my *Studies in American Indian Literatures* article drawn from the book also assisted my development of the project as a whole. Steven Moore adeptly assembled the book's index. The indexing was supported by a subvention grant from Emory College and the Laney Graduate School of Emory University. Bonnie Cobb's smart copyediting brought another level of polish to the prose. The wonderful team at MSU Press, including Julie Loehr, Kristine Blakeslee, Anastasia Wraight, Julie K. Reaume, Elise Jajuga, Annette Tanner, and Terika Hernandez expertly and efficiently carried the book through to production. The remaining limitations are all mine.

My high school English teacher, Cheryl Frarck, inspired me to write and to study literature; I am forever grateful that, thanks to the syllabus for her "Great Books" class, I entered academia thinking "great books" meant books that are great, including Maya Angelou's *I Know Why the Caged Bird Sings*. I still think that. I would not have embarked on this adventure were it not for the professors at Calvin College who introduced me to Native American literature and encouraged me to pursue graduate school. I am especially grateful to Brian Ingraffia, Linda Naranjo-Huebl, Gary Schmidt, Elizabeth Vander Lei, and the late William Vande Kopple.

From Calvin, through our days together at UConn, to the present, Zara Rix has been a faithful friend and the first person I turn to when I want smart advice about children's literature scholarship, writing, and life. Other friends who have kept me afloat with their encouragement, wisdom, and good humor include Levin Arnsperger, Rachel Birr, Miriam Brown Spiers, David Carlson, Ben Clary, Heather Gapanovich, Chris and Sarah Pallas, Christine and Jonathan Potter, Emily Mathes, Michelle Miles, Bambi and Matt Mroz, Margaret Noodin, Sarah Rasher, Carl and Jamie Schwendinger-Schreck, Caroline Schwenz, Patti Taylor, Martha Viehmann, and Melissa Tantaquidgeon Zobel. This book and I also owe a big debt to the preschool teachers at the First Baptist Church of Decatur, and the baristas at ChocoLaté Coffee.

I could not ask for a more supportive family. My dad, Jerry Suhr, taught me how to work hard, love hard, and laugh hard. The women who mothered me—my mother Shirley McQueen, my other mother Suecarol Schuler, and my grandmother Evelyn Suhr—have all inspired me through their love of reading, hearing, and telling stories. My in-laws, Deb and Jim Sytsma, are always eager to hear about my work, and Deb keeps me grounded with the insights and questions she draws from her daily experience working with Indigenous young people and their families. As I became a mother and lost my mother in the course of writing this book, I couldn't have made it through without my superhuman sisters MaryBeth Espinoza and Stacy Suhr. For feeding me with kindness, company, and lots of actual food, too, as I worked on this project, I am deeply grateful to all of my siblings, cousins, aunts, uncles, grandparents, nieces, and nephews.

My children, Rowan and Rosalind, have provided some lovely perspective. To read with them is pure delight, and their laughter is the best medicine on earth. My final and fullest thank you is for my husband, Nathan. I didn't know how deeply joyful life could be until he came along. I hope some of that joy comes across in these pages. I couldn't have done it without you, love.

———————————

An earlier version of some material from the book's introduction and first chapter appeared in *Studies in American Indian Literatures* 28.4 (2016): 25-52. Reprinted with permission from University of Nebraska Press.

The figure in chapter 2 is from *The Absolutely True Diary of a Part-Time Indian* by Sherman Alexie with art by Ellen Forney. Copyright © 2007 by Sherman Alexie. Used by permission of Little Brown Books for Young Readers.

Introduction

In November 2007, Sherman Alexie (Spokane/Coeur d'Alene) won the National Book Award for Young People's Literature with his novel *The Absolutely True Diary of a Part-Time Indian*. Alexie opened his acceptance speech by describing the importance in his childhood of Ezra Jack Keats's book *The Snowy Day*. Encountering the boy in *The Snowy Day*, "a black boy, a brown boy, a beige boy [was] the first time I ever looked at a book where somebody resembled me," he said. He went on to explain that he did not encounter any literature by Native American writers until he was in college. Having long faulted himself and other Indigenous authors for not reaching more young Indigenous readers, Alexie described the positive response to his YA title from young readers who identify with the text.[1]

The We Need Diverse Books movement of recent years has similarly emphasized the value of young people being able to see themselves in the books they read, and the resultant need for more children's and young adult literature depicting the lives of Indigenous people and people of color. Beginning as a Twitter campaign in 2014, We Need Diverse Books is now an established nonprofit that promotes literature by and about marginalized populations, supports authors, and advocates for changes in the publishing industry, while continuing to raise awareness about the large gap in the United States between demographics and representation in children's books.

While Alexie and those in the We Need Diverse Books movement are right to decry the underrepresentation of Indigenous people and other marginalized populations in children's and young adult literature, the emphasis on what is missing may obscure the reality of the small but significant body of Indigenous-authored young adult (YA) texts to which Alexie's high-profile *True Diary* belongs. For more than thirty years, starting with Jeannette Armstrong's 1985 *Slash* and continuing through and beyond Melissa Tantaquidgeon Zobel's 2015 *Wabanaki Blues*, Indigenous YA writings have been impacting young readers, remapping critical conversations in and beyond Indigenous studies, and reinventing young adult literature as we know it.[2]

YA has become an increasingly formidable literary scene in recent years, with a steady string of blockbusters proving that today's youth remain a hot market segment in the publishing world. The American Library Association (ALA) defines adolescent literature as encompassing three categories that Sheila Schwartz summarizes as "Books Written Specifically for Adolescents," "Books Written for General Trade Market Which Have Adolescent Heroes and Heroines," and "General Books of Interest to Young Adults" (Schwartz qtd. in Trites, *Disturbing* 7). While recognizing that other scholars use the YA label, often depicted as a subset of the broader category of children's literature, for texts that match any of the ALA's criteria for adolescent literature, Roberta Trites, a leading scholar in the field, limits the young adult literature designation to texts specifically targeting adolescents (*Disturbing* 7; "Theories and Possibilities" 2–3). Literary historians mark the emergence of YA literature as a distinctive genre in the mid-twentieth century: in 1942 with the publication of *Seventeenth Summer*, in 1951 with *The Catcher in the Rye*, or in 1967 with *The Outsiders* (Trites, *Disturbing* 9). The YA genre has been dominated since its inception by fiction, especially novels.

More recent YA titles, like the Harry Potter series and the Twilight Saga, have actually held appeal far beyond the youth market, but they have only doubled down on established YA thematics and plot progressions. Notwithstanding the market-driven, slippery nature of the YA label and the diversity of books encompassed by it, YA texts from the mid-twentieth century to the present largely conform to a set of common conventions. Narrated by or heavily focalized through an individual adolescent protagonist, these works depict adolescence as a fluid, potential-rich, and rebellious stage that young people begin to move out of as they come of age and come to terms with the social institutions that shape their worlds.

Considering the broadest definition of young adult literature as texts that capture the interests of young people, we would be hard pressed to identify a starting point for Indigenous YA. After all, Indigenous teens have been listening to stories and engaging written texts (texts like wampum belts, petroglyphs, and birchbark scrolls along with alphabetic texts) for as long as those stories and texts have been around. Moving into the early twentieth century—the period when the concept of "adolescence" took root in the literary, psychological, and popular imagination—Indian boarding-school narratives by the likes of Zitkala-Ša, Charles Alexander (Ohiyesa) Eastman, and Luther Standing Bear were usually directed at child or adult audiences, but also held appeal for teen readers. Teens also have been drawn to mid-century novels like Natachee Scott Momaday's *Owl in the Cedar Tree* (1965), D'Arcy McNickle's *Runner in the Sun* (1954), and Virginia Driving Hawk Sneve's *When Thunders Spoke* (1974) that were primarily geared toward a slightly younger readership. In the 1970s and early 1980s, many works of the Native American Renaissance in the United States and the parallel phenomenon in Canada featured adolescent experiences and would have appeal for teen readers, especially older teens, despite their being directed primarily at an adult audience. Some of those texts include Maria Campbell's *Halfbreed* (1973), James Welch's *Winter in the Blood* (1974), Janet Campbell Hale's *The Owl's Song* (1974), Leslie Marmon Silko's *Ceremony* (1977), and Beatrice Culleton Mosionier's *In Search of April Raintree* (1983). In addition to these and many other examples of widely circulated literary texts with appeal to adolescent readers, young people across Indian country have also encountered locally produced texts—radio programs, educational materials, theatrical performances, and so forth—made especially for their benefit.

Although the mainstream YA novel had solidified as a genre by the 1970s, Okanagan author Jeannette Armstrong's 1985 Red Power–movement novel *Slash* was the first novel by an American Indian or Canadian Aboriginal author written expressly for a teen readership and thereby falling under the narrow definition of YA literature. *Slash* was followed by several titles in the 1990s and early 2000s that engaged YA conventions while resting on either the middle-grade YA or adult YA line. Cynthia Leitich Smith's *Rain Is Not My Indian Name* (2001) and several titles by Joseph Bruchac, including *The Heart of a Chief* (1998) and

Skeleton Man (2000), are examples of the former. Some of the many titles in the latter category include Lee Maracle's *Ravensong* (1993), Linda Hogan's *Solar Storms* (1995), Richard Van Camp's *The Lesser Blessed* (1996), Thomas King's *Truth and Bright Water* (1999), and Eden Robinson's *Monkey Beach* (2000). We continue to see numerous middle-grade texts, like Louise Erdrich's Birchbark House series (1999–2016), Tim Tingle's *How I Became a Ghost* (2015), and Joseph Marshall III's *In the Footsteps of Crazy Horse* (2015), and adult texts, like Erdrich's *The Round House* (2012) and Erika Wurth's *Crazy Horse's Girlfriend* (2014) that carry crossover appeal for adolescent readers. At the same time, since the 2007 publication of Alexie's *True Diary*, we have also seen a burst of solidly YA titles, including, in Canada, Drew Hayden Taylor's *The Night Wanderer: A Native Gothic Novel* (2007), David Alexander Robertson and Scott B. Henderson's four-part graphic novel *7 Generations: A Plains Cree Saga* (2012), and Cherie Dimaline's *The Marrow Thieves* (2017), and, in the United States, Eric Gansworth's *If I Ever Get Out of Here* (2013), Joseph Bruchac's *Killer of Enemies* (2013), and Melissa Tantaquidgeon Zobel's *Wabanaki Blues* (2015).

When *Slash* appeared in 1985, the generic conventions of YA literature had been well established, including conventions regarding individual-community power dynamics. Roberta Trites convincingly argues that despite their consistent attention to maturation—influenced by the bildungsroman tradition—YA novels stand apart from both adult's and children's texts through their emphasis on power negotiations between individuals and social institutions, even more so than through their focus on adolescent growth (*Disturbing* 20). Trites and other scholars of young adult literature characterize the genre as typically representing as well as enacting a power dynamic by which young individuals are repressed by the institutions of their societies. While YA texts are known for their depiction of rebellious teenagers, they generally end with the halting or at least tempering of these characters' rebellion. "Adolescents do not achieve maturity in a YA novel," Trites explains, "until they have reconciled themselves to the power entailed in the social institutions with which they must interact to survive" (*Disturbing* 20).

Scholars of young adult literature maintain, moreover, that most YA texts depict adolescent protagonists as experiencing repression and the loss of individual agency as a result of that reconciliation (*Disturbing* 7–8, 34, 52; McCallum 71). In the more optimistic of these narratives, Trites explains, protagonists feel satisfied about reconciling themselves with their societies because of their hope that the societies will improve thanks to their own models of self-improvement (*Twain, Alcott* 143–44). In the less optimistic texts, protagonists become disillusioned about their ability to challenge the inevitable power of their societies' institutions, so they grudgingly or cynically accept that power and their place in society (*Disturbing* 16–20). In her book *Death, Gender, and Sexuality in Contemporary Adolescent Literature*, Kathryn James joins Trites in arguing that even those YA texts that most strongly resist dominant social norms typically end up simultaneously reinforcing them (James 73–111). While some scholars, such as Clare Bradford and Bonnie TuSmith, have acknowledged that Indigenous YA texts, along with African American and Latino/a YA texts, differ from mainstream texts in positively representing protagonists' coming of age as a communal experience, we have not yet seen this phenomenon fully theorized in general, nor in relation to the power dynamics of young adult literature.

YA literary studies scholars have attended not only to the power dynamics represented in YA texts but also to those operating in the relationship between young readers and the adults who produce and disseminate the texts. Like the power dynamics represented in YA literature, scholars generally characterize these dynamics as repressive, asserting that adult authors frequently use their narrative power to manipulate young readers into subject positions deemed appropriate by the authors and their societies (*Disturbing* 69–83; James 73–111; Cadden 146). In his seminal article "The Irony of Narration in the Young Adult Novel," Mike Cadden argues that adult authors frequently use their narrative position to disguise, manipulate, and abuse their authority over young readers (Cadden 146). Pretending, via their narration, that they are just like the teens reading their books, adult authors mask the age-based power hierarchy inevitably at play in their work. Moreover, other adults in positions of power—such as publishers, educators, librarians, and members of the media—often further repress young readers by packaging YA texts with proscribed interpretive frameworks that limit readers' agency.

Indigenous-authored young adult fiction of the last three decades significantly revises the conventions described above. While Indigenous YA texts, from *Slash* (1985) to *Wabanaki Blues* (2015), do tend to be strongly focalized through individual young Native protagonists who mature as they move from rebellion against, to reconciliation with their Indigenous communities, these protagonists experience an increase rather than a decrease in personal agency as a result of that reconciliation. Furthermore, their rebellion against colonial ideologies does not diminish but instead intensifies as the narratives draw to a close. The strong yet self-reflective narrative voices framing these protagonists' experiences prod young readers to bring their agency to this rebellion as well. In short, YA books are centrally concerned with young people finding their place vis-à-vis "the system." That both resonates and strikes a discordant note when Indigenous subjects are involved, because they are operating in multiple systems—their Indigenous societies and the colonial systems imposed on those societies—and because sovereignty (self-possession) is a *communal* issue for Native peoples in the Americas. Indigenous young adult texts are thus uniquely positioned to test the generic bounds of YA literature and the dominant discourses that the genre reinscribes.

The Red Power movements of the 1960s and 1970s correspond historically with the rise of young adult literature as a distinctive genre, and, like the YA conventions established in this period, the articulations of Native sovereignty from this era continue to reverberate. Galvanized by a myriad of local leaders along with widely known activists, like American Indian Movement (AIM) activists at the Wounded Knee occupation, and intellectual leaders, like Vine Deloria Jr., Indigenous people in Canada and the United States rallied to restore their sovereignty after a century of federal policies predominantly designed to diminish it. These policies included allotment, Indian agent oversight, the pass system, boarding/residential schools, relocation, termination, sterilization, and the "rounding up" of Native children to be adopted out of Native communities. Red Power activists believed in the inherent sovereignty of Indigenous people, but most also conceded that the United States and Canadian governments were not going away, at least not any time soon. Their sovereignty struggle therefore inhabited what Kevin Bruyneel calls a "third space" distinct from both the third world independence movements and the civil rights struggles of the period. Leaders in AIM and other Red Power groups wanted to restore sovereignty in two major ways. First, they wanted colonial governments to respect Native people as equal sovereign nations, reestablishing the treaty-making relationship ended in the United States in 1871 and in Canada in 1921, and returning resources of land, money, education, and governance that had been lost via broken treaties and other colonial practices. Second, they wanted to revive their own sense of inherent sovereignty that had been diminished by colonialist policies and internalized colonialism alike.[3]

In the decades following the Red Power movements, Indigenous communities across Canada and the United States saw a surge in Indigenous pride along with a limited but still significant body of federal legislation in support of Indigenous sovereignty. At the same time, as leaders of the Idle No More movement in Canada, the opposition to the Dakota Access Pipeline in the United States, and hundreds of lower-profile efforts starkly illustrate, the vision for Indigenous sovereignty articulated by leaders of the Red Power movements is far from fully realized. Indigenous communities continue to experience sovereignty as both a lived reality and something for which they must struggle. The realities and the struggles, moreover, are not just about sovereignty in the crucial but narrow legal/political terms set by colonial nation-states. Indigenous intellectuals and activists from Vine Deloria Jr. and Scott Richard Lyons to Niigaanwewidam Sinclair and Tokata Iron Eyes have indigenized sovereignty such that most Indigenous people understand it as being about their robust, holistic self-determination in every realm. Despite the broad adoption of this perspective, people across and within Indigenous nations, of course, have differing and at times clashing perspectives on how to exercise such sovereignty, perspectives influenced by a range of factors including national citizenship(s), clan membership(s), religious affiliation(s), political affiliation(s), recognition status, social class, and personal opinion.[4]

Overlapping histories of intertribal activism go along with overlapping literary traditions in the United States and Canada. I limit this study to texts by American Indian and Canadian Aboriginal writers because of the deep parallels in the Indian policies of the United States and Canadian governments, the related convergences in anti-colonial Indigenous resistance in both countries, and the simple fact that many Native communities—including those of the Okanagan and Anishinaabe authors I engage in this volume—inhabit both sides of the U.S./Canada border. This book focuses primarily on texts that fall under the narrow definition of YA literature as works written specifically for an adolescent (twelve- to eighteen-year-old) readership and exclusively on texts written since the mid-1980s that depict contemporary Native characters.[5]

Even though the YA texts featured in this book rarely use the word *sovereignty*, they all provocatively address the question of what sovereignty, holistically understood, can look like in the recent thirty-year period they represent and in the futures they suggest. While Armstrong's *Slash* explicitly tackles debates over the shape of Indigenous political self-determination in the immediate aftermath of Red

Power, the other texts in the study freshly imagine paths for Native sovereignty in a vast range of arenas, including culture, religion, education, economics, media, the arts, individuals' bodies, and personal relationships. As they foreground Native sovereignty, scholars in the Indigenous literary nationalism school have largely moved away from the focus on personal identity that had previously dominated the field of Native literary studies. As Indigenous YA texts render individuals' growth as more communal than most other YA texts do, they also reveal that concerns related to communal sovereignty are often actually intertwined with issues of personal identity. These texts thus prod us to return to questions of personal identity, but in ways that are intricately connected to, rather than severed from, political concerns.

While sovereignty may be the most important discourse for Native nations and Native studies over the last thirty years, it is not the only important discourse of this period for which Indigenous young adult literature offers an intervention. In the 1985–2015 timeframe of this study, neoliberal multiculturalism achieved widespread acceptance as the dominant discourse for managing diversity in the United States and Canada. In celebrating "cultural" differences while largely ignoring ongoing racism and colonialism, multiculturalism fails to acknowledge another influential discourse of this period: colonialist heteropatriarchy. In the late twentieth and early twenty-first centuries, violence against Indigenous women in the United States and Canada continued at a rate unparalleled by any other demographic, an unsettling reality that cannot be disentangled from the still deeply entrenched discourse of colonialist heteropatriarchy, over hundreds of years, that sexualizes and degrades Native women's bodies along with their lands. Literary criticism of the last thirty years, meanwhile, has seen hybridity develop as one of the most influential discourses in postcolonial studies, and in opposition to that discourse—or at least a certain strand of it—the subsequent rise of Indigenous literary nationalism, an approach that calls for nation-centered criticism that draws on and supports the cultures, intellectual traditions, and sovereignty of specific Native communities.

Published between 1985 and 2015, the Indigenous YA texts that I examine in this study intervene in the discourses described above as they engage issues related to sovereignty, colonialism, cultural adaptation, appropriation, intersectionality, and cross-cultural alliances. Combating a common misconception of children's and YA literature as being simplistic, accomplished author Madeleine L'Engle says, "You have to write the book that wants to be written. And if the book will be too difficult for grown-ups, then you write it for children." The young adult texts in this study are indeed rich works of literature that address pressing issues in complex ways, sometimes with greater nuance than their adult counterparts. The questions these texts enable us to deeply explore include: How can Indigenous individuals and communities heal from colonial traumas, renew cultural strength, and pursue political empowerment in the contemporary era? What are alternatives to multiculturalism, heteropatriarchy, and hybridity for theorizing diversity and building cross-cultural relationships? And what does young adult literature offer Indigenous writers, and what do Indigenous writers offer young adult literature as they tackle the above questions and more?

This book's foundational first chapter extends this introduction as I use my reading of Jeannette Armstrong's 1985 Red Power–movement novel *Slash* to elaborate on conceptualizations of Native sovereignty as they interact with power dynamics in young adult literature. Because the anti-colonialist rebellion of the novel's protagonist is bolstered via his ultimate reintegration with, and renewed commitment to, his Indigenous community, *Slash* significantly complicates the scholarship on power dynamics in YA literature, which characterizes YA protagonists as experiencing repression when they reconcile with their communities. As a text that simultaneously relays a heavy-handed message and invites questioning, *Slash* also troubles the common notion in YA literary studies that the oppressive meta-power dynamics at play between adult authors and young readers can only be countered via a relativistic multiplicity that disallows the privileging of any one subject position. Positioning *Slash* in relationship to the trend in the last decades of the twentieth century of Indigenous communities holistically pursuing sovereignty by focusing on internal community-building, I argue, moreover, that the novel's revisionary engagement with YA conventions illuminates ways that this approach to sovereignty can be at once uncompromising and dynamic.

Building on the broad theoretical framework that I develop in the first chapter, I focus in each subsequent chapter on a specific subgenre of YA literature. Like *Slash*, the school stories, romance narratives, and speculative texts that I engage here represent Indigenous communities as both strengthening and benefiting from young Indigenous individuals. As they join *Slash* in representing the mutual empowerment of individuals and their communities, these texts also all challenge colonial ideologies that seek to eradicate, assimilate, exoticize, and appropriate Native identities.

In the second chapter of the book, I argue that Sherman Alexie's *The Absolutely True Diary of a Part-Time Indian* (2007, with art by Ellen Forney) and Joseph Bruchac's *The Heart of a Chief* (1998) expand the school-story subgenre by going beyond typical arcs of rebellion and socialization in their representations of sustained resistance to mainstream multiculturalism. They especially challenge the tendencies within much of this discourse to mask white privilege and to portray Indigenous cultures as static—tendencies that, these novels show, contribute to the socioeconomic disenfranchisement and lateral oppression of Native people. Through their representations of avenues for Indigenous cultural dynamism, Alexie's and Bruchac's texts expose multiculturalism as a faulty discourse while also offering alternative approaches to cross-cultural learning.

I turn in the book's third chapter to Cynthia Leitich Smith's short story "A Real-Live Blond Cherokee and His Equally Annoyed Soul Mate" (2005) along with her novel *Rain Is Not My Indian Name* (2001), and Susan Power's short stories "Reunion" (2002) and "Drum Kiss" (2005). Through these narratives, which are actually more about the death of romance than romance itself, Smith and Power rewrite the interracial Indian romance. As they expose and critique the discourse of colonialist heteropatriarchy typically perpetuated in such romances, Smith's and Power's resistive romances explore complexities of intersectionality, internalized colonialism, self-awareness, and alliances. They also open new avenues for considering the importance of representational agency, especially for Indigenous girls and women.

The fourth and final chapter of the book focuses on how Melissa Tantaquidgeon Zobel's *Oracles* (2004) and Drew Hayden Taylor's *The Night Wanderer: A Native Gothic Novel* (2007) shake up the genre of speculative fiction, which has so often thrived on the appropriation of indigeneity, while also opening a provocative intervention in the discourse of hybridity. *Oracles* and *The Night Wanderer* go against the grain of hybridity as they strongly suggest not only that Indigenous individuals *can* pinpoint and privilege specific cultural identities—and the specific locations, relationships, and responsibilities associated with those identities—but also that they *ought* to privilege those specific identities over others. Failing to do so results in dire consequences (like dying or getting turned into a vampire) for the characters in these texts. *Oracles* and *The Night Wanderer* both also allude to tribally specific understandings of cultural dynamism and cross-cultural interaction, thereby opening possibilities for theorizing alternative Indigenous versions of hybridity. These novels thus contribute to the long-running debate in Native literary studies over whether aspects of cosmopolitanism can be reconciled with nationalism as they demonstrate how the cultural malleability often associated with cosmopolitanism can support Indigenous self-determination, but only under certain conditions.

While offering compelling stories along with nuanced generic and theoretical interventions, the Indigenous YA texts that I examine in this volume are not perfect. *Slash* reads as quite patriarchal at times despite Armstrong's stated intent to the contrary ("Jeannette Armstrong" 119). *True Diary* alternately mocks and idealizes queerness. Every text, except *Slash*, disconcertingly follows the "multicultural books" trend of including significant attention to white characters, with those white characters playing a strongly positive role in all but Taylor's novel.[6] None of the texts significantly address the complexities of status, recognition, and membership. And all of the texts at times romanticize Indigenous cultures even as they simultaneously provide extensive critiques of such romanticization.

Given publishing pressures—especially in the United States, where there are no large Indigenous publishing houses and the market for Native audiences is much smaller than in Canada—Native authors make compromises in their attempts to reach a broad readership. In the discussion period that followed his reading at the 2014 Native American Literature Symposium, Eric Gansworth spoke candidly about such negotiations as he worked on his first YA novel *If I Ever Get Out of Here*. He appreciated some of the ways his editor at Scholastic pushed him, noting how he grew as a writer by emphasizing plot and condensing his prose to conform to YA expectations. He was troubled, however, by some of the other compromises he made, including his revision to downplay his young character's relationships with his family members, even though his revision still resulted in a more substantial focus on those relationships than his publisher wanted and than is typical in YA fiction. Gansworth's negotiation with his publisher brings to the fore the complicated terrain that all Indigenous YA writers navigate as they simultaneously participate in and stretch the boundaries of mainstream YA literature.

In the coda of this book, I distill the mainstream YA conventions that the texts in this study deploy and challenge. I also articulate the unique Indigenous YA (anti)conventions that emerge through the study, and I explicitly engage the constraints of those (anti)conventions. Whose stories are *not* told in these texts? Which experiences are foregrounded and which elided? What issues and discourses go unexamined? I offer brief readings of Sherman Alexie's 2007 novel *Flight* and Melissa Tantaquidgeon Zobel's 2015 novel *Wabanaki Blues*, considering how these texts push the boundaries of *Indigenous* YA and thereby give us a glimpse into possible futures for Indigenous young adult literature and our engagement with it.

CHAPTER ONE

A Rebel with a Community, Not Just a Cause

Revising YA Power Dynamics and Uniquely Representing Indigenous Sovereignty in Jeannette Armstrong's *Slash*

An epic coming-of-age story that explicitly explores the meaning of Indigenous self-determination in the Red Power and post–Red Power era, Jeannette Armstrong's 1985 novel *Slash* provides a fruitful starting point for examining ways that Indigenous young adult texts imagine sovereignty and reimagine the possibilities of the YA genre. *Slash* negotiates YA genre expectations and contemporary understandings of Indigenous self-determination in ways that reverberate across much Indigenous YA literature.

Highlighting Armstrong's Canadian context, Craig Womack characterizes *Slash* as "a 'Red Power novel' about the sixties and seventies" and finds it "striking" that no equivalent text emerged in the United States ("Theorizing American Indian Experience" 400–401). *Slash* indeed provides a detailed and, at times, politically ambivalent treatment of Red Power and its aftermath through the lens of its protagonist/narrator, Tommy "Slash" Kelasket. Tommy describes his involvement in Red Power initiatives across Canada and the United States. Having left his Okanagan (Syilx) childhood home for Vancouver as a restless teenager, Tommy begins dealing drugs in the city, leading to a knife fight in a bar that earns him a stint in prison along with his nickname, "Slash." While recovering from the fight, he meets Mardi, a volunteer with the Indian Friendship Center and the Red Patrol who guides his initiation into Red Power. Like the patrols in Minneapolis that fostered the broader American Indian Movement, the Red Patrol in Vancouver monitored police treatment of Indigenous people while helping Indigenous individuals living on the streets. Inspired by Mardi and other activists who, as Mardi puts it, make a "third choice" outside the colonial assimilate-or-get-lost paradigm by pursing Indian pride and empowerment, Tommy participates in the 1972 Trail of Broken Treaties Caravan, which ended with the occupation of the Washington, DC, Bureau of Indian Affairs building, and the 1974 Native Peoples' Caravan across Canada, along with a host of lesser-known protests, occupations, and meetings.

Tommy's personal development parallels historical shifts in sovereignty activism as he moves from a position based in confronting colonial institutions to one based in internal community-building. Having earlier been estranged from his Okanagan community, in the second part of the novel he experiences an intense spiritual, cultural, and relational reintegration. This reintegration, coupled with numerous conversations with other Indigenous individuals, leads Tommy to part ways with some activists, including his own wife, Maeg, who, in the early 1980s, advocated for Aboriginal peoples' inclusion in talks surrounding the formation of Canada's new constitution. Instead, Tommy takes a position of total Indigenous autonomy and seeks to direct attention towards the renewing of his Okanagan community from within.

While I agree with Craig Womack that scholars—especially those based in the United States—ought to give *Slash* greater attention as a groundbreaking movement novel, I contend that the novel's equally groundbreaking young-adult status likewise merits more consideration (Womack, personal conversation). Armstrong created *Slash* as part of the Okanagan Indian Curriculum Project (OICP) for use in British Columbia high school history courses, and has frequently discussed her goal of reaching an adolescent audience with the novel. In an interview with Hartmut Lutz, she describes *Slash* emerging from her and her OICP colleagues' desire for "a tool to use in education" that could "give not just the historical documentation of that time" leading up to and during the Red Power movement, but that could also give readers, especially Indigenous young people, a sense of "what the people were feeling, what they dreamed, and what their pain and joy were during that time" (Armstrong, interview with Lutz 14–15). *Slash* went through ten printings between 1985 and 2008, reaching a large general audience in addition to many high school and college students in both literature and history courses (Armstrong, "Image" 145). Despite the novel's explicit targeting of teen readers and its engagement with YA genre conventions, previous scholarship has failed even to acknowledge *Slash* as a YA text.[1] Virginie Alba, Clare Bradford, Noel Elizabeth Currie, Matthew Green, and Katja Sarkowsky are among those scholars who overlook *Slash*'s youth audience and curricular context. Barbara Hodne and Manina Jones criticize these scholars for ignoring *Slash*'s didactic aims toward its juvenile audience, but even they do not identify *Slash* specifically as young adult literature or discuss it in relation to the genre. Reading *Slash* as a young adult text enables us to appreciate its revisionary engagement with YA conventions, especially those concerning power dynamics, and to examine the impact of that engagement on the novel's portrayal of Indigenous self-determination.

Slash's Revisionary Engagement with the Power Dynamics of YA Literature

Like most YA texts, *Slash* focuses on power dynamics at play between a young protagonist and the social institutions that impact his life. The novel follows one of the most common conventions of YA literature as it traces a character's movement from estrangement to reintegration with his community. *Slash* stands apart, however, through its representation of Tommy as being personally empowered rather than disempowered through his reintegration with his Okanagan community. The novel also dramatically diverges from many other YA works by depicting this reintegration not as marking the end or the taming of rebellion, but rather as invigorating an entire community's rebellion against co-lonialism. In addition to complicating the power dynamics typically represented within YA texts, through an Indigenous narrative voice that is simultaneously self-questioning and strong, fallible and privileged, *Slash* troubles the common understanding in YA literary studies that the oppressive power dynamics at play between authoritative writers and vulnerable readers can only be countered via multiplicity and relativism.

In terms of his Okanagan community, Tommy largely follows the pattern characteristic of YA protagonists as he moves from selfishness, rebellion, and estrangement to responsibility, reconciliation, and reintegration (Trites, *Disturbing* 20). He initially rejects the institutions of his Okanagan community not just by physically moving away but also by engaging in activities that disregard

Okanagan values: recklessly using drugs, having a chauvinistic attitude about his involvement with Red Power, and refusing to participate in Okanagan spiritual practices. As a result, he feels "lonely and left out," "like a stranger" to his family and home community, until he realizes his need to learn "what [he] really was, as an Indian" (179–80, 196–99).

Tommy's turning point from estrangement to reintegration comes during his stay at a camp dedicated to reconnecting Indian young people with traditional spirituality. His camp experience, coupled with his dialogue with other Indigenous people, leads Tommy to reinvest in his Okanagan community. He describes his revelation at the camp: "I learned that, being an Indian, I could never be a person only to myself. I was part of all the rest of the people. I was responsible to that" (202–3). Tommy returns home and immediately feels more connected to his family, community, and homeland than he has since childhood. "I knew I was home, really home," he writes, "and my land welcomed me" (206). Tommy's portrayal of his "home" here contrasts with the conflation of home with both nation and private property in dominant Canadian discourse, aligning instead with a tendency that Mavis Reimer identifies in Canadian Aboriginal children's/ YA literature of configuring "home as intergenerational connectedness, access to land, and political protest" (Reimer xvi). The Okanagan have a deep understanding of their land as Mother: source of their language and their life. Tommy feels welcomed not only by his immediate family but also by this Mother of his entire Okanagan nation and the Okanagan people who have lived on the land across generations.[2] Tommy's renewed sense of connection also entails a new approach to political action and a new sense of responsibility, which Tommy practices first by helping his father heal after a heart attack and then by throwing himself into work with his local community (206–8). To employ the term Roberta Trites uses in her discussion of typical YA plot progressions, by the end of the novel, Tommy has fully "reconciled" himself to the traditional institutions of his Okanagan society (Trites, *Disturbing* 20).

While Tommy follows a common YA pattern of reintegration, the fact that he experiences personal empowerment through his reintegration cuts against the grain of most YA texts as well as scholarly discussions of power in the genre. In *Ideologies of Identity in Adolescent Fiction*, Robyn McCallum observes that "adolescent fiction, and many of the discussions which surround it, typically assume and valorize humanistic concepts of individual agency, that is the capacity to act independently of social restraint" (McCallum 7). Yet, a certain kind of "social restraint" actually bolsters Tommy's individual agency. By accepting the restraints of his community and his responsibilities toward it, Tommy claims greater personal agency over choices regarding his everyday actions and political commitments. In his chapter on self-determination in *Power and Place*, Daniel Wildcat attests that it may sound like a contradiction to members of dominant Western societies, but "the more attentive one is to their community, the more self-determining they can be; the less attentive, the more selfish and self-destructing they will be" (Deloria and Wildcat 149). This is certainly true for Tommy. As he reflects on learning about responsibility at the camp, Tommy writes, "I saw then that each one of us who faltered was irreplaceable and a loss to all. In that way, I learned how important and how precious my existence was. I was necessary" (203). It is precisely by accepting his place in his community that Tommy finds value as an individual. He writes of this time of returning home, settling on his family's ancestral lands, and beginning to serve his people, "I had never felt so strong in all my life" (230). He feels strong as an individual because of his participation in his community.

That Tommy and his community are mutually empowered via his reintegration demonstrates the resistive and restorative nature of Okanagan interdependence. Traditionally, Okanagan children are raised by an extended family network, carefully attended to as individuals, and taught the laws of the people that center on the law "to learn to live and work in harmony with everyone and share with everyone in the community" (Armstrong et al. 14–15). In the first part of *Slash*, Tommy becomes divided from his Okanagan community through colonial schooling, his internalized sense of inferiority, his misdirected anger, and his buying into colonial attempts to weaken Indians with drugs and alcohol. His attempt to fight against colonialism as an individual estranged from his Okanagan community is not only unhealthy for him personally but also inherently ineffective because, the novel shows, colonialism itself has caused his isolation. In *Native Hubs*, Renya Ramirez contends that "Indigenous peoples sharing their past and contemporary experiences is a process of bringing back together or *re-membering* (a term recuperated by Guillermo Delgado-P, an Indigenous scholar) the Native social body that has been torn apart by colonization" (Ramirez 9). In reintegrating with his Okanagan community, Tommy joins them in remembering the community's interdependent way of life before colonization, the divisive trauma of colonization, and the resources they have within their own culture for healing from that trauma and moving forward. Through this reintegration and remembering,

Tommy's Okanagan community is able to re-member itself in a vibrant form that colonization was meant to destroy.

It is not new to the Okanagan (or many other Indigenous communities) to understand individuals as being empowered through connection to community, but this notion contrasts sharply with the repressive characterization of reintegration typical of mainstream YA literature (Trites, *Disturbing* 7–8, 34, 52; McCallum 71). In *Slash*, Tommy's reintegration into his Indigenous society not only empowers him personally but also bolsters his and his community's rebellion against colonialism. Returning home after his extensive travels, he recalls the way his Uncle Joe and Old Pra-cwa "talked about protecting our land and our ways," and, he writes, "I finally understood how that tied into the problems of our people" (206). He remembers that during his childhood days, his Uncle Joe had stressed the importance of maintaining cultural and spiritual traditions, and Pra-cwa had declared that "we are a people" with "rights [that] come from the Creator" (191, 209–10). In reconciling with the traditionalists in his Okanagan community, Tommy comes to accept their vision for sovereignty—based in a stance of complete autonomy from the Canadian government and a commitment to strengthening the people by investing in their traditional practices and homelands—and to freshly articulate that vision for young people in the community. The novel suggests that Tommy and his community most effectively resist colonialism when they focus on revitalizing Okanagan traditions, a move that challenges the "assimilate or get lost" colonialist policies that threaten their inherent right to self-determination (70, 208–54).

In depicting an entire Indigenous community fighting for self-determination against dominant colonial powers, *Slash* presents an additional layer of rebellion not found in most mainstream texts and not acknowledged by scholars of YA literature. Trites writes, "Power is a force that operates within the subject and upon the subject in adolescent literature; teenagers are repressed as well as liberated by their own power and by the power of the social forces that surround them in these books. Much of the genre is thus dedicated to depicting how potentially out-of-control adolescents can learn to exist within institutional structures" (*Disturbing* 7). Tommy becomes deeply dedicated to the institutions of his Okanagan and intertribal communities even as he works with others to further develop those institutions. However, Trites's conceptualization of power does not apply at all to Tommy's relationship with colonial institutions. By no means does Tommy "learn to exist" within colonial institutional structures. Instead, his reintegration with his Okanagan community prompts him to distance himself from those structures. As he and others in his community commit themselves to a holistic pursuit of sovereignty, they refuse to accept the blueprint for Indigenous communities given by colonial institutions. Not just in *Slash* but in all of the YA texts in this study, when Indigenous adolescent protagonists reconcile with their local communities, they become more deeply involved in their communities' resistance to colonial domination. Despite their awareness of the pervasiveness of colonial power, their grounding in their Indigenous communities gives them hope that they can resist that power and build their own power from within their communities.

Even the adolescent reform–novel tradition—the strand of YA literature that most stridently challenges dominant social norms (albeit while often simultaneously implicitly reinscribing those norms)—fails to account for the type of interdependent Indigenous empowerment found in *Slash*. As Trites explains in *Twain, Alcott, and the Birth of the Adolescent Reform Novel*, this tradition began with nineteenth-century works by the likes of Mark Twain and Louisa May Alcott, and it continues with many contemporary YA titles. In these texts, Trites observes:

> The protagonist is an ethical character who transcends his or her society by some form of self-reliance. . . . If the protagonist experiences growth—and s/he usually does—that growth provides a commentary as to how the society itself might also "grow" (i.e., improve). And the character's growth is a sign that the society can, indeed, potentially change. . . . These texts share a romantic faith in the ability of youth to improve the future. The message to readers is, invariably, "with self-improvement, you can improve the world." (143–44)

Like other protagonists in the adolescent reform–novel tradition, Tommy's growth as a character illuminates ways that his Okanagan and pan-Indigenous society can change for the better. As he comes to embrace an internally focused holistic approach to Indigenous self-determination, Armstrong clearly suggests that Indian country as a whole would do well to grow in that same direction. Tommy also believes that he and others can improve the world with self-improvement. Unlike other protagonists in the tradition, however, his version of self-improvement is the opposite of self-reliance. It is an acceptance of community interdependence and responsibility.

As he becomes a leader in his community, Tommy does not occupy this role as a transcendent social critic, as the YA protagonist-rebels in other reform novels do, nor does he stand apart as ethically superior to his community. In fact, his estrangement from his Okanagan community gives him a distorted view, not a transcendent one, and it is only when he reintegrates and learns from others in his community that he is able to understand what his society needs and how he can contribute to those needs. Moreover, while he does ethically transcend the dominant colonial society that he critiques, he is only able to do so with help from his Okanagan and intertribal Indigenous communities.[3] The adolescent reform–novel convention of an enlightened individual protagonist's conscious need to grow serving as a metaphor for society's need to grow (and paving the way for that growth) thus fails to account for the way in which Tommy's growth and that of his community are so completely intertwined. Unlike in the majority of YA texts, in *Slash*, the individual's growth does not come before or guide the community's growth; instead, the growth of both individual and community happens simultaneously, and they nurture one another. Tommy is most empowered when he commits himself to his community while participating in the dynamic development of that community. By extension, communities are at their strongest when they nurture individuals like Tommy while valuing the unique contribution of each individual's voice. YA literary theory's focus on negative institutional power and self-reliant individual power does not yet account for these unique power dynamics at play in *Slash* and many other Indigenous YA texts.

In deploying a strong first-person voice to represent her unique protagonist, Armstrong may draw criticism from scholars interested in YA reader/author power dynamics. In "The Irony of Narration," after characterizing most YA authors' use of narrative authority as manipulative and repressive, Mike Cadden argues that a writer can make this dynamic less repressive and more "ethical" by crafting a "self-conscious," "self-questioning" narrator who engages with "equal and multiple viewpoints," or, better yet, by creating multiple, diverse narrators. In Cadden's view, these postmodern strategies can displace the authority of the writer/narrator and empower young readers with greater interpretative agency. Cadden fails to acknowledge, however, that the first-person voice might actually empower readers when it represents those who have been silenced or marginalized (Cadden 146). As Margery Fee argues when discussing the use of first-person narration in *Slash* and other Indigenous literature, "This may not be a subversive tactic in a classic realist text or in the popular novel, but it is within the literary discourse of Canada" (Fee 172). Through first-person narrators, Fee contends, these texts "give a voice directly to those who generally are silenced"

(172). As the self-conscious author of his own story, *Slash*'s Tommy confronts the colonial silencing of Indigenous voices and models for Indigenous young people the crafting of a strong personal voice that resists colonialism and contributes to Indigenous sovereignty, including sovereignty over representation.

Armstrong is fiercely committed to Indigenous self-determination in the realm of representation and has frequently spoken of its importance for Indigenous young people. In an interview with Janice Williamson, Armstrong explains, "The suicide rates and problems our people are having are a result of being told you're stupid, ignorant, a drunk, you'll never amount to anything—just because you're Indian. To me, that's the biggest lie of all that needs to be dispelled. It's my vocation or commitment to do that" ("Jeannette Armstrong" 116). In Armstrong's view, dominant society's derogatory representations of Indigenous people have incredibly destructive effects. She therefore emphasizes, in the Williamson interview and other venues, the importance of Indigenous young people receiving healing and empowerment through accurate Native-authored representations of Native identity ("Jeannette Armstrong" 119–20; interview with Lutz 18; "Body of Our People" 16). This passion led her to fight hard to ensure Indigenous authorship of *Slash* and other OICP texts and to relay her novel in the voice of a strong first-person Indigenous narrator.[4]

In addition to offering a strong, self-determined Indigenous voice, *Slash*'s narrator/protagonist, Tommy, models the process of developing an empowered voice through struggle, dialogue, and writing. In the prologue, Tommy says that he is writing a fictional novel as a way to "examine" and attempt to "understand" how he has changed personally, along with "what changes our people went through during those times and what we are coming up against" (13). We are to understand that the character Tommy, not just the author Armstrong, is crafting a novel, and that he uses his writing process to think through ways that he and his community have changed and may continue to develop in the future. *Slash* thereby meets one of Cadden's criteria for ethical narration: drawing attention to its own construction (Cadden 146, 149, 153).

Beyond the prologue, as he develops his ideas and identity over the course of the novel, Tommy also develops his voice, from his vocabulary and cadence to his confidence and coherence.[5] His voice, like his identity, is always in process. In the first part of the book, Tommy often records instances when he is unsure about how to respond to different, sometimes competing perspectives he encounters (37, 42–43, 73–74, 131, 160). Reflecting on one such experience, he writes, "I couldn't seem to get the right words together" (131). In depicting Tommy's struggle—and sometimes failure—to find his voice, *Slash* assures young readers that they are not alone in their struggles to discover their voices. Tommy especially models for young Indigenous readers how to keep struggling for their voices by rooting themselves in their cultural traditions and engaging in constant dialogue with others in and beyond their communities. *Slash* also teaches young non-Native readers how to develop their voices by questioning colonialist perspectives and by listening to Indigenous voices that have too often been silenced.

In Cadden's framework, YA literature is more likely to empower young readers to question authority and engage diverse perspectives if it employs both multiple voices and meta-attention to reading and interpretation. These techniques, Cadden posits, open possibilities for readers to question the authority of narrators and to see "horizontal power relationships" at play in the texts, which may, in turn, enable them to see vertical power dynamics at play between themselves and the texts' adult authors (Cadden 146). Like other "more ethical" YA texts that Cadden discusses, *Slash* uses polyphony and metanarrative techniques in ways that enable readers to question authority within the text and within the author/reader relationship. *Slash* also goes further by teaching readers to question authority within larger societal narratives, especially colonialist ones.

A scene from early in the novel aptly illustrates how *Slash* empowers readers by representing multiple voices and drawing meta-attention to the process of navigating those voices. When Tommy and his siblings are about to begin attending school in town, where they will have white classmates for the first time, Tommy's father tells the children that the white students "will probably treat you mean and make fun of how you talk and how you dress and how you look" (23). His prediction soon proves true concerning white administrators and teachers, as well as students: The principal addresses the new Native students by saying, "You Indians are lucky to be here. We'll get along just fine as long as you don't steal from the other kids"; and a child on the playground says, "You frigging Injuns are nothing but thieves, full of lice, everybody knows that!" (23, 24). When warning his children about these disparaging perspectives, Tommy's father also teaches them to tell a different story: "Don't listen to them," he says, "Be proud that you're Indian. . . . We are the people who have every right to be here. We ain't sneaking in from somewhere and pushing our way in. Remember that every time one of them says anything bad to you" (23). Readers encounter variations on these competing stories and responses to them throughout the novel. By presenting competing narratives and interpretations—like that of Tommy's father—*Slash* teaches readers to think critically about the narratives they encounter and to pose their own interpretations.

In addition to building this "counter discourse," as Margery Fee terms it, to colonialist narratives, *Slash* demonstrates room for critical reading within the developing counter-discourse. As he brings a self-reflective, questioning attitude to his personal development, Tommy also frequently questions and changes his interpretations of others' perspectives. He often records an event or conversation and then later comments on how his original reaction to the incident has shifted, such as when he realizes his own parents had been trying to teach him the same things he searched for in his travels, or when his changing reactions to conversations with his cousin Chuck help move him away from a focus on confronting colonial power and toward an internal community-building approach to sovereignty (206–10, 139–42, 236–45).

In drawing meta-attention to this process of self-reflective interpretation, the novel teaches readers "interpretive strategies," a tactic that YA literature scholar Robyn McCallum says can empower readers to develop their own interpretive agency (McCallum 8). Following Tommy's model, readers learn to question their own initial interpretations and to raise questions about Tommy's and other characters' perspectives. Readers might connect scenes and question interpretations that Tommy does not question, making for a more dynamic and empowering literary experience. For example, even though Tommy gets the last word after his wife Maeg explains why she, unlike Tommy, wants to participate in the constitution talks, readers have the power to continue engaging Maeg's position and questioning Tommy's response to it because of the interpretive agency that Tommy has modeled for them (243–44).

Slash prods readers to bring their interpretive agency beyond the page as well. Just as Tommy illuminates the importance of dialogue in his own journey, he also suggests that those of his son's generation, to whom he addresses the narrative, should not receive his story as a fixed, authoritative guide. Tommy writes in the prologue that all Indian people "have the burden of individually deciding for our descendants how their world shall be affected and what shall be their heritage" (13). Throughout the rest of the novel, he demonstrates how Indigenous individuals do the best job of shaping the world for their descendants when they root themselves in, and commit themselves to, their local communities in a way that entails continuous questioning, reflection, and dialogue rather than blind allegiance. *Slash*, moreover, might inspire both non-Indigenous and Indigenous readers to bring the interpretative agency and questioning attitude they learn through their reading experience to their malleable individual perspectives, local communities, and larger societies.

While Cadden's discussion of literary techniques that encourage readers to expose and question discursive power focuses on novels and narrative theory of the late twentieth century, these same techniques have a much longer history in Indigenous storytelling traditions. The writers of *We Get Our Living Like Milk from the Land* explain how, through stories, Okanagan people remember their history, how they have survived as a people, and what laws of living have strengthened them. This rich body of stories, the *captíkwł*, is passed on orally from one generation to the next, and with each telling the community freshly imagines how to live out the values found in their history (Armstrong et al. 15). For the Okanagan and numerous other Indigenous communities, oral tradition is inherently communal, interactive, and dynamic; listeners bring their own interpretations, ideas, and questions to the stories as they hear them and as they adapt them for future audiences. Stories from Indigenous oral and written traditions, moreover, frequently draw attention to the simultaneously powerful and slippery nature of discourse. For centuries, Indigenous writers, from Samson Occom and Zitkala-Ša to Leslie Marmon Silko, Navaree Scott Momaday, and Lee Maracle, have drawn on these traditions in order to expose discursive power, resist narrative authority claimed by colonizers, and prod listeners/readers—especially Native audiences—to claim their own voices as they unmask and challenge oppressive narratives. In resisting oppressive discourses and encouraging audiences to keep critically engaging all of the discourses that they encounter once they have put the book down, *Slash*, then, not only mirrors techniques of contemporary ethical YA fiction but also carries on long-standing Indigenous narrative traditions.[6]

While *Slash* represents multiple voices and equips readers to critically engage those voices, it does not depict all of the perspectives it represents as equally valid, thereby parting ways with Cadden's charge that ethical narration deals with "*equal* and multiple viewpoints" (Cadden 148, my emphasis). The text teaches readers to challenge colonialist narratives by valuing Indigenous perspectives. Even though it equips readers to critically engage Indigenous voices—including Tommy's—the novel also clearly privileges those perspectives that align with Tommy's uncompromising and internally focused approach to sovereignty. *Slash* thereby carries on the didactic as well as the dynamic quality of Okanagan oral tradition. There is room for multiplicity, questioning, and change in that tradition, but the tradition is also meant to impart particular values. One story about a turtle, for example, teaches listeners "that we must not think of ourselves as individuals" but as interdependent members of the community, a value that *Slash* reflects via its revision of YA conventions regarding individual/community power dynamics (Armstrong et al. 15). *Slash* thus extends traditional Okanagan narratives through its own privileging of certain perspectives, as well as through its imaginative adaptability.

Does *Slash*'s privileging of Indigenous voices over colonialist ones, and certain Indigenous perspectives over others make it unethical? Does privileging certain positions over others always inevitably result in oppression? Is relativism a necessary component of ethical writing, reading, and living? Cadden is among a host of scholars in literary and cultural studies who suggest that multiplicity, hybridity, and relativism are indeed crucial components of both ethical societies and ethical works of art. Some scholars in Indigenous studies—including those who identify with American Indian literary nationalism—have critiqued this position, arguing that hybridity itself often operates as an oppressive discourse that denies the validity of particular Indigenous identities (and we could add narrative traditions) while undermining claims to Indigenous self-determination.[7]

Literature like *Slash* that equips readers to privilege Indigenous perspectives while critiquing colonialist ones can be understood as acutely ethical, especially given that colonialist perspectives are privileged almost everywhere else, including in most mainstream books for children and young adults. In contrast, most works of Indigenous YA literature join *Slash* in suggesting that some approaches to sovereignty are more effective than others, and that some degree of unity in diversity is necessary for strengthening Indigenous communities while resisting colonialism. Like *Slash*, the other texts that I examine in later chapters of this book adapt the conventions of the YA genre in order to resist colonialism as well as dominant discourses that are inextricably intertwined with colonialism, including discourses of heteropatriarchy, multiculturalism, and hybridity. Each of these discourses privileges dominant colonialist perspectives, even as the latter two overtly champion relativism. The more recent Indigenous YA texts that I examine in this volume continue in *Slash*'s vein by uncovering colonialist ideologies underlying dominant discourses, and by privileging Indigenous perspectives in ways that empower readers of the texts as well as characters within them.

Slash's Nuanced Portrayal of Interdependent Indigenous Sovereignty

A commitment to Indigenous self-determination necessitates the privileging of Indigenous perspectives, because the belief that Indigenous people have the right and ability to determine their own lives is foundational to the concept and practice of sovereignty. *Slash*'s general privileging of Indigenous voices, along with its specific vision for Indigenous self-determination as holistic, uncompromising, dynamic, and focused on internal community-building, largely aligns with and illuminates larger trends in sovereignty activism in the late twentieth century (and into the twenty-first century). The novel nonetheless adds important nuances for contemporary conceptualizations of Indigenous self-determination, and for the nationalism versus cosmopolitanism debates that have dominated Native literary studies for the last two decades. Specifically through its adaption of YA genre conventions, *Slash* uniquely foregrounds how Indigenous individuals and communities can mutually empower one another. It also uniquely presents dynamism, dialogue, coalition-building, and self-reflection as effective means to support Indigenous sovereignty, but only if Indigenous individuals and communities pursue such activities in the service of their primary investments in specific tribal/intertribal spaces, cultural practices, relationships, and responsibilities.

The approach to Indigenous political sovereignty emphasizing autonomy and internal community empowerment that Tommy comes to embrace in *Slash* was becoming the trend in many actual Indigenous communities in the United States and Canada at the time of Armstrong's writing, and it has become the prevailing approach in the decades since.[8] Vine Deloria Jr., one of Indian country's most influential scholar/activists in the second half of the twentieth century, supported the American Indian Movement (AIM) but was also critical of its emphasis on confronting colonial institutions. In *Tribal Secrets: Recovering American Indian Intellectual Traditions*, Robert Warrior analyzes the perspective on sovereignty that unfolds over Deloria's work. Warrior notes that in Deloria's 1969 *Custer Died for Your Sins*, "The time was coming, [Deloria] predicted, when the politics of confrontation would have to end and the work of building communities would have to begin" (Warrior 89). While agreeing with AIM leaders' legitimate grievances against the U.S. government, Deloria suggested that they ought to spend less time protesting that government's attacks on their sovereignty and more time actually living out that sovereignty by directly investing in the institutions of their own Native communities. Deloria's influence across Indian country surely helped to make his own predication a reality for many. "Because groups accomplish little by demanding that the dominating society change," Warrior observes, "Deloria advocates building communities and social structures through which those communities exercise political, economic, and spiritual power along with responsibility" (Warrior 92). Like Tommy in the final part of *Slash*, Deloria called on Indigenous people to stop asking for power, rights, and recognition from colonial governments—as if these things could be "given"—and to instead focus on revitalizing their communities by tapping into the power found in their own traditions (Warrior 91–92; Deloria, *We Talk, You Listen* 123).

Even though Deloria was critical of members of AIM for their emphasis on confrontation, he still supported them and saw their work as important (Warrior 89–90). Like Deloria, many in AIM and other Red Power groups encouraged Native people to revitalize their cultural and spiritual as well as political traditions. Moreover, many contemporary leaders credit Red Power with restoring Indigenous peoples' pride in their Indigenous identity, often characterizing this as the movement's most important contribution.[9] In *Slash*, as Tommy grows critical of the anger-driven confrontational approach of his own Red Power days, he also recognizes the movement's important restorative role. Near the end of the novel, he tells his son, Marlon, "You are an Indian of a special generation. Your world will be hard but you will grow up proud to be Indian. That will make you different than some of us. If I keep to the Indian path and protect your rights the way Pra-cwa explained [by practicing them], you will be the generation to help them white men change because you won't be filled with hate" (250). Tommy hopes that his son's generation, having inherited the restorative gains of Red Power, will progress in their pride and strength to the point that they will actually reverse the colonial trajectory of assimilation.

As the only Red Power–movement novel of its kind, *Slash* provides a window into how an individual might actually experience this restoration of self-pride while enacting the political shift Deloria advocated from a primary focus on confrontation to an emphasis on strengthening Indigenous communities from within. Tommy's experience at the camp, devoted to the revival of traditional spiritual practices, literally leads him home, and leads him to invest in relationships and institutions there to a degree he had never done before (202–8). After settling back in the Okanagan, Tommy still attends some protests and meetings focused on confronting colonial governments or planning for such confrontations.

However, he devotes relatively little time to these activities, especially in comparison to his traveling years. Instead, he prioritizes mentoring young people and program-building to support them, learning from family members and elders, spiritual activities, and time spent simply being present on his homeland and with his relations.

While his camp experience prompts Tommy to shift his personal approach to Indigenous self-determination, subsequent conversations with his relative, Chuck, enable him to more fully articulate his new approach and to advocate that others join him in pursuing it. We first meet Chuck, an older cousin who, like Tommy, grew up "with a real heavy emphasis on Indian values," sometime before Tommy's transformative time in the camp. After hearing Tommy rally a group of young Aboriginal men in British Columbia to prepare for the same kind of intense confrontations Tommy had seen in the United States at the BIA occupation, Wounded Knee, and elsewhere, Chuck criticizes Tommy for "feed[ing] anger and hate" and advocates that the people should instead develop a carefully planned strategy to pursue a big-picture "common goal" of empowerment (139–41). In response, Tommy feels "bitter" toward Chuck, because, at this point in the novel, Tommy still views aggressive confrontations with colonial institutions as the most important form of Indigenous resistance (139, 142).

Later in the novel, after Tommy's time in the camp leads to his reintegration with his Okanagan community, he encounters Chuck again and confides in him about his discomfort with the upcoming cross-Canada caravan and its goal of advocating for Indigenous inclusion in the talks about the new Canadian constitution (236–38). Affirming Tommy's wariness about the caravan and the talks, Chuck articulates the commitment to complete autonomy for Indigenous people—as opposed to "equal rights"—that becomes Tommy's own political position:

> They're going to Ottawa to give Trudeau shit for not letting them in on the talks. Can't you see how absurd that is? If they were going to Ottawa saying, "Bullshit to any constitution but our own, for each of our Indian Nations," the feeling would be much different. Eventually they will say that anyway, no matter what happens. The only thing is, it could happen a lot sooner. Does that set you straight? Watch things and see if I'm not right. (238–39)

Tommy does go on to "watch things"—the caravan, failing efforts to be included in the constitution talks in the months that follow, the old people's lack of support for the entire constitution effort—and concludes that "Chuck was right" (245).

In Tommy's experience, this belief that true Indigenous sovereignty means not playing by the government of Canada's rules aligns with his championing of internal community-building. *Slash* suggests that when Indigenous people restore their pride, revitalize their cultural practices, and renew their commitment to their communities, they naturally shift their primary focus away from confronting colonial institutions; their investment in Indigenous community itself becomes their primary means of resistance. Debates among Indigenous people in Canada more than thirty years after *Slash*'s publication over whether and how to partic-ipate in the residential schools truth-and-reconciliation process parallel debates about the constitution talks depicted in Armstrong's novel. Warning against an overemphasis on reconciliation, recognition, and rights, in her 2011 book *Dancing on Our Turtle's Back*, Anishinaabe scholar Leanne Simpson demonstrates an ongoing need to (re)focus Indigenous communities on building strength from within (Simpson 11–25). On reconciliation, she writes,

> For reconciliation to be meaningful to Indigenous Peoples and for it to be a decolonizing force, it must be interpreted broadly. To me, reconciliation must be grounded in cultural generation and political resurgence. It must support Indigenous nations in regenerating our languages, our oral cultures, our traditions of governance and everything else residential schools attacked and attempted to obliterate. (22)

While primarily approaching internal empowerment through the lens of Anishi-naabe intellectual traditions—especially concepts of resurgence—rather than reconciliation, Simpson also recasts reconciliation itself as chiefly about holistic internal Indigenous regeneration and settler support for it, underscoring the enduring relevance of *Slash*'s political discourse.

At the end of *Slash*, Tommy still recognizes that Indigenous communities need to confront policies of the dominant state that interfere with their ability to self-govern, and that their holistic empowerment further necessitates confronting dehumanizing colonial policies, discourses, and practices, especially those they have internalized. However, his overall attitude toward confrontation has turned inside out. Instead of focusing on masses of Indigenous people confronting colonial powers with justifiable rage, he nudges himself and other Indigenous people to honestly and respectfully confront one another, pushing one another toward the reintegration, responsibility, and dynamic interactions that will make them strong.

Concepts like dynamism, adaptation, fluidity, and hybridity are championed by advocates of cosmopolitanism who often alternately accuse nationalists of being essentialist and isolationist. Scholars like Craig Womack, Jace Weaver, Robert Warrior, and Lisa Brooks in *American Indian Literary Nationalism*, and Niigaanwewidam James Sinclair in "Tending to Ourselves: Hybridity and Native Literary Criticism" have responded to these accusations by articulating approaches to Indigenous nationalism that embrace cultural dynamism while promoting *critical* engagement not just with literature and criticism but also with tribal governments. These scholars demonstrate that we can recognize cultures as dynamic units that borrow from one another, acknowledge the multiple cultural affiliations of individuals, and discuss cross-cultural exchange without falling into the trap of seeing cultures either as overly static/reified or as so overly unstable/indefinable as to be meaningless. They suggest that the best expressions of Native sovereignty encourage dynamic development and self-critique within Native communities while simultaneously acknowledging the distinctive political status of those communities and their right to determine their own futures.

In offering a self-consciously young adult literary representation of an internally focused, resolute, and dynamic approach to Indigenous sovereignty coming out of and after Red Power, *Slash* not only anticipates the nationalist turn in Native literary criticism but also uniquely illuminates the various commitments at play in this approach to sovereignty, and the relationship among those commitments. First, through its reworking of YA conventions, *Slash* underscores the complexly collaborative nature of Indigenous individual and community empowerment. Like most YA protagonists, Tommy experiences a personal identity struggle. But his is not the torn-between-two-cultural-worlds identity struggle that scholars of Native literature once heavily emphasized (and some continue to emphasize), a practice criticized by scholars in the literary nationalist school who advocate for readings less focused on personal identity issues and colonial societies' influence on individuals, instead calling for and conducting readings informed by the history, culture, and politics of specific Indigenous nations. Tommy's identity struggle is a struggle to find his personal strength and his political philosophy in the context of his Okanagan nation and his intertribal activist communities. In demonstrating how Tommy's reintegration with his community empowers him personally while also enabling him to more effectively contribute to that community's collective empowerment, *Slash* foregrounds the importance of reciprocal relationship between individuals and communities in the pursuit of self-determination.

In addition to inviting us to consider old issues of personal identity in new, politically informed ways, *Slash* contributes to the conceptualization of Indigenous sovereignty through its representation of a hierarchy of commitments within its approach to self-determination, a move that clarifies and contributes to the long-running debate in Native studies and postcolonial studies about whether and how nationalism and cosmopolitanism can be reconciled. *Slash* portrays dynamism, dialogue, self-reflection, and coalition-building—practices often associated with cosmopolitanism—as productive for advancing Indigenous self-determination, but only when they are pursued in the service of a primary commitment to an uncompromising, internally focused, holistic vision of Indigenous sovereignty. During his time of physical and spiritual separation from his Okanagan community in the first part of the novel, Tommy moves all around North America, conversing with people from a diverse array of Native nations, and reflecting often about his personal experiences and political views. Yet Tommy is portrayed in this period as self-destructive, and as failing to make positive contributions to his Okanagan and intertribal communities. His dynamism, dialogue, self-reflection, and cross-nation relationships only become productive when he reintegrates with his Okanagan community, is strengthened by that community, and commits himself to the strengthening of that community from within.

Slash especially explores the value of dialogue in the pursuit of Indigenous sovereignty when the dialogue stems from a commitment to specific Indigenous communities and their holistic empowerment. In a sometimes jarring style, most of the novel consists of recorded conversations: Tommy's internal dialogues as well as his interactions with others. This style sets the novel apart from other literature in general and especially from YA literature. While the plot covers significant ground, *Slash* proceeds at a slower pace than most action-driven YA texts because of the lengthy conversations Tommy engages in with others and with himself as he reflects on his experiences. Moreover, while all of the conversations appear in English in the text, the novel signals that some are taking place in the Okanagan language, with fluent Okanagan-speaker Armstrong's translation of Okanagan forms of expression and knowledge into English adding to the multiplicity of voices that come across in the text.[10]

Other scholars who note the presence of these multiple voices in the text tend to focus on the voices' potential for challenging colonialism.[11] Margery Fee and Julia Emberley both focus on ways that the multiple voices in *Slash* form what Fee calls a "counter discourse" to dominant colonial narratives about Indigenous people. Armstrong's novel certainly develops counter-discourses to colonialism, but it also highlights the need for dialogue within the counter-discourses, as well as the need for discourses that are not focused on countering colonial voices at all, but rather on adapting Indigenous traditions in order to strengthen Indigenous communities on their own terms. Tommy opens himself up to his Okanagan and intertribal communities—and to the possibility of being strengthened by and strengthening those communities—through his conversations with others. By exchanging ideas, and sometimes disagreeing with one another, he and his conversation partners participate in shaping their communities' collective future. By conversing with a wide variety of people in his Okanagan community in an attempt to discern what the community needs most, how to meet those needs, and whether/how to confront colonial powers, Tommy also practices traditional Okanagan laws that center on mutual responsibility within the community (Armstrong et al. 14–15). While he respects a traditional age-based hierarchy, listening more when he is with older Okanagans and talking more when he is working with youth in the community, Tommy remains open to both giving and receiving critical feedback in all of his exchanges. This is genuine give-and-take dialogue that allows for disagreement, tension, and multiplicity.

Many of the same scholars who recognize the resistive potential of the multiple voices in *Slash* also read the novel as ultimately silencing these voices—and the dynamic possibilities they represent—since, in the end, the text so clearly privileges a single position on the constitution talks (Van Styvendale 209; Green 63–64; Fee 174). While these critics emphasize the singular nature of Tommy's approach to sovereignty—sometimes granting that we still hear multiple voices at the end of Armstrong's novel *despite* this singular approach—I contend that Tommy remains a fluid character at the end of his narrative *because* the approach to sovereignty he comes to embrace demands constant dialogue, movement, and growth. *Slash* does unmistakably privilege Tommy's position, and Armstrong might have served readers better with a more open ending, one that did not entail killing off Tommy's wife, Maeg, who represents an arguably still pro-sovereignty nuanced alternative to Tommy's position. However, Tommy comes to his position on the constitution talks through a great deal of dialogue, dynamic movement, and critical self-reflection. The novel suggests that such practices, when pursued in the service of a robust internal community-building approach to sovereignty, are not just permissible but also necessary for carrying out that approach. Yes, Tommy wants other Indigenous people to embrace his resistance to the constitution talks and the larger uncompromising, internally focused vision his position represents. But the novel suggests that Tommy's own journey as well as that of his community will continue beyond this point and beyond the book's timeframe. Even if the people come to a shared vision of what sovereignty means, it will still take a great deal of dialogue and self-reflective negotiation to carry that vision out.

Slash's engagement with the YA genre directly contributes to its unique portrayal of Indigenous sovereignty. The hierarchy of commitments within its approach to sovereignty comes to the fore through the novel's revision of YA conventions surrounding the power dynamics of individual/community reconciliation. The novel renders secondary commitments to dynamism, dialogue, self-reflection, and coalition-building as valuable at the precise point of Tommy's reintegration with his Okanagan community—a reintegration that coincides with and enables his deep investment in the primary commitment to strengthening his Indigenous community from within. In order to effectively understand, advocate for, and practice the holistic, internally focused approach to sovereignty championed by the novel, Tommy must dialogue with people in and beyond his community, reflect on his own and his community's actions, and be open to dynamically adapting those actions in response to what he and his fellow citizens learn from their ongoing dialogue and reflection.

We see evidence of Tommy's ongoing development and the importance of dynamism in his approach to sovereignty as late as the final chapter of the novel when he tells his friend Jimmy, "We are slowly learning decolonization. We got to recognize our solutions to some of those social problems are in progress already. We have our own interpretations as to how we function best" (223–24). In describing decolonization and self-determination as ways of being that Okanagan and other Indigenous people are "slowly learning," Tommy, like Vine Deloria Jr. and Scott Richard Lyons, casts sovereignty as a *process* of empowerment and renewal, not just an end (Warrior 91; Lyons 449). To borrow Warrior's words, Tommy, like Deloria, "recognizes that American Indians [and their counterparts in Canada] have to go through a process of building community and that that process will define the future" (Warrior 91). Tommy's process-based understanding of sovereignty comes across through both his actions and his words in the final third of the novel. Through its portrayal of Tommy's involvement in political meetings, after-school programs, family gatherings, and cultural events in his local community, as well as through intertribal protests, meetings, and other gatherings, *Slash* demonstrates that learning decolonization, discerning Indigenous-based solutions to problems, and interpreting how to function best as Indigenous communities are dynamic—and sometimes very difficult—processes. In the epilogue, as Tommy dedicates his story to his son and those of his son's generation, the novel further suggests that these future-defining, people-defining processes of sovereignty should continue well beyond Tommy's own generation (253).

Slash does not tell us how the generation of Tommy's son will specifically pursue this process of sovereignty. Many additional questions likewise remain unaddressed or not fully addressed at the end of the novel. When do conflicting political views within a Native community need to be resolved, and when can they remain unresolved as that community pursues its self-determination? Even regarding the constitution-talks debate, while *Slash* clearly privileges the anti-participation position, it simultaneously suggests some positive impacts for members of the community who advocate for participation, and the pro-participation camp is supported even by those like Tommy who disagree with them (236–37). The novel does not describe whether or how Tommy's Okanagan community ever resolved their differences over the constitution issue, nor does it address how the community dealt with other divisive issues. How can a community come together, pursue some common goals, and experience empowerment despite and/or through internal diversity of opinion as well as experience? *Slash* raises this question but does not fully answer it. Also, since the novel, like most YA texts, focuses on a single protagonist, Tommy, it does not address how other Indigenous individuals' unique identities and experiences uniquely shape their participation in the pursuit of self-determination, whether they hold dissenting views from others in their communities or not. Finally, regarding cross-cultural relationships and alliances, the novel leaves us with more questions than answers. How can intertribal communities support particular Indigenous nations and vice versa? *Slash* portrays the intertribal spiritual camp as positive because it leads Tommy home to focus on his Okanagan nation, but are there other productive ways for tribal and intertribal communities to support one another? And what about non-Native allies? As it focuses entirely on Okanagan and intertribal Indigenous communities—refreshing given the tendency to include significant white characters in multicultural children's and YA literature—*Slash* does not address this question at all. While largely aligning with *Slash*'s revision of YA conventions and its vision for Indigenous sovereignty, the other Indigenous YA texts examined in this volume uniquely tackle the above questions and raise many additional questions in the process.

CHAPTER TWO

Indigenous School Stories

Alternatives to Multiculturalism in Sherman Alexie's
The Absolutely True Diary of a Part-Time Indian
and Joseph Bruchac's *The Heart of a Chief*

lash's protagonist, Tommy, experiences a movement from confused anger under colonial influences to empowerment as a student and teacher of what he calls "Indian ways." Armstrong hoped to empower her readers as well—including her own grandchildren and the thousands of students reading *Slash* in school classrooms—by providing nuanced information about recent Indigenous histories along with a portrayal of "the heart of the people at that time" (interview with Lutz 14–15). Significantly, none of Tommy's positive experiences with education occur in formal school settings. The brief depictions the novel provides of these contexts reveal the harsh legacy of the residential school era and the racist, assimilationist ideology behind those schools. Like Armstrong, other Canadian Aboriginal writers focus on this legacy in their depictions of schools—understandable given that the last residential schools did not close in Canada until the late 1990s.[1] While I am interested in how these texts confront the residential schools' lasting impact, I focus my analysis in this chapter on texts by U.S.-based Indigenous writers who imagine positive ways that Native sovereignty can be advanced through formal school contexts even as they, too, expose the colonial ideologies continually at play in those contexts.

The 2007 illustrated novel *The Absolutely True Diary of a Part-Time Indian* by Sherman Alexie (Spokane/Coeur d'Alene) and the 1998 novel *The Heart of a Chief* by Joseph Bruchac (Abenaki) can be characterized as Indigenous young adult school stories. Each novel represents the fictionalized experiences of American Indian young people as they navigate the terrain of a predominantly white public junior high or high school. Whereas mainstream YA literature, like mainstream culture, has absorbed the rhetoric of neoliberal multiculturalism, Alexie's and Bruchac's novels enact tribal critical race theory as they critique multiculturalism—especially its tendencies to mask white privilege and to render cultures as static entities—and as they propose alternative models for conceptualizing diversity. They do this by both deploying and subverting conventions of mainstream school stories, and by robustly representing avenues for cultural dynamism, cross-cultural learning, and alliances that facilitate Indigenous empowerment.

Multiculturalism, Tribal Critical Race Theory, and the School Story

In the 1980s and 1990s, multiculturalism solidified in the United States and Canada as the dominant ideology, discourse, and, in Canada, official government policy for negotiating difference. It remains the dominant framework in both countries well into the twenty-first century. Adherents of multiculturalism characterize their approach as anti-racist since it encourages people to move past racial prejudices by simultaneously celebrating cultural diversity and embracing national/global unity (Bonilla-Silva and Embrick 7–8; Lyons 457; Saldanha 166). Critical race theorists and other critics of multiculturalism highlight the discourse's failure to account for ongoing racial inequalities as well as its conspicuous exclusion of material and political concerns in its definition of "culture" (Budde 248; Lyons 457; Prashad 38–40; Roediger 6–7; Melamed xvi–xvii; Saldanha 166–67). Government officials, educators, and others who push a multiculturalist agenda generally limit the parameters of culture to include ethnic identity, artistic expression, and, in the words of the Canadian Multiculturalism Act (CMA), "cultural heritage" (Melamed xix–xx; Saldanha 166–67; CMA 3.1). *True Diary* and *Heart of a Chief* must be understood against the backdrop of multiculturalism and critiques of it by tracing the historical development of multiculturalism as a discourse in Canada and the United States, especially the discourse's prevalence in government, education, and children's literature.

In 1988, just three years after *Slash* appeared, the Canadian House of Parliament passed Bill C-93, the CMA, pledging that the Canadian federal government would recognize and promote a greater appreciation for the "cultural and racial diversity of Canadian society," charging all federal institutions to do the same, and establishing a ministry position to assist in the act's implementation. While the CMA never explicitly defines "multiculturalism" or "culture," it implicitly characterizes multiculturalism as a fact of cultural diversity as well as a policy encouraging the appreciation of that fact in a way that reinforces a singular national identity among the "different cultures of Canadian society" (CMA 3.1.h).[2] Critics, including Louise Saldanha, Smaro Kamboureli, and Robert Budde, note that the CMA, along with the discourse advanced by it, characterizes "different cultures" as narrow, static, and apolitical entities that can be folded into the dominant national paradigm without upsetting it. While not a broadly legislated official policy in the United States, multiculturalism operates similarly there.

Despite their, at times aggressive, racializing of "worthy" and "unworthy" global citizens, proponents of multiculturalism often continue to characterize race as a thing of the past, positing that racism has already or will soon come to an end either via the simple fact of growing cultural diversity or via the harmonious coming together of different cultures—including the biological coming together represented in the children of interracial unions—under multiculturalist values (Roediger 3–8; Bonilla-Silva and Embrick 7–8).[3] In reality, as George Lipsitz observes, "Race is a cultural construct, but one with deadly social causes and consequences" (Lipsitz 2). By claiming that race and racism do not or will soon not exist and that we therefore do not need to discuss them, adherents of multiculturalism fail to address those deadly social causes and consequences of racial formation, thereby perpetuating the racist systems that exert their greatest force when they are least visible.

While race and colonization are off the table for adherents of multiculturalism, cultures are viewed not only as flavorful ingredients in the diversity soup (or, in Canada's preferred imagery, salad) but also as acceptable sites of blame for social problems. For example, while one would violate politically correct conventions if one blamed African Americans for being lazy because of their "race," one can be seen as legitimate when attributing underachievement among urban African American students to negative aspects of their home "culture" based on the dominant view that Robin D. G. Kelley discusses at length in *Yo' Mama's Disfunktional! Fighting the Culture Wars in Urban America* of the ghetto as a place of "pathologies" and "bad cultural values." Through a discourse that emphasizes the contributions that different "cultural heritages" bring to the national or global whole, adherents of multiculturalism feel entitled to police the actions of cultural groups and to designate those actions as "authentic" expressions of the group's cultural heritage or as corruptions of the culture that denigrate the cultural group and, possibly, larger national and global societies (Saldanha 167; Fletcher 102–3).

In the final chapter of *Represent and Destroy: Rationalizing Violence in the New Racial Capitalism*, Jodi Melamed joins critics like Elizabeth Cook-Lynn and Scott Richard Lyons in offering an Indigenous critique of multiculturalism. Cook-Lynn argues that multiculturalism is, by its "very nature," "in conflict with the concept of American Indian sovereignty" because of its focus on "spirituality and culture" rather than governance or nationhood (Cook-Lynn 91). Melamed builds on this insight, arguing that "By upholding an epistemological formation that separates culture and lands (turning culture into aesthetics and land into private property), multiculturalism has undermined indigenous land claims based on culture and enabled indigenous dispossession" (Melamed xxii). In the contemporary period of neoliberal global capitalism, multiculturalism paves the way for governments and corporations to exploit Indigenous lands and resources with impunity as they deny Indigenous people's land claims on the basis of perceiving them as just another "ethnic minority" (xxii).

Melamed characterizes multiculturalism as especially pervasive in literary texts as well as the study of those texts in institutions of higher education (xvi). However, multiculturalism arguably achieves its deepest influence in children's and young adult literature along with the study of such texts in elementary and secondary schools, where there is often not the strong counter to multiculturalism that Melamed identifies in university departments like ethnic studies and women's studies. In mainstream elementary and secondary schools, attention to Indigenous peoples rarely moves beyond what Daniel Wildcat calls "educational tokenism," the multiculturalist approach that highlights Indian crafts or snippets of Indian history in a small, discrete part of the curriculum (Deloria and Wildcat 38–39). Prashad, like Melamed, suggests that this tokenistic treatment of Indigenous cultures stems from the larger limited and limiting educational aims central to multiculturalism, contending that "multiculturalism (in most incarnations) sees the world as already constituted by different (and discrete) cultures that we can place into categories and study with respect" (Prashad 67). Yet, in neatly categorizing and studying cultures, educators and students fail to respect both cultural overlap and the material/political nature of cultures.

As Jeanette Haynes observes, in the field of education, "multicultural education" is a "continuum," with the "superficial" recolonizing ideology of mainstream multiculturalism on one end and multicultural education "as social justice" on the other; the social justice end is put into practice far less often than the superficial end, including when it comes to the treatment of Indigenous peoples in school curricula (Haynes 4). Tribal critical race theorists in the field of Indigenous education underscore the ongoing endemic reality of colonialism as it intersects with racism. They also examine how assimilation-based educational policies, along with multiculturalist ideology, mask this reality, and they advocate for, design, and implement education policies and practices based in Indigenous epistemologies and pedagogies (Brayboy 430–33, 436–40; Haynes 3, 8–11; Abercrombie-Donahue 28–43).

The limits of multiculturalism are strikingly revealed across bookstores in Canada, including the Toronto Centre for Children's Books, where, Saldanha observes, most texts in the multiculturalism section are white-authored, fail to address the material realities of race, and feature a white protagonist "who achieves maturity by learning, from a cultural 'other,' that 'we're all members of the same human family'" (Saldanha 168). Scholars like Doris Seale, Beverly Slapin, Debbie Reese, and Melissa Kay Thompson have identified a similar trend in so-called "multicultural" children's literature in the United States. The majority of widely marketed "multicultural" children's texts in Canada and the United States elide racial inequalities while reinforcing a view of non-mainstream cultures as static entities, available for appropriation by white young people and easily subsumed within a harmonious national or global family.

Even more disturbing to me than the predominance of multiculturalist ideology in children's literature is the tendency Saldanha identifies of readers—including critics, students, and teachers—to read multiculturalist perspectives into and/or to devalue children's texts that resist this ideology. Saldanha explains that literary scholars and even her own students respond to children's texts by non-white Canadian women in ways that are pedagogically consistent with neoliberal multiculturalism (Saldanha 174). These readers—students and scholars of literature—generally respond negatively to texts that expose present-day inequalities and challenge multiculturalist ideology. When they respond positively, they do so only by dismissing these critical elements, co-opting the texts in support of multiculturalism. Alexie's *True Diary* and Bruchac's *Heart of a Chief* capitulate to some mainstream "multicultural books" norms, including through their positive portrayals of white characters helping Native characters, a move that likely contributes to the books' mainstream acclaim. Yet, at the same time, both books offer strong, multifaceted critiques of multiculturalist ideology—critiques that have been almost entirely overlooked in the books' reception. Illuminating the critique of multiculturalism in these texts may contribute to a resistance against the kind of co-optive reading practices that Saldanha unveils. These novels offer an important counter to multiculturalism as YA texts frequently read in schools and especially as school stories, a subgenre of YA literature that generally reinforces dominant social norms, including those of multiculturalism.

_____

Most scholars point to Thomas Hughes's 1857 novel *Tom Brown's Schooldays* as launching the school-story genre. Beverly Lyon Clark explains that *Tom Brown's Schooldays* and the canonical school stories that followed it adhere to a predictable formula. Set in Britain's elite boarding schools for boys, the texts "feature an ordinary good-natured boy" and focus on his physical and moral adventures rather than classroom experiences (Clark 4.) Dieter Petzold analyzes how influential writers like Thomas Hughes and Rudyard Kipling represent the boarding-school boy "as a savage whose freedom they admire and envy even while they stress the necessity of his being 'broken in'" (Petzold 20). Such authors, Petzold explains, saw the elite British school as a space where young boys could be taught to accept authority without having their free spirits completely crushed (20). Though far less explicit and extreme in their mission, these schools were like Indian boarding/residential schools in their attempt to assimilate young people into a dominant society. Of course, for the upper-crust British boys—unlike their American Indian and Canadian Aboriginal counterparts—the means of assimilation was gentle and the dominant society into which they were being socialized was their own, the world that their parents wanted them to inherit.

Contemporary school stories have become a popular subgenre of YA literature. While they sometimes diverge from their traditional forebears in their settings and plots, they remain, as Roberta Trites argues, stories of socialization that allow for contained forms of rebellion while ultimately guiding their (more or less resistant) adolescent protagonists to embrace the status quo (*Disturbing* 32–36). Tison Pugh and David L. Wallace argue that even the Harry Potter series—the most well-known and among the most rebellious of contemporary school stories—"flirts with deconstructing normativity" but "simultaneously uphold[s] some of its most cherished values," particularly in regard to gender and sexuality (Pugh and Wallace 261). Nevertheless, the character Harry Potter pursues more radical avenues for rebellion than the majority of protagonists in mainstream school stories do; these protagonists may rebel, but, Trites observes, they eventually come to a form of "acceptable rebellion" that allows them to remain within the status quo of their educational institution and the other societal institutions it represents (*Disturbing* 33–34). Despite the plots of rebellion within their pages, then, contemporary school stories ultimately tend to reinforce dominant societal norms, including the norms of white privilege and multiculturalism.

While Alexie and Bruchac revise mainstream school-story conventions via their depiction of sustained rebellion against multiculturalism, it is important to recognize that contemporary Indigenous school stories also build on another body of work: narratives by Indigenous authors about experiences in Indian boarding/residential schools. *True Diary* includes an allusion to the lasting influence of boarding-school initiator Richard Pratt's assimilationist vision for Indian education, with one of the protagonist's white teachers confessing that, not so long ago, he beat children at the reservation school, having been taught to teach so as "to kill the Indian to save the child," "to kill Indian culture" (35). The 2013 YA novel *If I Ever Get Out of Here* by Eric Gansworth (Onondaga) stands out as a contemporary Indigenous school story (set in an off-reservation public junior high school) that more explicitly engages the legacy of Indian boarding schools. Lewis, the novel's young Tuscarora protagonist, has grandparents who went to Carlisle, the most infamous of these schools in the United States, and he does not shy away from detailing the horrors they experienced there (108, 113, 231). In his family, the boarding school is a "seventy-five-year-old ghost" that haunts Lewis as he spends much of the novel trying to decipher whether the grandparents of his new white best friend were teachers in one of these schools whose "object," Lewis succinctly puts it, "was to get us to ditch the things that make us, well, us" (178). Even when they don't implicitly or explicitly reference the boarding/residential schools, the legacy of those schools is always present in contemporary Indigenous school stories, just as it is always present in the schooling and the wider experiences of Indigenous people.[4]

Contemporary Indigenous school stories draw not only on the legacy of the schools themselves (and the intergenerational trauma perpetuated by that legacy) but also on the positive legacy of resistance reflected in boarding/residential school narratives from throughout the twentieth century. Indigenous children and young adults in the boarding/residential schools did not simply lie down and accept the dehumanizing and assimilationist ideology and practices of those schools; they resisted. Many resisted by writing. Early twentieth-century writers like Zitkala-Ša, Charles Alexander (Ohiyesa) Eastman, and Luther Standing Bear, and more recent writers like Basil Johnston, Shirley Sterling, and Tomson Highway, wrote stories that resisted the schools' assimilationist aims by revealing the horrors and hypocrisies enacted by school administrators in pursuit of that aim, and by arguing for the superiority of their own Indigenous cultures over the white society into which the schools were supposed to assimilate them.[5] The overt assimilationist rhetoric of the schools is echoed by the subtler assimilationist ideology that underpins the discourse of multiculturalism, including as it operates in contemporary education.

As stories that expose and critique contemporary colonialism while offering Indigenous alternatives to the colonialist paradigms of assimilation and multiculturalism, *True Diary* and *Heart of a Chief* can be understood as enacting tribal critical race theory. Critical race theory and tribal critical race theory both value stories as sources of knowledge and means for knowledge production. Articulating a key tenet of tribal critical race theory, Indigenous education scholar Bryan McKinley Jones Brayboy writes, "Stories are not separate from theory; they make up theory and are, therefore, real and legitimate sources of data and ways of being" (Brayboy 430). Indigenous school stories offer an important contribution in this vein. In Alexie's and Bruchac's texts, school does not just represent dominant institutions, as Trites describes the role of schools in school stories, but it is also one of the primary sites through which dominant colonial institutions and dominant ideologies operate. Schools in these novels also become sites of resistance, places where young people challenge racism and colonialism and where they begin enacting Indigenous pedagogies and Indigenous "visions for the future" (Brayboy 429).

Sustained Rebellion in *The Absolutely True Diary of a Part-Time Indian*

The Absolutely True Diary of a Part-Time Indian is Alexie's first explicitly young adult book, illustrated with dozens of cartoons by Ellen Fortney, with whom he collaborated closely. The novel unfolds from the perspective of Arnold "Junior" Spirit, an adolescent Spokane protagonist who, after opening his geometry textbook at his reservation school only to realize that it is so old his mother had used it when she was a student, decides to leave his reservation school to begin attending an all-white high school in the off-reservation town of Reardan. At Reardan, besides the Indian school mascot, he is "the only *other* Indian in town" (56). While attending Reardan, this protagonist, who goes by Junior at home and Arnold at school, continues to live at home on the Spokane reservation. Over the course of his first year at Reardan, Junior/Arnold writes and draws cartoons in the series of diary entries that make up the novel. He reflects on a range of experiences, including his struggles to get the more than twenty miles to and from school each day, the alcohol-related deaths of several close family members and friends, and his attempts to reconcile his relationship with his best friend, Rowdy, who hates him for going to Reardan.

The National Book Award for Young People's Literature, along with numerous other awards following *True Diary*'s 2007 publication, launched the novel into classrooms, libraries, and the front tables of bookstores across the United States. From the start, however, many called for the book's removal from such venues because of its use of vulgar language and portrayal of masturbation: typical censorship buttons for YA literature. When discussing *True Diary*, educators and librarians tend to focus their attention on these censorship issues, often because they appreciate the novel but fear repercussions for encouraging young people to read it. Meanwhile, among American Indian educators and in the Indigenous media, we see the usual debate surrounding Alexie's work about whether or not he perpetuates stereotypes of Native people. Finally, reviewers of *True Diary* for mainstream news outlets most often focus on Junior being "torn between" or "combining" two worlds (white and Indian), and/or they, like many educators, emphasize the universal nature of Junior's coming-of-age experience.[6]

In their attention to vulgarity, stereotypes, and Junior's supposedly bifurcated cultural identity, educators and critics of *True Diary* have largely failed to address the critique of white privilege central to the novel.[7] Although they have considered Junior's narrative as a YA coming-of-age plot, they have not read it as a school story. Yet, *True Diary* manipulates contemporary school-story conventions and portrays the harsh realities of a young Spokane person's life not to perpetuate stereotypes or portray a struggle between cultures, but rather to do something much more subversive than swearing or masturbation. The novel exposes white privilege as a dominant norm of the present—not just the past—and critiques not only white privilege but also some of the norms of multiculturalism, especially colorblindness and a static view of culture, that contribute to and mask that privilege.

Kerry Boland aptly reads Alexie's novel *Flight*, published the same year as *True Diary*, as embodying an unresolved tension as it oscillates between critiquing settler colonialism and presenting a universal apolitical posture in the vein of liberal multiculturalism that elides such critique (Boland). While I acknowledge that *True Diary* reflects a similar tension that is never fully resolved, I find the critique of multiculturalism more robust in *True Diary* than in *Flight*, especially as *True Diary* unveils the destructive role multiculturalist ideology plays in perpetuating internalized colonialism and lateral violence among Indigenous people. I focus my reading of *True Diary* on its critique of white privilege and multiculturalism, and not on the way it sometimes undermines that critique, because this focus has been largely absent in the novel's reception thus far, and it is critical for understanding the novel's contribution to young adult literature, the school story, and tribal critical race theory.

Multiculturalist ideology has pervaded the reception of *True Diary*. Reviewers in newspapers and teachers in online forums describe Junior as being torn between white and Indian cultures, blending those two cultures, and/or as held back by the culture of his reservation.[8] These characterizations support the multiculturalist understanding of cultures as apolitical, uniform, static entities and as acceptable sites of blame for social ills. If these readers understood cultures as more internally diverse and dynamic, they could see Junior as a Spokane kid who simply acts a bit differently than most other Spokane kids from his reservation when he chooses to attend an off-reservation school. The characterization of Junior as torn between or blending cultures likely stems from a surface reading of the novel's title and its most iconic cartoon, the one from Junior's first day at Reardan that shows his body divided down the middle into a "white" and an "Indian" half (57). The image (see figure) was reproduced on the cover flap of the first edition of *True Diary*; reviewers surely describe Junior as split between or combining cultures in part because Junior calls himself a "part-time" Indian and presents himself as a literal white/Indian composite in this cartoon.

Contrariwise, we could also see Junior's white/Indian cartoon, along with the rest of *True Diary*, as critically illustrating white privilege while reflecting Junior's struggle against internalizing white superiority and the dominant view

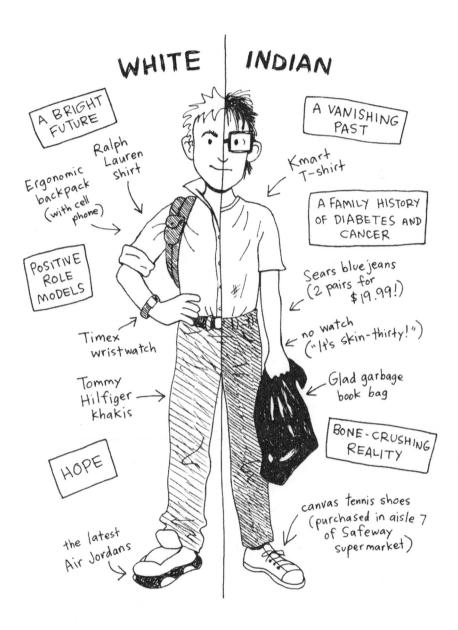

From *The Absolutely True Diary of a Part-Time Indian* by Sherman Alexie with art by Ellen Forney. Copyright © 2007 by Sherman Alexie. Used by permission of Little Brown Books for Young Readers.

of American Indian culture as singular, static, and inferior. With regard to the cartoon, critics oddly overlook two important facts: (1) the white side of the cartoon clearly depicts economic advantage and the related opportunities that come with it, and (2) Junior never actually gets any of the valuable possessions he draws on the white side. That everything on the white side remains a dream for him powerfully illustrates the persistence of white privilege.

Even before he begins attending Reardan, Junior demonstrates a deep awareness of the ongoing colonialism and systemic racism that multiculturalist discourse elides. In his second diary entry, "Why Chicken Means So Much to Me," he explains why he cannot blame his parents for his family's poverty. He writes, "And it's not like my mother and father were born into wealth. It's not like they gambled away their family fortunes. My parents came from poor people who came from poor people who came from poor people, all the way back to the very first poor people" (11). Junior's hyperbole emphasizes the intergenerational nature of his family's poverty—poverty that he clearly links to colonialism. His parents had dreams, he says,

> But we reservation Indians don't get to realize our dreams. We don't get those chances. Or choices. We're just poor. That's all we are.
>
> It sucks to be poor, and it sucks to feel that you somehow *deserve* to be poor. You start believing that you're poor because you're stupid and ugly. And then you start believing that you're stupid and ugly because you're Indian. And because you're Indian you start believing you're destined to be poor. It's an ugly circle and *there's nothing you can do about it.* (13)

Junior powerfully articulates here connections among colonialism, systematic inequality, and internalized racism. American Indians are poor because of colonialism, including the reservation system, which Junior later compares to "prisons" and "death camps" (216–17). The formation and later allotment of Indian reservations greatly reduced Indigenous landholdings. With the assimilationist imposition of private property and free-market capitalism—resisted by many—on reservations, Native people experienced further disenfranchisement due to U.S. government restrictions on Native economic enterprises on reservations, and rampant exploitation with impunity of reservation lands and resources by outsiders. As Melamed elucidates, in the era of global corporate capitalism, multiculturalism contributes to the further disenfranchisement of Indigenous peoples.

"By portraying all the world as the potential property of global multicultural citizens and treating indigenous people as ethnic minorities at best," Melamed explains, "neoliberal multiculturalism has made the appropriation of indigenous lands, territories, and resources by state governments and corporations appear democratic and fair" (Melamed xxii). Junior suggests that intractable poverty among Native people stems from these incarnations of historical and ongoing colonialism, along with Native people's internalization, at times, of the belief in white superiority that undergirds colonialism.

Through his time in Reardan, Junior comes to see some commonalities between the Spokanes on his reservation and the white people there, who had previously seemed completely alien to him. At the same time, his understanding of systemic inequality persists and deepens through his cross-cultural experience. While poverty remains a central concern throughout *True Diary*, Junior comes to see alcoholism as the most deadly consequence of the color line (Lipsitz 2). After the alcohol-related deaths of his dad's best friend, his grandmother, and his sister, Junior observes, "I'm fourteen years old and I've been to forty-two funerals. That's really the biggest difference between Indians and white people" (199). Junior calculates that the majority of those forty-two deaths were caused by alcohol (200). While showing that not all Indians are alcoholics—his mother has been sober for several years and his grandmother never drank—he depicts the real toll alcohol takes in many Indigenous communities.[9] He introduces readers to Spokanes who drink and die out of a despair caused by centuries of discrimination and attacks against their very existence. No one in his class at Reardan had been to more than five funerals (200). For Junior, realizing that his white classmates and the Indians on his reservation have some things in common also draws into stark relief the life-and-death disparities that remain.

Reviews of *True Diary* reflect multiculturalist ideology by ignoring these disparities or by attributing them to a supposedly corrupt reservation culture. Susan Carpenter's 2007 *Los Angeles Times* review does both. Carpenter attributes Junior's trials to his "culture that seems to revolve around alcohol and death" (par. 14). She then explicitly plays the colorblind card, claiming that the many tragedies Junior/Arnold experiences "are far removed from the lives of his peers at school, but they affect [him] in a way that isn't defined by black and white, or Indian versus non-Indian. As Arnold learns, the world isn't divided by color but by actions. You either step up, or you don't" (par. 15). Carpenter ignores the systemic colonialism-induced inequality at the root of the alcoholism and high death rate on the reservation. Instead, Carpenter joins the host of cultural critics who refuse to see racial inequalities in public life as race matters, instead attributing them to individual choice or "culture" (Prashad 42–44). Carpenter's comments suggest that Junior's reservation "culture" is wholly defunct and Spokanes themselves are fully to blame. In contrast, Junior clearly demonstrates that the tragedies he experiences—chronic hunger, his father's alcoholism, and the alcohol-related deaths of several loved ones—stem from his Spokane people's poverty, which stems from colonialism and ongoing systemic white privilege. Junior's world *is* very much "divided by color," and his individual actions do not change that.

In addition to missing the novel's antiracist, anticolonial critique, in focusing on the allegedly corrupt Spokane culture in *True Diary*, Carpenter also overlooks the positive aspects of Junior's reservation community. In the chapter "Red versus White," Junior explains how attending school in Reardan has helped him to appreciate his Spokane family, which is much more present for him than most of the white Reardan parents are for their children (152–58). He also frequently speaks highly of his grandmother and other members of his reservation community. Furthermore, in the novel's final chapter, which begins, "The reservation is beautiful" and ends with Junior reconciling with Rowdy, Junior recalls a past experience climbing the tallest tree on the reservation with Rowdy and thinking that from that view, the reservation "was green and golden and perfect" (219, 227). By ending the novel with an emphasis on beauty and reconciliation on the reservation, Alexie suggests avenues for actively resisting the "death camps" colonialist intentions for reservations within the reservation community, not just via escape from it.

Both on and off the reservation, white privilege and the discourses that mask it, including multiculturalism, clearly function as norms in Junior's school contexts. From the moment Junior throws his mother's old geometry book at Mr. P., the novel foregrounds inequality in education. In Junior's view, Spokane students needing to use the same books that their parents used because of their poverty is "absolutely the saddest thing in the world" (31). This epitomizes the disparity between their opportunities and those of students at other, more privileged schools (31). Junior also reveals ways in which multiculturalism masks these inequalities at both Wellpinit and Reardan. He describes the two types of teachers who work at his reservation school as "liberal, white, vegetarian do-gooders" and "conservative, white missionary saviors" (30). He observes, "Some of our teachers make us eat birdseed so we'll feel closer to the earth, and others hate birds because they are supposedly minions of the Devil" (30). Both types of teachers not only construct a singular, static cultural category of "the Indian"—"nature lover" and "Christian convert," respectively—but they also try to make the actual American Indian students in front of them fit their constructed molds. To draw on George Lipsitz's discussion of white privilege, they could hardly be more "controlling" or "condescending" in their embrace of Indians, which serves to perpetuate their own privilege (Lipsitz 118).

A similar perspective on American Indian culture (again, falsely in the singular) dominates at Reardan. No one in the school other than Junior seems disturbed by the Indian mascot, a stereotype of a savage Plains warrior, stuck in time and strikingly unlike the actual Spokane Indians living just a few miles from the school. Moreover, while we see no evidence that American Indian histories or cultures are studied in the curriculum at Reardan, we witness some of Junior's teachers making assumptions about him based on their view of American Indian culture as inferior and American Indians as less intelligent than whites. When Junior accurately corrects a teacher, Mr. Dodge, over his mistaken observation about the science of petrified wood, it takes the star white student, Gordy, to convince Mr. Dodge and the class that Junior is right. Moreover, after Mr. Dodge is convinced, he thanks Gordy but says nothing to Junior (84–86). "Yep, now even the teachers were treating me like an idiot," Junior laments (86). Even after he is clearly proven wrong, Mr. Dodge is unwilling to let go of his view of American Indians as inferior. At Reardan, the smart and athletic Junior poses a threat to the static, controllable, inferior view of American Indian culture held by white teachers and students and, thus, to the belief in white superiority inherent in that view.

Both schools that Junior attends—Wellpinit and Reardan—are dominated by white educators and by the ideology of white privilege. Junior has no formal schooling option that is self-determined by Spokane people or rooted in Spokane cultural values. The major differences between the schools are the student population (all Spokane on the reservation and all white at Reardan) and the resources for academic success (poor on the reservation and rich in Reardan). In contrast to the characterization in some reviews of the novel—like the claim in a *Publishers Weekly* review that "Junior must separate from his tribe in order to preserve his identity"—Junior does not abandon his Spokane community when he begins attending Reardan. Unlike most new-kid-in-school story protagonists, Junior does not move. He still lives on the reservation and attends Spokane cultural events after starting at Reardan. He does not run to Reardan in order to flee his Spokane community. Rather, he chooses to attend Reardan because it seems the only viable option for pursuing academic success and the opportunities that come with it.

While Junior embraces some social norms at Reardan, especially the school's valuing of academic achievement, he resists the school's attempt to socialize him and others into dominant norms of white privilege and multiculturalism. Although Junior initially attempts to perform whiteness at school, especially in going by "Arnold" rather than "Junior," hiding his poverty, and investing in the opportunities located in that white space, he ultimately rejects the system of white privilege as well as the dominant ideology that would identify him as less Indian for pursuing academic and economic opportunities. In this regard Junior moves to an ever stronger state of rebellion rather than toward socialization, or toward the more acceptable form of rebellion we find in most school stories. And unlike in texts such as *The Chocolate War*, where characters grow increasingly isolated in their resistance as their prospects for successful rebellion grow increasingly bleak, Junior finds increasing support among white as well as Indian allies.[10]

Junior's awareness and critique of some dominant norms of white privilege and multiculturalism develops over time. In the first part of his year at Reardan, as he exposes inequalities rooted in colonialism and racism, Junior also struggles against internalizing a sense of white superiority and a dominant notion of "authentic" American Indian identity. As a result, he often feels un-Indian and all alone, like he "was half Indian in one place and half white in the other," always feeling "like a stranger" in both Wellpinit and Reardan (118). After he has been attending Reardan for two months, Junior explains to his friend Gordy that people on the reservation call him an "apple" because they think he is "red on the outside and white on the inside" (131–32). Junior notes that "some Indians think you have to act white to make your life better. Some Indians think you *become* white if you to try to make your life better, if you become successful" (131). He feels like he does not belong anywhere because he is not white, nor is he Indian in a way that the dominant society would recognize as "authentic." Junior jokes as he is about to walk into Reardan for the first time that he cannot run away to go live in the woods "like a real Indian" because his allergies are too bad (58). Even though he is joking about the woods, being part of a Spokane community devastated by colonialism and then being labeled a traitor for leaving that community to attend Reardan does at times make Junior feel like he is not a real Indian. Wrestling with these feelings of being inauthentic and alone is a painful part of Junior's journey of resistance.

If Junior's own internalizing of dominant attitudes about Indian authenticity relates to his feelings of utter estrangement, then his rebellion against such dominant norms is intricately tied to the bonds he forms with other characters. It is only with the support of a few respected members of his Spokane community, especially his grandmother, and a growing number of white allies at Reardan, especially Gordy, that Junior is able to recover his sense of belonging and strengthen his rebellion. With the help of these allies, Junior resists socialization into the colonialist norms perpetuated within and beyond his school context, thereby surpassing the stunted rebellion we find in most school stories. With the help of his supporters, Junior begins to reject the idea that he is a tribal traitor. He identifies that idea's roots in internalized racism and comes to embrace a more dynamic view of cultural identities than adherents of multiculturalism offer. Both moves contribute to Junior's rebellion against socialization into a dominant society where white privilege and static understandings of culture are the norm and American Indians are therefore rendered choiceless, stuck in a static, impoverished state in which they must remain if they are to be considered fully Indian. As he grows increasingly critical of the idea that seeking success makes him white, Junior stops trying to hide his Spokane identity at school and bolsters his ties to his Spokane community, most notably as he grieves with his family over the many deaths of their loved ones and when he reconnects with Rowdy at the end of the novel.[11]

Junior's grandmother and a few others in his reservation community help him to challenge ideas about Spokane culture that come from internalized colonialism rather than from Spokane traditions. Just after the Christmas holidays, halfway through his year at Reardan, Junior's grandmother—one of about five Spokanes Junior knows who have never drunk alcohol—passes away after being struck by a drunk driver while walking home from a mini powwow on the reservation (157–58). In the buildup to announcing her death, Junior first explains why his grandmother was "the very best thing about Wellpinit" (154). Junior says that the "very best thing about [his] grandmother" was that "she was tolerant" (154). He goes on to discuss how his grandmother "held on to that old-time Indian spirit" that led Indians in the old days to "be forgiving of any kind of eccentricity" and, in fact, to celebrate "weird people" (155). Junior's grandmother traveled to powwows all over the country, she would talk to anyone, and she "was the only one who thought it was a 100 percent good idea" for Junior to attend Reardan (156). She was particularly excited about all the "new people" Junior would meet at his new school (156). Like his grandmother, Junior's parents, his dad's friend Eugene, and a few others on the reservation, "especially the grandmothers," think Junior is brave for attending Reardan, and they support him even as the vast majority on the reservation see him as a traitor.[12]

Since Junior's grandmother is traditional in the sense that she does not drink and frequently participates in cultural events, especially powwows, Junior can cling to her understanding of traditional Spokane culture when he is assailed by those outside and within his community who view Spokane culture as static, isolated, and intolerant of difference. From Junior's grandmother's perspective, these views are not traditionally Spokane, but rather they have been adopted from the colonizers. In her view, the "old time" view, the Spokane culture is strength-ened—rather than threatened—by internal diversity as well as by encounters with non-Spokane people. Still, even if he strongly believes his grandmother is right, it is hard for Junior to inhabit her perspective on the reservation when the majority, at one point, literally turn their backs on him, and perhaps even more so at school, where he feels far from his grandmother and his other Spokane supporters.[13]

It is important to acknowledge that Rowdy and some of the other Spokanes may have legitimate reasons, other than internalized racism, for criticizing Junior. For example, some may fault Junior for uncritically embracing a view of success that they think aligns more with dominant Euro-American capitalistic society than with traditional Spokane understandings of what constitutes a good life (a position they could take without necessarily disassociating Spokane tradition from all manifestations of capitalism, and without equating Spokane identity with material poverty). And Rowdy seems primarily upset because he feels Junior has abandoned him, putting personal dreams over their friendship. While *True Diary* might have done more to address these complexities, we can still learn much from its critique of the reductive, destructive association of Indian authenticity with poverty that Junior so fiercely resists.

Around Thanksgiving time, after months of intense loneliness at school and shortly before his grandmother's death, Junior befriends Gordy, whom he calls "the Genius White Boy" (91). Junior figures Gordy as an educator; he teaches Junior "how to read" (93–94). Gordy helps socialize Junior into certain school practices—how to study, read carefully, and embrace his excitement over books—but he does so in a way that enables Junior to be critical of dominant ideologies perpetuated within and beyond the school (94–98). In fact, as their friendship develops we see how Gordy's instruction in critical reading—paying close attention to words: who invents them, how they are used, and how they change in different contexts—extends to their "reading" of dominant discourses as well as books (94–95). For example, when Junior tells Gordy about some people on the reservation calling him an "apple," accusing him of acting white by attending Reardan and pursuing success, Gordy helps Junior to critique the logic in such thinking; if it were true that Indians become white if they achieve success, "then wouldn't all white people be successful?" Gordy says (131). Gordy goes on to explain that weird people used to be banished since they threatened the strength of their tribes, and assures Junior that "weird people still get banished" (132). Even though Gordy actually contradicts Junior's understanding of his own tribal tradition of embracing and celebrating weird people, he speaks powerfully to Junior's present reality; Junior feels banished by most of his Spokane tribe, whether or not they are straying from their traditions in doing so. Acknowledging that he and Gordy are both "weird," Junior declares, "Alright, then. So we have a tribe of two" (132). While Junior never feels as close to Gordy as he does to Rowdy, he and Gordy continue to develop a friendship centered around critical thinking.

Gordy, more often than Junior, is represented as the teacher figure in the boys' relationship, aligning, in many regards, with the white savior prototype of mainstream "multicultural literature." Yet, Junior teaches Gordy sometimes as well, with his critical-reading practice extending to messages he gets from Gordy. The most trenchant example appears in the chapter about the death of Junior's sister. Junior explains, "Gordy gave me a book by a Russian dude named Tolstoy, who wrote: 'Happy families are all alike; every unhappy family is unhappy in its own way.' Well I hate to argue with Russian Geniuses, but Tolstoy didn't know Indians. And he didn't know that all Indian families are unhappy for the same exact reason: the fricking booze" (200). The very title of the chapter, "Because Russian Guys Are Not Always Geniuses," reflects Junior's critical-reading practice, sharpened by his grief over the loss of his sister.

Building personal relationships with Gordy and others is a key part of Junior's rebellion because his experience of oppressive norms is both intensely personal and intensely isolating. Like Tommy in Armstrong's *Slash*, Junior is empowered through his connection to community. Unlike Tommy, Junior never travels away from his Indigenous community for long periods of time, nor does Junior become as estranged from his community as Tommy does. Yet, like Tommy, Junior finds personal strength via reimagining himself as a valuable member of his Native community and by reestablishing relationships in that community, especially with Rowdy. Junior differs from Tommy, however, in the degree that he is personally empowered through his actual and imagined integration into additional communities that include non-Native friends and allies, like Gordy.

While his deepest connections at Reardan are with Gordy and his girlfriend, Penelope, as the school year continues, more and more of Junior's white classmates come to support him. When a teacher mocks Junior for missing several classes after his grandmother and Eugene die, Gordy leads a protest by dropping his textbook loudly on the floor. Every one of Junior's classmates then joins him by dropping their books and leaving the room (175–76). By the time Junior returns to school after his sister's death, most of the Reardan community has come to support him. Junior writes, "All of these white kids and teachers, who were so suspicious of me when I first arrived, had learned to care about me. Maybe some of them even loved me. And I'd been so suspicious of them. And now I care about a lot of them. And loved a few of them" (212). On the one hand, the narrative too easily resolves here into a happy multicultural family, with no indication that this Reardan community will extend their embrace of Junior into a broader and more difficult alliance with the Spokane nation. On the other hand, Junior has led many at Reardan to at least begin questioning the dominant view of American Indians as inferior to whites, and he personally benefits from this community's support.

By the end of his year at Reardan, Junior has restored his sense of belonging. He recognizes the community he has formed at Reardan and begins restoring relationships—especially with Rowdy—in his reservation community. Junior's "huge realization" that he belonged to multiple "tribes" is key in this restoration. Junior realizes at the end of his school year that he was "not alone in [his] loneliness" (217). In what reads, on the surface, like a colorblind multiculturalist assertion, he writes, "I realized that, sure, I was Spokane Indian. I belonged to that tribe. But I also belonged to the tribe of American immigrants. And to the tribe of basketball players. And to the tribe of bookworms. And the tribe of cartoonists. And the tribe of chronic masturbators" (217). Junior says that upon realizing he belonged to all of these tribes, "I knew I'd be okay" (217). He knows he will be okay because he knows he will never be alone, even when away from the Spokane tribe, since he belongs to so many different "tribes."

Junior's list of multiple tribes simultaneously resonates with and challenges aspects of multiculturalism; the tension in the novel's treatment of multiculturalism is at its strongest here. The list celebrates diversity, downplays differences, elides anti-colonial resistance, and suggests that Spokane Indians are just another of many groups in America rather than a distinct sovereign nation. In many regards, this multiculturalist vision aligns with the shift in Alexie's thinking following the terrorist attacks of September 11, 2001. Alexie speaks frequently about how the attacks themselves as well as the climate of intolerance in their aftermath prompted a shift in his thinking—and in his work—away from militant nationalism and divisive tribalism and toward an embrace of tolerance and intercultural exchange.[14] In the poem "Tuxedo with Eagle Feathers" from his 2009 collection *Face*, Alexie launches an outright attack on Elizabeth Cook-Lynn and the literary nationalists associated with what he perceives as her brand of Indigenous separatism. He writes, "I wasn't saved by the separation of cultures; I was *reborn* inside the collision of cultures. So fuck Cook-Lynn and her swarm of professorial locusts" ("Tuxedo" 80). He then goes on to praise Haida artist/designer Dorothy Grant, "who blends traditional Haida symbol and imagery with twenty-first century fashion," creating the tuxedos with eagle feathers of the poem's title (80–81). This poem is interested in the individual sovereignty of the Indian artist rather than the tribal sovereignty espoused by Cook-Lynn and other Indigenous nationalists and critics of multiculturalism (79–80). The sovereignty imagined by the poem enables artistic autonomy and intercultural mixing rather than a separatist tribal nationalism. In *True Diary*, Junior is similarly depicted as needing to break away from what holds him back in his Spokane community and to embrace some aspects of the white culture at Reardan in order to pursue personal success. Like the speaker of "Tuxedo with Eagle Feathers," he experiences a sort of personal rebirth in the collision of cultures through his multiple-tribes realization.

Despite this multiculturalist tenor of Junior's epiphany, the way he imagines his membership in the multiple tribes on his list also, and at times contradictorily, challenges mainstream multiculturalism in at least three significant ways. First, for Junior, belonging to multiple tribes does not mean that all of the tribes blend together bringing an end to distinctions, unlike in the multiculturalist race-is-over dream. In belonging to all of the tribes, he is not torn between them and does not feel guilty about having multiple allegiances. Unlike in his earlier struggles over feeling like a tribal traitor or a part-time Indian, here Junior's belonging to many tribes is not figured as making him any less Indian. Instead, he is able to strongly assert that he "was a Spokane Indian" and that he "belonged to that tribe" alongside a host of other distinct, if sometimes overlapping, communities. While the tone of the list suggests a certain equity among these different groups, it does not necessarily erase the differences between them. Moreover, because Junior throughout the novel always references the Spokane when speaking of his "tribe" in the singular, the text subtly troubles the flattening tone of the list itself, signaling an important difference between the Spokane Indian nation and the other identity- and interest-based "tribes" to which Junior belongs.

Second, Junior's "tribes" are more dynamic, open, and internally diverse than the narrow, static rendering of cultures in the discourse of multiculturalism. By listing tribes such as "tortilla chips-and-salsa lovers" and "beloved sons" alongside "Spokane Indians," Junior suggests that Spokane Indians are as dynamic and internally diverse as these other "tribes" (217). He thereby starkly contrasts the multiculturalist view of ethnic cultures as closed entities that are defined by traditions from the distant past and that lose their authenticity if they adapt practices from other cultures.

Third, Junior's philosophy of multiple tribes counters multiculturalism by revealing the socioeconomic inequalities that multiculturalism masks, and creating space to challenge them. The tribes of "poverty" and "funeral-goers" would not appear on a list of ethnic-based cultures as defined by multiculturalism (217). The tribes Junior belongs to cut across lines of privilege. For instance, by recognizing his affiliation with the "tribe of poverty" as well as with the "tribe of teenage boys," Junior suggests that he has the right to pursue opportunities that other teenage boys—including wealthier ones—do, despite his poverty (217). Furthermore, Junior's list itself, with its "small-town kids" and "Pacific Northwesterners" as well as Spokane Indians and the poor, suggests alliances for naming and resisting inequalities. Many of the experiences Junior documents in his diary illuminate these possibilities. For instance, Gordy, the white, small-town farm kid, helps Junior, the Spokane Indian, to name and combat racism along with its links to poverty in their discussion of the apple complex (131–32).

True Diary neither fully embraces nor fully rejects multiculturalism. Instead, while it walks a slippery line (and sometimes slips), for the most part, the novel challenges multiculturalism by exposing racism and colonialism while critiquing the static view of cultures perpetuated by the discourse. In addition, the book presents the tolerance and cross-cultural exchange often associated with multiculturalism as traditional Spokane values, through the figure of Junior's grandmother. Though clearly in line with Alexie's larger critique of violent fundamentalism and separatism, the novel's figuring of cultural dynamism, internal diversity, tolerance, and movement among different cultures as traditional values of an Indigenous nation may expand rather than undermine understandings of Indigenous national sovereignty. *True Diary* as a whole, moreover, demonstrates that the ideologies of white privilege and multiculturalism are too powerful to be overturned by a lone individual or even a single small community, underscoring the need for allies to support Native nations.

In a discussion with American Indian students about Junior's multiple-tribes realization, Alexie characterizes Junior's many tribes both as unique communities to which Junior belongs and as allies for Junior's Spokane community. In his article "From Wellpinit to Reardan: Sherman Alexie's Journey to the National Book Award," Jim Blasingame includes the following words Alexie shared during his exchange with this small group of students from the Gila River Indian Community in Arizona:

> Our own elders have taught us that we're hated, and the truth is that we're not. People love Indians. Everywhere I go in the world, Indian people are admired. It worries me when we tell Indian young people to leave their hearts behind when they leave the rez because that implies that the world is a dangerous place for our hearts and it's not. There are so many allies out there, and if you don't bring your heart, you won't find them. (Blasingame 72)

Elsewhere, including in *True Diary*, Alexie exposes the problems of exploitative non-Native wannabes who "loved Indian people soooooooooo much" (*True Diary* 162). However, with the Gila River students, as in *True Diary*, Alexie emphasizes the importance of Indian young people opening themselves up to non-Native individuals and communities who actually care about them. As Junior says in *True Diary* after Roger and Penelope realize he is poor and their friendship begins to deepen, "If you let people into your life a little bit, they can be pretty damn amazing" (129). Importantly, in his exchange with the Gila River students, Alexie describes these non-Native people as "allies," thereby suggesting that when American Indian young adults open themselves up to people outside their communities, they open the possibility of building alliances that can advance the goals of Indigenous communities.

While Junior's journey is intensely personal, he depends on allies to seek his individual dreams and to resist dominant norms in a way that ultimately aims to strengthen not just Junior but also his entire Spokane community. The novel suggests that these non-Native communities become better allies to Native communities, or at least potential allies, when they too learn to resist the norms of white privilege and multiculturalism. The same proponents of multiculturalism who deploy a rhetoric of "diverse communities" also present cultures as static, apolitical entities. *True Diary* challenges the logic of multiculturalism by revealing how a blindness to racial inequalities and a static view of culture leads to isolation, not community-building, within as well as across cultural groups. In Junior's experience, honesty about ongoing inequalities and a dynamic view of culture foster a sense of belonging to multiple communities and enable alliance-building across cultural and racial groups.

While it critiques separatism, belonging is key in *True Diary*. The final scene of the novel underscores how Junior belongs to his distinctive Spokane community, and how that belonging can complement his movements beyond that community. As he and Rowdy play basketball—and reconcile their friendship in the process—Rowdy empowers Junior by giving him the title of "nomad" (229–30). Rowdy explains that Indians "used to be nomadic" (229). Most are not anymore, he adds, except for Junior (229). He says he had a dream about Junior traveling the world in which Junior looked happy and Rowdy felt happy for him (229). As Junior cries with gratitude, "'You're an old-time nomad,' Rowdy said, 'You're going to keep moving all over the world in search of food and water and grazing land. That's pretty cool'" (230). This conversation takes place away from any formal school context, but it builds on the resistance that Junior had been developing at Reardan, further enabling him to reject the ideology that positions his culture as static and him as either culturally inauthentic or a cultural traitor for pursuing success. Furthermore, as the nomad title draws on Indigenous traditions—albeit it in a problematically generic and romanticizing way—and is given on Junior's reservation by Rowdy, a fellow Spokane Indian, it firmly positions Junior's rebellion in an Indigenous context. While the idea of Junior being a nomad who travels and pursues personal success is, in some regards, quite individualistic, it takes the support of others—like Rowdy, Gordy, and Junior's grandmother—for Junior to embrace the pursuit. Moreover, Junior's supporters suggest that in remaining committed to his Spokane tribe while also leaving the reservation so as to learn from others, Junior carries on a community tradition and may enrich the tribe as a result.

In their chapter on *True Diary* and *Flight*, from the book *Sherman Alexie in the Classroom*, Heather E. Bruce, Anna E. Baldwin, and Christabel Umphrey call on educators to do antiracist work by addressing the colonial legacy of injustice and inequality depicted in these books (Bruce et al. 129–31). If teachers want to do this work, these authors argue, they will need "to do more than examine the stereotypes and the negative aspects of tribalism explored in Alexie's novels" (129). I would argue that scholars as well as students might pursue an antiracist and anti-colonialist agenda while also expanding their understanding of young adult and Native American literatures if they study *True Diary* as a uniquely rebellious school story, paying particular attention to the ways Junior exposes, critiques, and resists socialization into dominant norms of white privilege and multiculturalism. The nomad figure helps Junior justify his personal choices as a Spokane Indian, but it does not change Junior's own poverty, the precariousness of his hope, or the stark fact that dreams, choices, and chances remain out of reach for most people in his Spokane community. It would take allies far and wide, including those in privileged societies, to change that reality. While *True Diary* does not consider what such alliances may look like beyond Junior's personal situation, it may prompt readers to take that question to heart.

Collaborative Learning in *The Heart of a Chief*

Joseph Bruchac's novel *The Heart of a Chief*, published nearly ten years before *True Diary*, similarly shares some characteristics of contemporary mainstream school stories. Chris, the novel's eleven-year-old Penacook narrator/protagonist, is a new kid in school who tries to make friends and find his place while accepting certain norms of the school and rebelling against others. Like Junior's Reardan school, Chris's new school is predominately white and has an Indian team name and mascot, "the Chiefs." Chris is not, however, the only American Indian at his school. In fact, his Rangerville school is the only option Penacooks have from sixth grade on, so all junior high and high school–age Penacooks from Chris's small, fictional Penacook reservation take the bus with him to Rangerville. Chris, then, does not share Junior's struggle over being labeled a traitor for attending an off-reservation school. *Heart of a Chief* instead focuses on Chris's fight against the derogatory Indian mascot at Rangerville, and his response to divisions in his Penacook community over a proposed casino.

Heart of a Chief, like *True Diary*, diverges from mainstream school stories in its depiction of sustained rebellion against some of the norms of multiculturalism. Bruchac's novel does not critique white privilege to the degree that Alexie's does.

Instead, as Bruchac's protagonist, Chris, successfully marshals a direct challenge to his school's mascot, he joins *True Diary*'s Junior in also challenging the multiculturalist discourse behind the mascot, particularly its figuring of Indigenous culture as singular and static, with its parameters of authenticity determined by the dominant society. *Heart of a Chief* goes further than *True Diary* in imagining forms of cross-cultural learning and social action rooted in Indigenous epistemologies rather than multiculturalism. In contrast to most mainstream writers, Bruchac sets a substantial portion of his school story in a classroom environment rather than focusing on the social spaces of the school, enabling him to imagine what indigenized education can look like in a formal school context. Like *True Diary*, *Heart of a Chief* also extends beyond the school setting to a greater degree than most mainstream school stories do through its substantial focus on Chris and his family navigating the conflict in their reservation community over a proposed casino.

We are first introduced to the Rangerville mascot when Chris and his Penacook friends, Belly Button and Gartersnake, watch their other Penacook friend, Pizza, play football on the Rangerville Junior High team. Chris explains that the Rangerville Chiefs "paint their cheeks like phony Indians before every game and shout out war woops when they take the field. Lots of people on the Rangerville side join in, and they also do the tomahawk chop like on television" (54). He goes on to describe the signs some fans make with "ugly cartoon Indians on them holding tomahawks" that say "SCALP 'EM CHIEFS" (54). When Pizza scores a touchdown and fans actually start chanting "SCALP 'EM, INJUN, SCALP 'EM," Chris realizes "what it is like to be excited and depressed all at once" (59). Belly Button tells him that high school games are even worse. The high school team is called "the Big Chiefs," and their mascot, "who is never a real Indian, dresses in buckskin with a Plains Indian headdress and runs up and down the sidelines leading people in the tomahawk chop" (55). By the end of the game, after Pizza has scored the third touchdown, Chris, Gartersnake, and Belly Button are the only Rangerville fans not joining in the "SCALP 'EM" chant and tomahawk chop (60). Chris imagines that his Penacook friends feel the same way he does, "proud and empty at the same time" (60).

During a presentation about Indian team names and mascots that Chris and a group of his language-arts classmates give near the end of the novel, Chris points out that supporters of "the Chiefs" say that giving the Rangerville team an Indian name is "meant to honor Indians" (129). Yet, as Chris's critique of the mascot and of other celebrated representations of Indians at his school demonstrates, in their attempt to "honor Indians" these non-Natives fail to pay any attention to actual living Native people. Instead, they construct their own image of Native Americans based on stereotypes from other dominant representations and then defend themselves as preservers of "true"—meaning static and singular—Native American culture when they come under critique. Like the adherents of multiculturalism that Prashad describes, these members of the dominant society view the culture of "others" as something they have the authority to define, control, and police (Prashad 67).

At Chris's school, these issues extend beyond the Indian mascot. During a provocative early exchange between Chris and Mr. Dougal, the homeroom and language-arts teacher for whom Chris later gives the presentation on Indian team names and mascots, Bruchac exposes the way in which teacherly authority and multiculturalist discourse combine to perpetuate a colonialist perspective that positions Indians neatly in the past. Mr. Dougal announces that the class will be discussing *The Sign of the Beaver*, a book, Chris notes, that he has read before and that "is about my people" (19). It is clear to Chris that Mr. Dougal "loves the book" (19). "Like a lot of teachers in Rangerville," Chris observes, "it seems he admires Indians in the past and doesn't really pay much attention to those of us who are still here. Or maybe he thinks that this book should make us feel proud we are Indian" (19). When Chris raises his hand to say that there is "something wrong" about the book, Mr. Dougal attempts to silence him, saying, "I have been assured that it is an accurate portrayal of the times. It's a balanced view of both the settlers and the Native Americans, wouldn't you agree?" (20). Chris knows that "Wouldn't you agree?" really "means that a teacher knows more than you do and it is time to shut up" (20). In other words, Mr. Dougal claims that *The Sign of the Beaver*, a dominant representation of American Indians, has the final authority. Chris, a living Penacook person, has no right to critique it. Like the advocates of Indian mascots that legal scholar Matthew Fletcher discusses in his work on Indigenous critical race theory, Mr. Dougal seems to judge Chris as ignorant at best and an inauthentic Indian at worst. He sees Chris as an unworthy critic of a representation that to him clearly celebrates "real" Native people (Fletcher 23, 102).[15] The academic language of "accuracy" and "balance" bolsters Mr. Dougal's position. Chris's earlier comparison of the Rangerville school building to a "maximum security prison" resonates here as Mr. Dougal attempts to police Chris's discourse (11). Chris says that Mr. Dougal looks at him like "a hawk about to dive down on a rabbit," a violent metaphor for the control and silencing that Mr. Dougal attempts to enforce.

Yet, Chris, feeling bolstered by his ancestors, refuses to fold (19–20). He pushes his rebellion beyond the usual acceptable limits of the school story when he assures readers, "But I am not a rabbit," and tells Mr. Dougal and the class that the end of *The Sign of the Beaver* is wrong since "the Indians just go away" (20). In reality, he says, "We didn't go away. They tried to drive us off the land. They put bounties on our scalps. They burned our villages. But we didn't go away" (20). Mr. Dougal is silent for a long time, and then he actually concedes that Chris has made "a good point" and says he would like to discuss it more sometime (21). Chris's perhaps unrealistically significant influence on Mr. Dougal continues from this point, with Mr. Dougal eventually becoming an ally in Chris's opposition to the school mascot.

While many teachers at Rangerville praise dominant representations of American Indians and do not "pay much attention" to the American Indians still in their midst, their view of American Indian culture nevertheless affects their interactions with real Penacook students. Bruchac does not address white racism against American Indians as explicitly as Alexie does. However, like *True Diary*, *Heart of a Chief* suggests that teachers and students at Chris's school harbor attitudes of white superiority that are closely tied to their view of American Indian culture as static. Since the Penacook students at Rangerville are neither "authentic" Indians of the past nor privileged whites, they are seen as inferior by many at the school. Early in the novel, Chris describes the Penacook students as little fish in a sea of sharks (11). As Chris enters his homeroom and takes a seat, he quickly learns that "It's an unwritten rule that Indian kids who don't want to get in trouble sit in the back" (14). A white student sitting near the seat Chris has chosen—near the front of the room—stares at Chris and motions for him to move, and Chris does, sliding into a back seat and putting his head down (14). On his first day of school, then, Chris is literally put in his place by a white student. At Rangerville, the norm is for whites to have the power, including power over Penacook students and representations of them. It is no wonder that when the school principal asks Chris why no Penacooks have complained about the school mascot before, Chris replies, "Maybe they didn't think anyone would listen" (131–32). In a space that privileges white voices and socializes students to do the same, Penacooks have understood that their voices would not be heard. Although Chris slouches to the back of his classroom on that first day, later the same day he moves back up to his seat in the front, a movement of resistance to dominant ideologies that continues in his exchange soon after with Mr. Dougal about *The Sign of the Beaver* and throughout the rest of the novel (19).

From the very beginning of *Heart of a Chief*, through a discussion of his use of the English language, Chris figures his Penacook society as dynamic and developing, but not assimilating. He explains in the first chapter that he has some knowledge of the Penacook language and that he keeps learning more from Doda (his grandfather) and from the Penacook land, which "keeps the language" (2). "Things are not always so clear in English," Chris says, as they are in Penacook. Yet, he goes on to say that he will tell his story primarily in English since, as his Auntie says, "it is our language too" (3). "In our family," Chris explains, "we've been speaking it for about four hundred years" (3). For Chris, using English requires him neither to abandon the Penacook language and the values associated with it, nor to embrace all of the social values of the Euro-Americans. Instead, like many Indigenous authors of boarding/residential school narratives, Chris uses English to challenge dominant norms, to disseminate Indigenous cultural values, and to advocate for his Indigenous nation. For Chris, English is not a lingua franca that melts away all distinctions, as in the multiculturalist vision of a race-free future, but rather one of the many resources he embraces in order to express his distinctive Penacook identity at home and at school.

Chris's stance on language lines up with the argument Simon Ortiz makes in his 1981 essay "Toward a National Indian Literature: Cultural Authenticity in Nationalism," reprinted in the 2006 landmark book *American Indian Literary Nationalism*. Ortiz writes,

> The indigenous peoples of the Americas have taken the languages of the colonial-
> ists and used them for their own purposes. Some would argue that this means
> that Indian people have succumbed or become educated into a different linguistic
> system and have forgotten or have been forced to forsake their native selves. This
> is simply not true. Along with their native languages, Indian women and men
> have carried on their lives and their expression through the use of the newer
> languages, particularly Spanish, French, and English, and they have used these
> languages on their own terms. This is the crucial item that has to be understood,
> that it is entirely possible for a people to retain and maintain their lives through
> the use of any language. There is not a question of authenticity here; rather, it
> is the way that Indian people have creatively responded to forced colonization.

And this response has been one of resistance; there is no clearer word for it than resistance. (Ortiz 256–57)

In their preface to *American Indian Literary Nationalism*, coauthors Jace Weaver, Craig Womack, and Robert Warrior describe Ortiz's treatment of language as foundational to their literary nationalism project, praising the way that Ortiz values older Indigenous languages while also claiming "English as an Indian language" in contrast with "the omnipresent cliché that Indian people are the victims of English" (Weaver et al. xviii). English has, of course, been used to oppress Native people, not least of all in Indian boarding schools where children were beaten for speaking Indigenous languages. Yet, as K. Tsianina Lomawaima and Teresa L. McCarty point out, many students from the boarding schools (not just those who published stories about their experiences) used English to "remain Indian," transforming the language into one of intertribal community-building and resistance to colonialism.[16]

In his own school context, Chris builds on these appropriations of English as he also uses the language to foster alliances with non-Native students to support the interests of his Penacook community. At the same time, he subtly suggests Penacook-language preservation as one of those community interests via his brief reference to the distinctiveness of the Penacook language as able to express some ideas more clearly than English, and as uniquely connected to the Penacook land base (2). While this suggestion is somewhat bolstered by Chris's later depiction of himself and his friends using some Penacook words in their conversations, *Heart of a Chief,* like all of the texts in this study, falls short of offering an in-depth exploration of the role that Indigenous-language maintenance and revitalization can play in Indigenous empowerment. Neither does *Heart of a Chief* reflect a substantial influence from Penacook vocabulary or linguistic structures. Readers will need to look elsewhere, such as to Louise Erdrich's Birchbark House series, or to the growing number of children's and young adult titles being published in Indigenous languages, for this deeper kind of engagement with Indigenous languages, which could lead to a more nuanced picture of Indigenous linguistic resistance in regard to multiculturalism and beyond.[17]

In addition to figuring his own use of English alongside the Penacook language as a traditional practice, Chris highlights other ways his family extends Penacook traditions into contemporary times and dominant spaces. For example, he shares his grandfather's equation of traditional Penacook hunting—a way of working on behalf of the community—with "new ways" of hunting, including Chris's father, Mito, "hunting" for a Harvard MBA that would help him "find ways to bring jobs to Penacooks," a contemporary manifestation of working on behalf of the community (75).[18] Adherents of multiculturalism who problematically associate the pursuit of higher education with Euro-American society might see a neutral blending of cultures at play here, or they might characterize Mito as compromising his authenticity as Penacook. However, with the imagery of hunting, Chris clearly situates Mito's pursuit in a Penacook framework.

Chris's group of four Penacook friends further demonstrates his embrace of the dynamism of Penacook culture. His group calls themselves "the Rainbow Coalition," because, Chris explains, "we hang out together and all look so different" (39). Chris is the only one in the group who "looks Penacook" in a stereotypical way (36). Gartersnake has a Penacook mother and an absentee Norwegian father (36–37). Belly Button, the only one in the group "who has an actual mother and father both alive and living together" is, Chris says, "living proof of the fact that Penacooks adopted all kinds of other Indians into our tribe" (38). "He looks just like a Pueblo Indian," Chris explains (38). Finally, Pizza has a deceased Penacook father and an absentee African American mother (38–39). He lives with his dad's sister and her children (39).

On the surface, the "Rainbow Coalition" name resonates with multiculturalism even more than *True Diary*'s "multiple tribes." Yet, contrasting with multiculturalism, in his historical Rainbow Coalition, to which Bruchac likely alludes here, the Reverend Jesse Jackson certainly did not elide the ongoing realities of racism as he sought to bring the nation of the United States together for a more inclusive and just future. Chris's group also troubles multiculturalism's singular, static take on cultures since all of the very different-looking members of this Rainbow Coalition belong to the same Indigenous nation. The fact that they all seem to fully belong as citizens of the Penacook nation enables the novel to avoid the complex, contentious terrain of blood quantum and tribal membership. The group nevertheless challenges multiculturalism in striving to embrace their internal diversity and the malleability of their nation that it reflects.

While the members of the Rainbow Coalition generally embrace their own diversity as Penacooks, they, like Junior in *True Diary*, also at times struggle with dominant notions of cultural authenticity. In an early exchange, Gartersnake calls Chris "Tonto," and when Chris tells him never to do that again, Gartersnake responds, "At least you look Indian" (36). We see Gartersnake's internalization of dominant understandings of culture in his use of the name Tonto, as well as in his insecurity about his own Indian identity because of his physical appearance. In another early scene, the entire Coalition comes under the influence of a static view of culture as they talk about Katie, a new girl in school who claims to be Indian, and they wonder what kind of Indian she is (23). They look at one another: "Four reservation kids," and we know "what kind of Indian we are. The kind of Indian you don't see in Hollywood movies" (23). The Coalition sees themselves as the kind of Indian "who gets ignored at best and treated like dirt at worst. The kind of Indian who lives in second hand trailers or in old houses with no insulation. The kind of Indian who ends up in foster homes or whose parents fall off the wagon and get killed in car accidents or just disappear. The kind of Indian who knows that hope rhymes with nope" (24). While they could use these observations to marshal a critique of colonialism, racism, or inequality—as Junior often does in *True Diary*—in this instance they instead embrace their markers of poverty and despair as signs of cultural authenticity. They are "real Indians," they think, because of the hardships they experience on the reservation, and, without knowing anything about Katie's background, they label her an inauthentic Indian by contrast, a "Cherokee Princess" who does not belong in their club (23–24).

Even as Chris's group of friends is sometimes influenced by dominant un-derstandings of Indigenous cultures, at other times they resist such views. They sometimes shorten their "Rainbow Coalition" title to "Coalition," a word implying alliance for political resistance. The novel suggests ties to larger movements, too, as when Chris tells us that Gartersnake "has been reading about the American Indian Movement lately," and that his own family subscribes to the activist newspaper *Akwesasne Notes* (21, 100). The other members of the Coalition support Chris in his challenge of the school mascot as well. When their families disagree about whether or not a casino is a good idea for their reservation, a major rift develops in the Coalition. However, the rift is temporary, with the group's reunification representing how their larger Penacook nation can come together out of a shared respect for one another and for the sacred lands on their reservation even if they disagree about gaming.

Like the derogatory Indian mascot at his school, Chris and his friends see the "Cherokee Princess" complex as a threat to Indigenous self-determination. While the Coalition is too quick in labeling Katie a Cherokee Princess—thereby them-selves taking on the dominant practice of simplified cultural classification—they do reflect a legitimate concern. As he and his friends talk about Katie, Chris recounts his father explaining the term "Cherokee Princess" as referring to someone who claims Indian identity because their great-great-grandmother "was a real Cherokee Princess" (24). In the two pages he devotes to this topic, Chris reveals how individuals playing the Cherokee Princess card claim Indigenous heritage (often falsely) and take on the dominant society's view of American Indian culture as singular, static, and something that those in the dominant society have the authority to define and control. Those with a Cherokee Princess complex misrepresent and simplify Indigenous lineages, government structures, and gender dynamics in order to preserve a simpler representation of American Indians that better serves the purposes of Euro-Americans. When Chris finds out that Katie actually has a strong connection to her Indigenous heritage—her father is from the Akwesasne Mohawk Reservation—he apologizes to her. She becomes a powerful ally to Chris, along with the Rainbow Coalition, in resisting dominant views of American Indians. In fact, she helps convince the language-arts group in which she and Chris both participate to do the project on Indian team names and mascots.

As Chris and his allies challenge the school mascot, they offer a provocative alternative to multiculturalism for cross-cultural engagement. Chris lays the foundation for this in the "Talking Stick" chapter. After Mr. Dougal randomly divides Chris's language-arts class into groups for a research project on a "controversial topic," Chris's group—which includes Chris, Katie, and five others—chooses him as their leader (94). Chris asks his group if they are willing to use "Penacook rules" as they discuss potential research topics: "when one person is talking, no one else can interrupt them," and "everyone has to agree with whatever we decide." Chris clarifies, "If even one person doesn't agree, we can't come to a decision" (95). The group agrees to the rules and, at Chris's suggestion, uses a pencil as a "talking stick" to help enforce the first rule: only the person holding the pencil can talk (95). "Everyone is really serious about [this rule]," Chris observes, "as if we were sitting in a real council" (96). When the pencil comes to Katie, she suggests the topic "using Indian names for sports teams." Chris, who gets the pencil last, explains that he had the same idea (97). Through their Penacook discussion methods, everyone in the group comes to agree that they want to use this idea for their project (95–99). Because they "are all listening so close to what each person has to say," the group does not realize until after they come to their decision that the rest of the class has stopped talking and is fixated on them (98).

Once all of the groups tell Mr. Dougal their topics, Mr. Dougal addresses Chris: "Thank you, Mr. Nicola, for your group's topic and for this lesson in participatory democracy" (98). As they leave the classroom, the members of Chris's group look at one another and smile. "We all know that the circle we made hasn't been broken," Chris observes (99).

In this "Talking Stick" chapter, Chris shows his fellow students, as well as his readers, how American Indian cultures can be brought into mainstream classrooms in ways that move beyond tokenism. In the rhetoric of the dominant society, when cross-cultural interaction moves beyond tokenism, then either all cultural distinctions are lost or the authenticity of the othered culture has been polluted. In the dominant discourse, it is always the othered culture that is polluted by borrowing from the dominant culture. That the dominant culture itself borrows from other cultures in anything other than tokenistic ways is rarely recognized. In a school context, a multiculturalist approach to cross-cultural interaction treats token aspects of othered cultures as objects of study, encourages assimilation of othered cultures into the dominant culture—with minor exceptions, insisting that individuals from othered cultures adhere to mainstream values and ideologies while maintaining tokenized "customs"—and dismisses othered cultures as inauthentic because they have changed over time and have adapted features perceived as belonging to the dominant culture. In contrast, Chris brings to his group not a token aspect of Penacook culture to study, but rather an entire Penacook-based method for social interaction that everyone in his group—and, it turns out, everyone in his class—can learn from. Chris thereby resists tokenization, assimilation, and the notion that cultural exchange only goes one way, from the dominant to the othered culture.

Throughout *Heart of a Chief*, Chris illuminates how the approach that he introduces to his classmates is rooted in Penacook cultural traditions. He frequently describes the way in which elders in his community, especially his grandfather, Doda, teach him to listen respectfully to others and to be patient with them. He also recounts Doda explaining to him how Penacooks traditionally chose their sagamons and made decisions by unanimous consent (77–78). "When you vote, majority rules and minority feels like fools," Chris says, summarizing Doda's sentiments as well as his own (78). They both wish that their people "followed the old ways more." It is these "old ways," adapted for contemporary times, that Chris brings to his classmates, and that Chris and his family work to sustain in their Penacook community (78).

The Penacook method for interaction that Chris introduces to his classmates is a step toward what Vine Deloria Jr. and Daniel Wildcat call "indigenizing education." In *Power and Place*, Deloria and Wildcat contend that indigenizing education requires major shifts toward valuing Indigenous philosophies and methodologies rather than just adding information to the curriculum about Indigenous peoples, a vision that aligns with the tribal critical race theory that has come after and been influenced by Deloria and Wildcat's work. Wildcat observes that, at the post-secondary level, some mainstream scholarship has begun to value traditional Indigenous knowledge; however, in mainstream elementary and secondary schools, Indigenous peoples by and large still receive only token attention (Deloria and Wildcat 38–39).[19] Chris's talking-stick circle does not in itself transform his school's curriculum to make it based "on a foundation of American Indian metaphysics" as hoped for by Wildcat and Deloria and as actually pursued now by many tribal schools and some public schools with large Native student populations (Deloria and Wildcat 9).[20] But Chris's circle does go some way in indigenizing education, first by revealing the limits of dominant Western worldviews—reflected in the usual combative method of group decision-making that Chris eschews, as well as in the school mascot his group decides to challenge—and second by its enacting of a small but important part of an "indigenous metaphysical system," the Penacook method of consensus-building.

Bruchac represents cross-cultural listening with unrealistic ease, but he does, at points, begin to acknowledge more complexity. As Chris and his research group have lunch together on the day before Thanksgiving break, they have a difficult conversation about Thanksgiving, with Chris and Katie explaining to the others why the holiday is "different for Indians" (109). They tell the rest of the group how the phony Indian costumes kids wear at school around Thanksgiving make them feel like their people are being made fun of, and they lament the versions of history told about Thanksgiving in school that highlight the Pilgrims' experience but fail to include the related stories of how Europeans subjected Native people to enslavement, smallpox, and war (109–10). When one of the group members, Alicia, asks, "So do Indians hate us?" Chris answers with a story Doda told him about a Penacook man confronting a white neighbor who burned down his house, destroyed his field, and shot his dog (110–11). The Penacook man tracks the white man down, but instead of attacking him, he just asks the man if he is the one who burned down his house, destroyed his field, and shot his dog. Then, when the white man confesses to the crimes, the Penacook man says, "Well, you better not let that happen again" (111). The group is silent at first. Then they laugh, and Chris thinks about "how wise Doda is" (111).

The Penacook man in Chris's story lets go of the white man's criminal actions too easily, with Bruchac sidestepping basic concerns about the limits of truth and reconciliation that even young readers could engage. The discomfort of Chris's classmates is too quickly alleviated, with these characters in the novel and Bruchac's readers missing out on the learning they could have experienced if they stayed longer in a more realistically uncomfortable cross-cultural exchange. The novel effectively elides historic and contemporary colonial violence here by acknowledging it too simply and briefly. Still, Doda's story becomes a somewhat productive, if problematic, metaphor for how Chris's white classmates can honestly confront the historical mistreatment of American Indians at the hands of Euro-Americans while also focusing on how they can be allies of Native people in the present. In Chris's own interpretation, Doda's story demonstrates that "it isn't just what was done in the past that's important; it's also what we do now" (111).

The alliance-building that develops among the members of Chris's research group extends outward as the group finds allies in the school, town, and reservation communities. At the invitation of the research group, representatives from all of these sites come as guests to Mr. Dougal's class to see their presentation on Indian team names and mascots. Among the guests are two men—Muskrat Mike, the Penacook DJ for the reservation radio station, and Coach Takahashi, Chris's gym teacher—who already support the efforts of Chris's group to change the team name (126). Before the day of the presentation, Chris finds out, to his surprise, that Coach Takahashi is the one who has been taking down the "CHIEFS FOREVER" signs some students had been putting up in protest against the forthcoming presentation (119–20). As a Japanese American whose relatives were put in internment camps during World War II, Coach Takahashi says he understands how "portraying people as less than human, demeaning them in words and images" can lead to bigger harms (120–21). Takahashi's support is thus represented as rooted in a common experience of racial oppression along with a common understanding of the powerful role dominant representations play in that oppression. The other, presumably white, guests at the presentation—the school principal and assistant principal, four school board members, and the sports reporter from the town paper—enter Mr. Dougal's classroom unconvinced that Indian names for sports teams are a problem (126). However, as a result of the presentation, they come to support the group's stance. Just a week after the presentation, following negotiations with the principal, school board, and student athletes, the newspaper announces a contest for a new name (143–44). Chris's research group and the Rainbow Coalition will campaign for "the Rangerville Moose," with Chris confident that they can get many students to vote for it (144). *Heart of a Chief* suggests that the cross-cultural collaboration that began during the first meeting of Chris's research group will continue, and not just as they campaign for the new mascot, because the group members have become friends who listen to, respect, and care for one another.

Unlike most mainstream school stories, Indigenous school stories tend to provide a substantial investment in non-school spaces, with their protagonists' sustained resistance to dominant norms spilling over into locations beyond the school. Since Rangerville school sports teams involve parents, school board members, and local citizens, Chris and his friends must engage these communities in order to successfully pursue their challenge to the "Chiefs" because the ideologies of white privilege and multiculturalism that prop up the derogatory mascot permeate multiple spheres of the dominant society and, to a certain degree, of marginalized communities as well. Like Alexie's *True Diary* and other Indigenous school stories, *Heart of a Chief* also gives substantial attention to the Indigenous home community of its protagonist. Chris, like Junior, spends as much time telling readers about his experiences on his reservation as he does describing events at school. Moreover, like Junior, Chris resists the internalization of dominant norms he sees in his reservation community. With allies among his Penacook family and friends, Chris works to revive the same traditional Penacook approach to social interaction—based on respectful listening and mutual consent—that he introduces to his classmates at school.

Throughout the novel, members of Chris's Penacook community, especially Doda, discuss ways that dominant society values have influenced Penacook society, government, and approaches to the casino question. As the Penacooks' governmental structure becomes more like the dominant society model of democracy, privileging the majority view and the votes of individuals, Doda and other elders see among the people a growing obsession with money, a disregard for sacred land, and a general impatience with their fellow Penacooks. When Chris and his Rainbow Coalition friends see that surveyors have staked the sacred island on the reservation for the casino, Chris leads the group in ripping up the surveyor stakes and burning them (41–42). When the reservation police and fire department arrive, Chris gives a passionate speech about the island being the heart of the Penacook people (45–46). Later, Chris overhears his auntie telling his dad that people are saying he talked "like a Sagamon" and inspired people with that speech (63). However, despite appreciating his reverence for the island, Doda reprimands Chris for burning the surveyor stakes before learning more about the situation first (48). "Stones don't get impatient," Doda says, suggesting that Chris needs to learn more from the land he has professed to be the Penacooks' heart (48).

Even before ripping up the surveyor stakes, Chris acknowledges potential benefits as well as drawbacks to a casino: "how it would bring jobs into the community on the one hand and how gambling can mess people up on the other" (40). After the incident with the stakes, he learns to listen more patiently and respectfully, not just to the land but also to his fellow Penacooks, including those who support the casino. Belly Button's dad helps him more fully understand the reasoning behind different positions on the casino: how some Penacooks see a casino as essential for the community's economic viability while others feel a casino—no matter where it is built—would be "against our traditional way of life" (50). Belly Button's dad further complicates matters by sharing his knowledge of other reservations where casinos were mismanaged. The Mohawks had even taken up arms against one another in their division over a casino, he observes (50). Belly Button's dad concludes, "A casino will divide us" (50). Chris and his family grow increasingly concerned about the bitter divisiveness already present in their community over the casino issue. Chris wonders, "What have I started?," as these divisions become intensely personal, causing a rift in the Rainbow Coalition (49–53).

In the end, Chris's family uses their proposal for the casino to unite the people in a way they have not experienced for years. In the second to last chapter of the book, Bruchac brings together Chris's commitment to Penacook values, his growing patience in listening to the land and the people around him, and his understanding of Penacook culture as dynamic. As he walks on the island, a birch leaf falls onto Chris's cheek, and he thinks about how that leaf will feed other growing trees in the natural cycle he has been learning about in science class at school (146). Chris suddenly realizes then that there is a connection between that cycle and "our old Penacook idea of the sacred circle of life" (146). In basic terms Bruchac would have done well to flesh out, this realization highlights the potential relevancy for Penacook epistemology in science education. It also brings into focus, for Chris, an idea that had been brewing in his mind: the new casino could go on his family's land on the edge of town rather than on the island. The house on that land had burned down the year before Chris was born, killing his aunt, uncle, and cousins (71). It has been an abandoned "ghost house" since, especially affecting Mito, who is driven to further despair (and drink) whenever he looks at it (71–72). In being neglected, the land, Chris realizes, has been "kept out of the cycle, even though it is near the main highway. But if it was to be used in the right way, it could save our island" (146). Chris thanks the birch leaf before heading back to the mainland to share his idea. His family embraces the idea and then presents it before the chief, the tribal council, and the community as a way to reconcile the need for more income in the community with the need to protect the sacred island (147–52). When the decision comes to a vote, every person present agrees to the proposal. Even though they are technically voting, they effectively enact the traditional consensus-building approach since everyone agrees to the same decision and feels good about it.

On the cover of the 2001 Puffin edition of *Heart of a Chief*, the publishers ask, "Can one boy make a difference?" The book answers with a resounding "yes." Chris makes a big difference in both his school and reservation communities in just a few short months. At the same time, the novel complicates the "one boy can make a difference" paradigm advanced by the publisher. First, Chris does not make a difference by himself. The collaboration of his classmates and family are key. This sets Chris apart from the protagonists of mainstream YA texts who are often isolated in their resistance to dominant norms. Second, despite the relative ease with which Chris and his allies solve the mascot and casino problems, and despite Bruchac's failure to engage some major complications that would likely arise with both of these issues, *Heart of a Chief* does reveal some of the complexity involved in Chris's pursuits. Even as it makes consensus look too easy and avoids the hard question of how communities can remain unified and strong when they hold significant and irreconcilable differences, as they always do, the novel does present and take seriously contrasting perspectives on the casino. We get glimpses of the real grappling Chris's school community experiences over the mascot issue and, perhaps most significantly, we see the members of Chris's research group struggle to maintain honest, productive cross-cultural relationships in the face of misunderstanding, white guilt, and the pressures of dominant discourses.

Bruchac unrealistically allows Chris to avoid some important complexities, but the novel is still realistic enough to hearten young readers, including Indigenous readers, who have experienced more than their fair share of defeat. Paulette Molin, in *American Indian Themes in Young Adult Literature*, legitimately faults

Heart of a Chief for representing solutions to complex problems as occurring too easily and too quickly (Molin 34–36). Nevertheless, readers might be inspired by the novel's combination of touching on some complexities while depicting significant victories. Is the model of cross-cultural collaboration represented in *Heart of a Chief* deceptively simple? Yes. Is it a model that might inspire readers to work across cultures in order to rebel against dominant norms and support Indigenous communities? I think so, especially where it is engaged in classrooms with educators informed by tribal critical race theory.

As they challenge the dominant discourse of heteropatriarchy as well as multiculturalism, the YA romance texts by Cynthia Leitch Smith and Susan Power that I will discuss in the next chapter sharply illuminate some of the complexities—especially related to cross-cultural collaboration, intersectionality, and internalized oppression—left unexplored by both Alexie and Bruchac. At the same time, Smith's and Power's texts will further illuminate the anti-colonial resistance, Indigenous empowerment, cultural dynamism, and respectful alliances that are central to Alexie's and Bruchac's Indigenous school stories.

CHAPTER THREE

Not Your Father's Pocahontas

Cynthia Leitich Smith's and Susan Power's Resistive Romance

In *The Absolutely True Diary of a Part-Time Indian,* the main character satirizes "Indian romances." Upon learning that his sister wanted to write romance novels and that she enjoyed reading "the Indian ones," Junior observes that these books "always featured a love affair between a virginal white schoolteacher or preacher's wife and a half-breed Indian warrior. The covers were hilarious" (37–38). Then he composes his own cover for a book titled "Savage Summer" starring a long-haired, buff Indian man holding a large-breasted, fair-haired woman. Junior lists alternate titles alongside his drawing of the couple: "Apache Heart," "Lummi Lust," and "Yakama Yearning." With labels in the margin, he also draws attention to the woman's cleavage, the man's "huge half-breed muscles," and the man's hair, "blowing in the wind" (38). It is no wonder that Junior pokes fun at these popular "Indian romances" given that they adhere to the multiculturalist ideology that *True Diary* critiques. As Junior's satiric book cover illuminates, popular Indian romance novels propagate a static view of "Indian culture" in support of colonialist fantasies that commodify Indian bodies for white protagonists as well as readers.

Interracial couples can at once support and threaten multiculturalist ideals: On the one hand, such couples epitomize multiculturalist aspirations like tolerance, the overcoming of difference, and the dream of a race-free future achieved via racial "blending." On the other hand, they call into question the multiculturalist characterization of cultures as separate, static entities. Interracial relationships have the potential not only to deplete supposed cultural purity but also to illuminate the inequalities that multiculturalism obscures. As Frances Gateward argues in an essay on the portrayal of interracial romance in teen films of the late twentieth and early twenty-first centuries, these threats to multiculturalism are usually overcome in teen movies either because the interracial relationship ends or because the non-white person abandons his or her own cultural community in order to fully devote him/herself to the white partner, much like the half-breed hero of the popular Indian romance novel does. In a 2005 article examining interracial romances in contemporary children's books by Ann Rinaldi, Anton Ferreira, and Julia Holland that depict Native Americans as well as other Indigenous groups from a colonialist perspective, Donnarae MacCann similarly contends that "The cross-cultural relationships" in these texts "serve to contradict and soften plotlines that are a blend of hostility, disrespect, and condescension toward non-Westerners" (MacCann 205–6). MacCann sees these texts as part of a larger trend in many popular children's books of using representations of interracial couples to mask imperialist perspectives.

Gateward and MacCann, like Alexie's Junior, highlight an othering of non-white people and an assimilation impulse evident across many mainstream portrayals of interracial romance. This tendency to at once exoticize and attempt to assimilate perceived Others has been core to the agenda of settler colonialism in the United States and Canada from the start. In this chapter, I read young adult texts by Cynthia Leitich Smith (Muscogee) and Susan Power (Dakota) that I characterize as *resistive romance*. While representing romantic relationships— usually Native/white relationships—these texts resist the exoticize/assimilate tendency, especially as it has been advanced through the discourse of colonialist heteropatriarchy that pervades dominant Euro-American/Canadian narratives of interracial Indian romance.

The Pervasive Legacy of Pocahontas

Colonialist heteropatriarchy has exerted influence in dominant narratives of the last two and a half centuries about Pocahontas: the co-optation, suppression, and erasure of Native women's voices along with the exoticize/assimilate tendency evident in these representations of Pocahontas continue to influence YA romance as well as Indian policy in the United States and Canada. The discourse of colonialist heteropatriarchy goes back to the earliest days of European exploration of the Americas, when European writers characterized "the New World" as a female subject destined for penetration, conquering, and settlement by a male-coded Europe.[1] The influence of this discourse and the sexual violence it perpetuates continues to the present day.

As it pertains to mainstream interracial Indian romances, the discourse of colonialist heteropatriarchy goes back at least as far as early Euro-American representations of Pocahontas. The historic Matoaka, nicknamed Pocahontas, was the daughter of Chief Powhatan. At the age of seventeen, in 1612, she was taken prisoner by the English at Jamestown. She married Englishman John Rolfe in 1614, taking the name Rebecca Rolfe; traveled to England in 1616; and died at age twenty-one in 1617 just as she was beginning the journey home. Not until after she died did John Smith relay the well-known and likely fabricated story of Pocahontas rescuing him in 1607 when she would have been just ten or eleven years old. As Robert Tilton demonstrates in his book on representations of Pocahontas, Euro-Americans have been using their portrayals of Pocahontas's relationship with her husband John Rolfe and, much more so, her relationship with John Smith to promote colonialist ideologies for the last four hundred years. Like representations of interracial romance in contemporary "Indian romance novels," teen films, and children's/YA literature, representations of Pocahontas demonstrate the contradictory colonial impulses to emphasize Indians' otherness—out of fear of miscegenation as well as an adherence to a Euro-American exceptionalism that justifies manifest destiny—and to encourage Indian assimilation into white society.

Tilton explains that early-eighteenth-century Pocahontas narratives emphasized her relationship with her husband John Rolfe as much as her relationship with John Smith. Historians of the period framed the marriage of Pocahontas to Rolfe in nostalgic terms, as "proof that a merging of the two peoples and two cultures [English and Indian] was, or at least had been, possible" (Tilton 12). These commentators suggested that if Pocahontas and Rolfe's model of intermarriage had been followed more widely, the colonies might have averted the "animosity between the races" (12). From the perspective of European settlers in this period, Pocahontas had "turned her back on her people and her title" as she "converted, married an Englishman, and produced a son" (12). Narratives of this time equated Pocahontas and other Native women with Native lands, both of which were seen as destined for consumption by Euro-American men. In the period leading up to the American Revolution, they figured Pocahontas and her descendants as enabling a uniquely American identity distinct from Europe, through an Indian woman, but in a way that demanded the ultimate erasure of her Indian identity and society.

For these early Euro-Americans, marriage became a solution for racial conflict not through a mutual exchanging of cultural knowledge, but rather when Indians adopted the ways of their European partners and thereby eased the way of manifest destiny. Tilton thus characterizes this nostalgia for miscegenation as a "fantasy of absorption of the established peoples into the culture of the newcomers," a fantasy that carried over into later representations of Pocahontas, and later policies of assimilation, even as representations produced during the late eighteenth century and after would emphasize Pocahontas's relationship with John Smith rather than her marriage to Rolfe, reflecting a desire to avoid the topic of actual miscegenation (Tilton 3–4).[2]

The quintessential dominant Euro-American narrative of Pocahontas emerged after the American Revolutionary War and into the Romantic period of the nineteenth century. In this narrative, which persists to the present day, the "Indian Princess" Pocahontas rescues John Smith out of love for him (Tilton 85). As Tilton explains, this narrative was attractive to Euro-American settlers for a number of reasons. In this account, "The Indians are defeated not solely by the superior arms of the Europeans, but also by the irresistible sexual attractiveness of their charismatic leaders" (85). Moreover, Pocahontas is depicted in this narrative as "a convenient scapegoat for the subjugation or destruction of her culture," displacing the blame from Euro-Americans (85). Euro-Americans romanticized the "passing of the Indian" and mythologized Indians like Pocahontas who aided white settlers (51–52). They justified the massacre of "bad" resistant Indians by raising up the example of Pocahontas, the archetypal "good" Indian—good because she went against the interests of her own people in order to seek absorption into the settler society that was destined to take the Indians' lands (51–52). The virtuous and friendly Pocahontas was also represented as contrasting with the threateningly sexual Indian "squaw" woman as well as the dangerously resistant "savage" Indian man. Tilton argues that, despite its historical inaccuracies—actually because of those inaccuracies—this quintessential Euro-American Pocahontas narrative became foundational for the genre of the American historical romance, a genre that continues to influence mainstream literature, including YA romance.

It would be difficult to overstate the influence of the colonialist-inspired Pocahontas narrative in contemporary North American popular culture, especially youth culture. Children's books, school curricula, and the hugely popular 1995 Disney movie about Pocahontas by and large support the dominant narrative described by Tilton. The ideologies of Euro-American exceptionalism, manifest destiny, and American Indian assimilation underlying that narrative continue in contemporary YA romance texts ranging from Ann Rinaldi's historical novel *The Second Bend in the River* (1997) to Stephenie Meyer's wildly successful Twilight Saga (2005–2008). In their essay "Biting Bella: Treaty Negotiation, Quileute History, and Why 'Team Jacob' Is Doomed to Lose," Judith Leggatt and Kristin Burnett argue that, despite Meyer's presenting "a positive, if stereotypical, image of the Quileute people," and despite her characters' demonstrating "more respect for the treaties" (between the Quileute and the Cullen family of vampires in the Twilight novels) than the United States government ever has historically, the saga's love triangle between Bella (white), Edward (white/vampire), and Jacob (Quileute/werewolf) ultimately results in a shift of power and land away from Native people and toward "newcomers," thus supporting the manifest-destiny ideology of the dominant Pocahontas narrative and the American historical romance (Leggatt and Burnett 28, 31, 41–44). The American historical romance depicts one culture replacing another, and that movement of erasure via death and/or assimilation continues in the romance stories of contemporary YA literature.

These dominant narratives of interracial Indian romance have had a broad and devastating impact on Indigenous people, especially women. Along with wars, massacres, coerced treaties, and violated treaties, the colonial governments of the United States and Canada have implemented policies like allotment, residential/ boarding schools, termination, and relocation, all designed to take Indigenous land and all justified, at times, with reference to romantic narratives of vanishing Indians of the past and "good Indians" of the future, with the "good Indians" seen as sacrificing themselves on the altar of assimilation for the future of their people and, more importantly, the colonial nation.

Romance narrative paradigms of exoticization, assimilation, and "good Indians" vs. "bad Indians" also carry over into the contentious arenas of tribal recognition and membership. Since long before Europeans colonized the Americas,

Indigenous people were, of course, marrying—for love, for political reasons, and by force—across lines of nation and clan, and negotiating related affiliation(s) through a range of matrilineal, patrilineal, and other frameworks. Colonial institutions of Europe and later the United States and Canada imposed their own criteria for membership onto Native communities in an effort both to advance patriarchy and to diminish Indigenous populations. Many Indigenous nations have either never been "recognized" or "given status" by the United States or Canada, or have seen their recognized status revoked. Moreover, historically, the least accommodating individual members of recognized nations were also the least likely to make it onto the official colonial government's rolls.

Colonial policies that define Indian status based on blood quantum have sought to "absorb" Indians of mixed ancestry, conveniently diminishing the ranks of potentially resistant tribal nations and the federal government's treaty responsibilities to the members of those nations. Some view tribal/band governments that continue to use blood quantum to determine tribal membership as internalizing destructive colonialist perspectives, while others cast the practice as based in Indigenous nations' own self-determined values. We see the same divided response to the many tribal/band governments that terminate membership for women and/or men who "marry out" of the tribe. Under the 1876 Indian Act in Canada, First Nations women who married outside of their Indigenous nation were denied Indian status by the federal government until Bill C-31 overturned that policy in 1985. Some Indigenous governments continue that policy. Even in communities where "marrying out" does not result in official exclusion, Native people, especially Native women, who have romantic relationships with non-Natives are sometimes viewed by both Native and non-Native people as seeking assimilation (for better or worse, depending on who is making the assessment) and/or selling out their tribal communities, a notion that Smith and Power both challenge in their work.[3]

In addition to its broad influence over policies and attitudes, the discourse of colonialist heteropatriarchy underlying dominant romance narratives results in a great deal of direct sexual violence against Indigenous women. Native women in both Canada and the United States experience sexual violence much more frequently than women of other populations do, most often at the hands of white men. In 2007, Amnesty International issued a report entitled *Maze of Injustice* that revealed that one in three Native women in the United States will report being raped in her lifetime, and that many more experience but do not report rape; that 86 percent of rapes and other instances of sexual assault upon Native women are committed by non-Native men; and that few of these cases are ever prosecuted, because of jurisdictional problems. Amnesty's 2004 report *Stolen Sisters* documented similar experiences for Indigenous women in Canada. Despite some legislation and activist campaigns addressing these issues in recent years, violence against Native women continues at high rates and remains massively under-addressed, starkly illustrating colonialist heteropatriarchy's deep influence.[4]

Some Indigenous young adult texts directly represent sexual violence while interrogating colonial legislation and policy that enables such violence. Some of these texts include Louise Erdrich's *The Round House* (2012), Beatrice Culleton Mosionier's *In Search of April Raintree* (1983), Eden Robinson's *Monkey Beach* (1999), and Joseph Bruchac's *Hidden Roots* (2004).[5] The texts that I examine by Cynthia Leitich Smith and Susan Power do not focus on colonial sexual violence in the realm of personal experience, law, or policy. Instead, they focus on the realm of representation, especially in terms of romance. They resist colonialist heteropatriarchy and the violence it perpetuates by critiquing the central tenets of the discourse that have been advanced through dominant romance narratives, and by depicting powerful female Native voices that offer alternatives to the discourse.

To recap, the dominant Pocahontas story and other mainstream Indian interracial romance narratives perpetuate colonialist heteropatriarchy in several regards: by erasing via the assimilation impulse and/or exoticizing differences between Indians and Euro-Americans; by subjecting Native people to Euro-American gender hierarchies and sexual norms; by rendering Native women and their lands as rapable sites for Euro-American/Canadian consumption; by depicting "good" Indians as those who willingly open themselves to colonial consumption and who assist colonial projects; by blaming Native women for the demise of Native people because of their promiscuity, betrayals, and general complicity in advancing Euro-American conquest; and, at the meta-level, by presenting themselves as definitive narratives rather than taking into account the voices of actual Native people. Smith's and Power's resistive romance stories challenge all of these elements of colonialist heteropatriarchy. As I analyze these stories, I aim to advance critiques of colonialist heteropatriarchy and mainstream Indian interracial romance narratives while further illuminating the strong ties between them.

YA Romance, Death, and the Death of Romance

I define young adult romance broadly and simply as any YA text that represents romantic love. Smith's and Power's texts diverge from the typical conventions of YA romances in ways that reflect an innovative repurposing of the subgenre. These texts are *resistive romances* not only because they challenge the colonialist heteropatriarchy of dominant romances but also because they resist YA romance itself, rejecting elements that are generally central to the subgenre. To begin with, most of Smith's and Power's texts do not represent the development of an adolescent romance. In fact, Smith's novel and both of the Power stories I discuss here are premised on the death of a romantic relationship via the death of the white (usually male) romantic partner in a Native-white relationship. These deaths are not tragic endings to romance stories, as sometimes happens in mainstream romances; rather, they are deaths that have occurred before the narrative even begins. It is the simultaneous absence and ghostly presence of romantic partners within these texts that makes Smith's and Power's resistive romance possible. Through their invocation of dead romances, they effectively put to death the colonialist heteropatriarchy of the mainstream interracial Indian romance while bringing to life an alternative discourse that critiques colonialism, empowers Native women, and fosters relationships—usually non-romantic ones—that advance Indigenous self-determination.

To appreciate Smith's and Power's repurposing of YA romance, one must understand the typical features of the subgenre in general, and especially the tropes related to the treatment of death. In *Reading the Adolescent Romance*, Amy Pattee describes the typical trajectory of a popular YA romance novel. A passive adolescent female protagonist, who is not ethnically marked and who does not talk about social-class differences, seeks social recognition via a heterosexual romantic relationship. While avoiding explicit sex, the novel suggests that the protagonist experiences growth through her romantic relationship. As in other genres of YA literature, the protagonist's growth ultimately results in her adherence to dominant social values, particularly those of heteropatriarchy (Pattee 54–63). While Pattee focuses on popular YA romances, scholars like Roberta Trites and Kathryn James demonstrate that alternative YA romances, even the most transgressive ones, tend ultimately to reinforce dominant social norms, including those of heteropatriarchy.[6] While Smith's and Power's protagonists are chaste and experience growth, in all other aspects they part ways with the typical heroines of mainstream YA romance. The protagonists in Smith's and Power's texts mature not through romantic relationships but rather through their representations of their own and others' romances of the past. That growth, moreover, does not result in their adhering to heterosexual patriarchal norms, but instead moves them to ever deeper critiques of colonialist heteropatriarchy and ever greater empowerment as young Native women.

The protagonists of Smith's and Power's texts are able to grow in these resistive ways largely through their treatment of death, which troubles broad YA conventions. In *Death, Gender, and Sexuality in Contemporary Adolescent Literature*, Kathryn James identifies patterns regarding the treatment of death across a wide and diverse body of young adult literature. Three of her observations are particularly relevant here. First, James observes that the association of death with women, a link deeply engrained in European and Euro-American/Canadian arts, persists in the realm of realist YA romance literature (James 27, 73–111). Second, James contends that in realistic YA texts, simultaneous experiences with death and romantic/sexual awakening lead adolescent protagonists to grow, often by negotiating a crisis in their personal gender identity that generally results in their embrace of heterosexual patriarchal norms (73–111). Third, if they do not embrace those heterosexual patriarchal norms, characters in these texts die! Not always, but often, and even in texts that graphically represent and in some regards celebrate transgressive sexual behavior, "the death of the protagonist occurs as the result of a violation of the [heterosexual patriarchal] rules governing sexual experience" (89, 73–111).

YA texts tend to associate death with women, and the dominant interracial Indian romance associates death with Indian women in particular. After all, it is by dying to her life as an Indian princess and then literally dying young that the Pocahontas of the dominant story enables her own mythologizing as a figure of manifest destiny. In stark contrast, Smith and Power use death to turn the dead Native woman/conquered territory association on its head since it is most often the white male romantic partner who is passed/past in their texts. His death, moreover, opens space for Native female voices that tell their own stories in ways that challenge colonialist heteropatriarchy and advance Native empowerment. Rather than growing toward an embrace of heteropatriarchy, Smith's and Power's protagonists' experiences of death and romance, and especially their own representations of dead romances, enable them to grow increasingly critical of colonialist heteropatriarchy, and even, at times, to interrogate and attempt to recover from their own complicity in the discourse. Theirs are not personal crises over gender identity so much as communal crises over the harmful effects of this discourse. Even though these protagonists' resistance to colonialist heteropatriarchal norms also encompasses much more than their personal experience of gender and sexuality—and they are thus much more transgressive than typical YA romance characters—they do not die for their transgressions. Instead, the deaths they represent become productive sites for enabling self-reflection, self-representations, and alliances that empower the individual characters as well as their larger Indigenous communities.

Confronting Exoticization in Smith's "A Real-Live Blond Cherokee and His Equally Annoyed Soul Mate"

While no one literally dies in Cynthia Leitich Smith's short story "A Real-Live Blond Cherokee and His Equally Annoyed Soul Mate," the symbolic death of colonialist representations anchors the plot as well as the romance. As the story unfolds, Jason—the narrator and titular real-live blond Cherokee—falls for Nika, an apparently Irish American girl. Nika comes into the Austin, Texas, costume shop where Jason works to ask for his help with her school history report on Native Americans. When Jason refuses, finding Nika's request "mildly offensive," Nika leaves just as "a trio of very frat-looking guys" walk in. As the guys rent a "Wild West Indian costume" along with some others, apparently for Halloween, Nika returns, confessing to Jason that she had not really come in to ask for help with a report but rather to ask him out. "I've never asked out a guy before," she explains, "and I needed an excuse to talk with you." But she has "lost absolutely all interest," she says, on account of Jason's rudeness (37). As she storms out, she recognizes one of the frat boys and exits the store with him, leaving Jason baffled. He spends the rest of the day thinking about Nika until he finally finds out where she lives and literally runs to her house, where he finds her in the backyard beside a smoking metal garbage can. Nika explains that Chad, the frat boy with whom she left the shop, is her brother, "kind of protective . . . sort of annoying. But good" (40). Upon realizing that Nika is not burning leaves, as he first assumed, but rather the Indian costume that Chad had rented, Jason is moved. As Nika says that she is thinking of taking up Wicca, Jason reaches out to touch her hair and lift her chin. With Jason presumably about to kiss Nika, the story ends with him thinking that she will make a good witch.

The effects of colonialism are never far from Jason's mind, and they form the basis for his and Nika's "annoyance." The story begins with Jason declaring, "I'm a swear-to-God, card-carrying, respectably thick blood Oklahoma Cherokee" with a "tribal ID" to go with his "sandy blond" hair (33). He also explains that his mother's mother is the full-blood Cherokee, immediately adding, "No, I didn't call her a 'princess,' and don't make fun of my gramma" (33). He recognizes that "every 'take-me-to-your-sweat-lodge' wannabe claims he's a Cherokee" via an Indian princess grandma, and he feels the need to immediately challenge that myth while simultaneously asserting his own Indian identity. If they are not purported descendants of Pocahontas, wannabes indeed tend to claim a Cherokee princess ancestor, on their mother's side, firmly positioning themselves in the line of "good," "civilized" Indian women who supposedly supported the colonialist goals of the Euro-American settlers they married. Like Joseph Bruchac in *The Heart of a Chief*, Smith recognizes the pervasiveness of the Cherokee Princess complex and tackles it head-on. Through Jason's rant, Smith suggests that the complex is most annoying to those who actually have Cherokee grandmothers and are active members of the Cherokee nation.

A costume shop is the perfect setting to interrogate dominant representations of Indians. Jason explicitly draws the connection between the Indian costume and the broader policing of Indian identity by the dominant society—a policing that erases real American Indian people like him who do not adhere to stereotypes. The costume represents how Indians are either denied recognition because of their lack of authenticity or exoticized as completely Other, relics of history available for consumption and appropriation by Euro-Americans/Canadians. Jason describes the costume as "ugly, cheap, and ridiculous looking—suede fringe and purple feathers on the obligatory pseudo-Plains headdress" (35). He calls attention to the fact that the costume represents a version of Native identity that is wholly an invention of the colonial imagination. The dominant society casts Plains Indians as the most authentic of Native peoples, but Jason's description of the costume clearly shows that it does not reflect an actual Plains Indian identity, but rather the fictional "Plains Indian" that non-Natives most enjoy "playing."

Jason grips the counter as one of the frat boys "held the costume up to himself, and—as if that wasn't enough—started making 'war whoops'" (35). Jason explains his distress: "Maybe the minstrel show of an Indian costume was no big deal, not by itself. But it was one of a million little things (not to mention a few biggies), and they just kept on coming . . . like everybody who didn't believe in blond Cherokees . . . like a pretty stupid girl [Nika] who thought I was exotic" (36). With the language of "minstrel show," Jason suggests a link between playing Indian and performing blackness, provocative given that blackface is no longer acceptable in most circles while "red face" is, as Halloween and Thanksgiving celebrations make clear. He also directly links this type of appropriation with the exoticizing and authenticity policing that he has personally experienced numerous times. When Euro-Americans define authentic Indianness as conforming to their own exoticized images—epitomized in the costume—they also deny authenticity to the likes of Jason, and really to all living Native people, none of whom fit the costume image that Jason aptly classifies as "ridiculous."

Even though the scene is short, when they play at being Indian with the costume, the frat boys in this story reflect attitudes that cut across a long and complex history of Euro-Americans "playing Indian" in order to appropriate the perceived natural, adventurous, authentic spirit of "the Indians" while simultaneously denying the existence of, or at least the authenticity of, actual living Native people. In their attraction to the costume, their mocking, and their war whoops, these young men enact what Philip Deloria calls a "dialectic of simultaneous desire and repulsion" that has been central to Euro-Americans' playing Indian since the eighteenth century (P. Deloria 3). As it enables both the belittling and the appropriating of Indian identity, such play embodies the colonialist ideologies evident in the dominant Indian interracial romance.[7]

So where does Jason and Nika's budding romance fit into all of this? As the title suggests, both characters are "annoyed." It becomes clear over the course of the story that Jason's "annoyance" over the Indian costume and all that it represents is actually a deep anger, hence his being moved to the verge of tears when Nika burns the costume. As Jason watches the flames in Nika's backyard, he writes, "I rubbed my eyes. 'It's the smoke,' I explained, surprised by how much the gesture affected me. Glad that somebody else got it for once, that it wasn't up to me to deal alone. I understood now why I'd had to find her" (40). Jason sees Nika as an ally in his resistance to colonial representations of Indians. He had to find her because she shares his "annoyance." Even though she is non-Native, she understands how damaging representations like the Indian costume are, so much so that she is willing to scorn her own brother, lose money (she says she'll pay for the costume), and probably break some city ordinances by burning the costume. Jason sees Nika as a good match because she supports his anti-colonialist cause without questioning his authenticity, and without trying to appropriate an Indian identity for herself.

The burning of the Indian costume represents the death of one kind of romance narrative, the Pocahontas kind that perpetuates colonialist heteropatriarchy through its stereotyping, deriding, and appropriating of Native identity. With the costume still burning at the end of the story, this symbolic death occurs at the exact same moment that Nika and Jason's romance is born, just as they are about to kiss. The story suggests that their romance will counter the kind of romance represented by the costume; theirs is a resistive romance from the start. They come together because of their shared disdain for the ideology reflected in the costume. By initiating the burning of the costume, Nika helps move them from mere annoyance to resistance, and as the story ends, we are left wondering where this resistance will take them next.

Jason suggests that Nika understands why the Indian costume is such a problem because she has Irish heritage, and Irish identity, like American Indian identity, has been exoticized, mocked, and appropriated by the same dominant Euro-American society in which the Irish have also gained entry after a history of marginalization. As the costume burns, Jason looks at Nika and "saw hints of my grandmother. Not my Cherokee grandma, my Irish one." He continues, "The one with the green eyes people sing about on the street corners and in late-night bars. The one who was annoyed by the Celtic fad and framed four-leaf clovers. The one who couldn't stand the folks who flocked to see *Lord of the Dance*. Wannabes, Gramma called them. Gramma with her iced evergreen eyes" (41). In saying that his Irish grandmother was "annoyed by the Celtic fad," Jason implies that Nika, too, is annoyed by the exoticizing, tokenizing, and appropriating of Irish identity, and that this personal experience fuels her solidarity with him. The examples Jason gives of "Irish culture" put up for consumption by the dominant society may seem mild, but Smith gestures here to dark histories of colonialism in Ireland and oppression against Irish Americans that enable this contemporary exoticization and appropriation. Jason's suggestion of an American Indian/Irish anti-colonialist alliance also speaks to—and may prompt readers to learn about—the real history of American Indian/Irish alliances.

While Jason's suggestion of a shared experience of exoticization holds to a certain degree, the Irish/Indian analogy can only be taken so far given the relatively enfranchised position of contemporary Irish Americans. Significantly, Nika herself never declares an Irish identity, let alone an alliance with Jason and other American Indians based on her Irishness. She may be motivated by empathy—and romance—rather than parallel experience; after all, her brother

Chad shares her Irish heritage but sees no problem with the Indian costume. In the end, a corresponding experience of being seen as Other—whether because of her Irishness, Wiccan aspirations, or general alternativeness—might contribute to Nika's alliance with Jason, but as readers we do not actually know whether this is the case. We just know that Jason's perception of a shared experience or exoticization contributes to his feeling of connection with Nika.

The critique of exoticization in "A Real-Live Blond Cherokee" becomes more complicated when we consider Jason's own complicity. Even as he sharply criticizes stereotypes of American Indians and recalls his grandmother's annoyance over stereotypes of the Irish, Jason makes several stereotype-based judgments of Nika throughout the story. Smith thereby demonstrates how Native people can internalize the very dominant perspectives that they condemn, and she reveals potential pitfalls to the alliance symbolized by Jason and Nika's romance. Jason describes Nika as "Little Miss Gentrification" before she even speaks (34). After refusing her request for help on her report, he says, "She was harmless. Mildly offensive, definitely intrusive, but no different from a thousand other spoiled teenage girls when it came to things like Indian identity or, say, the fact that she was sporting dyed red hair, a gauzy green dress, two nose rings, and an infinity tattoo, which, in this neighborhood, made her a walking cliché" (34). He also notes that she has green eyes that remind him of someone, but he can't remember who (34–35). When she returns to the store for their second encounter, he again fixates on "those iced evergreen eyes" and also notices that her "female power symbol" necklace was "a little more mystic than you'd find at the neighborhood herb store" (36). In their final encounter, Jason observes that Nika has changed out of her "quirky urban princess ensemble" in favor of a T-shirt and shorts (40). He also notices, in contrast to his original assumption, that her red hair color is natural, not dyed, and that it "was a deeper red, more alive" than he had first thought. And he is again drawn to her eyes, this time realizing that they remind him of his Irish grandmother (41). Finally, as he runs his hand "down the curve of her freckled cheek," Jason thinks approvingly of Nika's desire to explore Wicca, remarking in the last line of the story, "At least she had the witchy looks for it, I thought, the classic coloring" (41).

While some of Jason's emphasis on Nika's appearance comes from his growing attraction to her, his descriptions also repeatedly stereotype and exoticize her. Some of his assumptions are explicitly undone. It turns out that Nika does not share other spoiled teenagers' assumptions about Indian identity, and her hair color is natural. Yet, as Jason abandons some of his stereotypes, in other ways he comes to exoticize Nika more and more, particularly in terms of her Irishness. In fact, she becomes more than the neighborhood cliché precisely through exoticized Irish traits: her "mystic" female power necklace, her "alive" red hair, her "iced evergreen eyes," her freckles, and her pale skin. Some of the ways Jason exoticizes Nika in terms of her Irishness parallel the exoticization of American Indians as "spiritual" and "close to nature." His fixation on the color of her eyes, hair, and skin belies his own frustration with others' attention to his own blond hair in their policing of his Cherokee identity; yet Jason never registers the irony.

At the end of Smith's story, the budding romantic relationship and Native/non-Native alliance that it represents remain precarious. In the immediate context of the romance, if Nika is passionately annoyed about exoticization, she is going to be annoyed at Jason's exoticizing of her. In the larger world of Native/non-Native alliance, exoticization will only further colonialist aims. Moreover, the conflating of divergent cultural experiences not only overlaps with the colonial project of cultural assimilation but also impedes true alliance work in support of Indigenous empowerment. For, if experiences are rendered too similar, allies cannot address the unique effects of colonization on particular communities, or those communities' unique values and goals. "A Real-Live Blond Cherokee" marshals an interracial romance to illuminate the pervasiveness of exoticization and the role it plays in furthering colonialism, but it does not answer the question of how allies can find common ground without erasing or exoticizing their differences. For that, we must turn to other resistive romances.

Building Alliances by Challenging Dominant Representations, Enacting Self-Representation, and Practicing Self-Critique in Smith's *Rain Is Not My Indian Name*

Unlike Jason, Rain, the protagonist of Smith's novel *Rain Is Not My Indian Name*, is at times quite self-aware about her own complicity in ideologies of colonialist heteropatriarchy. *Rain* is able to provide a more nuanced critique of this discourse because of the protagonist's self-reflection, because the novel form provides more space for this critique to unfold, and because the novel begins with the death of a budding interracial white/Indian romance, via the literal death of the white male partner. That death opens rich terrain not only for critique but also for a young Indigenous woman's self-fashioning and refashioning of dominant representations.

Rain Is Not My Indian Name is narrated by its fourteen-year-old protagonist, Cassidy Rain Berghoff, who goes by her middle name and lives in the predominantly white fictional town of Hannesburg, Kansas. Rain describes herself as "Muscogee Creek-Cherokee and Scots-Irish on Mom's side, Irish-German-Ojibway on Dad's" (20). The novel opens with her remembering the New Year's Eve night on which her white best friend and would-be boyfriend Galen died in an accident on his way home from an outing with her, and the following day, her New Year's Day birthday, when she learned of the death. As the story then jumps ahead six months to June, we learn that Rain has closed herself off from everyone other than her family. We also learn that her mother had died a few years earlier, that her father is at a military base in Guam, and that she and her older brother Fynn live with their grandfather, who is away on a Las Vegas vacation for the few days over which the novel is set.

Some characters experience romance as the novel unfolds: Fynn becomes engaged to his white girlfriend Natalie, who also lives with the family, and Rain's grandfather gets married in Vegas to a widow he meets there. However, the novel focuses on Rain's need to finally "do some living" after Galen's death and the death of their short-lived romance. The novel is structured by dated chapters intermingled with undated journal entries in which Rain records memories of Galen and her mother along with anecdotes that convey what it is like to be American Indian in Hannesburg. Rain's experiences center around the science and technology–based camp that her science teacher Aunt Georgia puts on for Native young people in the town. Rain, once an avid photographer, has not been taking pictures since Galen died. When Natalie asks her to shoot photos of the camp for the town newspaper that Natalie edits, Rain agrees, a decision that opens the way for her to form new relationships and to move on after her loss.

In contrast with the YA protagonists described by Kathryn James whose experiences with death lead them to a gendered identity crisis and an ultimate embrace of heteropatriarchal norms, as she deals with Galen's death, Rain grows by critiquing dominant norms—especially dominant representations of Indian girls and women—and by deepening a variety of relationships, especially with family members and the people she meets through Indian Camp. Rain does not experience an identity crisis, gendered or otherwise. She asserts, "Being a mixed-blood girl is no big deal. Really. It seems weird to have to say this, but after a lifetime of experience, I'm used to being me" (113). Unlike her dad, who suffers from internalized racism, and the non-Natives in town who frequently tell Rain she doesn't "seem Indian," Rain is comfortable with her identity (113).[8] She does not have a problem with who she is, but other people do, their problem stemming from Rain's failure to conform to dominant representations of American Indian women. Rain does not resolve the crisis others face over her identity by conforming to dominant understandings of Indian women, but instead challenges the crisis itself, directly as well as indirectly, through her own dynamic, honest, self-critical representation.

Early in the novel, Rain says that she thinks the most likely reason for Aunt Georgia putting on the Indian Camp "had something to do with the way Hannesburg schools taught about Indians and, because of that, the way it sometimes felt to be an Indian in Hannesburg schools" (13). The nature of the dominant representations of American Indians that Rain references here, along with the hurtful effects those representations have on Native young people are illuminated throughout the novel as Rain records thoughts, conversations, and journal entries. In Hannesburg schools, Indians are both exoticized and erased, paraded around as ridiculous stereotypes for Thanksgiving and then ignored the rest of the year. As Rain puts it,

> At school, the subject of Native Americans pretty much comes up just around Turkey Day, like those cardboard cutouts of Pilgrims and the pumpkins and the squash taped to the windows at McDonald's. And the so-called Indians always look like bogeymen on the prairie, windblown cover boys selling paperback romances, or baby-faced refugees from the world of Precious Moments. I usually get through it by reading sci-fi fanzines behind my textbooks until we move on to Kwanza. (13)

In this passage, Rain captures the tendency in the dominant society at large, as well as in her school curriculum, to represent Indians with exotic extremes—scary savages, hot hunks, or pathetic children—and to reproduce those representations for popular consumption. Just as non-Native people in the dominant culture eat at McDonald's, buy romance novels, and collect Precious Moments figurines, they consume dominant representations of American Indians, claiming ownership over Indian identity based on those representations while either ignoring or challenging Native people who do not match the representations. Around this same point in the novel, Rain also recognizes how these same dominant representations get perpetuated in the kind of "Indian Camp" programs that are very different from Aunt Georgia's, the kind "where a bunch of suburban, probably rich, probably white kids tromped around a woodsy park, calling themselves 'princesses,' 'braves,' or 'guides'" (12).[9] A sci-fi fan with dirty blond hair, black nails, and a love of photography, Rain clearly does not match. While exoticized so-called Indians are conjured up every Thanksgiving—as they are in the interracial Indian romance novels that Rain joins Alexie's Junior in mocking—there is no room in the Hannesburg school curriculum or in the other kind of "Indian Camp" for the histories or contemporary experiences of actual Native young people like Rain who don't "seem Indian" according to dominant representations. While I do not classify Smith's novel as a school story, since it does not focus primarily on Rain's experiences in her public school or at Georgia's educational camp, the text joins Indigenous school stories, like Bruchac's *Heart of a Chief*, in critiquing colonialism, including as it is advanced in schools, and in imagining an indigenized educational space, via Indian Camp.

While addressing the presence of dominant representations of Native people in her school and town, Rain explicitly highlights Pocahontas's starring role. In the chapter titled "Malibu Pocahontas," as she gears up to reveal her Indian identity to the reporter covering Indian Camp with her, unsure of how he will respond, Rain explains that she and Fynn frequently get asked questions like "What are you?" and "How much Indian are you?" She doesn't mind as much when Native people ask, because they "show respect for the tribal affiliation, for my family" and because "they never follow up with something like 'You don't seem Indian to me'" (48). "I've never asked about the phrase 'seem Indian,'" Rain continues, "but I figure it involves construction-paper feathers, a plastic paint pony, and Malibu Pocahontas" (49). Especially in the post–Disney movie era, Rain aptly associates Pocahontas with other objects used to "play Indian." The example of a Malibu Pocahontas Barbie doll especially speaks to the dominant society's tendency to position Pocahontas as an exotic princess who epitomizes dominant feminine ideals while enabling a sexualized exploitation of the fertile lands with which Pocahontas and other Native women are associated.[10]

In her journal entry at the start of the Malibu Pocahontas chapter, Rain recalls a third-grade assignment to give a report on "an important person." "I got it in my head that I wanted to pick an Indian woman," Rain writes, "and a trip to the library narrowed my choices to Sacagawea or Pocahontas. I chose former Kansas senator Nancy Kassebaum instead" (44). With the dry humor of this brief remark, Rain reveals an utter lack of variety in dominant representations of Native women. The only two Native women in the town library are from the distant past and are most often praised—in children's books and school curricula—for the ways they helped white men and furthered the manifest destiny of Euro-Americans. For a girl like Rain, interested in the distinctive communities of her living family members, the library has nothing to offer when it comes to representations of Native women.

As Smith's novel explicitly confronts the dominant representation of Native women as Indian princesses, with Pocahontas standing in as the virtuous ideal woman/assimilated Indian, it also implicitly challenges the dominant representation of Native women as "squaws": sexually promiscuous and less than fully human subjects who invite sexual exploitation by Euro-Americans and thereby threaten the stability of Euro-American families and, by extension, Euro-American society.[11] As the novel moves toward its climax, Rain visits Galen's mother, Mrs. Owen, with the intention of confronting her about her vocal opposition, as a mayoral candidate, to town funding for the Indian Camp. Instead, they only discuss Galen, and Rain is confused when Mrs. Owen says that people talked at Galen's funeral—and are still talking—about Rain and Galen "running around" on the night Galen died (95–96). Natalie later clarifies that rumors have been circulating alleging that Rain and Galen were not just running around but "fooling around" (98). Rain does not directly attribute the rumors to her Indian identity. Given that people "expect that kind of behavior" from the "Blue Heaven [trailer court] girls" but not someone "from an Old Town family" like her or Galen, Rain sees how the rumor would appeal to the townsfolk as especially juicy: "a supposed, scandalous sighting of a fourteen-year-old Old Town girl with Mrs. Owen's dead son—that was practically poetry" (98–99). Rain gets at something other than her Old Town middle-class status, however, when she writes, "I could see where some people would especially want to believe that about me" (98). Given the way she exposes dominant assumptions about Native Americans throughout the text, and given the shame in her own family—particularly expressed by her father and his mother—about being Indian, Rain suggests here that some townspeople want to believe she fooled around with Galen because that belief would adhere to a dominant stereotype that marks Indian girls, like trailer court girls, as sexually promiscuous. As Rain explains in the journal entry that closes the novel, "what really happened" the night of Galen's death was just one simple kiss (135).

Smith's novel also addresses, albeit with a light touch, attitudes regarding Native people who date non-Natives. After the third day of Indian Camp, Rain accompanies Dmitri Headbird, a local Ojibwe boy and one of the campers, to his trailer house, looking to buy a gift from his family of artists and traders for the baby she has learned Fynn and Natalie are expecting. After Dmitri refers to Natalie as "the white girl" and remarks that his own brother is dating a Kiowa girl, Rain concludes, "Either Dmitri was telling me that he didn't approve of Fynn's choice or just that he himself had a preference for Indian girls." Rain continues, "Other than his sister and—if I wanted to be generous—Queenie, the only local Indian girl near his age happened to be me" (73). (Earlier that day, at Indian Camp, Rain's African American "ex second best friend" Queenie had revealed her family's recent discovery that one of her great-grandfathers was Native [70].) While the attention in this passage quickly turns to a potential romance between Rain and Dmitri, Rain's initial wondering if Dmitri disapproves of Native-white romances remains significant. Given the novel's ultimate suggestion that a romantic relationship between Rain and Dmitri is likely, and given the way that Dmitri and Rain's pre-romance corresponds with Rain's learning to move on from Galen's death, one could argue that Smith kills off Galen—Rain's white romantic interest—in order to make room for a better, Native/Native romance. Such a reading would correspond with Kathryn James's reading of many YA texts depicting death as punishment for the transgression of social norms, in the context of Indigenous communities that see interracial romance as taboo, as well as in relation to the dominant society's continuing anxieties about miscegenation.

Such a reading is complicated, however, by Galen's earlier support of Rain's investment in her Indigenous communities, recounted in Rain's journal entries. In fact, one reason that Rain misses Galen so much is that he would "always step up with the smooth thing to say" in response to people who told Rain she did not "seem Indian" or made other comments about Native people that made her uncomfortable (49). While the gender dynamic is reversed, Fynn and Natalie's relationship also challenges critiques of Native/white romance since Natalie, like Galen, supports Fynn's and Rain's ties to their Indigenous communities, and she wants her expected child to belong to those communities as well (62, 77). Through their struggles, as Rain roots for Fynn and Natalie's relationship, Smith's readers are drawn to do the same.

In addition to considering Native attitudes toward Native/non-Native romantic relationships, *Rain* also raises questions about how exoticized or derogatory understandings of Native people contribute to non-Native people's desire to either date or avoid dating them. At one point, Rain wonders if Natalie has moved in with

Fynn to rebel against her parents' suburban life. She hopes this is not true, and, even if it is partially true, she still wants Natalie and Fynn's relationship to succeed and still sees Natalie as part of the family, a source of mutual support (64). Rain also admits that "there was a time when I wondered if my being Native was the reason [Galen had] never made a first move on me." But, she says, "the rest of my heart knew better" and that it was instead Galen's mother—and her rule barring Galen from dating anyone—that held him back (133). While she attributes better motives to Natalie and Galen, she is led to question their intentions because of the negative representations of Native people that plague her town.

In one of her journal entries, Rain records a conversation she overhears between Aunt Georgia and Jordon "the Flash" Guller, Natalie's college-student intern who covers Indian Camp with her. Georgia tells the Flash that the goals of the camp are "To give these kids a chance to get together, learn a thing or two, build a bridge. Maybe we'll catch a movie." She chuckles and adds, "Oh, and to have fun. Eat up my cooking" (56). The campers—who include Spence (Aunt Georgia's grandnephew from a suburb of Oklahoma City), Dmitri and his twin sister Marie (who are fairly new to the area), Queenie, and eventually Rain herself, despite her initial refusal to participate beyond taking photos—indeed eat together, write in their journals (in part to generate material to put on a website that Fynn, a web designer, will teach them to make), and build an actual weight-bearing bridge out of pasta. When the Flash asks about the challenges of the program, Georgia talks about the short time span, "diverse group," and her own inexperience. "Maybe I should be doing it differently somehow," she says. "But mostly, I just think these kids need one another" (56). Rain concludes her journal entry, "I wasn't sure what Aunt Georgia meant, and she didn't explain" (56).

Yet, given Rain's sense, discussed earlier, that Georgia's motivations had something to do with dominant representations of Indians in Hannesburg and their effects on the Indian young people there, and given Rain's focus on those effects throughout the novel, we can surmise that countering those effects is one reason the campers need one another (13). Indian Camp is a place where they can escape dominant representations for a while and just be themselves without having their identities questioned by non-Natives. The presence of the Flash mitigates that escape element, but the campers are still able to express themselves and do activities together in a unique space outside of school or other dominant institutions. They also offer one another support and build strength as a community in a way that offers healing from the hurtful impact of dominant representations while enabling them to challenge the ideologies behind those representations and work toward sovereignty over their own self-representations.

Rain frequently emphasizes how small a minority American Indians are in Hannesburg. She tells the Flash she knows of nine Indians in town: "me, my brother, my uncle, Aunt Georgia, and the Headbirds" (48–49). By coming together as a small intertribal community, the campers not only escape feelings of isolation and invisibility but also build pride rooted in their actual heritages, interests, relationships, and collaborative accomplishments, thereby overcoming some of the shame that they—like Rain's father—may have experienced as a result of colonialist attitudes regarding Indians. In addition to their literal pasta bridge, the campers build bridges of connection between one another, creating an intertribal alliance in Hannesburg that promises to continue beyond the camp. Meanwhile, the campers' planned culminating trip to the Leech Lake Ojibwe reservation in Minnesota (the primary reason they seek funding from the town) opens a route for building additional bridges of support between the budding Hannesburg intertribal alliance of Indian Camp and other Indigenous communities.

The campers most clearly confront dominant attitudes and claim representative self-determination as they write and draw in their journals, as they articulate the value of Indian Camp at a town council meeting that includes a vote on funding for the camp, and as they contribute their voices, and in Rain's case her photos, to the newspaper feature on Indian Camp assembled by the Flash. Over the course of just a few days, the campers develop relationships, build individual as well as communal strength, and begin offering Hannesburg a self-determined view of Native Americans.

Because of the attention Indian Camp gets in both town politics (much to Rain's chagrin) and the town paper (with Rain's assistance), the camp becomes a site not just of intertribal alliance-making but also of opportunities for Native/non-Native interaction and alliance. Mrs. Owen and the Flash represent possibilities for alliance while also shedding light on how both exoticizing American Indians and erasing differences between Native and non-Native people can present obstacles to alliance-making. In spearheading the opposition to Georgia's request for $1,340 from the Hannesburg city council for Indian Camp (a move she seems to make in an attempt to wrangle votes for a second attempt to get elected mayor, having recently lost an election), Mrs. Owen deploys classic multiculturalist, anti–affirmative action rhetoric, declaring in a letter to the editor, the "highest respect for Native American culture" while questioning, as a "fiscally responsible citizen," whether "it is the place of our city to finance a special program that serves only one small ethnic group" (33). This rhetoric reflects a simultaneous othering and erasure since the logic goes: this small minority of "other" people should not get "our" (read "white citizens") tax dollars because "they" are not really that different from "us" and they therefore do not need the "special" treatment merited by a unique or uniquely oppressed population. Many have characterized such an anti-affirmative stance as colonialist.[12] Smith's novel complicates that characterization, but only slightly. The Republican Fynn declares that Mrs. Owen is right that "the city can't afford to allocate that much for programs like Indian Camp." However, Rain suggests that Fynn's stance stems from internalized colonialism when she tells Natalie that the only reason she can think of for Fynn not "completely supporting Indian Camp"—even though he had nagged her for weeks to sign up—is that "he took after Dad," whose shame about his Indian heritage Rain frequently draws attention to (117).

Fynn, like Rain, is most upset by the way Mrs. Owen drags Rain into her political agenda. Mrs. Owen makes an obvious reference to Rain in her letter to the editor when she emphasizes the small number of camp participants in part by pointing out that "the only local Native American child who's an honor roll student" does not plan to take part (33). Rain herself had divulged that information two days prior to the letter's appearance in the paper when she ran into Mrs. Owen on her first trip to the grocery store in months. Rain feels "stuck in the middle" by her "big mouth": "If I did nothing," she writes, "it would look like I was siding with Mrs. Owen. If I joined Indian Camp, it would look like Aunt Georgia had pressured me—something she'd never do" (34). Natalie gets Rain out of the bind by getting her to shoot photographs of the camp for the paper, and by banning Rain from joining the camp since doing so would be a "conflict of interest" (36–37). In her letter, Mrs. Owen dehumanizes Rain, using her, along with the other Indian young people in town, as a tool to further her political prospects. She similarly dehumanizes Rain at other times by reducing her to the derogatory stereotypes of Native women evident in the rumors circulating about her and Galen. Mrs. Owen's big challenge is to see Rain as human—as her late son's best friend and a multifaceted young woman—and to humanize the Indian Camp participants by recognizing their unique, and often difficult, experiences as American Indians in Hannesburg that result in their need for the camp.

In the end, Mrs. Owen donates space to Dmitri and Marie to sell wild-rice soup as a fundraiser for the Leech Lake trip (129). Rain speculates about her motivation: "For votes maybe or to soothe a guilty conscience. Or maybe it was an act of kindness" (129). Regardless of her motivation, Mrs. Owen has become an ally rather than an adversary, even if the campers' need for an ally to help with fundraising is a direct result of her getting the town to reject their funding request. That Mrs. Owen might have underhanded motivations highlights the way in which non-Native individuals and groups can sometimes ally with Native people out of personal interest rather than solidarity; in other words, the ideologies of colonialism do not always prevent non-Native/Native alliances in the pursuit of short-term goals, even as they certainly deter long-term alliances and big-picture anti-colonialist work. Whether Mrs. Owen will become a long-term ally, whether she will confront her colonialist perspectives, and whether she will reconcile with Rain remain unanswered at the end of Smith's novel.

The Flash shows more promise as a long-term ally because he is open to learning from the campers and allows their self-representations to replace his own stereotypes, at least in part. The novel gives significant attention to his learning process. After the first day of camp, when Rain tells him that she knows of "nine Indians living in town," the Flash responds, "They prefer 'Native Americans'" (48). Even after Rain reveals her own Indian identity, the Flash still uses the term "Native Americans" and refers to Indian Camp as a "Native American Youth Program" despite Georgia and the campers always using the term "Indian Camp." This contrasting terminology just scratches the surface of the Flash's expectations butting against the actual experience of the campers.

While the Flash never changes his terminology, he does develop greater respect for the campers' perspectives, and attempts to incorporate their self-representation into his news story. When he and Rain first meet to go to Indian Camp, and Rain says that she needs to ask permission to shoot the story, the Flash does not understand why they should ask and trivializes Native peoples' concerns about being represented by others. Looking at Rain's camera, he asks, "Will they think you're trying to steal their souls or something?" (39). Instead of acknowledging a history of non-Natives—from photographers to anthropologists—exploiting Native people through their representations of them, the Flash instead evokes a stereotype of Indians being superstitious of technology, particularly imprudent given the camp's science and technology focus. However, as the Flash begins to get to know Rain, Georgia, and the campers, despite still sometimes trying to "feed lines," he also increasingly listens carefully and records what they say, even when he is surprised by their words or does not fully understand them.

The Flash's struggle to reconcile his previous knowledge of Native Americans—based wholly on dominant representations—with the campers' self-representations comes to a head near the end of the novel as he interviews Rain for his story. (Rain becomes "fair game for a source" once she joins the camp and Natalie fires her.) During this exchange, the Flash asks Rain several times about why Georgia had the campers build a pasta bridge. Georgia had told him about "fostering teamwork" and drawing on her expertise as a retired science teacher, but he still does not understand (112–16). "What does bridge building have to do with Native American culture?" he asks (114). Rain jokes with him, asks if he understands "how weird it is to be an Indian in Hannesburg, Kansas," and finally challenges the Flash to "Think of it like this: How is bridge building not an Indian thing?" (112–15). The Flash is finally stymied. He trips over his words: "Well, Indians . . . You just don't think . . . Well, maybe *you* do. I just always thought of Native American culture being . . ." (115). Rain jumps in to tease him in her "best Hollywood Indian voice," saying, "Bridges not for white man only" (115). The Flash finally gets it. Rain suggests that the reason for building the bridge has everything to do with the Flash failing to understand why Indians would build bridges: dominant representations of Indians—including representations of Indians as nature-bound creatures of the past divorced from technologies like bridge-building—have plagued Indian young people. The camp provides a space for them to get away from those representations as they build a literal bridge as well as a bridge of relationships with one another that will give them the strength to confront those representations going forward. The Flash accepts Rain's answers and decides to run her pictures, along with material from his interviews, despite Natalie's having officially fired Rain as the photographer for the story. In so doing, the Flash becomes an ally in furthering Native self-representation, helping the campers to counter dominant representations of Indians in the town of Hannesburg even as he continues to wrestle with the impact of such representations on his own perspective.

Although we expect that the Flash will attempt to accurately convey the campers' views in his news story, he is still an outsider, and his presence, as well as his forthcoming news story, raises anxieties about non-Native involvement in the representation of Native people. After watching the Flash interview Marie and Dmitri, Rain feels that she has "made a mistake by pulling the *Examiner* into

Indian Camp" (66). She "wondered then if Marie and Dmitri weren't exactly shy. Maybe they felt like they shouldn't have to explain themselves. Like they didn't particularly care if Hannesburg got a glimpse into their lives. Aunt Georgia was always polite, but she didn't seem overly thrilled to have the Flash around all the time" (66). As he interviews Marie and Dmitri, the Flash seems to have taken Georgia's hint that, as Rain says, "it might be best for an outsider to leave the details alone" regarding the spiritual significance of the Ojibwe wild-rice harvest; he does not press them to share about this as they describe their experiences growing up in Minneapolis and on the Leech Lake Reservation (58, 66). Still, they appear uncomfortable during the interview, lending weight to Rain's concerns. If Georgia had wanted the camp to be an escape from the non-Native gaze, her desire remains unfulfilled thanks to the Flash and his story. In the end, the possibility of the newspaper coverage of the camp positively putting forth Native perspectives and challenging dominant representations in Hannesburg seems to trump concerns about the possibility of the Flash and his coverage of the camp encouraging as well as enacting an exploitative, exoticizing white gaze on Native people for non-Native consumption. These tensions are not, however, wholly resolved; Smith thereby prompts her non-Native readers to consider critically their own experiences of learning and talking about Indians.

The hope for Native/non-Native alliance represented by the Flash and Natalie (and, possibly, Mrs. Owen) is tempered by Galen's death. As I have already argued, Smith does not suggest that Galen has died because of his being romantically involved with and allied with Rain. Nevertheless, he remains dead, marking the absence of a potential non-Native ally in the white-dominated Hannesburg schools and other institutions of the town. After all, neither the Flash nor Natalie will be attending school with Rain and the other Hannesburg campers. I maintain that Galen's death opens space for Rain's critique of colonialist heteropatriarchy and her pursuit of Indigenous self-representation that is supported by Native and non-Native allies. At the same time, Galen was an ally to Rain—a white male who challenged colonialism—and his death troubles Rain's hope for immediate allies in her school context as well as a larger hope for certain kinds of Native/ white alliances, particularly those based in romantic partnerships. I nevertheless read the ending of *Rain* as optimistic about Native/non-Native alliances since the collaborative self-representation coming out of Indian Camp—through the campers' website and their fundraising efforts for the Leech Lake trip, as well as the newspaper story—have the potential to inspire Native/non-Native alliances in the town that go beyond individual relationships like that of Rain and Galen. Moreover, as Rain deals with Galen's death, she enacts self-critique and self-representation in ways that open further possibilities for effective alliances.

———————————

Like Jason in "A Real-Live Blond Cherokee," Rain is at times complicit in colonial- ist postures that exoticize, deride, or erase differences in perceived Others. Unlike Jason, Rain gives frequent critical attention to her own complicity, a unique feature of Smith's novel that offers a model for the sort of self-awareness and openness to growth necessary for healthy alliances across lines of race, culture, class, gender, and sexuality in resistance to racism and colonialism. Such self-critique is necessary not only for alliance-building—Native individuals and communities need to overcome colonialist ways of seeing themselves as well as others if their relationships with allies are to be long-lasting and effective in resisting colonial- ism—but also for the dynamic growth of Indigenous communities. Even when they are not channeling the ideologies of colonialism, the different voices within Indigenous communities—let alone voices across Indigenous and non-Indigenous communities—are bound, at times, to clash. Taking on a self-critical posture, along with a willingness to learn and change, enables individuals and communities to challenge oppression, strengthen their ties with one another, and grow. Rain models such growth via self-critique as she begins forming new relationships and reconciling old ones during Indian Camp, especially with the Flash, Dmitri, Queenie, and an additional character named Lorelei.

Paralleling the frat boys' and Jason's mutual exoticization (of Indians and the Irish, respectively) in "A Real-Live Blond Cherokee," Rain's reaction to the Flash's revelation that he is Jewish aligns with the responses she gets when people discover that she is Indian. When Rain asks the Flash if he has "any idea how weird it is to be Indian in Hannesburg, Kansas," the Flash responds by asking if she has "any idea how weird it is to be Jewish in Hannesburg, Kansas." Surprised, Rain asks, "You're Jewish?" and the Flash answers, "My whole life." "But you don't seem . . ." Rain starts, stopping herself before she is clearly about to say "Jewish" (114). This comes after Rain has repeatedly expressed frustration with those who tell her she does not "seem Indian." Unlike Jason, however, Rain immediately catches her gaffe and reprimands herself. A few minutes later, when the Flash confesses that he has "never even met a Native American before this summer," Rain admits, "all I know about Jewish people, I learned from *Fiddler on the*

Roof (115–16). Recognizing that her understanding of Jewish people is based on stereotypes, Rain wants to change.[13] She wants to see the Flash for who he is, just as she wants him to see her when he looks at her, not his stereotypes: "It wasn't funny, how clueless both of us were," Rain says. "But laughing worked better than medicine" (116). As they laugh, their relationship deepens, and we sense that it provides some of the inspiration for Rain to move on with her life, confronting the townsfolk's assumptions about her head-on and with a good sense of humor.

Rain's relationship with Dmitri is the most romantically charged and among the most revelatory about Rain's prejudices regarding social class. Rain's pejorative notions about the residents of the Blue Heaven trailer court does not disappear when Dmitri takes her to his home there, but the visit does lead her to question some of her assumptions. Even though Rain has grown up in Hannesburg, she had never been to the trailer court prior to this visit. Standing in front of the trailer while Dmitri runs inside to get a dream catcher for her to consider buying as a present for Natalie and Fynn's baby, Rain recounts, "I took my first close look at Blue Heaven." Observing the "cement porches" and the "sunburned, half-naked little kids" who "played with matches and ash snakes on gravel drive-throughs," she notes, "I held on tight to my camera and my two crisp twenty dollar bills, fresh from the cash machine" (71). Rain sees the sorts of bodies and behaviors she expects to see based on dominant representations of poor people. Since they do not dress or play according to the middle-class norms of Rain's neighborhood, Rain assumes the worst of the children, that they are likely to steal from her. Rain is an Old Town girl, not "the kind of girl who hangs out in the trailer park" (71).

Rain's assumptions begin to shift when she steps into Dmitri's trailer. She is surprised that the trailer is much bigger than she expected and feels "more like a house" than a camper (72). She is also impressed by the artwork Dmitri's family makes and by their deep investment in their Ojibwe heritage, ashamed that she does not know more about that side of her own family (73). As Dmitri's home and Dmitri himself challenge Rain's ideas about the lower-class residents of her town, Rain begins confronting her complicity in class-based prejudice, opening avenues for cross-class alliances within and beyond American Indian communities.

Rain initially expresses anxieties about Dmitri's cultural authenticity as well as his social class, remarking, "dream catchers are kind of . . . trendy, don't you think?" when he offers to sell her one, but she quickly overcomes these anxieties, moving to the opposite end of the spectrum by valorizing what she sees as his cultural authenticity relative to her own (71–73). Rain's questioning of Queenie's cultural authenticity is only slightly more complicated. When the Flash asks Queenie what she, an African American girl, is doing at Indian Camp, Queenie explains that her aunt Suzanne "has been tracing our family tree for the reunion next month, and, come to find out, one of my great-grandfathers was a Native American" (70). Rain records her reaction: "The word *cousin* sneaked onto my tongue, and I didn't like the way it tasted. As if stealing Galen hadn't been enough [Queenie had dated and broken up with Galen prior to his last special night with Rain], now Queenie was barging in on my cultural territory. Granted, she was no guru-seeking, crystal waving, long-lost descendant of an Indian princess, but still . . ." (70). At the time, Queenie does not even know what "tribe, Nation, or band" her great-grandfather belonged to, but Rain does not pass judgment on her for this (70). When Rain later learns that Queenie's great-grandfather was Seminole, she says this made her "a pretty close cousin after all" (133). In Rain's eyes, Queenie is not an Indian princess wannabe any more than Dmitri is a dream catcher wannabe. She initially did not want Queenie to invade her cultural territory like she had invaded her relationship with Galen, but she quickly becomes self-critical on this front and even praises Queenie for discovering her Native heritage and joining Indian Camp as one of the positive ways Queenie (unlike herself and Mrs. Owen) has healthily moved forward after Galen's death (126). Ultimately, Rain accepts Queenie's claim, embracing her as a cousin, not just an ally.

Smith could have used Rain's questioning of Queenie's claim to Native identity as an opportunity to engage complex issues regarding Native identity and cultural appropriation, but she does not. Should Queenie be able to enroll in the Seminole nation? Check the "Native American" box on her college applications? Participate in intertribal Native communities beyond Indian Camp? Publish as an American Indian author? Even though it deeply engages issues related to dominant and Indigenous representation, the novel's engagement with dominant as well as Indigenous understandings of Native identity is limited. As I discuss in this book's coda, Indigenous YA literature largely avoids deep engagement with these core questions about who "counts" in what ways in Indian country, in material and legal as well as symbolic and psychological terms.

While Rain does not ultimately question Queenie's claim to Native identity, she does raise questions about her own complicity in colonialist heteropatriarchy in her treatment of Queenie, and gestures toward their shared need to resist the discourse given its destructive effects for both African American and Native

American women. Rain had broken off her friendship with Queenie a few months before Galen's death when, as Rain understood it, Queenie dumped Galen for another guy just before a school dance. The events of the novel come to a head on July 2nd—two days before Galen's July 4th birthday, which Rain has pledged always to remember—at Indian Camp, when Rain accidentally breaks the campers' pasta bridge and her camera, then gets into a fight with Queenie. Rain calls Queenie "the star" of Galen's funeral—Queenie read a poem at the funeral, whereas Rain could not even bring herself to attend—and Queenie reveals that Galen actually broke up with her before that dance, not the other way around. Rain storms off, but they begin to reconcile their friendship the following day at the town council meeting when Queenie smiles at Rain for raising her hand to be counted as a camper. Rain spends the night of July 3rd and morning of July 4th making a memorial website for Galen, uploading some of her photos along with Queenie's funeral poem, and feeling relieved that she has finally discovered a good way to remember her late friend's birthday. Spence is the one who delivers Queenie's poem to Rain along with the message that Rain can use it on her website, as requested, under the condition that she help the campers rebuild the broken bridge (123).

Shortly after this moment that confirms the girlfriends' reconciliation, we are reminded of the reason for their conflict in a somewhat sarcastic but still significant remark by Spence. When Rain asks him for his opinion on her Galen website, Spence replies, "I don't know," continuing, "It depends. Are you girls ever going to stop fighting over this dead white guy and give me a shot?" (123). Spence's remark is tongue-in-cheek but also true. Queenie and Rain have been torn apart, during a time when they both really could have used a friend, by their feelings for Galen, and Rain's incorrect belief that Queenie hurt Galen by dumping him. Galen had "let me think the worst of Queenie," she later recognizes, and she "blamed him for that." "But," she says, "I let it burn through, and I let it go. Blame wasn't something I cared to hold on to" (134). While she releases her anger with Galen for tearing her and Queenie apart, she continues to interrogate her own role in that rift. She had prized Galen—her white male best friend—over Queenie, her "second best friend," even before Galen's death, and had kept shutting Queenie out after his death because of her blind commitment to him. Even though Galen himself had resisted colonialist perspectives, in putting him on a pedestal at the expense of her friendship with Queenie, and especially in clinging to him after his death in ways that compromised her own vitality as well as her ability to contribute to her

Native community, Rain had become complicit in the ideologies of colonialist heteropatriarchy so often associated with the generic "dead white guy" humorously referenced by Spence.[14] Spence's off-the-cuff comment therefore deeply affects Rain. After recovering from the shock of it and realizing that Spence may actually be romantically interested in her, Rain says, "It was time for me to start focusing on what was happening now and what might happen in the future" (124). Rain realizes that she must not only pay attention to, but also actively participate in the present and future, including by joining the members of the Indian Camp in building relationships and creating resistive self-representations.

Rain most clearly confronts her own investment in the ideologies of colonialist heteropatriarchy in her shifting attitudes toward, and budding relationship with, Lorelei, a character we meet early in the novel on Rain's first grocery-store outing in months. Introducing Lorelei, who staffs the checkout counter, Rain says, "Between her bleached bangs and Salvation Army outfit—a checked halter top and faded cutoffs—she looked the part of her reputation. Around town, folks called her 'the Lorelei Express,' and not because she's fast at the cash register. Fynn had actually dated her, back when they were juniors in high school" (18). By saying that Fynn "had actually dated her," Rain registers alarm clearly tied to Lorelei's lower-class position and related reputation for sexual promiscuity.

Lorelei's class position and the town's—and Rain's—sexualized representation of her intersect again during Rain's trip with Dmitri to the trailer park. Rain is driven away not only by the thought that she is being disloyal to Galen by spending time with Dmitri, but also by the fear that someone might have seen her come into Dmitri's trailer house alone with him "and what they might say" (75). When she had first entered the trailer park, clutching her camera and her cash as she eyed the "half-naked" children playing, Rain had thought, "I wasn't the kind of girl who hung out at the trailer park. I didn't want a reputation like Lorelei's" (71). In Hannesburg, lower-class girls like Lorelei who live in and/or "hang out" at the trailer park are perceived as sexually promiscuous, their poverty and promiscuity described in inextricably connected terms. Rain is complicit in the oppression of these poor young women via her perpetuation of the dominant representations of them that serve to reinscribe Rain's privilege as a middle-class girl from a respectable neighborhood.

Later, when Rain finds out that people have been gossiping about her alleged sexual relationship with Galen, she says, "I wondered if this was how it felt to be Lorelei" (99). She develops empathy for Lorelei and begins questioning her complicity in the town's representation of Lorelei once she realizes that the same assumptions people make about Lorelei have been falsely made about her because of her Native identity. Through Rain's developing perspective on Lorelei, Smith demonstrates the overlap in dominant representations of "Indian girls" and "trailer court girls" along with the hurt those representations cause. Like Native women in dominant narratives, especially those of interracial romance, poor white girls are represented in and beyond Hannesburg as sexually promiscuous, out of control—unable to respectably control their expressions of sexuality and unable to resist men—complicit in their own exploitation, and responsible for their communities' struggles over issues like teen pregnancy and their resultant entrenched poverty. In her simple line about wondering if her own feelings coincided with Lorelei's, which comes after her frequent critiques of dominant representations of Indians as well as her portrayal of her own complicity in dominant representations of "trailer court girls," Rain opens an avenue for a crucial alliance in the fight against colonialist heteropatriarchy.

Rain's relationship with Lorelei and the budding Native women/poor women alliance it symbolizes remains tentative at the end of Smith's novel because of the depth of Rain's, and possibly Lorelei's, internalization of dominant assumptions. Resisting their own complicity in such assumptions will need to be an ongoing process. Right after she empathizes with Lorelei based on her shared experience of having rumors spread about her, Rain wonders if Lorelei is responsible for spreading the rumors, possibly out of her lingering anger about losing Fynn (99). If this is true, then Lorelei herself has been complicit in perpetuating the ideologies of colonialist heteropatriarchy, demeaning another young woman—significantly an Indian girl—because of her feelings for a man. When Lorelei asks Rain, in another checkout-counter scene near the end of the novel, if she is going to watch the Fourth of July fireworks, "Maybe with a certain retired teacher's visiting nephew [Spence]? Or that new boy from the trailer park [Dmitri]?," it is unclear whether she is looking for gossip, making assumptions about Rain as an "Indian girl," and/or just being friendly (131). Rain still clearly suspects Lorelei of gossiping, and she likely still carries additional dominant assumptions about Lorelei and other poor women despite having questioned those assumptions and empathized with Lorelei over the rumors. Smith thus underscores the difficulty as well as the necessity of marginalized women from different communities confronting their own complicity in colonialist heteropatriarchy if they are to form alliances that effectively resist it.

When Lorelei asks about Rain's romantic prospects with Spence or Dmitri for the Fourth of July, Rain replies, "I've got plans with another male. A wild one. We're going to run like night creatures and howl at the moon" (131). The wild male is actually her dog, Chewie, with whom she watches the fireworks, but her remark is meant to rile Lorelei through its mockery of the dominant assumptions about Indian girls that Lorelei might be drawing on in her question (131–32). Rain's remark suggests that humor provides one avenue for Native women and poor women to confront and resist their complicity in one another's oppression. Such humor is certainly important for Rain's own self-critique.

In terms of her personal grieving process over Galen, Rain adheres to a common pattern in YA texts that bring together photography with themes of death. In *Disturbing the Universe*, Roberta Trites draws on Roland Barthes's theorizing of photography as always relaying a subtext of death since every photo moves a person from a subject position toward an object position as it captures someone who is dead or who will eventually die (Trites, *Disturbing* 135). Rain is empowered through her position—in her case, a return to her position—behind the camera; her engagement with the subject-object relationship of photography, as she looks at photos of Indian Camp as well as photos of her and Galen, helps her to mature in a way that enables her to process her grief (*Disturbing* 123–24). Rain's use of photography, along with other avenues of representation, like her journal entries, relates to her developing anti-colonial critique as well as her participation in the resistive community of the Indian Camp. Drawing on Susan Sontag's work, Trites attests, "For characters who take pictures instead of becoming involved, photography can become a source of complicity, a way to approve tacitly that which they might not otherwise be able to change" (126). While photographing Indian Camp gets Rain back behind her camera for the first time since Galen's death, it also distances her from the campers. Taking pictures of them rather than joining them is yet another way in which Rain is, for the first part of the novel, complicit in the dominant repression of Native women's vitality and voices; her commitment to avoiding a "conflict of interest" initially stifles her own ability to directly participate in the empowering camp experience even as she is ultimately drawn in.

By completing her memorial website to Galen, joining Indian Camp, and adding her voice as well as her photos to the campers' self-representation, Rain begins to more fully contribute to the empowerment of her intertribal community while experiencing a restoration of the personal agency she lost in the period of intense grief following Galen's death. Rain moves from passively looking at her photos of Galen and valorizing him as a perfect subject to actively editing those photos and creating the tribute website. This work renders Galen as simultaneously a dead object that Rain can finally lay to rest and a more fully human—in other words, imperfect—subject who instead of having a debilitating hold over her can now, through Rain's memories, contribute to her dynamic growth.

Photography is a medium through which Euro-Americans have associated Native people with death, a phenomenon epitomized by Edward Curtis's huge and hugely popular body of photography that represents Native people as belonging to an already dead or quickly vanishing past. This is evident in the outdated, culturally inappropriate dress, the lighting, and the coloring of Curtis's photos as well as the stoic faces he requested of his Native subjects. While Rain's website—featuring photos of Galen—firmly positions a white boy in the realm of the dead (where he belongs), her photos of Indian Camp do the opposite. Her photographs for the newspaper's feature story portray the campers, a small but diverse community of Native people, living very much in the present as they explore science and technology, write in their journals, and solidify their intertribal alliance. Her images become even more powerfully tied to present-day concerns in her community when they are coupled with her words, recorded by the Flash, about why Indians in Hannesburg need to "build bridges."

Rain's grandfather, also a photographer, says that a darkroom is "a place of possibilities. Using filters, papers, and chemical mixes, the photographer can reproduce, rediscover, and reinvent realities" (45). Over the course of the novel, Rain moves along this spectrum from reproducing to rediscovering to reinventing dominant representations, especially of Native people. She comes to reinvent such representations not only in her photography but also in her journal entries—which frequently describe dominant representations and their effects—and her attention to the self-representation of other Native characters as seen in Dmitri's drawings, Marie's speech to the town council, Fynn's web design, and the artwork of Dmitri's parents.

Rain's embracing of her own and others' self-representation is one of the most important threads in Smith's novel. She becomes empowered as she confronts dominant representations of Indians with her own self-representations, and as she makes allies with others in part by allowing their self-representations to replace the dominant representations that she has internalized. While Rain begins the novel as a passive character, consumed by her mourning for Galen, unlike other heroines of YA romance, she becomes anything but passive by the end of the novel. She is the one with the camera, the speech, and the pen; the one determining her town's gaze through her photos of Indian Camp; and the one determining our gaze as readers. Like Tommy in *Slash* and Junior in *The Absolutely True Diary of a Part-Time Indian*, Rain assumes agency over her own self-representation. Smith thus constructs a multifaceted resistive romance by beginning with the death of an adolescent romance, by deeply challenging the colonialist heteropatriarchy of the dominant interracial Indian romance, and by providing strong Native voices, especially the Native female voice of Rain herself.

Empowered Indigenous Female Voices in Power's "Reunion"

Even more than *Rain Is Not My Indian Name*, Susan Power's story "Reunion" focuses on the representational power of Indigenous girls and women. It does so through a story of interracial romance that is sure to disturb some readers for its surface parallels with dominant narratives of white/Indian romance. Unlike *Rain Is Not My Indian Name*, "Reunion" is not at all about the romantic relationships of its young adult protagonist. Instead, and in keeping with a major strand of Indigenous young adult literature, the story focuses on the romance of the protagonist's parents.[15] "Reunion" appears in the nonfiction section of Power's 2002 collection *Roofwalker*, but it blurs the lines of fiction and nonfiction as the story of a young Susan Power imagining her parents' first meeting.

Addressed to Power's mother, "Reunion" begins, "Mama, I am eleven years old, sitting in an empty corner of the school library, playing God" (166). Because she misses her father, who has died six months earlier, the young Power decides to "play God" by imagining and writing the story of her parents meeting. Her pen carries all of them back to 1935. Her mother, at ten years old, is leaning against the marker for Sitting Bull's grave when her father, "twenty years old and a Hamilton College man," drives up in his car (167). The young author is tempted to "tease you young people," her parents, by telling them how they will marry in twenty-five years and keep their promises until the man dies, but she does not. Instead she "direct[s] you both to speak" (167). Her father speaks of the "beautiful country." As her mother tells him stories, the young Power knows that she wishes she could touch "the thick brown waves of his hair" (167–68). Her father describes his family: "His ancestors traveled to the North American continent in the early 1600s" (168). But he "is not a storyteller and hasn't much to say," so instead he reads to her mother from Emily Dickinson (168). "You trust this dapper young white man with a flair for the dramatic, I can tell," Power tells her mother (168–69). She wants to keep her parents there by Sitting Bull's grave, but she knows she cannot if they are to marry and give her life, so instead she has her father give her mother his Phi Beta Kappa Key and go on his way (169). Then Power transitions back to the story's frame: "Mama, I am eleven years old, sitting in an empty corner of the school library," she reminds us again, but, having written the story of her parents meeting, she caps her pen, "because I no longer need to comfort and distract myself by playing God" (170). Power recalls telling her mother, after school, about the story she wrote back then, and concludes by crediting her mother with inspiring her to keep telling her own stories (170–71).

On the surface, "Reunion" adheres to dominant romance plots about white men and Indian women in which the power—sexual and political as well as narrative—lies entirely with the white men. Like so many settlers, soldiers, anthropologists, educators, and priests before him, the well-educated, privileged white man in this story is drawn to Indian country and to an Indian girl over whom he would seem to have all the power. He is, after all, ten years her senior, the adult in an adult/child, romantically charged relationship that will disturb readers who recall white men sexually exploiting Indigenous women and girls throughout history, their colonial project extending to these girls' and women's bodies as well as their lands. The long history of this exploitation—"romantic" only in the realm of sanitized Euro-American/Canadian representation—like the romantic narratives that support it, extends back (and beyond) the seventeenth century when the ancestors of the man in Power's story came to North America.

Yet, the man in "Reunion" is not just another white man. He is Power's father, and this is her story, not his. Despite a superficial resemblance, he is not the man of manifest destiny. In "Reunion," as well as other nonfiction stories, Power shows how he supports her, her mother, and their Native communities. Moreover, when we read closely, we see that Power's mother, not her father, has the power in the story that the young girl pens in the library as well as in the nonfiction frame about the girl's actual family life. The mother Power imagines as a ten-year-old girl is not an exotic enchantress luring the college man in, but rather a smart girl with agency. She chooses to speak to the man even though she does not have to;

she could tease him by pretending she cannot speak English, as she likes to do with other white tourists (167). The young Power whispers in her mother's ear, "Yes, someday you will gather him in," making the mother the primary actor in creating the romantic union of the future (168). The mother possesses the power of representation as a storyteller, and the power of inspiration as the girl's mother. At the end of the story she writes in the library, the young Power says to her mother, "You say you aren't particularly smart, that you haven't done very much in life, but my father and I know that this is just another one of your stories" (170). She finishes the story with this praise for her mother:

> You read so many books—you are my encyclopedia. You recite the history of my ancestors without pause, without forgetting a single detail—you are my memory. You speak up when others are afraid to—you are my voice. You notice what so many people would like to ignore—you are my vision. You imagine that I can do anything I decide upon—you are my dreams. You've shown me where the spirits hide—you are my imagination. You've challenged me to change my corner of the world—you are my conscience. (170)

Thus, a story that begins as a way to remember a lost father instead becomes an honor song for a living mother. She stops writing because she has remembered that her incredible mother is still there for her as a source of incredible inspiration.

In contrast with her mother's own humility, Power and her father recognize the woman's important contributions, including as a gifted storyteller. Power demonstrates a deep appreciation for her mother's stories—and calls on her mother to recognize her power as a storyteller—not only in the long paragraph of praise that concludes her story about her younger self but also in the final lines of the larger story's frame. "You help me keep my father alive," the adult author Power tells her mother. "You encourage me to tell my own stories. You say that I must have inherited the words from my father. But when I close my eyes searching for inspiration, it is your voice I hear chanting in the dark" (171). Her father has a great reading voice, she has told us, but he is "not a storyteller" (168). It is the Native woman, not the white man, who has the power of representation in this story. This, more than anything else, sets it apart from dominant narratives of white/Indian romance. Inspired by her mother, Power brings representational power to her own writing, most provocatively in "Reunion" by demonstrating that even the well-worn story of the older white man and young Indian girl—a story used to further colonialist aims since those first seventeenth-century narratives about Pocahontas—can be reappropriated by an Indigenous woman for the empowerment of Indigenous women. Just because the story of the older white man and the younger Native woman has often been used to disempower Native women, promote manifest destiny, and justify colonialism, this does not mean that the story must do these things.

Through her treatment of romance in "Reunion," Power uniquely builds on other Native thinkers' discussions of the importance of Indigenous self-representation. For example, like many of the contributors to *Reinventing the Enemy's Language*, the landmark anthology of Native women's writing edited by Joy Harjo and Gloria Bird, Paula Gunn Allen prefaces her selection by highlighting the importance of Native women's self-representation. Allen says, "I write because I am aware that whoever controls the image controls the population; that those who define us determine not only our lives, but our concept of our very selves, and that colonization begins and ends with the definer, the contextualizer, and the propagandist" (Harjo and Bird 151). "Reunion" enacts a powerful anti-colonial resistance as Power takes control over an image and a narrative—that of white/Native romance—that has limited Indigenous women's opportunities as well as their self-concepts, repurposing this story so as to empower Indigenous women. In "Rhetorical Sovereignty," Scott Lyons writes, "As the inherent right and ability of people to determine their own communicative needs and desires in the pursuit of self-determination, rhetorical sovereignty requires above all the presence of Indian voices, speaking or writing in an ongoing context of colonization and setting at least some of the terms of the debate" (Lyons 462). "Reunion" enacts rhetorical sovereignty through its self-reflexive crafting of a Native female voice that changes the terms not so much of a debate as of the genre of Indian romance, as Power displaces the genre's typical emphasis on white (male) appropriation of Native (female) bodies and lands with an emphasis on her empowering relationship with her mother and her own self-determined story.

Girlfriends and Ghosts in Power's "Drum Kiss"

The narrator of Power's fictional short story "Drum Kiss" is, like the young Power of "Reunion," an eleven-year-old American Indian girl who finds empowerment by telling a story of Native/non-Native romance. Published in the 2005 *Moccasin*

Thunder collection, "Drum Kiss" is set in the Uptown Chicago neighborhood where Power grew up, primarily populated at that time by American Indians and white Americans from Appalachia. The story is narrated by Fawn, a Winnebago girl who longs to be friends with another Winnebago girl, the beautiful and confident Gladys, and her group of American Indian girlfriends. Gladys and the other Indian kids stand up for Fawn when white kids at school pick on her—mostly because of Fawn's poverty—but Fawn is too shy and, in her estimation, too boring to be their friend. That all changes during a Halloween party at the Indian Center when Fawn surprises herself by telling Gladys and the other girls a captivating story to explain how the center came to be haunted. Fawn begins by explaining, "This isn't just a ghost story . . . it's also a romantic one. A story of hillbilly love" (148).

She goes on to tell the love story of a couple who meet at the Indian Center: Ronnie, a sixteen-year-old blond-haired, green-eyed girl whose family moved to Chicago from the Appalachian Mountains, and Kunu, a Winnebago boy from Wisconsin. Both Ronnie's and Kunu's parents disapproved of their relationship, but, Fawn says, Ronnie "decided to turn Indian as much as she could because our ways aren't so different from theirs, but there were just a lot of things she didn't know, such as the drum being off-limits to women, being an energy she shouldn't mess with" (149). Ronnie loves watching Kunu and his relatives at the drum, and at one Indian Center powwow, not knowing any better, she leans down and not only touches but kisses the drum after the men finish playing (149). As she sits on the steps of the center, "crying because she hadn't meant to break a taboo and anger the love of her life," a spirit, whom she at first mistakes for Kunu, comes and sucks the life out of her, punishing her for kissing the drum (150). Ronnie's ghost haunts the center now, Fawn explains, crying and searching for Kunu (150). That is why Kunu, a real person known to Fawn and the other girls, does not come to the Indian Center much anymore; he is afraid Ronnie's ghost will "come after him just as the spirit came after her" (150).

Gladys and the others like Fawn's story. At the end of "Drum Kiss," Fawn tells us that she is friends with them now, and even though other kids at school still pick on her, it "doesn't bother me anymore" (151). She has sleepovers with her new friends and tells them stories; "no one thinks [she is] boring anymore" (152). But, Fawn says, she keeps some stories to herself, like what she believes to be the real story about who haunts the Indian Center. Ronnie was just an invention of her imagination, she explains; there are really two ghosts at the Indian Center, the ghosts of her own deceased parents, who have been looking for her since their death and have finally found her. "They looked for me and looked for me because they love me," Fawn writes, concluding her story: "I believe in them and magic and miracles, and it is all a little easier to have faith in now that I am twelve" (152).

Telling the story of Ronnie and Kunu empowers Fawn by strengthening her ties to an intertribal community at the Indian Center and at her school. The themes of self-representation, alliance-building, and Indigenous female empowerment that I have been addressing throughout this chapter come together here. Fawn tells a story of a now dead Native/non-Native romance, and this directly leads to her becoming a more confident young woman and a more fully connected member of an Indigenous community that supports her in the face of attacks from white classmates. Like Smith's *Rain Is Not My Indian Name* and her own "Reunion," Power's "Drum Kiss" is a resistive romance both through its countering of the ideologies that usually underlie the white/Native romance plot that it reappropriates, and through its departure from the typical conventions of YA romance, including the genre's central investment in protagonists' growth toward heteropatriarchal norms via direct romantic experience.

Like Rain and the young Power of "Reunion," Fawn herself is primarily interested in relationships with friends and family rather than a romantic partner; she tells a romance story not because she is personally interested in a romantic relationship, but in order to connect with a group of girls who become friends and supporters.[16] These new friends help Fawn to resist the discrimination she faces at school, and to experience further empowerment as a storyteller. She tells herself the alternative "true" version of the story of the Indian Center ghosts—her deceased parents—in order to connect with her parents and experience further empowerment through their love for her. Gladys and her girlfriends, along with Fawn's parents, are the only love interests in the larger narrative of "Drum Kiss" despite the Native/white male/female love story that Fawn repurposes en route to stronger connections with these other characters.

The complexities of "Drum Kiss" extend beyond its undermining of conventional romance plots. Like many of Power's stories in *Roofwalker*, it gives a bleak picture of the prospects of healthy, long-lasting romance between Native men and Native women. It also offers as much warning about alliance-making as it does hope. These complications make it a good story for helping us to avoid an oversimplified reading of resistive romance in Indigenous YA literature, and to understand colonialist heteropatriarchy in more nuanced terms. The only Native men Fawn expresses an interest in are her deceased father and her fictionalized version of Kunu, who partners with a white woman and is then debilitated by a fear that isolates him from others. Fawn does not suggest any romantic prospects between any living Native men and Native women. While one might dismiss this fact because of the story's brevity and/or Fawn's age—as an eleven-turning-twelve-year-old girl she may or may not yet have meaningful romantic interests of her own—it is significant when read in the context of Power's larger body of short stories in which the absence of viable men, especially viable Native men, is a common theme. "Reunion" and other nonfiction stories feature Power's positively portrayed white father, but other stories show men—most often Native men—as threats to the well-being and even survival of their female partners. Alcohol abuse and violent behavior, in particular, mark these men as unsuitable partners. Throughout these stories, Power suggests that many Native men have internalized harmful colonialist attitudes about masculinity and the appropriate treatment of women. She also suggests that these men do not deserve the affections of Native women, hence her sometimes focusing, as in "Drum Kiss," on female/female and interracial relationships.[17]

"Drum Kiss" further troubles colonialist heteropatriarchy—internalized and otherwise—through its suggestion of a homoerotic link between Fawn and Gladys. Fawn emphasizes Gladys's physical beauty to a degree that implies a possible sexual attraction; she certainly has some kind of crush on the girl. Since this suggestion remains tentative and undeveloped, "Drum Kiss" does not lend itself to extensive analysis as a queer Indigenous text in the ways that the adult texts that Mark Rifkin discusses in *The Erotics of Sovereignty* do. Widely distributed Indigenous YA texts featuring GBLTQ/Two-Spirit protagonists have yet to appear.[18] Nevertheless, "Drum Kiss" does enact what Rifkin calls the "queering" of colonialist and heterosexual norms through its emphasis on Fawn and Gladys's resistive female/female relationship as well as through its revision of a colonialist heterosexual romance narrative in the service of Native female empowerment.

In terms of alliance, despite the story of Native/non-Native romance that Fawn tells, in the larger context of "Drum Kiss" Fawn is only concerned about building relationships with other American Indians: seeking friendship with Gladys and her crowd, trying to protect her grandmother from the ailments of aging, and doggedly holding onto her belief that her parents are still around and still loving her even though they have died. Like *Rain Is Not My Indian Name*, "Drum Kiss" shows how a local intertribal community can be a source of strength and resistance for a young Native girl. "Drum Kiss" has less hope, however, for the prospects of Native/non-Native alliance. The only non-Native characters Fawn describes outside of the Ronnie/Kunu story are the white kids who bully her at school. Fawn does not reference any real-life romances, friendships, or alliances between the white and Indian people in her world. Like *Rain Is Not My Indian Name* and "A Real-Live Blond Cherokee," "Drum Kiss" shows that exoticizing and/or erasing differences can be hindrances to effective alliance. Fawn herself does both in her hillbilly love story, fixating on Ronnie's Celtic features and asserting that Ronnie's and Kunu's cultures "aren't so different," even as she also attributes Ronnie's death to her ignorance of differences between the way she and the Winnebago see the drum. We could say that Ronnie's story serves as a warning to potential non-Native allies that they need to show greater respect for Indigenous cultural traditions, but Ronnie has tried to learn all that she can and to be respectful of Kunu's Winnebago community. In the end, then, "Drum Kiss" signals that Native/non-Native alliances are a difficult and complicated business even when all of the parties involved have the best of intentions. The challenges of such alliances will become more fully illuminated in the next chapter as we turn our attention to Indigenous speculative fiction, and to texts that are more concerned with the troubling than the promising elements of Indigenous/non-Indigenous relationships.

CHAPTER FOUR

That's One Story

Reworking Hybridity through Melissa Tantaquidgeon Zobel's
and Drew Hayden Taylor's Speculative Fiction

R eaders often think of highly canonical novels like James Fenimore Cooper's *The Last of the Mohicans* as historical fiction, because they have accepted as historical elements that are actually quite speculative. Interrupting this paradigm, Indigenous writers are increasingly turning to speculative fiction to recast their histories, their present realities, and their futures on their own terms. Mohegan author and direct descendant of the seventeenth-century Mohegan sachem Uncas, Melissa Tantaquidgeon Zobel sees this turn as especially important for Mohegans, who have been marked as an extinct people of the past by Cooper's false depiction of Uncas as the last of his tribe ("Magical Futurism"). While Zobel challenges Cooper's account from a historian's vantage point in her 1995 nonfiction work *The Lasting of the Mohegans*, the speculative approach of her 2004 novel *Oracles* enables her not only to reinscribe Mohegan presence in the past but also to imagine the Mohegans as a vibrant nation and vital contributors to the world of the future. While Zobel transports us to the future, Anishinaabe author Drew Hayden Taylor, in his 2007 book *The Night Wanderer: A Native Gothic Novel*, marshals the speculative form to take us back through hundreds of years of history from an Anishinaabe vantage point, while underscoring the life-saving relevance of that viewpoint for characters, and readers, of the present. Contrasting with both the historical fiction of the canon and mainstream speculative fiction, Zobel and Taylor leverage the speculative YA platform to tackle real, pressing issues facing contemporary Native communities, from youth suicide and environmental degradation to economic exploitation and cultural appropriation.[1]

"Speculative fiction" typically serves as an umbrella term for genres that transcend straight realism, including science fiction, fantasy, utopia/dystopia, horror, and fantastic realism. The genre lives on the margins of the literary world, from where it often subverts the dominant norms of mainstream society as well as mainstream literature. Many writers of European descent have used speculative works to critique elements of the colonial enterprises they represent; however, their texts too often simultaneously rely on stereotypes of Indigenous peoples while reinscribing colonialist practices. Indigenous cultures are romanticized, exploited, and appropriated across speculative literature, including in the early-twenty-first-century flood of YA novels about vampires, shape-shifters, and the undead.[2] In their novels, Zobel and Taylor write back to this trend, using the tools of speculative fiction to exaggerate and thereby illuminate these colonialist practices in their darkest extremes.[3]

In her article about the 1995 vampire novel *Eye Killers* by Aaron Carr (Laguna/Navajo), Rebecca Tillett suggests a link between romanticization, appropriation, and exploitation. Drawing on Gerald Vizenor's work, she argues that the "widespread perception of Native American absence" stemming from the white invention of the "indian" as a romanticized figure of the past makes way for white exploitation and appropriation of Native lands, resources, and cultures (Tillett 149–58). *Eye Killers*, Tillett contends, exposes this dynamic by portraying malicious European and Euro-American vampires who suck the blood of American Indians as an allegory for neocolonialism, specifically the vampiric consumption by global corporate enterprises of Indigenous lands, resources, and bodies in the American Southwest.[4] These issues similarly come together in *Oracles* through the novel's representation of pervasive non-Native consumption of Native spirituality that is foundational to the dominant global economy, media, and government of Zobel's world, and in *The Night Wanderer* through its depiction of the historic fur trade, the tradition of Indigenous cultures-as-entertainment in historic Europe, and the literal blood-sucking of a European vampire. *The Night Wanderer* also highlights contemporary forms of exploitation evident in dominant representations of Canadian history as well as in economic relationships between Indigenous and non-Indigenous Canadians.

Judith Leggatt observes that even mainstream science-fiction texts that are set in the future and feature positive Indigenous characters tend to associate Indians with the past and portray their cultures as static (Leggatt, "Critiquing" 128–29, 133–34). While occasionally falling prey to romanticization themselves, Taylor and Zobel challenge this nostalgic stance toward Indigenous people by representing particular Native communities of the present or near future as complex, dynamic, and internally diverse. It is actually through their negative depictions of Indigenous characters—the leading vampire of Taylor's story and a sell-out antagonist of Zobel's—that these authors advance a more complicated critique of colonialism than Carr does, even as they also imagine positive paths forward for their Native nations.

Reworking Hybridity by Homing In from Home

Through their revisionary engagement with the speculative genre, *Oracles* and *The Night Wanderer* also offer new ways for approaching hybridity, a discourse that has been deployed in Native literary studies, postcolonial studies, and be-yond—including in speculative fiction and "multicultural literature"—in ways that support or fail to sufficiently challenge the appropriation of Indigenous identities, cultures, and resources. In his 2010 essay "Tending to Ourselves: Hybridity and Native Literary Criticism," Niigaanwewidam James Sinclair joins the authors of *American Indian Literary Nationalism* (Weaver et al. 2006) in challenging notions of hybridity that insist on the equality of an individual's multiple subject positions. By not allowing for the privileging of any one identity, Sinclair argues, such notions threaten Indigenous sovereignty.

In *American Indian Literary Nationalism*, Jace Weaver, Craig Womack, and Robert Warrior define their approach as much by what it is not—freewheeling hybridity—as by what it is: a broad nationalist methodology centrally concerned with questions about "what links [Native] literature to communities" (Weaver et al. xxi). They characterize the deployment of hybridity by the scholar Elvira Pulitano and her protégées as "freewheeling" because it champions a relativism that denies Indigenous people the possibility of identifying, articulating, and privileging their Indigenous subject positions—especially in relation to their Native nations—and because it allows non-Natives to appropriate Native iden-tities. When no one and everyone is "free" to claim an Indian identity, the idea of distinctive sovereign Indian nations loses all meaning. Like Weaver, Womack, and Warrior, Sinclair argues that freewheeling hybridity theorists' insistence that Native people cannot, or at least should not, privilege certain subject positions over others constitutes an attack on the continuance and self-determination of Native communities (Sinclair 250–51).

Sinclair is especially critical of the tendency in hybridity theory to unilaterally emphasize the Native mediation of Euro-American/Canadian practices as if cultural exchange only occurs in one direction, from the colonizer to the colonized. In his view, when critics like Pulitano insist that Native writers acknowledge Western influences and suggest that all Indigenous identities are so mediated as to never be specifically Indigenous in any significant way, they ignore "500 years of power dynamics" (Sinclair 250–51). Such critics, Sinclair maintains, perpetuate colonialism by insisting that Native people can only be meaningfully identified in relation to their participation in the cultures of their colonizers. Sinclair demonstrates that we can recognize cultures as dynamic, nonessential units that borrow from one another, acknowledge individuals' multiple cultural affiliations, and discuss cross-cultural exchange without rendering cultures as so overly unstable as to be meaningless.

"This is not an argument for cultural purity but a position on tribal sovereignty," Sinclair writes of his critique of hybridity and his position that Native peoples can name, claim, and privilege their Native identities (251). Weaver, Womack, and Warrior similarly assert throughout their volume that their brand of nationalism is not isolationist or exclusionary, that it embraces cultural dynamism, and that it promotes *critical* engagement with tribal governments as well as with literature and criticism. Zobel and Taylor shed further light on this balanced approach as their narratives make the case, even more explicitly and starkly than Armstrong's *Slash* does, that Indigenous sovereignty can flourish through an embrace of self-critique, dynamism, and alliances, but only if those are rooted in the integrity of Indigenous nations, their internal strength, and their uncompromising self-determination.

Positioning hybridity as antithetical to Native sovereignty, the contributors to *American Indian Literary Nationalism*, especially Womack, characterize it as an irrecoverable concept.[5] Sinclair takes a different position. Seeing potential possibilities as well as pitfalls for hybridity, he insists that the term "should not be disregarded" but "must simply open up to allow for an Indigenous interpretation, and re-working" (Sinclair 244–55). He thereby provocatively suggests that the right approach to hybridity could complement rather than contradict Indigenous literary nationalism and the movement's commitment to Indigenous self-determination.

Zobel's and Taylor's novels provide just the sort of Indigenous reworking of hybridity called for by Sinclair. Via reappropriating the speculative form, *Oracles* and *The Night Wanderer* critique freewheeling hybridity while offering alternative approaches that support Indigenous sovereignty. On the surface, they seem unlikely sources for theorizing Indigenous hybridities. Of all of the YA texts addressed in this volume, they are the most skeptical about cultural adaptation and cross-cultural exchange. In fact, unlike in most of the texts discussed in the previous two chapters, Native/non-Native interaction never leads to good for the Indigenous people portrayed in *Oracles* and *The Night Wanderer*.[6] Yet, as the readings that follow demonstrate, these novels' critical attention to cross-cultural engagement actually proves crucial for their intervention. In their reworking of hybridity, these books insist on the value of specific cultural identities, responsibilities, and boundaries. They suggest that expressions of hybridity that align with those values will not only allow for but also actively encourage rootedness, accountability, and continuity *alongside* some degree of fluidity and exchange. These novels also illuminate how the alternative Indigenous hybridities they depict can support Native people's efforts to confront the ongoing manifestations of colonialism that freewheeling hybridity, like multiculturalism, too often elides and that speculative fiction too often reinscribes.

———————————

Through their deep investments in specific places—geographic places along with the communities, histories, and traditions attached to those places—and in protecting the boundaries that delineate those places, Zobel and Taylor also expand approaches to home, movement, and agency in children's/young adult literary studies. While scholars who examine both Native American literature and children's literature have identified a common home-away-home pattern in the works they study, in a 2011 *Children's Literature* article, Michelle Pagni Stewart draws attention to some significant differences between the discussions in these respective fields, including in relation to the stability of "home." Stewart contrasts William Bevis's influential assertion that in Native American novels "the place itself has not changed" with a parallel landmark study revealing that when young characters in children's literature experience a movement from home, away, and back home again, they return to a "new home" that has changed during their absence (Stewart 145–47). This movement is heightened in the genre of speculative fiction as children and adolescents travel to different worlds, returning to homes that have changed in ways exceeding what would be possible in realist texts. In Stewart's view, "what makes Bevis's notion of homing in so significant is the fact that home is what it always was; the protagonist himself is the one who has changed, in his realization that home is where he belongs, among the community and a part of the place, its history, and its traditions" (147).

Stewart contends that most Indigenous texts for children and young adults, including *Rain Is Not My Indian Name*, *The Absolutely True Diary of a Part-Time Indian*, and *The Night Wanderer*, stand apart from most children's literature and diverge from the pattern Bevis identifies in Native American texts for adults since the characters in these works are not estranged from Native identities and thus "do not need to home in" (Stewart 147). Stewart's concluding characterization of the protagonists in these texts as "comfortable" inhabitants of dominant societies who sometimes occupy "liminal" positions contradicts that earlier central claim (148). I find the earlier characterization more accurate, if incomplete. The protagonists of most Indigenous-authored YA texts, including *Oracles* and *The Night Wanderer*, have not only "not truly lost sight of" their Indigenous "heritage and roots," but they are also consistently and firmly rooted in the living spaces and communities attached to those heritages (Stewart 148).

The adolescent protagonists of *The Night Wanderer* and *Oracles*—and all of the other texts in this study other than *Slash*—align with Stewart's assessment in that they do not leave home and are not estranged from their communities. However, I argue that they do still "home in" in the sense that they more deeply realize, as Stewart summarizes Bevis's notion of homing in, "that home is where [they] belon[g], among the community and a part of the place, its history, and its traditions" (147). This is especially true of *Oracles* and *The Night Wanderer*, in which the young adult protagonists are already deeply rooted in their Indigenous communities. As they mature, they embrace their rootedness and make it their own. In other words, they transition from a relatively passive experience of being rooted to an active homing in through which they intensify their commitment to their Indigenous home, with home construed as including community and traditions as well as place.[7] It is through their representations of this homing in *from* home that *Oracles* and *The Night Wanderer* interrogate and rework hybridity. They also join the texts I have discussed in previous chapters in challenging the relativist positions of YA literary critics who, like hybridity theorists, often read the privileging of certain places and perspectives over others as necessarily oppressive, and who often suggest that young adult protagonists sacrifice agency if they settle, either literally or metaphorically, in a single place.[8]

The readings that follow provide examples of how we as critics can articulate Indigenous hybridities—and thereby reconcile some features of cosmopolitan criticism with literary nationalism—by beginning our theorizing with Indige-nous-authored literary texts and the specific Indigenous traditions they represent. Young adult literature provides a particularly fruitful site for this theorizing because identity formation is a core concern both of the genre and of hybridity. Indigenous speculative literature, too, is uniquely positioned to offer contribu-tions to an Indigenous reworking of hybridity given the genre's ability, as Brian Atteberry says, to "make the familiar seem new and strange" and to "clarify philosophical and moral conflicts" (Atteberry 3–4). YA literary studies and speculative literary studies are also sites where Indigenous approaches to hybridity can offer important interventions, advancing our understanding of these genres' complicity in the romanticization, appropriation, and exploitation of Indigenous peoples while also opening alternative possibilities that more strongly support Indigenous empowerment and Indigenous senses of home.

Rooted and Responsible at "The True Center of the Universe"

The first novel by Mohegan writer, historian, and tribal medicine woman Melissa Tantaquidgeon Zobel, *Oracles* is hard to categorize but includes features charac-teristic of science fiction, fantastic realism, and post-apocalyptic fiction.[9] Zobel describes the book as part of a genre she terms "magical futurism," with its setting in the not-so-distant future enabling its engagement with a host of issues relevant to the Mohegan and other contemporary Indigenous communities, including cultural/spiritual appropriation, environmental degradation, globalism, gaming, the promises and perils of technology, and the struggle to maintain and adapt cultural traditions.

Oracles centers on the fictionalized Yantuck tribe of the northeastern United States, a thinly veiled stand-in for the Mohegans. We learn near the beginning of the novel that "For most Yantuck Indians, Big Rock Casino down in Fire Hollow had been apex of their reservation" (4). In contrast, "Only a select few still believed that nearby Yantuck Mountain remained the true center of the universe. Of that loyal group, fewer still were chosen to become medicine people and serve as the mountain's sacred guardians." Protagonist Ashneon Quay is "the youngest of those elite oracles" (4). In an early scene, Big Rock Casino burns down as Ashneon, at ten years old, watches from Yantuck Mountain. The novel then jumps ahead to Ashneon at twenty-two years old. She has joined her grandmother Winay and great-uncle Tomuck, who raised her and are teaching her tribal medicine, in seeing Yantuck Mountain as central; it is her training ground as well as her home. As the novel progresses, she increasingly homes in on the mountain as Tomuck teaches her to listen to the woods and the artifacts housed in the small museum the family maintains there (71). Ashneon's ability to hear spirits speaking through trees and artifacts is "magical" in the sense that it reveals the world as more enchanted than the average person realizes, but in the context of traditional Mohegan culture, this ability is also a realistic element.

Ashneon possesses the unique magical ability to travel freely to and from the world of the dead, where she can directly communicate with those who have passed over. Most Yantucks think Ashneon is "delusional," inventing her journeys to the Spirit World as a way to cope with the loss of her parents, both of whom died just after she was born (25). Although they deride her for her claims about visiting the dead, this tribal majority most often does not give Ashneon much attention at all. Instead, still reeling from the loss of the casino, they focus on trying to find a way to profit from the "New Light Corporation," the New Age–like movement that dominates the media, economy, and mainstream culture of Zobel's futuristic world. The New Light Corporation has a monopoly on "the cy," the enhanced television/internet—complete with smells—of Zobel's slightly sci-fi world. Unlike most people, Ashneon, Tomuck, and Winay are not glued to the cy. They instead focus on Ashneon's training, the museum, the educational programs they lead for visiting schoolchildren, and staving off New Lighters and tribal members wanting to make a profit by turning Winay and Tomuck into New Light Oracles.

While Ashneon's grandmother and great-uncle have no interest in the New Light business, her cousin Obed does. *Oracles* is centrally concerned with Obed's rise as a New Light Oracle, Tomuck's death, and Ashneon's attempts to get Obed to act more responsibly. Obed finally transforms after his practice of dark magic on Yantuck Mountain nearly kills him. Ashneon dies shortly thereafter, killed due to an ectopic pregnancy after having married Tashteh, the medicine man of the neighboring Patuxet tribe. The novel ends with Obed as a Yantuck medicine man, working with Winay and his mother, Nuda, to train the next generation of Yantuck medicine people, his own young children, who show promise for revitalizing the tribe and the planet by using the cy to advance timeless Yantuck values. The novel's strongest warning is aimed at "Obed's kind," those who would attempt to exploit Yantuck Mountain and the tribe's connection with it for personal glory and profit.

Like its fictional Yantuck Mountain equivalent, Mohegan Hill is integral to Mohegan identity. In *Medicine Trails: The Life and Lessons of Gladys Tantaquidgeon*, Zobel describes Mohegan Hill as a "magical" place "where Mohegan spirit looms large." She continues, "Mohegans are not simply tied to the hill. They are of it. Gentle spirits protect those who live here. In each generation, some serve as its chosen caretakers" (*Medicine Trails* 9). Medicine people like Zobel and her great-aunt Gladys Tantaquidgeon before her are traditionally understood to be caretakers of Mohegan Hill who listen to the "whispers of all the beings who reside there"—spirits speaking through trees, plants, tribal artifacts, and dreams, along with the little people and other beings on the hill—in order to gain wisdom that helps them care for, protect, and advise the tribe (*Medicine Trails* 9; Guest Lecture). Mohegan Hill, like the fictitious Yantuck Mountain, houses a small museum of significant tribal artifacts. That Tantaquidgeon Museum (the oldest Indian owned and operated museum in the United States), along with the rest of Mohegan Hill, serves as the primary training ground for Mohegan medicine people.[10] The environmental dystopian setting of *Oracles* further heightens the importance of Mohegan Hill/Yantuck Mountain; the mountain is home to one of the only stands of trees left on the "entire eastern seaboard" (51).

Over the course of the novel, we see the mountain's persistent power and its ability to empower those who root themselves on it. The novel also clearly demonstrates that, while they may profit in the short term, bad fortune awaits those who neglect the mountain or attempt to exploit it, whether by centering their identity too much in the casino or by participating in the free-for-all New Light movement. Zobel started writing *Oracles* in the late 1990s at the height of the New Age wave and just after the Mohegan opened Mohegan Sun Casino, now one of the largest-grossing gaming facilities in the world (Zobel, Guest Lecture). Given the centrality of Mohegan Hill in Mohegan culture, and given the anxieties expressed by Zobel and other spiritual leaders of the tribe that the community might come to identify too fully with the casino—despite their concurrent belief that the casino could strengthen the cultural continuance along with the finances of the tribe—we can read the novel as a warning for Mohegan readers to stay rooted on Mohegan Hill, just as the Yantuck are at their best when rooted on Yantuck Mountain (Zobel, Guest Lecture).

Despite its warnings about cultural/spiritual appropriation and its positive representation of rootedness, a surface reading might cast *Oracles* as invested in freewheeling hybridity's celebration of the "in-between spaces" of multiple, fluid, and equally valid cultural identities, especially given the book jacket's description of Ashneon as "caught between two worlds." In many regards, Ashneon is just the sort of mixed-blood character who cosmopolitan critics find so appealing. Her father's side of the family is Euro-American; her mother's is Irish as well as Yantuck. Zobel frequently reminds us that Ashneon has turquoise eyes. Ashneon, however, never characterizes herself as torn between Euro-American and Yantuck worlds, or even as a mixture of cultures. Although she questions whether or not she is cut out to be a medicine woman, she stays planted firmly in her Yantuck identity and grows increasingly committed to Yantuck Mountain and the particular traditions it embodies. Her eyes, we learn, represent multiple allegiances of a different sort. We first hear about her eye color when, at the age of ten, she mysteriously remembers the day after she was born. Her mother had died due to labor complications, and her father died in a car accident while driving the newborn Ashneon home the next day. Ashneon would have died as well, but Winay appeared, rescuing her granddaughter from the flames of the crash and from the mythical giant who was trying to beckon Ashneon into the fire to join her parents (12). Staring into Ashneon's "deep turquoise eyes," the giant agreed to let the baby go with her grandmother but only on the condition that she would, from that day forward, belong to the "two worlds" of the living and the dead (12–13). In this life, she could "visit the Spirit World at any time," and once she dies, she "will be called upon to aid the living" (13). The giant declared that her fiery turquoise eyes would constantly remind Ashneon that she is "only one step away from the brightest fire and light of the universe" (13).

Personally, then, Ashneon is caught between the world of the living and the Spirit World rather than between cultures. At the same time, when read in the context of the entire novel, Ashneon's turquoise eyes participate in a literary tradition that problematically attributes special powers and insights to those with mixed heritages.[11] Ashneon herself demonstrates some interest in her Irish as well as her Yantuck ancestry. Even more significantly, Zobel emphasizes cross-cultural intersection by starting the book with an "ancient Yantuck story" and then interrupting her main narrative at various points with "an ancient Greek story," "an ancient Irish story," and "an ancient Mali story." These four ancient stories share key features, especially giants and little people. These figures also occasionally make their way into the main narrative of the novel, and they are never given culturally or nationally specific labels, like "Yantuck giants" or "Irish little people," when they do. Zobel thereby suggests here, in contradiction with her emphasis elsewhere on the distinctiveness of spiritual entities in specific geographic/cultural/national spaces, that Yantuck, Greek, Irish, and Mali people refer to the same giants and little people in their stories, implying that these ancient figures freely cross cultural and geographic as well as chronological boundaries. Ashneon and her surrogate parents, Winay and Tomuck—all sympathetic characters—also frequently assert that "real medicine people are the same everywhere," sharing qualities that transcend national and cultural lines (26, 33, 45, 107). Thus, the magical and spiritual elements at the heart of Zobel's novel—Ashneon's communication with the dead, the actions of giants and little people, and the practices of medicine people—are associated with the crossing of cultural boundaries, even as the text denounces the New Light Corporation's cross-cultural version of Indigenous spirituality.

Oracles joins recent freewheeling hybridity criticism (and multiculturalism) in celebrating the crossing of cultural boundaries. Still, in its thorough denunciation of the cosmopolitan vision represented by the New Light Corporation, the novel critiques several of the core elements of freewheeling hybridity that it, at times, also advances: the emphasis on the infinite instability of cultural identities, the claim that individuals should not privilege certain cultural identities over others, and the oppressive characterization of attempts to control cultural meanings. In its treatment of New Light, *Oracles* shows that Indigenous individuals can and should privilege specific, identifiable cultural spaces, traditions, and communities; not doing so leads to grave harm. "Real medicine people" are shown to be "the same" in part because they access universal realities through attachment and accountability to their specific communities. Zobel most fully teases out the significance of rootedness and responsibility by contrasting Ashneon with her cousin Obed, who during his time as a New Light Oracle embodies hybridity at its worst. At the end of the novel, the young, emerging leaders of the Yantuck nation—Obed's children Skeezucks and Aquinnee along with their friend Anaquah—pursue an even more dynamic approach to culture than their predecessors, practicing an Indigenous hybridity based in Mohegan history rather than cosmopolitan theory.

The mountain functions as a key player in the war of words between Ashneon and Obed that unfolds over the course of the novel. As the cousins debate which one of them is taking the better course, Ashneon repeatedly argues for the privileging of Yantuck Mountain; she contends that exercising accountability toward the mountain and the Yantuck community who are inseparable from it is the most important task for a Yantuck person, especially a medicine person. In contrast, Obed casts Ashneon's privileging of the mountain and her attempt to protect it from the New Light Corporation as close-minded and selfish. As a New Light Oracle, he equally values the medicines of all places and refuses to commit himself to the community of any single place; to do otherwise, he contends, demonstrates an unenlightened exclusivism.

We learn early in *Oracles* of Obed's involvement with the New Lighters, but his big debut comes at Tomuck's funeral (20). In addition to his rising fame as a New Light Oracle, Obed has also been "slated by inside sources" to be Tomuck's replacement as a Yantuck medicine chief and is thus selected to give Tomuck's eulogy (84). Ashneon is disgusted both by the performance Obed gives at the funeral—he eulogizes Tomuck's journey to "Mother Earth and Father Sun" with language and rituals that "made no sense" for Yantucks even though they impressed the crowd of Obed's New Light followers—and by her budding realization that he is using dark magic to achieve his power (86–90). While Ashneon does not confront Obed at the funeral, her thoughts during it set the stage for her and Obed's subsequent encounters.

Ashneon observes that the audience for the funeral included people from around the world: "Hundreds of Obed's kind," "All natives from somewhere, but all abandoning their unique traditions for a generic path absent of accountability to any nagging grandmother, demanding uncle, or judgmental spirit lurking atop an ancestral mountain" (89). In jumping on the New Light bandwagon, these individuals have abandoned their ties to their places of origin, their communities, and the "discerning teachers" who would have guided them in the deep, meaningful, and responsible use of their own medicine traditions (89). Ashneon's belief that Obed is like these other New Light followers in that he has neglected Yantuck Mountain and his Yantuck community, including his own children, fuels all of her rhetorical attacks that follow.

In the chapter "Miracle," Obed's late wife Danugun appears to Ashneon in a dream. Ashneon reveals her belief that Obed is tapping into "the medicine of far-off places with far-flung claims" because he wants to bring Danugun back from the dead and knows that he cannot do that with Yantuck medicine since it "can't upset the balance" (110). Ashneon laments that Obed has not listened when she has tried to explain that "If he would just believe in the mountain," he might access the power to talk with Danugun as she does (110). Stymied, she asks for the help of Danugun, who replies that Ashneon will know what to do when she wakes (111). The next morning, Ashneon goes to Nuda's house, where former Big Rock Casino CEO Ryan Tianu is confronting Obed and his New Light disciples about Obed's aim to replace Tomuck as the Yantuck medicine chief. Ryan tells Obed that the Yantuck do not need him bringing the "fool's medicine" of the New Lighters to them; indicating Ashneon, he says, "We have real medicine here" (111–12). Ashneon joins in, denouncing Obed's use of Wiccan medicine on the mountain "to help you get your way" (112–13). Obed shoots back that he knows Ashneon believes in the value of medicine from all places (112). She agrees that "real Medicine People are the same everywhere." "But," she adds, "they do not all derive their medicine from the same places. Nor are they all real. This mountain is your home and you never gave it a chance" (113).

Ashneon continues to emphasize the centrality of Yantuck Mountain to her medicine when Ryan asks her to show everyone what real medicine is by crossing to the land of the dead, and she responds, "By staying here on the mountain, I found my answers. Not by running away. I may be able to show Obed how to talk to his wife, Danugun, if he'll let me. But I cannot show him how to meddle with people's thoughts and desires using dark, foreign medicine or how to bring his wife back to life for good. That sort of magic won't work on this mountain" (113–14). Foxon, Obed's most enthusiastic New Light follower, chimes in: "I appreciate your traditional, conservative views. But Obed has far surpassed the limitations of your fundamentalist, indigenous medicine" (114). In this case, Obed disregards this enlightened-New-Light vs. backwards-Ashneon rhetoric long enough to accompany Ashneon to Danugun's grave (114).

Unlike in Ashneon's previous visits to the Spirit World, during this one Danugun swaps places with Ashneon, momentarily appearing to Obed and the other spectators gathered around her grave (114–15). It quickly becomes clear, however, that Danugun does not get through to Obed, and that none of the New Lighters are willing to accept the real medicine of a specific place. Foxon, other New Lighters, and even most other Yantucks say that Ashneon's miracle was somehow fabricated; she was just "putting on her sideshow for money, to capture a prime Oracle position" (116–17). Obed joins in, calling Ashneon "grief-stricken and delusionary" and even selfish for trying to protect Winay from her destiny as a New Light Oracle (125–26). Obed thus fails to accept Ashneon's claims about the power of Yantuck Mountain, even when Ashneon and Danugun show him that power firsthand.

Shortly after the Danugun incident, as Obed continues his New Light antics (including doing pseudo-yoga moves for a "bamboozled media" and "enraptured" cy audiences), Winay surprises Ashneon by confirming Obed as the next medicine man of the Yantuck (125, 130). Obed's dark magic has affected even this strong-willed medicine woman. Given his new position of leadership within the tribe, Ashneon tells Obed—and the audience of New Light disciples and cy reporters who follow him everywhere—that she assumes he will be attending an upcoming tribal meeting. "We have some serious issues before our community," she says—issues that should be discussed "privately" (131). Obed replies by saying that he will not attend this or any other tribal meeting because they are "closed to outsiders" (131). "When the tribe opens up its meetings to the world, then I will return to them," he says (131). "I believe I represent many people now and that I belong to many people," he proclaims, arguing that the Yantuck tribe needs to catch up with his enlightened stance (131). He asserts, "We Yantuck need to move beyond our petty nationalist divisions and realize we are all members of the human race, part of the universal union of light!" (131). Obed's attitude here epitomizes nationalist critics' concerns about where freewheeling hybridity can lead. Whereas Ashneon casts local responsibility as the primary duty of a tribal leader, Obed refuses to even recognize the particular identity of his tribal nation, let alone invest in its specific needs.

Ashneon and Obed's war of words comes to a head when Obed finally confesses to Ashneon that he is experiencing constant noise in his head, pain, and nightmares as a consequence of using dark magic to propel his Oracle fame (134–35). He defends himself, saying, "Yes, I have tried new things. I have questioned. I have *lived*, Ashneon, not just followed the Yantuck lesson plan for life, like you. I wanted more than just this tiny mountain and its small-minded Indians" (136). Ashneon responds, "Well you got more and look at you, you're a mess and you still wound up back here anyway. That says it all. I was always satisfied with this mountain. If you saw it fully, you wouldn't find it so limiting" (136). Obed replies, "This mountain may limit you more than you know" (136). He can run to the tops of mountains and even fly, he explains, something he is sure Ashneon cannot do (136–37). "I'll fly down this mountain and far away from here," he says, before he runs down the mountain path, tumbles over granite steps, and splats onto the highway (137). He clearly did not believe Ashneon's claim that dark magic would not work on Yantuck Mountain (114). Instead, it takes a literal and dramatic encounter with the mountain itself to rattle him out of his New Light haze.

Winay had foreshadowed Obed's fall early in the novel, telling Ashneon, "When Indians walk away from the Creator and start running toward the dollar, it's much worse than for other folks. But, when our very own medicine family starts running there . . ." (21). The ellipses here suggests that words cannot express how terrible Winay thinks it is for members of her medicine family to abandon the Creator in an effort to make money. Drawing on her experience as a medicine woman, Zobel has glossed this passage by explaining that it is worse for Indians than others to abandon their specific tribal traditions because they ought to "know better." Zobel claims to have personally met people like Obed who experienced dire consequences, including death, as a result of doing tribal medicine for personal profit, or trying a New Age practice through which they indiscriminately opened themselves up to all kinds of spirits, bad as well as good (Guest Lecture).[12] Obed does not die as a result of his fall—the impact injures his pride more than his body—but he might have died from his headaches or been completely incapacitated by them without Ashneon's intervention. After Obed's fall, with the help of the Patuxet medicine man Tashteh, Ashneon performs a ceremony to undo the dark magic that gave rise to both Obed's headaches and his fame. She calls on the spirits of Yantuck Mountain to "return the spell to the land it came from, harming no one of that place" and to let any remaining "negative energy" from the spell "enter me, and only me, never again harming anyone or anything of this or any place" (140). The ceremony works. The noises in Obed's head vanish, along with his New Light following, and Ashneon charges her cousin to be grateful without divulging the details of the ceremony she selflessly carried out on his behalf.

After his big fall, Obed loses his positions as Yantuck medicine chief as well as New Light Oracle and sinks into a pathetic depression. Ashneon visits him at Nuda's house two weeks after the fall during this slump. At their visit, Obed questions Ashneon's commitment to her duties over her personal happiness; he thinks she should take care of herself by marrying Tashteh, who Obed claims is obviously in love with her (144). Yet, Obed has clearly gained a greater respect for Ashneon and Yantuck Mountain. Shortly after their visit at Nuda's, they tap into the power of the mountain to bring Danugun alive once more, and she prods Obed to start prioritizing their children (145–46). "She insisted that I move on for Aquinnee and Skeezuck's sake," Obed recalls after the encounter. "Something about their heavy task" (146). After this encounter, Ashneon insists that she and Obed serve together as Yantuck medicine people (146). Thanks to his encounter with Danugun and the hard lessons he learned through his fall, we imagine that, going forward, Obed will stay accountable to Yantuck Mountain and his community there, a possibility further suggested at the end of the novel as Obed joins Winay and Nuda in training his children to be the next Yantuck medicine people—a training based in the forest and museum of the Mountain.

Throughout *Oracles*, Zobel reveals a major difference between the generic spirituality of the New Light approach, represented by Obed, and the traditional Yantuck-specific approach, represented by Ashneon: whereas advocates of the former please the masses by telling them what they want to hear, advocates of the latter speak locally grounded truths that are sometimes difficult to hear.[13] Obed eventually comes to accept the hard truths that he cannot bring Danugun back from the dead, that he needs to swallow his ego and accept Ashneon's help, and, above all, that he needs to be responsible to his Yantuck community. Over the course of the novel, Ashneon also encounters two significant unpleasant truths about herself: first, that her own coauthored anthropology article about "The Weekum Medicine Legacy" may be partially to blame for drawing the New Light attention to Yantuck Mountain; and second, that her marriage to Tashteh would violate the "age-old fact" that "Medicine People are not supposed to marry one another," because "Too much energy concentrated in one place is always dangerous—dangerous to the couple, dangerous to those around them, dangerous to the universe" (48, 152). Ashneon is receptive to the first truth. It leads her to distance herself from the academy and her coauthor, a romantic interest as well as collaborator. However, she ignores the second truth. She marries Tashteh and dies, the novel suggests, as a direct result of failing to heed the traditional warning.

Ashneon presumably would know this hard truth about medicine people marrying, having trained her entire life with Winay and Tomuck. Why she fails to heed its fatal warnings remains a mystery. Does she place her happiness over her duties in this instance? Did the ceremony she perform to cure Obed fill her with negative energy that clouds her vision? Also, why doesn't Winay remind her granddaughter about the taboo, since speaking such truths appears to be one of the duties of real medicine people? While Zobel leaves these questions unanswered, she clearly suggests that Ashneon acts uncharacteristically irresponsible in marrying Tashteh. Very early in the novel, Winay tells Ashneon that "maintain[ing] the balance" in the universe is the "only job" of medicine people (11). In marrying Tashteh, Ashneon upsets that balance, endangering not only herself but also, according to the old law, the entire Yantuck community and everyone in the universe. *Oracles* thus shows that prioritizing one's specific place and accountability to the community and teachings of that place is a daunting task, even for our fiery heroine.

While *Oracles* strongly suggests that Ashneon's death results from her violating the ancient law against medicine people marrying, it also subtly offers an additional reason. Nuda scolds Winay as she laments the tragedy of Ashneon's death: "You always told me that all things happen for a reason. Now here I am, reminding you of it" (163). The focus in the remainder of the novel on the young, emerging Yantuck leaders—Anaquah, Skeezucks, and Aquinnee—implies that the reason for Ashneon's death is to open the way for this next generation of leaders, whose more dynamic approach to cultural continuance provides a more viable path forward for the entire Yantuck nation, not just the staunch traditionalist holdouts on Yantuck Mountain.

Zobel herself identifies this as a core message of the novel. She sees Obed and Tomuck as representing two extremes, and wanted the novel to show the "middle path" of the younger, emerging Yantuck leaders as a better option (Guest Lecture). For most of the novel, Obed represents the extreme of those who are so willing to adapt their cultural traditions in order to appease others and profit themselves that they neglect their responsibilities to their specific communities and jeopardize the sovereignty—and even survival—of their people. At the other end of the spectrum, Tomuck represents those who resist any kind of change, even when change could enrich the community or is necessary to protect the people (Guest Lecture). Ashneon comes to align herself with Tomuck's separatist position of rejecting all kinds of technology, commerce, and "book learning" as products of colonial societies that can only bring harm to the Yantuck tribe. Ashneon dies, Zobel contends, because the tribe needs different kinds of leaders—leaders like Anaquah, Skeezucks, and Aquinnee, who promise to find a balance between the two extremes of their predecessors (Guest Lecture). These young people take a dynamic approach to Yantuck culture and are cross-culturally engaged even as they remain rooted in, and primarily accountable to, their Yantuck home. Zobel sees *Oracles* as clearly championing this "middle path." When asked how we should read Anaquah's position, articulated in direct contrast to Tomuck's, that the Yantucks "have to change our ways to survive" by learning to use the cy, the technology of the dominant society, Zobel points out that, unlike Tomuck and Ashneon, Anaquah survives (*Oracles* 58–59, 160; Guest Lecture). "She is the future," Zobel concludes, and that "says it all" (Guest Lecture).

I am not as convinced as Zobel is that *Oracles* so clearly marks Anaquah's position as superior to Tomuck's and Ashneon's. Yes, Tomuck and Ashneon die, but the narrative leads us to sympathize with Ashneon's position for most of the novel, and in opposing Tomuck and stressing adaptability, Anaquah's views seem to align with Obed, who we are led to critique. Nevertheless, while a comparably brief and underdeveloped portion of the novel that in some regards contradicts other aspects of the book, *Oracles*'s concluding attention to Anaquah, Skeezucks, and Aquinnee's dynamic approach to their culture does offer some seeds for imagining an Indigenous reworking of hybridity. For thirteen generations, the Mohegan have looked to their leader Uncas as modeling an approach to cultural adaptation and cross-cultural interaction that strengthens the Mohegan nation, this even as they have simultaneously struggled to come to terms with Uncas's controversial alliance with the English, and his complicity in the massacre of his Pequot relatives. The emerging Yantuck leaders of *Oracles* carry forward the positive values that many Mohegans associate with Uncas as they interact with their elders, negotiate their own cultural positions, and use the technology of the dominant society in an effort to enable a strong future for the people of Yantuck Mountain and beyond.

In 1635, the Pequot *sagamore* (subchief) Uncas and his followers parted ways with the Pequot nation over disagreements about how to engage the English. Uncas became sachem of the new, separate band who called themselves the Mohegan, meaning Wolf People, the old Lenni Lenape name for Uncas's clan (Zobel, *Medicine Trails* xi). As Zobel records in *Medicine Trails*, Uncas "pledged his friendship, along with that of his descendants, to the English" (xi). In the short term, this stance led the Mohegans to side with the English against their own Pequot relatives in the Pequot War (1636–1638), and led the Mohegans and the English to mutually recognize one another's sovereignty in the Treaty of 1638 (*Medicine Trails* xii). In the long term, Uncas set a precedent for mutual tolerance between the Mohegans and the state of Connecticut that continued into the nineteenth century. Zobel identifies the "maintenance of Uncas's friendship with the non-Indian" as among the many ancient Mohegan customs that carries forth into the present (*Medicine Trails* xii-xiii). The "Our History: Uncas, Sachem and Statesman" page of the Mohegan Tribe's official website calls Uncas's decision to part ways with the Pequot "controversial." One need only view the Pequot War exhibit at the Mashantucket Pequot Museum for a much darker view of the Mohegan leader. Even contemporary Mohegans have sometimes had a hard time accepting Uncas's decision to cooperate with the English, especially given that the English so often failed to uphold their treaty promises and other agreements. As Zobel explained in a talk on tribal history and culture, in the 1960s especially, tribal members sought to distance themselves from Uncas's legacy; however, many tribal members in the twenty-first century understand Uncas as a diplomat ahead of his time who cooperated with the English in order to ensure the survival and sovereignty of his people (Zobel, Mohegan History and Culture Presentation). As Zobel put it in our 2015 interview, Uncas "created a relationship with the outside community that we believe bonded us permanently into good relations with our non-Indian neighbors. Uncas bound us to cooperate without compromising. We [Mohegans] take this promise very seriously. We believe that this approach helped us survive the colonial era, but we also see it as a positive force for good in the world" (83).[14]

In her guest lecture in a Native American literature course I taught, Zobel drew a direct connection between Uncas's legacy and the dynamic "middle path" of the young, emerging Yantuck leaders in *Oracles*. Zobel wanted the adaptability represented by Uncas to come across positively in *Oracles*. "People should know their history and traditions but not be stuck in old ways," Zobel said. "That's a fine line, and a hard one to balance" (Guest Lecture). While we do not know whether Anaquah, Aquinnee, and Skeezucks will be able to balance these values in the long term—the novel ends when they are all still very young—in the short term they advance Uncas's legacy of adaptability as they imagine new ways of carrying traditions into their world.

The twelve-year-old Anaquah demonstrates her understanding of the "fine line" between continuity and change when she first appears in *Oracles*. In an exchange with Tomuck during her class trip to the Yantuck museum, after telling Tomuck that the Yantuck need to change and learn to use the cy in order to survive, she goes on to compare the cy to the smallpox epidemic that ravished her people "back in the 1600s." Like the smallpox virus, she explains, "the components of the cy are small but powerful" (58). Therefore, "we had better make friends with them," she says, "make them work for good, or they will destroy the natural world and us along with it" (58–59). She asserts, "We have to change, Chief. We have to get past our cyphobia. We Yantuck Indians should be accustomed to change and realize that technology and nature are not natural enemies" (59). Anaquah shows respect for Tomuck here, calling the medicine chief "Chief" and responding to his questions clearly and honestly. She also demonstrates an understanding of her people's history, both distant and recent. After she explains how and why she thinks the Yantuck have to change, Tomuck responds, "But I am sure you understand that not all change for our people has been good—like the way our people changed so much they forgot about the natural world altogether for a while. What have you learned about that part of your tribal history?" Anaquah says that her father, the former casino CEO Ryan Tianu, who later confronts Obed, has told her how the Yantucks destroyed much of the natural environment on their reservation as they developed the casino and other economic enterprises. Further honoring Tomuck, she concludes, "He says you saved the people and the mountain, Chief" (59).

Anaquah thereby differentiates her call for adaptability from the likes of "Obed's kind" and the greedy, casino-obsessed Yantucks before him—perhaps including her own father before he altered course—who pursued change for selfish reasons and brought harm to the Yantucks and their environment. She seems to strike the "balance" Zobel describes in association with Uncas, being grounded in her community but able to adapt in order to confront new challenges. Anaquah may not change Tomuck's position, but *Oracles* suggests that the spirits of Yantuck Mountain and beyond favor her perspective. During the museum visit, she is watched closely by a wooden Hobbo statue who later communicates with Ashneon, and she is cheered on by a little red-haired boy who appears to be a magical little person from Ireland; he shows up again at the end of the novel to get the bear club from Winay in order to help Aquinnee and Skeezucks in their new roles as medicine people (58, 60–62, 170).

Near the end of *Oracles*, but before Obed's twin children Aquinnee and Skeezucks are officially selected as the next Yantuck medicine people, the twins join Anaquah in acting on her idea to use the cy for good. Aquinnee and Skeezucks still have their doubts about Anaquah's attempts at "cybersalvation," but they believe in her vision enough to contribute to a cy message intended to entice people to both protect and increase what is left of the natural world (159–61). Aquinnee composes a "Celtic-Andean melody" that plays as the screen flashes an image of planet Earth sprouting green patches, joyous birds, and words like "Fly with Us" and "Spread the Message" meant to "entice would be members" of a new organization called "Winged Messengers" devoted to the rejuvenation of the natural environment (160). Unlike in her treatment of the New Light Corporation, and aligning with her presentation of the ancient Yantuck, Greek, Irish, and Mali stories, Zobel does not trouble the cultural blending and appropriation at play in the creation of this commercial, which, according to the description in the novel, features Celtic-Andean music and birds that could be from anywhere, with no identifiable Yantuck elements. Instead, Zobel's characters emphasize the universal nature of their message while figuring that very universality as based in Tomuck's assertion that all things are connected," and all individuals are a "part of nature," "like it or not" (55).

Yet, unlike the actual environmentalist television commercials of the 1970s that used images of sad Indians to promote the cause, this cy message is being crafted by Indigenous people, and their desire to restore the natural world is drawn from their Yantuck community while also relevant for the entire universe. Do Anaquah, Aquinnee, and Skeezucks use their agency to craft a vaguely Indigenous message to protect the privacy of their specifically Yantuck cultural knowledge? Such a move would contrast with the New Light Corporation's "international freedom of religious information" law requiring communities to share knowledge without any regard for how that knowledge will be used, and with freewheeling hybridity's disregard for claims of privileged access to cultural knowledge (*Oracles* 39). Or does the cy message these characters create simply reflect their own complicity in the amorphous appropriation of Indigenous cultures that much of the rest of the novel critiques? Or are they self-consciously deploying a problematically pan-Indigenous rhetoric so as to appeal to an audience, more interested in that audience's actions than their motivations? That the novel leaves these questions unanswered and does not spend more time considering them is unfortunate, especially in an era when actual Indigenous young people face challenges of balancing the specific and the universal, and of making rhetorical appeals that are ethical as well as effective as they increasingly turn to video, music, and social media platforms to advance environmentalist aims.

Instead of grappling with the way they bring together different cultures, Anaquah, Aquinnee, and Skeezucks characterize their work as a bringing together of "old and new." While we do not see Ashneon demonstrating any enthusiasm about the cy throughout *Oracles*, Anaquah argues that Ashneon "knew the old ways to protect the planet, but she also knew the cy had the potential to save it" (161). Their own experiences with Ashneon lead the twins to believe Anaquah when she concludes that Ashneon "just never figured out how to mate the old and the new" before she died (161). Anaquah describes the cy message as the "answer to the paradox Ashneon struggled with" (161). The cy message also represents an answer to the larger question *Oracles* raises about balancing continuity and change. The cy message does not so much reflect a balancing of old and new as a bringing together, a "mating" as Anaquah puts it. Anaquah, Aquinnee, and Skeezucks bring old truths into a new medium and bring their old tribally specific values to an international audience whom they attempt to recruit for their cause. While they adapt by using a technology of the dominant society, their primary aim is to share Yantuck principles with members of the dominant society, much like Tomuck, Winay, and Ashneon share Yantuck knowledge with the visitors to their museum, or Chris in *The Heart of a Chief* shares Penacook discussion methods with his classmates.

While problematic and too briefly described, the cy message nevertheless represents a form of Indigenous hybridity. As an attempt by young Native leaders to influence people across the world with Yantuck perspectives, the cy message diverges from both the dominant appropriation of Indigenous cultures and the emphasis on the dominant-to-marginalized direction of cultural exchange furthered by the discourse of multiculturalism as well as freewheeling hybridity. Furthermore, the novel's positioning of these young Yantuck (Mohegan) leaders as potential saviors of the future contrasts starkly with Cooper's depiction of historical Mohegan extinction. In her article on "Apocalypse as Protest in Indigenous Speculative Fiction," Roslyn Weaver argues that "Apocalypse offers an opportunity for indigenous writers to reinscribe the unwritten future with themselves as a significant part of the landscape" (Weaver 102). *Oracles* does precisely that.

Whereas the cy message in *Oracles* highlights the importance of adaptation to new technologies, the very end of the novel emphasizes cultural continuance. As Nuda, Winay, and Obed begin initiating Aquinnee and Skeezucks in the ways of Yantuck medicine, our narrator observes that "Until humanity's last gulp of breathable air, the people of Yantuck Mountain would continue much as they always had. The thirteen moons would cycle each year. The rocks would continue to mark the sites of ancient miracles, and the blazing sunshine would allow the glorious trees to grow ever thicker; thus, the Yantuck had done their job" (165). Carrying on "much as they always had" is cast here as the Yantucks' principal role. As they exercise their age-old relationships with one another and with their environment, one of their primary responsibilities is not to change too much.

The narrator suggests that Skeezucks and Aquinnee will excel as the new Yantuck medicine people because they "carry magic from both sides of the Atlantic," having Irish as well as Yantuck ancestry (169). But it also seems that these young recruits will, like Ashneon, privilege their Yantuck ties. Winay gets the last word in *Oracles*, describing the stars she gazes at with her grandniece Aquinnee as "Your real family . . . , your true parents, grandparents, cousins, and relatives back to the beginning" (170–71). She then speaks of the turtle rattle, given to Aquinnee to symbolize her status as a medicine woman recruit, and of Grandfather Turtle, concluding with "You do remember how the world began, don't you?" (171). Being a good Yantuck leader, Winay suggests, means traveling through history, back to the beginning. Earlier, while discussing ancient stones and artifacts at the museum, Winay says, "A journey through time is at once the most challenging and worthiest of adventures" (63). The vision statement adopted by the Mohegan Council of Elders in 1997 describes the Mohegan Trail of Life as "circular" and suggests that achieving "wholeness" requires Mohegan people to home in on their history, actively bringing the past into the present and future. This crossing of temporal borders touched on in *Oracles* is valued by the Anishinaabe as well, and is central to the Indigenous hybridity imagined by Drew Hayden Taylor's *The Night Wanderer*.

Discovering That History Is "Right Here" at Otter Lake

Drew Hayden Taylor's 2007 *The Night Wanderer: A Native Gothic Novel* centers on two protagonists: a 350-year-old Anishinaabe vampire who goes by Pierre L'Errant, and Tiffany Hunter, an angsty sixteen-year-old Anishinaabe girl living on the small fictional Otter Lake First Nations reserve in central Ontario. While Taylor avoids using the word "vampire" until the last pages of the novel, from the start, readers have no shortage of obvious hints. The novel opens with Pierre's meticulously planned flight from London to Toronto. As he observes the northern lights shining through the airplane windows, the narrator tells us that he had seen those lights dance over "more than a dozen countries during his infinite wanderings," and that "Many of those countries no longer existed, or had changed in name and form, as had he" (1). Such ominous statements quickly start sharing space with more playful prose. Pierre's thoughts about choosing the perfect flight, one that would "take off at night, and land at night," are instructive: "This kind of flight was called the 'red eye,'" Pierre recalls. "He loved the irony" (3).

We meet Tiffany a few pages later as she rides in a car with Tony Banks, her white boyfriend of just one month—her first boyfriend, and, she thinks, a good catch; Tony was "tall, good-looking, and had his own car" (9). Since her mother, Claudia, left with a white man just over a year earlier, Tiffany has been fighting constantly with her father, Keith, and while she loves both her dad and her Granny Ruth, who lives with Tiffany and Keith, she "longed for the stability that disappeared with her mom" (17–20). Sitting in her room after Tony drops her off, Tiffany thinks, "School sucked. Life in this house sucked. The only shining light was her new relationship with Tony" (28). Tiffany's and Pierre's paths cross when Keith rents Tiffany's room to the stranger on account of the family's financial hardships. Keith tells Tiffany, through a note, that she needs to move to the basement temporarily to make room for the European visitor. This fuels another fight, but in the end Tiffany does not have to surrender her room because Pierre, of course, prefers the dark basement himself.

Taylor's novel takes place over just four days. Interspersed throughout the narrative of daily events we hear Pierre's story of growing up on the shores of Otter Lake as a curious boy named Owl. After sneaking away to join the French fur traders, he had ended up in Montreal and then France, longing for home and dying young from the measles. He was turned into a vampire as he breathed his last by another vampire who was "intrigued" by the boy from a "new land" (180). So began Pierre's centuries of "wandering" and feeding on the blood of countless victims. He has returned to his Anishinaabe homeland to fast and purify himself before facing the sunrise in a ceremony that will end his vampire existence once and for all.

Tiffany encounters Pierre a few times throughout the novel, but focuses more on her troubles with Tony, her dad, and her friends. Her relationship with Tony becomes strained when he takes her to a bush party and spends most of his time talking with other people, including another girl, Julie, who he claims is just an "old friend." The next day, Tiffany's worst fears are confirmed; Tony is cheating on her with Julie. With Tony out of the picture, Keith furious at her for hiding a bad school progress report, and her friends mad at her for ditching them for Tony, Tiffany reaches a low point and calls her mother, with whom she has not spoken in months. Her low point dips lower when Claudia reveals she is pregnant. From Tiffany's viewpoint, her mother is starting "a new life" without her (151). The next morning, Tiffany gets into a fight with Keith, threatens to commit suicide, and runs away. Keith and Granny Ruth search for her all day, but it is Pierre who finds her in the woods, where he shares his life story and convinces her to come home. With Pierre also having nearly killed Tiffany in the woods, his willpower weakened by his four-day fast, the novel ends with him completing his sunrise ceremony (215).

In the only full-length essay published thus far on *The Night Wanderer*, Donna Ellwood Flett astutely positions the novel within "the rise of nationalism, the historic emergence of the Gothic genre, and the play of power in the world literary field" (Flett 26). However, Flett's analysis fails to account for the novel's biting critique of freewheeling hybridity. At the end of the novel, just before Pierre tells Tiffany his life story and while Tiffany is still considering suicide, they discuss the old lakeside Anishinaabe village site where they are standing. Tiffany does not know that Pierre is drawing on firsthand knowledge as he describes what the village "was probably like" (200). After Pierre points out that "generations of your ancestors" have stood in the same place, Tiffany confesses, "Sometimes I don't know what being Anishinaabe means." "According to Tony and his father, it has something to do with taxes," she says. "For my father, its [*sic*] hunting and fishing and stuff like that. My grandmother believes its [*sic*] all about speaking Anishi-naabe. Then there are land claims and all sorts of political stuff that I don't really understand." Pierre "nodded solemnly" and replied, "Yes. It's all those things. And none of them" (201). Citing this passage, Flett argues that "What those nebulous definitions do is open the door to flexibility, change, and transformation—a move into a contemporary world rather than a condemnation to a rigid past" (Flett 36). In Flett's view, Taylor's novel ultimately offers "the assertion that perhaps modern young Aboriginal people should 'bend and blend' a bit in order to make a better and newer life for themselves and their people" (38).

Departing from Flett's analysis, I read *The Night Wanderer* as condemning, rather than promoting, a "bend and blend" view of Anishinaabe culture. Just prior to the passage Flett cites, Pierre idealizes the customs of the ancient village, and while he says that "what it means to be Anishinaabe" is "all" and "none" of the things Tiffany lists, his story shows that the most important source of meaning for the Anishinaabe is their connection to the past: their lands and the ancestors who, for millennia, have carried on their traditions there. Pierre's personal story, moreover, epitomizes the dark side of cross-cultural interaction and adaptation. While he has learned many lessons in his wanderings, lessons he passes on to Tiffany, he wishes he had never left Otter Lake and never become a vampire. He sees that Tiffany is curious like him and that she wants to leave the community, just as he did when he was a boy. He seeks to redirect the girl's curiosity literally to the ground beneath her feet so that she will not become a wanderer like him.

Taylor's novel is at once even more pessimistic than *Oracles* about the impacts of cross-cultural contact on Indigenous people and more explicit in depicting a specific Indigenous approach to cultural change. *The Night Wanderer* offers a critique of freewheeling hybridity by sharply exposing the colonial power dynamics that hybridity theorists often eschew; the only examples of Native/non-Native interaction in the novel involve the exploitation of Indigenous people. Like *Oracles*, *The Night Wanderer* also departs from freewheeling hybridity by positively presenting the privileging of a particular cultural identity. Pierre may have "all kinds of blood in his veins," but he clearly privileges his Anishinaabe identity. *The Night Wanderer*, moreover, uniquely imagines an Indigenous hybridity that values crossing borders of time and adapting stories within one's own society more than crossing borders of geography or culture.

As he lies dying in France before the vampire arrives to turn him, Owl opens a window and looks westward: "That was where his land and his people were. He would die looking in the direction of home. A place he never should have left" (161). Before turning into a vampire—and long before assuming the name Pierre L'Errant—Owl's life had taken a miserable turn, and not just because of his illness. Exploiting his youthful curiosity—and superb canoeing skills—the French fur traders had taken Owl to Montreal and then on to France (129–32). Lured by the traders' stories of adventure, the boy had snuck off from his village to join them, planning to return home with "great gifts" as well as apologies for deceiving his family (130). After months in France, all Owl wanted was "to go home" (146). Everything about France was different, and "Owl had long ago become tired of different" (146). The boy missed home and "was beginning to hate white people" for not letting him return and for exploiting his Anishinaabe identity. He sat alone all of the time, other than when the king beckoned him to parade before the "strange people" who "wanted him to talk Anishinaabe, sing some of their sacred songs, and prance around like some animal" (146). While he laments his own complicity—he did initially leave his home voluntarily—Owl resents the persistent exploitative power the French exercise over him.

As the king, the center of French colonial power, directly asserts control over Owl's actions and his expression of Anishinaabe culture, Owl's experience in France symbolizes the larger colonial exploitation his people would experience as the French and English came to settle and assert their power in the boy's homeland. His personal experience becomes an even more dramatic metaphor for colonialism when the European vampire turns him. The vampire exercises his power by laying claim to the boy, making Owl "the first of your kind to join my kind," the first Indigenous person from the Americas to become a vampire (180). In the larger context of Taylor's novel, the vampire metaphor here of colonial exploitation, appropriation, and assimilation could hardly be clearer. Owl/Pierre's experience of vampirism is exceptional: a colonial vampire literally sucks the boy's blood and appropriates the boy's body/identity/future for "his kind." Nevertheless, as *The Night Wanderer* weaves together allusions to Pierre's vampire nature, episodes from Pierre's former life as the boy Owl, and Tiffany's contemporary day-to-day experiences, Taylor suggests parallel manifestations of colonial exploitation in all three threads. Before leaving his homeland, Owl had dreamed of seeing the world beyond his village, but "those dreams Owl treasured so much would eventually become nightmares" (77). While no one from Tiffany's contemporary Otter Lake community is turned into a vampire, the nightmares of colonialism still haunt them.

From early on, *The Night Wanderer* suggests parallels between historical and contemporary experiences of colonial exploitation. On the first evening we meet her, as Tiffany sits in her room thinking about Tony, her history book is next to her, opened to her assigned reading on the fur trade. The narrative toggles between Tiffany's thoughts about the fur trade and Tony, specifically his obsession with using her Indian status card to avoid paying sales tax. Tiffany ponders how what "she remembered most" about her "first days with Tony" was "his astonishment over her status card when it came time to pay for things" (29). She recalls how she had offered to let him use the card on an early date, explaining that "Status Natives don't pay sales tax." It was "some treaty thing, she assumed" (30). She had just wanted to do Tony "a favor," and brushes off her cousin/best friend Darla's warning that some people "will take advantage of you for doing that" (31). Tony had gone on to do just that, using the card constantly, including at a jewelry store where be bought two bracelets, one for Tiffany and one supposedly for his mother (32). As they left the store, Tiffany, who had been growing increasingly uncomfortable about Tony using the card, had asked him to stop, and he had apologized, promising it would not happen again (32–34). As she falls asleep on that first evening of the novel, seven days after the visit to the jewelry store, with the bracelet from Tony "still comfortably wrapped around her small wrist" and "the history book tossed on the floor," Tiffany thinks happily of Tony, "the only shining light" in her life (28, 34).

The parallel suggested in this early scene grows increasingly evident in light of later revelations regarding Owl/Pierre's experience with the fur traders and Tony's infidelity. At both the beginning and end of this scene, Taylor emphasizes the bracelet's treasured position on Tiffany's wrist compared to the history book's neglected position on the floor, foreshadowing the drama that ensues between Tiffany and Tony (29, 34). Tiffany fingers the bracelet as she thinks: "All this fur-trading stuff happened so long ago, what possible relevance could it have in her life now?" (29). "Those days were long gone," she thinks, "and though she was proud of her Native heritage, she found the annual powwow events quite culturally satisfying enough, thank you very much" (29). As the fur traders exploited the likes of Owl and paved the way for colonial exploitation on a grand scale, it will turn out that Tony's exploitation of Tiffany's Anishinaabe identity via his use of her status card extends further than Tiffany had originally realized; he gives the second bracelet to Julie, thereby betraying Tiffany through the very means he had used to take advantage of her (106). When Tiffany later confronts Tony about Julie, he evasively talks about how he and his dad think Tiffany's family should have to pay taxes like "all Canadians" (136–37). As he breaks up with her, it becomes "horribly obvious" to Tiffany that Tony is seeing Julie, and that this is the real reason for the breakup (137).

By talking about taxes, Tony hides behind one colonialist perspective, the idea that Native people have undeserved "special rights"—an attitude that dismisses the treaty-recognized sovereignty of Anishinaabe and other First Nations—in order to avoid admitting his old colonialist practice of using an Indigenous girl for his own ends, and then dumping her when she no longer proves useful. Tiffany is more interested in Tony than her history homework, but it turns out that the historical colonial exploitation of the fur trade was also playing out in her relationship with Tony. She tosses aside the history book when that book might have helped her see the exploitation evident in her pretty bracelet.

Tiffany's textbook itself, however, manifests another version of colonial exploitation. The pictures of the fur trade in the book "had been drawn by Europeans, and the Native people looked like demented savages. They weren't the people she knew or had heard about. Therefore, why should she care?" (30). Tiffany tries to see herself, her father, or her grandmother in the faces of the Indians in her textbook, but she cannot (30). These are not the Indians of the present that Tiffany knows or the Indians of the past that she has "heard about," presumably through stories shared by her grandmother and other elders in the community. Through their "demented savages" representation of Native people, the producers of Tiffany's textbook exploit Indigenous peoples, histories, and cultures in order to give a dominant version of Canadian history that justifies settlement. Taylor thus joins other Indigenous authors discussed in this volume in drawing attention to the ways colonialist agendas are advanced by schools and school curricula.

Tiffany gestures toward yet another form of exploitation exercised by residents of the predominantly white town of Baymeadow, home to the school that assigns Tiffany's textbook. At one point, she ponders the tensions between Baymeadow and Otter Lake, and the many residents of Baymeadow who think of Native people as "lazy, alcoholics, and other unpleasant descriptions" (111–12). Although Tiffany does not draw the connections herself, her musings suggest that people from Baymeadow use this derogatory attitude toward Native people to justify their economic exploitation of Otter Lake, and to dismiss Otter Lake citizens' pushing "issues like land claims, hunting and fishing rights," much as Tony and his dad disparage Native peoples' "special" privileges regarding taxes (111–12). Given her history textbook's participation in the colonialist perspectives that pervaded Canadian history and that continue to pervade the town where the book is assigned, Tiffany needs an alternative, Anishinaabe perspective on history, something that Pierre is poised to offer as no one else can.[15]

As the exploitative power dynamics of colonialism saturate both Pierre's and Tiffany's stories, *The Night Wanderer* suggests that if Native people are interested in self-preservation and self-fulfillment, as well as in the health and sovereignty of their communities, they should be wary about crossing cultural boundaries. Even before he became a vampire in Europe, Owl/Pierre had thought of his Anishinaabe homeland as "a place he never should have left" (161). He attributes his leaving as a boy to his "dangerous" curiosity, and recognizes himself in Tiffany, who was "a curious sort, regardless of what her teachers told her," especially about "the possibilities beyond the reserve boundaries" (98, 104). One of her "biggest fears" is that she will never leave, but the novel suggests she will be better served by staying (112). Of course, if Pierre had not left his community, he would never have been turned into a vampire and would not be alive hundreds of years later to encourage Tiffany to stay in her community. Nevertheless, he clearly presents his own story as an example of what Tiffany should not do. His leaving enabled further colonial exploitation, just as Tiffany's dating outside the community did.[16]

The Night Wanderer's negative portrayal of those who leave the community extends beyond Pierre and Tiffany as well. Tiffany's mother abandons her responsibilities to her family. We learn that Keith left the reserve for a while when he was young. He tells Pierre that he "wanted to see the world" so he moved to the city, but "it only lasted a year and a half. It was too fast there. Missed the quietness of the woods." He "finally realized this was my home" (89–90). Granny Ruth is interested in the rest of the world, especially Monaco and Italy, but having spent her entire long life within just a couple of hours of her home, she has a deep connection to the land, language, and culture of her people (168). Granny Ruth is the most stable, positive presence in Tiffany's life, a character trait tied to the fact that she has not left.

Pierre sees the curiosity of young people as inevitable and not entirely negative (87, 129). Remembering children playing during the maple syrup harvest when he was just an ordinary boy, Pierre thinks that it was okay for the children to get in the way, because "A child who wasn't curious, or excited, was a sad child indeed" (87). Thus, instead of trying to extinguish Tiffany's curiosity, Pierre attempts to redirect it away from the outside world and toward her own Anishinaabe location. Especially as he speaks with Tiffany at the old Anishinaabe village site, Pierre demonstrates that Tiffany does not need to leave the reserve in order to feed her longing for connection and curiosity. Instead, she can be fulfilled by looking closely at the land and deeply through time, homing in to connect with the rich history of her own people.[17]

The final encounter in *The Night Wanderer* between Pierre and Tiffany illuminates the novel's representation of an Indigenous hybridity grounded in a specific community/place and invested in temporal border-crossing as a means to deepen connection with that community/place. Pierre is less than sympathetic when he first finds Tiffany in a treehouse in the woods several hours after she has delivered her ominous suicide threat and run away. Tiffany complains about her dad making her life "crap," and Pierre responds, "You know nothing. You are a young, self-obsessed girl who does not care about those around her" (184). Tiffany pushes him out of the treehouse and bolts toward the lakeshore. When Pierre finds her on the shore, he is kinder but still insists that Tiffany has a relatively good life for someone contemplating suicide; many "would dream of" having such a life that includes shelter, food, friends, family who care about her, and a home on the land "where your people have always lived" (195–96). Pierre digs in the dirt by the shore and pulls up some ancient arrowheads. To some, an arrowhead is "a simple hunk of rock," but for him and Tiffany, he says, it is "a heritage. A history" (197). Then, like a good history teacher, he leads the girl in a line of questions until Tiffany realizes that they are standing on the old Anishinaabe village site that she had heard was "somewhere around here, hundreds of years ago" (197–98, 116). In an earlier encounter by the lake, Pierre had given Tiffany some arrowheads from there, and Tiffany had said that he might have found that old village (116). Pierre has easily found the village, his childhood home. As Pierre and Tiffany keep digging, they find a spearhead and more arrowheads, and they talk about how they would have been used (197–98). When Tiffany asks Pierre what he thinks the village was like, and he replies, "I thought you weren't interested in history," she responds, "This isn't history. This is right here" (200).

Earlier in the novel we see how history is "here" in the present via ongoing forms of colonial exploitation, but in this scene Pierre focuses on positively portraying his boyhood home. He seems "almost happy" for the first time in the novel as he describes the village:

> Just think, Tiffany. For hundreds or even thousands of years, Anishinaabe people have lived here. They hunted, laughed, played, made love, and died in the village that once stood here. And in that same village over those same centuries were hundreds and possibly thousands of young girls just like you, asking the same questions. Standing right where you are standing. (200)

He goes on to tell Tiffany "what this place was probably like," describing family huts, good fishing and hunting, and peaceful days. His own nostalgia having built up over hundreds of years, Pierre avoids any mention of the hardships or the Indigenous cross-cultural encounters, both peaceful and violent, that Anishinaabe people experienced before European colonization. Instead, he describes a "very happy existence," with "children playing in the sunlight. Being told stories by their parents and enjoying life" (200). When Tiffany says it is "hard to picture those days," Pierre tells her that "generations of her ancestors" have stood just where she is standing; they breathed the same air, climbed the same trees, and sat on the same rocks as she did (200–201).

This is when Tiffany says that she sometimes does not "know what being Anishinaabe means" and lists what it means for Tony's family, her father, and Granny Ruth, the passage Flett cites to support her "bend and blend" reading. After Pierre says it is "all" and "none" of those things, Tiffany focuses on picturing the village, and "found herself half believing she had been living here, a long time ago" (201). Tiffany then tells Pierre that his "all" and "none" answer "doesn't help much." "But," she continues, "this [imagining the old village] is amazing. It really is. You know, I've heard these stories all my life but—." Pierre interjects, "You thought they were just stories. You must remember, all stories start somewhere." Feeling the spearhead in her pocket, Tiffany remarks, "I bet this place is full of stories" (201).

Pierre then launches into his own story. He tells Tiffany that it is true, told to him by his great-grandfather, to which Tiffany replies, "Granny Ruth says all her stories are true too" (203). Pierre "h[eld] back nothing, glad to rid himself of the memories," and Tiffany feels at once scared by the many tales of murder and sympathetic for the murderer. She could "feel the longing of this wanderer, the pain of not being able to return home" (205). When Pierre finally finishes the story, Tiffany exclaims, "A Native vampire! That is so cool!"—the first time the word "vampire" appears in the novel (206). Pierre continues, telling how the story ends with the wanderer "getting bored" and coming home "as a Native man" to fast and purify himself before dying at a special spot while watching the sunrise (207–8). Pierre tells Tiffany, "I believe you and this 'bored vampire,' as you call him, have much in common. You both have responded to incidents in your life rather drastically. Bad and misdirected decisions were made" (208). Then, in a moment of weakness, he nearly kills Tiffany, slamming her against a tree and offering to help her die (209). He quickly stops himself, though, dropping Tiffany and apologizing as he runs away (209–10). Pierre has stunned Tiffany, but his offer to kill her has also made her realize that, contrary to her recent suicidal thoughts, "She didn't want to die" (210). As she takes off on a panicked run toward home, she trips, hitting her head on a rock (210–11). A freshly composed Pierre reappears, assuring her that he will not hurt her, and carries her home (211–13).

This final encounter between Pierre and Tiffany suggests that connecting to an Anishinaabe community across time is central to "what being Anishinaabe means." Tiffany is riveted by her feeling of connection to the old village site, and talking with Pierre at the site transports her through time. Their conversation about what it means to be Anishinaabe occurs precisely as Tiffany is experiencing this feeling of connection to the past, suggesting that the feeling itself answers her question. Tiffany has "heard these stories" about the village before, but, as Pierre says, they were "just stories" to her before, rather than a living, active presence with which she could identify. Tiffany, it seems, could satiate a lifetime of curiosity with the stories of the village site, so she does not have to risk further exploitation by leaving her Anishinaabe community for that pursuit. Even more importantly, those stories have the power to fulfill Tiffany's longing for connection. She has heard them before, but talking with Pierre at the village site enables her to connect with the community of the past described in those stories and to connect more deeply with the contemporary community that shares those stories.

As Pierre tells his story, Tiffany identifies with the vampire's "longing" for home. Tiffany's last name is Hunter—ironic, since Pierre is the ultimate hunter. However, the name "Hunter" also resonates with Tiffany's unconscious hunt for a meaningful connection with her Anishinaabe community. Her final encounter with Pierre highlights the parallels between both characters' homing-in movement from isolation to community. After he shares his story, Pierre explicitly claims that he and Tiffany have "much in common," especially in terms of their "bad and misdirected decisions." Pierre's bad decisions are obvious. The novel suggests that deciding to take her own life would be the worst decision Tiffany could make, but it also points to other poor decisions that contributed to her suicidal thoughts: placing all of her hopes in Tony, estranging herself from her family and friends, and pining too much for the outside world rather than investing in the Anishinaabe history and community all around her. These are not just personal decisions; they reflect the ongoing manifestations of colonialism, internalized and otherwise, addressed throughout the novel. But Pierre's emphasis on personal decisions helps Tiffany restore her sense of personal agency. As she cried herself to sleep the night before running away, Tiffany had thought, "The world was a terrible place, with terrible people in it. And there was nothing she could do about it" (151). Her experience with Pierre helps her to realize that one thing she can do is intentionally look for the beautiful, not just the terrible, in the place where she lives, in the people of the past, and, by extension, in the people of the present.

Connecting with her Anishinaabe history indeed moves Tiffany toward a recommitment to her present-day Anishinaabe community. As Pierre and Tiffany find spearheads and arrowheads at the village site, Tiffany says, "Dad would love this stuff. Granny Ruth too" (199). When Pierre responds, "But I thought you didn't care about them," Tiffany tells him to "drop it" (199). Tiffany's care for, and longing to reconnect with, her family is evidenced in the final words she and Pierre exchange in the woods after she falls. "I don't want to be alone out here," she says (211). "Would you like me to take you home?" Pierre asks (211). Tiffany nods, and Pierre says, "Then I will take you home" (212). Tiffany has been alone in the woods all day and has felt alone for some time: abandoned by her mom; isolated—partly because of her own decisions—from her dad, her friends, and Granny Ruth; and then rejected by Tony, the only person to whom she had clung. Pierre's repetition of the phrase "take you home" emphasizes the importance of Tiffany's impending reconnection with her contemporary community, the next stage of her homing in.

While Pierre intends all along to right the wrongs of his personal past by returning home to die, his encounters with Tiffany give him an additional opportunity to change his legacy. At one point, as Pierre walks, weak with hunger, through the woods of Otter Lake, he looks at an old tree and wonders if he had known the tree as a boy. He concludes, "It was unimportant. The past was the past. Pierre had long ago given up the notion of changing the past, for it was a harsh mistress, and it would change for no one. Only the present and the future were his to mold" (145). On the surface, this line of thinking contradicts Pierre's emphasis on the richness of the past as he talks with Tiffany about the old Anishinaabe village. In her reading of *The Night Wanderer*, Flett insightfully reads Pierre as transformed from villain to hero by acting as an elder who initiates Tiffany into the history and values of her people more fully than any regular tribal elder could (Flett 29–30). Flett focuses more, however, on how Aboriginal peoples in Canada need to "transcend" the history of colonialism, the "horrors of the past—dispersal and relocation; repression and imprisonment; disease and epidemics; death; loss of culture, community, language, and family" represented by Pierre (Flett 28, 31). In dying, she says, Pierre "symbolically washes away the sins of the past," just as the "hauntings" of the past must be "dissected, analyzed, and transformed or cast off" by Aboriginal peoples in Canada today so that they "can move forward and grow" (30–31). While Pierre certainly represents broad-scale colonial traumas of the past, I take issue with Flett's suggestion that the vampire's primary role is to represent this colonial past along with the need to process it and move forward. Flett overlooks both the novel's portrayal of *contemporary* manifestations of colonial exploitation, and its strong emphasis on young people like Tiffany forming *positive* connections with the past.

The Night Wanderer's seemingly contradictory messages about moving on from the past, learning from the colonial past, and connecting with the Anishinaabe past come together in Pierre's transformation of his personal regrets. Pierre's thoughts in the woods about how he cannot change the past come just after a statement regarding his determination to change via ending his existence as a vampire and just before a passage about Owl/Pierre longing for home in France (146–47). Pierre's statement about the unchanging "harsh mistress" of the past seems primarily related to his personal regrets. During his flight that opens the novel, we learn that Pierre has decided to return to his homeland because "It was time to deal with the past. And one thing he was sure of: no matter how long ago the past occurred, it colored the present and the future" (5). His poor personal decision to leave with the fur traders has led to centuries of shame-filled, lonely wanderings. In returning home, he seeks healing from the trauma he experienced after making that decision, as well as purification from the countless sins he has committed as a vampire. Yet, the past also becomes part of his purification; as he walks in the lands of his childhood, he experiences a flood of "cherished memories" that help to restore his primary identity as an Anishinaabe man and prepare him for his death. Helping Tiffany connect with that Anishinaabe past—and, by extension, her contemporary Anishinaabe community—becomes an additional way that Pierre changes his legacy, a way "to color the present and the future" for good before he dies. It is also a way for Tiffany to experience healing from her own complicity in colonial exploitation and from the pain of her somewhat self-inflicted isolation.

Tiffany's literal and symbolic "return home," her connecting with her Anishinaabe community across time, can be read as the "birth" Pierre anticipates coinciding with his death. At the old village site, when describing the end of the wanderer's story, Pierre explains, "Among his people there is an understanding of how the circle of life operates. With every death, there is a birth. He understood this and since he was born in that far-off village, that was where he should end his existence" (207). With Pierre's death at the end of the novel, readers anticipate a new birth for Tiffany. She has decided not to kill herself and has instead begun making a fresh, life-affirming connection with her community. Her connection to her community across time renews Tiffany's strength in part because it gives her "perspective," one of Pierre's favorite words (116). Connecting with countless ancestors who lived in the same place and asked "the same questions" helps her move out of loneliness, self-absorption, and self-pity. Her improved state has the promise to positively affect those around her—for instance, by contributing to the healing of rifts in her family caused by her mother's departure.

Through its depiction of Tiffany's journey, *The Night Wanderer* joins texts like the comic series *7 Generations: A Plains Cree Saga* and the short films of the We Matter Campaign, which tackle Indigenous youth suicide head-on while offering hope to young people whose inheritance of intergenerational colonial trauma leads them to have the highest suicide rates in the world. Like the 7 Generations series, featuring a young Cree protagonist whose failed suicide attempt leads him to an encounter with seven generations of his people's history, Taylor's novel portrays deep engagement with history as crucial both for understanding how intergenerational trauma influences high youth suicide rates, and for empowering young people to overcome the isolating despair that can lead to suicide. Investing in history can lead young people to deepen their personal identification with ancestors across time and make more meaningful connections with their present-day communities, which they understand better as a result of learning about the traumatic as well as the life-giving aspects of their collective history.

While literally life-saving, Pierre's portrayal of Anishinaabe history is also problematic, reflecting a romanticized, static view of Anishinaabe culture. All of the dramatic, primarily traumatic, changes that Pierre has experienced have occurred abroad. His contrasting static depiction of Anishinaabe history extends beyond his nostalgic description of the village site. As he walks around Otter Lake, he notices some differences, like the lakeshore having shifted as a result of the government installing a lock system, but he overwhelmingly emphasizes how the place, the people, and even the smells of his homeland have not changed in the last 350 years (58, 60, 76, 86–87, 94, 115). He draws on this idea of sameness in order to help Tiffany connect with her ancestors who walked the same paths and thought the same thoughts as she does.

If we focused only on Pierre's descriptions of Otter Lake, we would be hard-pressed to align *The Night Wanderer* with the emphasis on cultural dynamism in both hybridity criticism and literary nationalism. In keeping with the home-away-home pattern identified by Bevis, Pierre returns to an Anishinaabe home that has not changed despite his being away for centuries. However, the novel suggests a more dynamic approach to Anishinaabe culture, and an additional aspect of its Indigenous hybridity, in its positioning of Pierre within Anishinaabe storytelling traditions. Pierre has changed dramatically during his travels, but his most important change comes during his final stay in his Anishinaabe homeland, especially via Granny Ruth's dynamic storytelling. Through Granny Ruth's wendigo story, Taylor suggests that a dynamic approach to culture is Pierre's only hope of salvation. In his own writing of the novel, Taylor extends these principles of dynamism beyond the context of traditional stories, pointing to positive possibilities of cross-cultural interaction that are not apparent within the novel itself.

On the day Tiffany runs away, before looking for her, Pierre talks with Granny Ruth. The perceptive elder tells Pierre that he is "a very weird man" who seems to have "the weight of the world" on his shoulders (167). After discussing his travels, Pierre wonders "what you do when you've seen it all," confessing, "Sometimes, you've seen enough. Sometimes, you just want to sleep." "Metaphorically, of course," he adds (169). Pierre smiles at Granny Ruth's "feistiness" as she chastises him for saying such things (169). Then she asks him if his grandparents "ever told [him] about the wendigo" (169). He nods and describes the wendigo:

> Demons. Or monsters. Cannibals whose souls are lost. They eat and eat, anything and everything. And everybody. They never get satisfied. In fact, the more they eat, the bigger they get, and the bigger their appetite becomes. It's a never-ending circle. They become giant, ravenous monsters marauding across the countryside, laying waste to it. They come in the winter, from the north. (170)

Pierre is not a giant from the north, but the parallels between his own experience and his description of the wendigo are clear. From the start, Pierre describes himself as a "monster." He wants to return home to finally put an end to the "never-ending circle" of death that has constituted his vampire life (4). Pierre's description of the wendigo aligns with Tiffany's understanding. Early in the novel, as she drives through the woods with Tony, Tiffany thinks about the spooky stories she has heard regarding the northern woods of the reserve, including ones about "wendigos who were cannibal spirits that ate anything and everyone" (16). She "wondered what Otter Lake would do if a real-life monster came out of those woods and into the village" (16). Taylor thereby sets readers up to see Pierre as a wendigo, with Pierre first entering the reserve "from the north" through those same woods (44–45).

In response to Pierre's description of the wendigo, Granny Ruth offers her own version. "That's one story," she says. "Another says they were once humans who, during winter when food was scarce, had resorted to cannibalism. By eating the flesh of humans, they condemned themselves to aimless wandering, trying to feed a hunger that will not be satisfied" (170). Pierre is listening "too intently" to notice when she slips into Anishinaabemowin, adding, "Some say the only way to kill one is to burn them in a fire, to melt their frozen heart. Only then will they be destroyed and free" (170). When Pierre asks why Granny Ruth is "telling me this now," she all but admits to knowing the vampire's true nature. She observes that Pierre is "doing quite a bit of wandering" and that it seems "there's something in [him] that's not satisfied" (170). In reply, "'L'Errant is French for the Wanderer,' was all he said."

Whereas Pierre's wendigo story is really just a description of the monster's physical appearance and behavior, Granny Ruth's is a real story, with a beginning, a middle, and an end. Pierre later tells Tiffany at the old village site, "You must remember, all stories start somewhere" (201). Granny Ruth's story starts with sympathetic human beings who, like Pierre, become monsters as a result of forces beyond their control combined with their own bad decisions. The wendigos of Granny Ruth's story look and act like the ones Pierre describes—eating and eating, but never becoming satisfied. The difference is that her version renders the wendigos in a sympathetic light and includes a way for them to become free of their miserable existence.

In telling her wendigo story, Granny Ruth participates in an Anishinaabe tradition of dynamism in the realm of storytelling and offers Pierre an Anishinaabe framework for understanding his experience. In an article on Anishinaabe story-telling as a practice of cultural sovereignty, Lawrence Gross explains, "Anishinaabe myth"—an umbrella term he uses for traditional stories—includes a "number of versions of different stories" along with a number of acceptable interpretations. "A plurality of readings can be acceptable," Gross attests, "as long as they are in concert with the accepted value system." He continues, "Some of the values of the Anishinaabe can be found in the concept of *bimaadiziwin*, the Good Life. Although the Anishinaabe themselves are loath to establish a limited, set definition of this term, some of the parameters of the Good Life include humility, generosity, and kindness" (Gross 128–29). In *Dancing on Our Turtle's Back,* Leanne Simpson defines *bimaadiziwin* as "living life in a way that promotes rebirth, renewal, reciprocity and respect" and stresses that "living in a good way is an ongoing process" (27). While she does not explicitly discuss *bimaadiziwin* in relation to storytelling, in another section of the book, she joins Gross in emphasizing the relational and "dynamic" nature of Anishinaabe oral storytelling, with stories changing based on the storyteller's context and her/his understanding of the audience's needs (Simpson 34).

Granny Ruth's version of the wendigo story enacts the values of generosity and kindness, opening a path of rebirth for Pierre and unknowingly prodding him to carry the *bimaadiziwin* she extends to him forward to Tiffany. Whether or not she fully understands Pierre's true nature, she generously offers the story to him with sympathy, and as a way for him to look with greater kindness upon himself. As a respected Anishinaabe elder, she tells the story as a way of embracing Pierre as a member of the Anishinaabe community. He may have become a monster with a hunger that is never satisfied, but there is still a place for him in the Anishinaabe world, and still an avenue for his redemption. While Pierre would have known that watching the sunrise would kill him, as it would any vampire, Granny Ruth's description of fire that simultaneously destroys and frees the wendigo gives Pierre an Anishinaabe way—and a more hopeful way—of approaching his coming death. Granny Ruth suggests that, in dying, Pierre will not only end a terrible cycle of death but that he will also be "free"—free to join his ancestors not as a monster but as a fellow soft-hearted human being. As Pierre later begins to tell Tiffany his story, she tells him that Granny Ruth says all of her stories are true. By embracing the truth of Granny Ruth's story, Pierre, like Tiffany, is able to move from isolation to community. He becomes connected to his Anishinaabe community as he identifies with other Anishinaabe-turned-wendigos. He tells Tiffany of the Anishinaabe ancestors he knew as a child and whom he will join upon his death. By drawing Tiffany into this community with him, he further adapts the wendigo story told by Granny Ruth, providing himself with an even greater opportunity for redemption than Granny Ruth had imagined.

The cultural adaptation positively represented at the conclusion of *Oracles* involves Native young people adapting technologies of the dominant society to advance Yantuck values at home and abroad. In contrast, the positive representation of cultural dynamism within *The Night Wanderer* is wholly internal; Granny Ruth's retelling of the wendigo story adapts Anishinaabe traditions in a way that helps an Anishinaabe man, Pierre, and, it turns out, an Anishinaabe girl, Tiffany. Beyond some fleeting references to friends Pierre has met during his travels, the content of *The Night Wanderer* paints a bleak picture of cross-cultural interaction.

While positive cultural adaptation in *The Night Wanderer* is restricted to the Anishinaabe community, through his own exercise of the Anishinaabe tradition of dynamic storytelling in his production of the novel, Taylor demonstrates that self-determined Anishinaabe cultural dynamism can benefit from engagement with non-Anishinaabe people as influences and allies. In his practice as a writer, and in the generic form he developed in *The Night Wanderer,* Taylor enacts and extends an aspect of the uniquely Indigenous form of hybridity represented in the novel: the Anishinaabe tradition of adapting stories in ways that further Anishinaabe values.

I risk alienating myself from the literary nationalist school by characterizing Taylor's engagement with Euro-American/Canadian literary forms and with non-Anishinaabe collaborators as acts of hybridity. In *American Indian Literary Nationalism*, Weaver, Womack, and Warrior adamantly oppose critics who argue that Native writers engage in hybridity when they use the English language or forms, like the novel, that have been used by writers of European descent. Characterizing such acts as "hybrid," they contend, fails to account for Native people's influence on the English language and the literary world; it also denies Native artists' agency in the process of adapting their own cultural expressions by engaging with other cultures, just as all artists—and all people—have always done.

Taylor's process as a writer and the form of his novel, however, much like the content of his and Zobel's novels, foster an understanding of Indigenous hybridity that contrasts with freewheeling hybridity, aligning more with what the authors of *American Indian Literary Nationalism* call "transformation" or "adaptation" (Weaver et al. xix, 240–44). In this Indigenous reworking of hybridity, Indigenous agency is central, Indigenous perspectives are privileged, and cross-cultural exchange goes in both directions. In the way that Granny Ruth adapts the Anishinaabe wendigo story and thereby extends Anishinaabe values to Pierre—and ultimately to Tiffany and their entire community—Taylor adapted the wendigo story along with European gothic traditions and the international vampire genre (both of which may draw some influence from Indigenous cultures) in order to produce a novel that forwards Anishinaabe values.

In interviews, Taylor has discussed drawing inspiration from Native as well as non-Native writers.[18] In his interview about *The Night Wanderer* with Cynthia

Leitich Smith, he says, "Basically, because I am bi-cultural (half Native, half white), I like combining or exploring examples of each culture. So for this book, I took a European legend and indigenized it." Unlike in much of his work that draws attention to his own mixed heritage as a "blue-eyed Ojibway," *The Night Wanderer* presents Tiffany, Pierre, and other Indigenous characters as only Anishinaabe, with no attention to other ancestry and no positive connection to outside cultural influences.[19] Yet, as Taylor explains, his own bicultural identity influenced his choice to combine European and Anishinaabe forms in *The Night Wanderer*. The influence of both the European gothic tradition and the vampire genre would have been clear in Taylor's original title for the book: *A Contemporary Gothic Indian Vampire Story*. As he explains in his interview with Smith, he unhappily changed the title at the request of his publisher, who may have been attempting to keep Pierre's vampire nature a secret from less-aware readers.

Taylor's use of European and international literary traditions influences Flett's characterization of *The Night Wanderer* as promoting a "bend and blend" approach to Aboriginal cultures (Flett 38). Taylor's use of the word "indigenize," however, to characterize his work reflects an Indigenous agency and a favoring of the Anishinaabe stance that cannot be accounted for by a freewheeling hybridity discourse of "blending" or "mediating." By indigenizing literary traditions with roots in cultures other than his own, Taylor instead participates in the Indigenous reworking of hybridity that I have theorized from his and Zobel's novels. In this reworking, Indigenous individuals and communities actively privilege their specific Indigenous place while being critically engaged with that place, as well as with people and cultures beyond that place.

In addition to discussing his engagement with non-Native literary traditions, in his interviews Taylor praises non-Native as well as Native mentors, and credits many non-Native readers, theater audience members, grant makers, publishers, and distributors who make his work possible.[20] He frequently discusses the problem of cultural appropriation—he has written several characters with differing takes on the issue—but he says in his interview with John Moffatt and Sandy Tait that there are many ways for non-Native allies to be involved in the world of Native literature without "crossing the line."[21]

Non-Indigenous allies can support the rhetorical sovereignty of Indigenous writers even when that sovereignty results in texts like *The Night Wanderer* that are wary about cross-cultural alliances. In exploring a range of ways that Native/non-Native contact has led and can lead to harm for Native people, *Oracles* and

The Night Wanderer enable us to extend the consideration of pitfalls to effective alliances begun in the previous chapter of this volume. The Indigenous hybridities reflected in these novels, moreover, gesture toward new Indigenous approaches to alliance. As they push the boundaries not just of young adult literature but of Indigenous YA, the texts I turn to in my coda also build on *Oracles, The Night Wanderer*, and the other texts discussed in this book in expanding our understanding of what alliance can mean for Indigenous people of the present and future.

Alexie's *Flight*, Zobel's *Wabanaki Blues*, and the Future of Indigenous YA Literature

W hile acknowledging the influence of nation-specific and intertribal literary traditions on Indigenous young adult literature—such as boarding/residential school narratives in chapter 2 and Anishinaabe hermeneutics in chapter 4—this book has also defined Indigenous YA literature in terms of its engagement with the YA genre. My analysis has highlighted ways that all of the texts in this study both conform to and resist established YA conventions as they portray contemporary Indigenous experiences. The texts solidly align with YA tropes through their focus on individual adolescent protagonists who mature as they come of age by negotiating their own identities and agency in relation to their immediate communities, along with the larger societies in which they participate. The texts also all follow the typical YA plot progression of tracing protagonists' movements from estrangement to reconciliation with community.

They certainly make contributions—to YA literature as well as to the various discourses in which they intervene—through their adherence to YA norms, but the texts stand apart, collectively forming a unique *Indigenous* YA genre, through their chafing against common YA features. We can distill the mainstream conventions and Indigenous (anti)conventions addressed in each chapter of this volume as follows: (1) YA literature characterizes reintegration as repressive, but Indigenous

YA stories show individuals who are empowered through connection to communities; (2) YA literature, like the larger dominant society, has absorbed the rhetoric of multiculturalism, but Indigenous YA critiques multiculturalism and proposes alternatives for defining, inhabiting, and learning from different cultures; (3) mainstream "Indian romances" have been recolonizing, and YA romance similarly perpetuates colonialist heteropatriarchy, but the resistive romance of these stories paints a more complicated picture of alliances, intersectionality, and internalized colonialism while foregrounding Indigenous women's representational empowerment; and (4) YA speculative fiction joins canonical historical fiction in cementing Indians in a nostalgic past, but Indigenous fiction uses speculative elements and Indigenous hybridities to address real contemporary issues facing Indigenous people, including the very kind of appropriation commonly reinforced by both speculative fiction and hybridity theory. While focusing on particular subgenres and discourses in each chapter, I have attempted to illuminate ways that the moves articulated above resonate across Indigenous YA literature. While we have seen how these works at times advance the very YA norms that they also resist, their significant challenge to these conventions nevertheless marks them as unique.

In addition to reflecting the (anti)conventions described above, Indigenous YA texts also tend to overlap in terms of the types of communities they depict and the range of issues they address. Although they represent a variety of Indigenous communities, all of the protagonists in the texts I have discussed are enrolled members of Native nations whose sovereignty is recognized by the federal government (in the limited ways that Canada and the United States recognize sovereignty), and all of them have strong ties to a Native community.[1] Content-wise, these texts tackle colonialism and its intersections with other forms of oppression, Indigenous self-determination, identity, adaptation, and cross-cultural interaction in a range of ways. But there are many issues within and beyond these topics that they do not deeply engage, including those related to recognition, enrollment, multiple citizenships, adoption, and foster care.

Having attended to the complex ways the texts examined in this study tackle issues of importance to Native people, I anticipate that the Indigenous YA literature of the future will fill in these gaps and others. In so doing, these works will also likely press against the (anti)conventions of *Indigenous* YA literature just as the texts previously discussed in this volume have expanded the boundaries for YA literature. These works have yet to be seen, but I predict their arrival, in part because I see glimpses in this direction in two very different twenty-first-century works: Sherman Alexie's 2007 adult/YA crossover novel *Flight*, and Melissa Tantaquidgeon Zobel's 2015 YA novel *Wabanaki Blues*.[2]

In form and content, Indigenous YA literature is centrally concerned with relationships between young Native individuals and the Native communities to which they belong. Yet, estrangement from Native community is a reality for many Indigenous people, especially those who have been fostered or adopted out as a result of colonialist policies that continue to influence child welfare practices in both the United States and Canada.[3] Alexie's *Flight* features just such estrangement. It is not the only work to do so. Other adult/YA crossover texts, like Beatrice Culleton Mosionier's *In Search of April Raintree* (1983) and Richard Wagamese's *Keeper'n Me* (1994), similarly represent experiences of individuals who have been removed from their Native communities and placed with non-Native families. But the protagonists in these other works ultimately restore connection with Indigenous community. In Mosionier's novel, the Métis sisters April and Cheryl remain in contact with family members even after they are removed from their parents' custody, and the second part of the novel represents their integration into an intertribal community in Winnipeg. Wagamese's *Keeper'n Me* depicts its adult protagonist's life-affirming return home to the Anishinaabe family and reserve community from which he was removed when he was just three years old. In contrast, Zits, the half Native/half white protagonist of *Flight*, never joins a present-day Native community.

Zits's Native American father, whose tribal affiliation(s) Zits does not even know, abandoned him as he was being born, and his white mother died of breast cancer when he was six years old. He has since had twenty different foster fathers, including two Indian ones who were "bigger jerks" than the eighteen white ones (9). Zits has learned all about Indians, mostly from television, because "it makes me feel more like a real Indian," he says, but the closest thing he has to a Native community are Seattle's homeless Indians with whom he sometimes gets drunk (7). At the beginning of the novel, Zits is ashamed, angry, hardened, violent, and afraid to form relationships with others. Early on he befriends an even angrier white boy, Justice, who convinces Zits to open gunfire in a bank. After spraying the bank lobby with bullets, Zits is shot in the head and wakes up in the body of a white FBI agent in Red River, Idaho, in the 1970s. Most of the novel consists of Zits's experience time-traveling into the bodies of others. After the FBI agent, he inhabits an Indian boy at the Battle of Little Bighorn, a nineteenth-century white Indian tracker in the U.S. Army, a contemporary white pilot, and, finally, his own drunken Indian father. When Zits comes to, he is still alive in the bank lobby, and he learns, along with Alexie's readers, that he actually has not shot anyone. He leaves the bank and turns his guns over to Officer Dave, a policeman who watches out for Zits. He then accepts Dave's proposal to live with Dave's brother and his wife, who want to adopt him. Zits's experience of time travel teaches him that "all life is sacred," that violence is not the answer, and that all people possess darkness as well as beauty (162–63). By the end of the novel, Zits has experienced a newfound connection to humanity, he has emotionally softened, and he is ready to give his new family a chance.

The lack of a Native community in this novel is striking. A therapist once told Zits that he had "attachment issues": "'All you know about is absence,' he said. 'And you're always looking to fill that absence'" (27). Alexie thereby prods us to contemplate the nature of Native community through its absence. In the assessment of the authors of *New World Orders in Contemporary Children's Literature*, "fiction concerning itself with the disorders and fractures of modern communities tends to propose better futures indirectly, by extrapolation from undesirable and negative forms of society" (Bradford et al. 122). Through Zits's time travel, and more importantly his reflection on the experience, Alexie clearly suggests a better future for everyone, a future in which people see one another's humanity and are therefore less violent and more honest with one another. In terms of Native community, *Flight* presents Zits's lack of one as negative—this absence contributes to his isolation and anger—while simultaneously showing many forms of Native community to be undesirable: in addition to his mean Indian foster dads and his own damaged, alcoholic father, Zits realizes through his time travels that Native people can be as violent, vengeful, and duplicitous as their white counterparts. *Flight* thus raises but does not answer questions about how a better future can come to Native individuals and communities.

That, prior to his time travel, Zits learns about Native people almost entirely through television and books underscores the limits along with the possibilities of forming connection via texts. In his National Book Award acceptance speech referenced in the introduction to this book, Sherman Alexie describes his experience of feeling connected to an empowered and empowering Native community of writers through his encounters with Native literature.[4] And he joins many of the other writers discussed in this book in frequently speaking of his desire to encourage and inspire young Indigenous readers through his work. A Native novel, James Welch's *Winter in the Blood*, is one of the three paperbacks that Zits has read dozens of times. Welch's work, which features a young Native man's struggle to renew relationships and recover from personal trauma, and other texts that Zits engages may enable him to understand himself better and to form meaningful ties with other Native people. But these forms of connection are not the same as belonging to the kind of immediate, physically present Native community for which Zits longs.

While he does not join a Native community, *Flight* ends with Zits in the process of forming a community with Dave's brother Robert and his wife Mary, his new foster parents, along with Dave, who promises to remain a supportive friend. Alexie decidedly does not mark Zits's new family as Indigenous. Because of her physical features, Zits wonders if Mary is "a little bit Indian," but he does not ask her. Mary might be Native, she might be connected with a Native community, and she might eventually draw Zits into that community, but we do not even know if she is Native, and the novel suggests that her possible Native identity is inconsequential, at least in the short term. What matters is that Mary, Robert, and Dave are present, caring for Zits, respecting him, and inviting him into a "permanent" relationship (175–77). In terms of Indigenous YA conventions, we see mutual empowerment within Zits's new family, with the novel suggesting that they need him as much as he needs them to experience healing from the pain of their pasts and to lend each other strength as they move into the future. But the lack of a clear Indigenous community here complicates Indigenous YA parameters. Can we characterize a community as a "Native community" if only one member of the community is Indigenous? Can a Native individual's pursuit of self-determination contribute to larger struggles for Indigenous empowerment even if that individual never becomes part of a larger Native community and never directly contributes to the well-being of such a community?[5] How can literature inspire estranged Native young people to (re)connect with Native community? And how can allies support these estranged individuals beyond caring for them personally as Robert, Mary, and Dave care for Zits? I eagerly look forward to the future YA texts that will address these questions that *Flight* raises but does not answer.

———————————

In addition to tackling these questions about what Native community means for estranged individuals, what is next for Indigenous young adult literature? Melissa Tantaquidgeon Zobel's 2015 YA novel *Wabanaki Blues* suggests some provocative possibilities. Published thirty years after Armstrong's *Slash* set the course for Indigenous YA literature and its treatment of sovereignty, *Wabanaki Blues* invites us to imagine what can happen when Indigenous self-determination and the centrality of Indigenous perspectives are presented as givens, the starting point for a text rather than something for which the Indigenous characters must struggle. In her book *The Common Pot*, Lisa Brooks asks,

> What happens when we put Native space at the center of America rather than merely striving for inclusion of minority viewpoints or viewing Native Americans as *part* of or on the *periphery* of America? What does the historical landscape look like when viewed through the waterways and kinship networks of the northeast, with Europe and its colonies on the periphery? What happens when the texts of Anglo-American history and literature are participants in Native spaces rather than the center of the story? What kind of map emerges? (Brooks xxxv)

By casting Native space and Native stories at "the center of America," *Wabanaki Blues* offers a literary version of Brooks's academic/cartographic project. Zobel's novel makes us view contemporary American and, really, global issues—everything from the state of blues music to climate change—through the lens of the "waterways and kinship networks of the northeast." The book depicts texts and people from Anglo-America, and Afro-Caribbean America, as "participants in Native spaces," especially the Connecticut River valley and the surrounding areas of the Wabanaki confederacy. Wabanaki perspectives are shown as central, moreover, not just for the region or for America, but for the entire universe.

Wabanaki Blues unfolds as a double mystery. The novel's protagonist and narrator, Mona Lisa LaPierre, is Mohegan through her mother's father, "Grumps"; Abenaki through her mother's late mother, Bilki; and French Canadian on her father's side. She lives in Hartford, Connecticut, and is a talented blues musician, inspired by other musicians in her working-class, largely Afro-Caribbean neighborhood. The novel begins on her last day of high school, the day students "remember Mia Delaney, the senior who never made it out of here alive," and, having seen Mia's ghost that day, Mona spends much of the rest of the novel attempting to solve that eighteen-year-old murder case (3). Mona's parents also announce, on this final school day, that she will spend the summer with Grumps at his cabin in Abenaki territory in northern New Hampshire. To her surprise, Mona finds clues about Mia's murder in New Hampshire, where she also becomes entangled in a band, a romance, and the second major mystery of the novel surrounding her family's role in an ancient Wabanaki prophecy about a hunter and a great bear.

Having never heard the term Wabanaki before her summer in New Hampshire, Mona learns from a book shortly after her arrival there that it means "people of the dawn land" and "refers to the ancient confederacy of the Mi'kmaq, Maliseet, Passamaquoddy, Abenaki and Penobscot tribes of the northeastern United States" (61). She later learns from the Mohegan Grumps, who has chosen to stay in Bilki's Abenaki home country even after her death, that the Wabanaki confederacy also includes the Mohegans, who "used to live further north" (115). Mona has been well-grounded in her Mohegan culture through a lifetime of tribal camp and other events; over the course of the novel, Grumps and Bilki, with whom Mona frequently converses even though she has passed away, guide her initiation into Abenaki life and into stories and spaces shared across the Wabanaki dawn land.

At one point, in response to Bilki's question, "Where is home?," Mona thinks about Hartford, the Mohegan Reservation, and Abenaki territory as "appropriate answers" (89). To return to the concept of "homing in" discussed in the previous chapter, Mona's experience complicates that concept as she considers all three of these spaces home, as she homes in on all of them, and especially as she comes to better understand the links among them. Zobel's novel also thus engages the experience, underrepresented in Indigenous YA, of having multiple tribal affiliations. Like Rain in Cynthia Leitich Smith's *Rain Is Not My Indian Name*, Mona is completely comfortable with her mixed identity. In addition, even though "the United States Government forced [Mona's mother] to pick a single tribe" for enrollment, Mona feels an equal sense of belonging in her Abenaki, Mohegan, and intertribal/interracial urban communities (21). That she comes to appreciate a deep interconnectedness among her multiple communities further complicates notions of home, membership, and belonging.

The multiple communities and narrative threads of *Wabanaki Blues* come together in an ancient story told across Wabanaki territory about a hunter and The Great Bear. The Great Bear is not an ordinary animal, but, as Grumps reverently describes him, "the most ancient and powerful creature in all these woods, in the whole world, in fact" (52). In the ancient story, a hunter must kill The Great Bear so that his blood and fat can drip down in order to change the color of the leaves in autumn and bring joy to the people as they face the bleak season of winter. As Mona's great-aunt explains, "Forever after, the constellations of The Great Bear and The Hunter remained among the stars to remind us that every fall a sacrifice must take place to renew autumn's glory. The Hunter must take the Bear's life, to repaint the leaves and bring color into our world" (318).

It takes the entire novel for Mona to realize that she is destined to assume the role of the hunter in this story. The novel ends with her hitting and killing The Great Bear with her truck as she attempts to flee from this destiny and "get away from New England for a while" (324). Instead of escaping New England, she saves it, her crash with The Great Bear causing the unusually dull autumn leaves to burst into vibrant color, with implications for broader environmental and social renewal. Instead of escaping her destiny, she takes her first step away from the fallen Great Bear and, in the final words of the novel, declares, "I no longer walk a finite woman's trail. I am one with the circle, one with the universe. I am in step with it all. Toe heel, toe heel. I soar into the cosmos and cross a chain of stars, in gold, crimson, and stellar blue. I ride an icy comet to The Hunter constellation and call it home. I wave to a million starry ancestors and their light shines through me. Toe heel, toe heel, toe heel . . ." (325). The novel thereby ends with a Wabanaki story, and a young Wabanaki woman as center and savior of the universe, across time and space.

The themes of connection, balance, and sacrifice in the Great Bear story prove critical in Mona's approach to Mia's murder case, which she does eventually solve, and in all of the novel's many other subplots involving Mona's romantic relationships, music career, family, and neighborhood. The Great Bear story also speaks to the importance of Indigenous knowledge for the literal survival of the planet, including in the face of the kind of climate change alluded to in the lack of fall color before Mona and The Great Bear enact their sacrifice. In our 2015 interview for *Studies in American Indian Literatures*, Zobel explains, "*Wabanaki Blues* focuses on a traditional regional story about bears that speaks to changes in our planet and our universe. It seemed to be a good time to tell this story" ("The View from Crow Hill" 93). As Mona drives back and forth between Hartford and northern New Hampshire along the Connecticut River, readers come with her to see this entire northeast region as an interconnected Indigenous space. Grumps's description of this waterway highlights its connection to other land and water across the globe. As he tells Mona about the four New Hampshire lakes that feed the river, he explains, "Their water flows south into the Connecticut River that runs through your hometown of Hartford into The Great Salt Sea" (45). This image of water connecting different parts of the region with the globe, coupled with the emphasis in the Great Bear story—including as Mona experiences it—on interdependence among humans, other beings on earth, and stars in the galaxy, highlight how everyone on the planet and in the universe is connected. The Great Bear story, *Wabanaki Blues* suggests, is relevant for everyone because everyone is related and everyone's survival depends on maintaining the health and balance of the whole.

Wabanaki Blues's emphasis on interconnectedness does not erase distinctions, as evidenced in the unique, detailed descriptions the novel provides of Mona's Hartford neighborhood, Abenaki territory, and the Mohegan reservation. The novel's approach to interdependence, moreover, contrasts with multiculturalism and cosmopolitanism because it, like the other Indigenous YA texts discussed in this volume, privileges an Indigenous perspective. As we have seen, *Wabanaki Blues*'s approach to interconnection comes from a specific Wabanaki story. Mona exercises a hybridity similar to the Indigenous hybridities represented in *Oracles* and *The Night Wanderer*, one concerned with dynamically bringing the traditions of a specific Indigenous community into the present for the benefit of that community and others. Even more so than in her earlier novel *Oracles*, in *Wabanaki Blues*, Zobel places dominant society in a position of marginalized dependency in this process. Whereas the emerging leaders at the end of *Oracles* use the technology of the dominant society to share their Yantuck values, Mona is prepared to fulfill the universe-saving Wabanaki Great Bear prophecy by engaging Afro-Caribbean, Mohegan, and Abenaki cultures rather than the dominant white-settler society of her context. In addition, while Euro-American characters—including both of Mona's love interests—as well as Afro-Caribbean American characters have major roles in the novel, they depend on a variety of Wabanaki stories and spaces to understand their experiences in addition to relying on the Great Bear story for their continued existence.

As Mona dances among her star ancestors at the conclusion of *Wabanaki Blues*, Zobel does not explain why everyone in the northeast and the universe needs the Great Bear story and Mona's participation in it. She just imagines us into a reality where that is the case. In this reality, Indigenous stories, Indigenous knowledge, and Indigenous people are central to the survival and flourishing of everyone in every place. *Wabanaki Blues*'s greatest contribution to Indigenous YA rests in this portrayal of an indigenized universe.

In what has become a rallying cry for Indigenous young people in recent years, pop singer Inez Jasper of the Skowkale First Nation, in her song "Dancin' on the Run," belts lyrics that resonate with Indigenous YA literature's emphasis on resistance, community, and empowerment:

> No matter what they say, we gonna dance together.
> No matter what they do, we gonna dance together.
> No matter what they want, we gonna dance forever.
> Me, you dancin' on the run.

And they are going to keep on writing, too. We do not even know what is next for *Wabanaki Blues*—it is the first book in a trilogy, and, at the time of my writing, the other two are yet to be published—let alone what else is on the horizon for Indigenous YA literature. But, finding inspiration from their communities, their unique engagement with the world, and the YA texts that I have discussed in this book, Indigenous young people will surely rise up and produce the next generation of Indigenous YA literature, a body of work that promises to continue stretching the possibilities of Indigenous expression, the YA genre, and the way we read, think, and move in this world.

Notes

Introduction

1. Alexie's 2013 *Brooklyn Rail* interview with Williams Cole is one of many venues in which he discusses his readership. Alexie tells Cole, "Well, the reading literary public are white, middle-class and upper-class college-educated women. That's who my readers are. I mean, I do a reading at a bookstore and 70% of the crowd will be white women." He goes on to say that he also does readings on Indian reservations in an attempt to reach that audience. Alexie often speaks of wanting to make his work more accessible, especially to American Indian young people, and wishing that other Native writers would do the same. In a 1997 interview with John Purdy, Alexie famously summarized his views, saying, "If Indian literature can't be read by the average twelve-year-old kid living on the reservation, what the hell good is it?" ("Crossroads" 7). In a 2001 interview with Joelle Fraser, Alexie expressed anxiety about not reaching as many Native readers as he would like: "Tonight I'll look up from the reading and 95% of the people in the crowd will be white. There's something wrong with my not reaching Indians." He goes on to describe his forays into filmmaking as an attempt to reach a larger American Indian audience. However, it was not until the publication of *True Diary*, ten years after his Purdy interview, that Alexie reached a wide-enough audience of young Native readers—along with other young readers, including readers of color—to

ease his anxiety over his readership. In addition to the acceptance speech itself, Alexie's 2007 Stamford, CT, reading, his 2008 television interview with Enrique Cerna, his 2011 *Wall Street Journal* essay "Why the Best Books Are Written in Blood," and his 2012 *Think Out Loud* radio interview with David Miller are among the many venues in which he has described responses to *True Diary* from young readers who recognize themselves in the text.

2. Regarding terminology, I follow common conventions in Indigenous studies, using the term "Indigenous" when referring to Indigenous peoples around the world, and using "Indigenous" and "Native" interchangeably when discussing people indigenous to the lands of North America, including both Canada and the United States. While "Native" can carry derogatory associations in Canada, many Indigenous studies scholars there continue to use the term in a respectful manner. Still, I generally use "Canadian Aboriginal" (rather than "Native") when discussing all of the Indigenous peoples of Canada, who include First Nations (referred to as "Indian" in some Canadian government contexts), Métis, and Inuit people. I use "Native American" and "American Indian" interchangeably for Indigenous peoples in the United States mainland. Native Hawaiians and Alaskan Natives have unique histories and relationships with colonial governments, as well as unique literary and activist traditions that are unfortunately beyond the scope of this project. Whenever possible, I use the names of specific Indigenous communities when discussing the writers, texts, histories, and traditions of such communities. Many tribes and bands ("tribes" and "bands" themselves being problematic terms but ones frequently used by Native communities as well as colonial governments) frequently have numerous names, with numerous spelling variations. I attempt to match my usage with that of the authors I study and/or with that of the respective Indigenous governments.

    I use the term "intertribal" rather than "pan-tribal" or "pan-Indian" to describe collective relationships and actions of multiple tribes or bands. Like Deanna Reder, I hope to invoke the spirit of the term intertribal as it is used to describe intertribal dances at powwows that bring together diverse Indigenous people who are encouraged to express their individuality even as they contribute to a unifying communal event (Reder ix).

3. In his book *The Third Space of Sovereignty*, Bruyneel theorizes that titular space, "between civil rights and decolonization," pursued during the Red Power era, by focusing on three texts: Vine Deloria Jr.'s first book, *Custer Died for Your Sins: An Indian Manifesto*, published in 1969; the Indians of All Tribes document stating

the claim to Alcatraz Island, which American Indians occupied from 1969 to
1971; and the American Indian Movement (AIM)'s *Twenty Point Position Paper*
produced during the 1972 Trail of Broken Treaties caravan and the subsequent
occupation of the Bureau of Indian Affairs offices in Washington, DC (Bruyneel
123-69). See Paul Chaat Smith and Robert Warrior's *Like a Hurricane: The Indian
Movement from Alcatraz to Wounded Knee* for a book-length history of AIM.

4. See Vine Deloria Jr.'s *Custer Died for Your Sins*, Scott Richard Lyon's "Rhetorical
Sovereignty," Niigaanwewidam James Sinclair's "Tending to Ourselves," and
the videos "Rezpect Our Water: Sign Our Petition" and "She Is Standing Up
to the Dakota Access Pipeline for Herself and Her People," featuring Standing
Rock youth Tokata Iron Eyes, for examples of American Indian and Canadian
Aboriginal leaders articulating holistic understandings of Indigenous sovereignty.
For further discussion of the meaning of sovereignty and how Indigenous
sovereignty has been recognized, limited, and undermined by legislation, court
decisions, and other acts by colonial federal, state, and provincial governments,
see Bruyneel's *The Third Space of Sovereignty*, David Wilkins and K. Tsianina
Lomawaima's *Uneven Ground*, Mark Rifkin's *The Erotics of Sovereignty*, David
Elliott's *Law and Aboriginal Peoples in Canada*, and Jo-Ann Episkenew's *Taking
Back Our Spirits*.

5. My work intersects with Doris Seale and Beverly Slapin's books *A Broken Flute*
and *Through Indian Eyes*, Paulette Molin's book *American Indian Themes in
Young Adult Literature*, Clare Bradford's book *Unsettling Narratives*, and Debbie
Reese's blog *American Indians in Children's Literature*. These sources provide
broad analytical surveys of texts by non-Indigenous as well as Indigenous authors
who represent Indigenous characters in books for young readers. By critiquing
stereotypes and colonialist perspectives in texts by non-Native writers—including
award-winning texts commonly integrated into school curricula—and by
promoting texts that offer accurate, nuanced representations of Indigenous
people, these scholars make crucial contributions to K–12 education and popular
culture as well as children's/YA literary studies. While I build on their work, my
project stands apart by focusing exclusively and deeply on Native-authored texts.
This is the first book-length project to focus exclusively on Indigenous-authored
young adult literature.

6. A comparative review of Indigenous publishing contexts in Canada and the
United States is beyond the scope of this project. Nevertheless, it is worth noting
that the two texts in this study that negatively depict white characters (*The Night*

Wanderer) or almost entirely avoid white characters (*Slash*) were both published in Canada. These features of the texts are likely related to the fact that Canada, unlike the United States, has large, longstanding Indigenous presses, including Theytus, the publisher of *Slash*, and the fact that Canada has a larger potential Indigenous readership for Indigenous-authored books.

Chapter One. A Rebel with a Community, Not Just a Cause: Revising YA Power Dynamics and Uniquely Representing Indigenous Sovereignty in Jeannette Armstrong's *Slash*

1. *Slash* clearly falls under the narrowest definition of young adult literature—texts written specifically for adolescent readers—given that it was produced as part of the Okanagan Indian Curriculum Project for use in high school classrooms, and given that Armstrong frequently discusses her desire to reach teens with the novel. See, for example, her interviews with Victoria Freeman, Hartmut Lutz, and Janice Williamson ("The Body of Our People"; interview with Lutz; "Jeannette Armstrong").

2. The Okanagan view of land as Mother inspires the title of *We Get Our Living Like Milk from the Land*, an Okanagan history book coedited by Armstrong et al. In "Land Speaking," Armstrong discusses the significance of the Okanagan land as the source for the Okanagan language as well as a teacher who enables the survival and flourishing of the people (175–76).

3. He does not address the implications for YA literary theory, but my reading here otherwise aligns with Matthew Green's argument that "it is possible to conceive of Slash [Tommy] as a role model and teacher without suggesting that he has risen *above* the rest of the Native community. On the contrary, as we have seen, it is precisely because Slash has come to recognize his position *within* the community that he can speak confidently and insightfully" (Green 65).

4. Armstrong discusses her contested but ultimately successful effort to ensure Indigenous authorship for *Slash* and other OICP texts in her interviews with Janice Williamson and Hartmut Lutz ("Jeannette Armstrong" 121–24; interview with Lutz 27–29). She also addresses, in both these interviews, her decision to narrate *Slash* with a strong male voice that could empower Indigenous readers and challenge the internalization by some of those readers of dominant patriarchal notions of masculinity ("Jeannette Armstrong" 119–20, 123; interview with Lutz 18).

5. Armstrong describes her careful attention to the development of Tommy's voice

in her interview with Karin Beeler ("Image, Music, Text" 146).

6. As several critics discuss, we also see stylistic evidence of oral-tradition influences in *Slash* (Morton 20-23; Jones 55–59; Emberley 131). Armstrong discusses *Slash*'s engagement with oral tradition in her interviews with Kim Anderson and Karin Beeler ("Reclaiming Native Space"; "Image, Music, Text").

7. In "Tending to Ourselves: Hybridity and Native Literary Criticism," Niigaanwewidam James Sinclair overviews critiques of hybridity from Indigenous studies while also calling for an Indigenous "re-working" of the concept.

8. While he personally takes issue with "sovereignty" as an imposed European paradigm, including in his landmark *Peace, Power, Righteousness: An Indigenous Manifesto*, in his *Companion to American Indian History* entry on sovereignty, Taiaiake Alfred also credits Native sovereignty movements of recent decades with working to "restore [Indigenous peoples'] autonomous power and cultural integrity in the area of governance" and to "rejec[t] the models of government rooted in European cultural values" (Alfred 465). He acknowledges, further, that "In the past two or three generations, there has been movement for the good in terms of rebuilding social cohesion, gaining economic self-sufficiency, and empowering structures of self-government within indigenous communities. There has also been a return to seeking guidance in traditional teachings, and a revitalization of the traditions that sustained the great cultural achievement of respectful coexistence. People have begun to appreciate that wisdom, and much of the discourse on what constitutes justice and proper relationship within indigenous communities today revolves around the struggle to promote the recovery of these values" (472–73).

9. In an interview with Hartmut Lutz, Armstrong explains that a major motivation in writing *Slash* was to pass on the feeling of "renewal"—renewed commitment to Indigenous traditions as well as renewed pride in being Indian—that came out of Red Power (14–15).

10. Grauer, Morton, and Emberley address the influence of Okanagan language and oral tradition in *Slash*. Early in the novel, when describing the challenge Okanagan young people face at the predominantly white town school, Tommy observes, "Most of us Indian kids talked English different too" (25). *Slash* positively represents the ability to speak the Okanagan language, to use English to express unique Okanagan concepts, and to connect with the land from whom Okanagan people traditionally understand they receive their language (Armstrong, "Land Speaking" 175). The novel does not, however, explicitly address language

revitalization as a way to unify people in the midst of divisive political debate (even as it does represent dance in those terms) or as part of the broad project of renewing the community's strength from within, a surprising omission given Armstrong's commitment to the language (*Slash* 138; Grauer).

11. Matthew Green and Clare Bradford devote entire articles to analyzing the "polyphony" or "multiple discourses" of *Slash*, and they both consider how the presence of multiple voices in *Slash* works to expose, reinscribe, and/or challenge dominant colonialist narratives. Margery Fee, Manina Jones, Katja Sarkowksy, and Nancy Van Styvendale similarly address the presence of multiple voices in the novel.

Chapter Two. Indigenous School Stories: Alternatives to Multiculturalism in Sherman Alexie's *The Absolutely True Diary of a Part-Time Indian* and Joseph Bruchac's *The Heart of a Chief*

1. According to the opening summary volume of the *Final Report of the Truth and Reconciliation Commission of Canada*, the last federally administered residential schools closed in 1996, while some of the religious schools continued later into the 1990s (353-63). Negative depictions of formal K–12 schooling that illuminate the impact of the residential school era can be found in many Canadian Aboriginal texts, including Eden Robinson's *Monkey Beach*, Beatrice Culleton Mosionier's *In Search of April Raintree*, Lee Maracle's *Ravensong*, and Drew Hayden Taylor's *The Night Wanderer*.

2. That the policy of multiculturalism is meant to reinforce a singular national identity is evident in the repeated use of the singular "Canadian society" in the section outlining the policy (CMA 3.1). Furthermore, while the CMA at times refers to the "cultural heritage" of those with "different origins" or "cultures" in the plural, it also refers to "Canadian heritage" in the singular, as in the central declaration that the Canadian government will "recognize and promote the understanding that multiculturalism is a fundamental characteristic of the Canadian heritage and identity and that it provides an invaluable resource in the shaping of Canada's future" (CMA 3.1.b, 3.1.g, 3.1.h).

3. David Roediger traces the notion that racial mixture will end racism back to at least the mid-nineteenth century but identifies a fresh incarnation of the idea in the multiculturalism that began developing in the United States through the 1990s (8).

4. Other Indigenous YA texts, such as Eden Robinson's *Monkey Beach* and David

Alexander Robertson and Scott B. Henderson's 7 Generations saga, address
ongoing impacts of boarding/residential schools, but, unlike Bruchac's, Alexie's,
and Gansworth's books, I do not categorize these texts as contemporary school
stories, because they do not focus substantially on contemporary school
experiences.

5. For discussion of anti-assimilation resistance in boarding-school narratives by
early-twentieth-century American Indian writers—including Zitkala-Ša, Eastman,
and Standing Bear—see K. Tsianina Lomawaima and Teresa L. McCarty's *To
Remain an Indian*, Amelia Katanski's *Learning to Write Indian*, Ruth Spack's
America's Second Tongue, and Jessica Enoch's "Resisting the Script of Indian
Education." Sam McKegney's *Magic Weapons* and Jo-Ann Episkenew's *Taking
Back Our Spirits* address resistance in mid-to-late twentieth-century narratives by
Canadian Aboriginal writers.

6. Regarding censorship, *True Diary* was listed on the American Library
Association's Office for Intellectual Freedom (OIF) "Best of the Banned" list for
the 2011 annual Banned Books Week. In their article on these books, the OIF
notes that *True Diary* "faced heated challenges in schools and libraries" for the
following reasons: "offensive language; racism; religious viewpoint; sexually
explicit; unsuited to age group." Alexie has frequently responded to these
censorship campaigns by speaking out against book-banning on his website, www.
fallsapart.com. The National Council for Teachers of English (NCTE) English
Companion site (among the most popular sites that high school English teachers
in the United States use for sharing ideas) includes several discussions of *True
Diary* that encapsulate the major concerns of educators while also reflecting
debates about stereotypes among Alexie's Native readers. Teachers, here, ask for
advice in justifying their inclusion of *True Diary* in the curriculum (or explain that
they simply avoid it) because of the novel's censorship buttons. They also praise
the novel for engaging reluctant readers and male readers. In terms of curriculum,
they primarily focus on getting students to personally connect with the novel's
universal themes related to the adolescent experience (loneliness, belonging,
multiple identities, etc.). In one forum, Ann Baldwin, coauthor of *Sherman
Alexie in the Classroom*, contributes to the discussion by pointing out that many
Native students and parents (including in the setting where she teaches) take
offense at Alexie's work because they see it as perpetuating stereotypes. Baldwin
encourages other teachers to contextualize the novel with additional sources on
contemporary American Indian cultures. Sammie Bordeaux, a Rosebud Sioux

tribal member, responds to Baldwin by describing a positive experience teaching *True Diary* at a tribal college on the Rosebud Sioux reservation. Bordeaux disagrees with the charge that Alexie's work perpetuates stereotypes and speaks of her students identifying with Junior's experiences while appreciating Alexie's humor and sarcasm. I discuss examples of mainstream reviews of *True Diary* later in this section.

7. Exceptions to this trend include Allison Porzio, in her article on *True Diary* in the *English Record*, along with Adrienne Kertzer in her *Children's Literature* article on the novel, and Heather E. Bruce, Anna E. Baldwin, and Christabel Umphrey in their chapter on *True Diary* and *Flight* in the NCTE book *Sherman Alexie in the Classroom*. Both Porzio's article and the NCTE book chapter call attention to *True Diary*'s exploration of white privilege. Neither, however, offers an in-depth discussion of it. Bruce, Baldwin, and Umphrey focus on Alexie's engagement with tolerance. Porzio discusses *True Diary*'s treatment of racial and class inequality, but she does not substantively analyze the intersections of these two types of inequality. Kertzer provocatively suggests that *True Diary* challenges dominant discourses (despite Clare Bradford's reading to the contrary), illuminating a subtle anti-colonial critique in the novel via its allusions to historical figures like the infamous Indian-boarding-schools forefather Richard Pratt and Civil War General Sheridan, known for his declaration that the "only good Indian is a dead Indian" (Kertzer 59–62). Kertzer also draws attention to Junior's critiques of Indian stereotypes while also reading the novel, particularly Forney's cartoons, as sometimes reinforcing the very stereotypes that it at other times calls into question (61, 65–72). Kertzer does not, however, provide an in-depth focus on Alexie's critique of white privilege and multiculturalism.

8. For example, in their reviews of *True Diary*, Carpenter and Trinoskey both speak of Junior as adapting to "white" and "Indian" "worlds." In addition, despite quoting Alexie at length, with Alexie characterizing both himself and Junior as Indians with non-Native allies (not as people torn between white and Indian), in his *ALAN Review* article, Jim Blasingame claims that *True Diary* "is largely about striding two cultures" (72).

9. Whenever interviewers ask Alexie to respond to charges that his work perpetuates stereotypes of alcoholic Indians, Alexie always vehemently denies the suggestion that alcoholism among Indians is a stereotype, and reiterates his interest in confronting the brutal realities of alcoholism, poverty, and despair that plague American Indian communities. See, for example, his interview with Enrique Cerna.

10. In *Disturbing the Universe*, Roberta Trites contends that rebellion is ultimately put in check by *The Chocolate War*. The protagonist, Charlie, asks, "Do I dare disturb the universe?," and readers, Trites argues, are likely to answer "no" given the dire consequences Charlie experiences for his rebellion. At his 2007 reading in Stamford, CT, Alexie described Cormier's *The Chocolate War* as a favorite book and key influence, and he described reading several additional YA authors— including Laurie Halse Anderson, Sara Zarr, Walter Dean Meyers, J. D. Salinger, and M. T. Anderson—in preparation for writing *True Diary*, interesting given that these particular writers have often used school settings to critique dominant society, albeit in the limited ways that Trites addresses.

11. Junior's growing critique of associating success with whiteness overlaps with the title character of Jeannette Armstrong's *Slash* revealing as a lie the notion that assimilation into the dominant society will lead to success for Indigenous people. Although Junior focuses on combating the idea that pursuing success makes him "white," he also demonstrates that performing whiteness—a partial attempt at assimilation—in his early days at Reardan mitigates neither his poverty nor the discrimination he experiences.

12. Junior references the grandmothers when he describes his experience trick-or-treating on the reservation. Most people, he says, "called me names and slammed the door in my face" (79). Yet, he says, "plenty of people were happy to give me spare change [for the homeless]. And more than a few of them gave me candy *and* spare change." He goes on to note that "A few folks, especially the grandmothers, thought I was a brave little dude for going to a white school" (79).

13. The Wellpinit fans jeer at Junior and then turn their backs on him when he enters the Wellpinit gym with the Reardan basketball team (143–45).

14. In an interview with Sarah T. Williams, excerpted in Williams's article "Man of Many Tribes," for example, Alexie explains how after 9/11, "I saw the end game of tribalism—it ends up with people flying planes into buildings. I've worked hard since then to shed the negative parts of tribal thinking, which almost always involve some sort of fear," which leads to violence. He continues, noting that "*Indian Killer* is very much a tribal and fundamentalist book. I've really disowned it." Williams, along with Heather E. Bruce, Anna E. Baldwin, and Christabel Umphrey in their chapter from *Sherman Alexie in the Classroom*, analyzes this shift from *Indian Killer* and other earlier works by Alexie to the more recent novels *Flight* and *True Diary*, both of which emphasize empathy, tolerance, and Native/non-Native collaboration.

15. In his depiction of debates over Indian mascots, Fletcher demonstrates that non-Native proponents of mascots often see the Native American protesters as the ones with the problem. The proponents claim to be celebrating Native "culture." Influenced by a supposedly colorblind multiculturalist approach, they see their American Indian critics as wrong for characterizing mascots as racist since they see race and racism as belonging to the past. Moreover, they often accuse their American Indian critics of being inauthentic Indians—because their culture has adapted and modernized—who know less about "real" traditional Native American culture than they do and thus have no right to decide whether or not a mascot accurately represents Native American culture (Fletcher 22–29, 93–124). This attitude is not new. See Philip Deloria's *Playing Indian* for an extensive discussion of non-Native people "acting like Indians" while policing the "authenticity" of actual Native people from the 1700s to the present.

16. In *America's Second Tongue: American Indian Education and the Ownership of English, 1860–1900,* Ruth Spack similarly argues that in the wake of oppressive English-only boarding-school education, because of Native peoples' creativity and resilience, "English as a shared language has engendered a pan-tribal political and social environment that has empowered Native people in ways policymakers never imagined. In place after place there is a rich story to be told by Native people of how they have taken ownership of English and shaped it to accommodate new and powerful forms of expression" (178).

17. Bruchac himself has increasingly written and published in his Western Abenaki language in recent years, but *Heart of a Chief* was published before this turn. By writing entirely or almost entirely in English, the authors featured in this study are able to reach wide audiences. Yet, as Chris himself observes, some concepts just do not come across as "clearly" in English as they would in an Indigenous language. See Margaret Noodin's *Bawaajimo: A Dialect of Dreams in Anishinaabe Language and Literature* for a discussion of the expansive influence of Anishinaabemowin—including how the conceptual aspects of the language intersect with the technical aspects—in the Birchbark House series, along with other works by Erdrich and additional Anishinaabe authors. Numerous grassroots language-revitalization programs have led to the demand for and production of Indigenous-language texts, including the children's book *Awesiinyensag: Dibaajimowinan Ji-Gikinoo'amaageng* by Anton Treuer et al. Written entirely in Anishinaabemowin and published by Heid and Louise Erdrich's Wiigwaas Press (a press created to promote Ojibwe-language publishing) in 2010, *Awesiinyensag*

drew unprecedented national attention to Indigenous-language publications when it was selected as Minnesota's Best Read for 2011 by the Library of Congress, making it the single official selection to represent Minnesota publications at the National Book Festival that year.

18. *The Heart of a Chief* suggests that Mito had completed his Harvard MBA and begun doing some work on behalf of the tribe before his wife passed away and his despair drove him to alcoholism (62, 69). At one point, Chris recalls, "it looked like [Mito] would be chief here, like Doda had been. Before he started drinking so much" (69). Like Alexie, then, Bruchac confronts the reality of alcoholism in American Indian communities. In typically optimistic Bruchac fashion, the conclusion of *The Heart of a Chief* suggests that, despite failed previous treatment attempts, Mito's most recent stint in a treatment facility, coupled with his family's renewed investment in the community via the casino project, will result in a long-term recovery.

19. Saldanha similarly critiques the limited attention given to Aboriginal communities and communities of color in Canadian schools, arguing, "What is absent from current articulations of multiculturalism is the profound potential of multiple and dynamic knowledges to mutually and substantively transform the national space" (174–75).

20. Indigenous ways of knowing and being are centralized in a variety of unique ways in many tribally run schools. Ricky White, superintendent of the Circle of Life Academy on the Anishinaabe White Earth Nation discusses one example in the March 28, 2017, broadcast of the radio program *Native America Calling* titled "Culture in the Classroom for School Success." White describes a holistic approach that includes optional daily smudging, parental involvement, language and traditional arts instruction by elders, and trauma counseling. In that same broadcast, Joe Carrier, director of the Native American Education Department at Detroit Lakes Public Schools describes his attempt to foreground and value Indigenous perspectives in his public-school setting.

Chapter Three. Not Your Father's Pocahontas: Cynthia Leitich Smith's and Susan Power's Resistive Romance

1. Susan Scott Parrish's article "The Female Opossum and the Nature of the New World" offers one insightful analysis of this phenomenon.

2. Even though Thomas Jefferson is infamous for his claim that Indians could be assimilated into Euro-American society via intermarriage whereas African

Americans could not, Tilton observes that during the Jeffersonian era, when the "fantasy of absorption" was revived in Pocahontas narratives by again depicting her marriage to Rolfe, it was "always in the form of either a nostalgic looking back to the earliest days of the colonies when it could have happened, or a looking ahead to when it might someday occur. There was clearly no room in the present for such a union" (3). The dominant Euro-American aversion to miscegenation that would strengthen through the nineteenth century was already strong in this earlier period. See Jolie Sheffer's *The Romance of Race* for a discussion of attitudes toward miscegenation in the late nineteenth and early twentieth centuries. In many regards, the earliest Euro-American representations of Pocahontas that positively focus on her marriage to Rolfe align with the late twentieth- and early twenty-first-century articulations of triumphant multiculturalism via mixed-race subjects that Roediger discusses in *Colored White*, including ways that these subjects are valued only insofar as they are perceived as assimilating to dominant Euro-American norms.

3. Some of the many texts that address these complex issues regarding recognition and membership include Jo-Ann Episkenew's *Taking Back our Spirits*, Jill Doerfler's *Those Who Belong*, Kim TallBear's *Native American DNA*, and Tracey Deer's documentary film *Club Native*. Andrea Smith's *Conquest* and several essays in the 2011 *Queer Indigenous Studies* collection (Driskill et al.) address the colonial imposition of patriarchal values on Native communities.

4. In the United States, federal rather than tribal courts generally have jurisdiction over crimes committed by non-Natives on Native land, and there are contradictory federal policies regarding tribal jurisdiction over sexual crimes. The 2010 Tribal Law and Order Act sought to address some of these jurisdiction problems that make sexual violence against Native women a largely unpunished crime, but implementation of the law has been slow, with sexual violence continuing at a high rate and continuing to go largely unprosecuted. In the afterword to her 2012 novel *The Round House* (which focuses on a boy's quest for justice after a white man rapes his Anishinaabe mother), Louise Erdrich summarizes some of the findings of the "Maze of Injustice" Amnesty report and references several other sources that discuss related problems along with organizations working to address them. Sarah Deer's 2015 book *The Beginning and End of Rape: Confronting Sexual Violence in Native America* provides one of the most extensive treatments of jurisdiction, sentencing, and justice issues on this topic. Jo-Ann Episkenew discusses sexual violence against Indigenous women

in Canada—and references many additional studies—in *Taking Back Our Spirits*. After years of robust Indigenous activism surrounding missing and murdered Indigenous women in Canada, the Canadian government finally agreed to conduct a public inquiry on the topic in December 2015. At the time of this writing, the pre-inquiry process has finished, but the inquiry itself (along with any concrete justice measures that may emerge from it) has yet to transpire. See the "National Inquiry into Missing and Murdered Indigenous Women and Girls" page of the Government of Canada website for more information.

5. *The Round House, In Search of April Raintree*, and *Monkey Beach* all appeal to adults as well as adolescents, thus falling under a broad rather than narrow definition of young adult literature. *Hidden Roots* is directed primarily at middle-grade readers.

6. While Pattee focuses on the Sweet Valley High (SVH) series that ran from the 1980s through the early 2000s, her characterization of popular YA romance, particularly as reinforcing conservative, heterosexual "middle-class" norms, cuts across the genre. Pattee traces the dissemination of these values starting in the junior novels of the 1940s and 1950s that served as precursors to later YA romances, and continuing through contemporary YA texts, including the 2008 revival of the SVH books (Pattee 11, 24, 33, 170–73). Pattee describes the newer SVH books as differing from other twenty-first-century YA romances because, whereas the heroines of the other texts come into their own as young women through capitalist consumption, the heroines of the SVH books still achieve their new subject positions via romance (173). As Naomi Johnson focuses on other popular YA romance texts, like the Gossip Girls, A-List, and Clique series, in which "acts of consumption to prepare for romantic relationships" are the primary focus "rather than the relationships themselves," she joins Pattee in observing a broad tendency across popular YA romance to reinforce heterosexual patriarchal norms (N. Johnson 59). In "Queer Discourse and the Young Adult Novel," Roberta Trites argues that even gay YA literature tends to reinforce heterosexual norms by repressing the very queer discourses it seeks to liberate and celebrate ("Queer Discourse" 143–44, 149). In *Death, Gender, and Sexuality in Contemporary Adolescent Literature*, Kathryn James similarly argues that the texts that most strongly attempt to resist heterosexual patriarchal norms still end up reinforcing them either by depicting death as a punishment for transgressing those norms or by stabilizing femininity as normative (or dead) (James 111).

7. See Philip Deloria's *Playing Indian* for an analysis of this phenomenon among a

wide range of groups across United States history, from the Boston Tea Party to the New Age movement. Debbie Reese, Doris Seale, Beverly Slapin, and Matthew Fletcher are among those who critique this phenomenon in children's literature, school curricula (including Halloween and Thanksgiving activities), and sports mascots.

8. Beverly Slapin highlights this aspect of the novel in her *Broken Flute* review, observing that "Cassidy Rain Berghoff is not troubled by who she is; rather, she's bothered by other people's perceptions of Indians," setting her apart from the protagonists who suffer from "mixed blood identity crises—'walking in two worlds'—that white authors love to write about" (Seale and Slapin, *Broken Flute* 392). I read Rain's father as having internalized racism against Native Americans, because he tells Rain that photography is her future and "A person shouldn't let her heritage hold her back," as if her Native heritage is a hindrance to cast off rather than a point of pride (61). Rain also recalls him critiquing one of her brother Fynn's college entrance essays about the family as being too "personal" and then Fynn changing the "Native American/American Indian" boxes he had checked to "White" (92). Rain's father may have picked up this shame from his mother, who always said she was "just Irish" or "Black Irish," disregarding her Ojibwe ancestry (20).

9. See Deloria's *Playing Indian* for a discussion of the historic development of these kinds of camps that continue to be operated today by organizations like the Boy Scouts, Girl Scouts, and YMCA.

10. Smith heightens this association by conflating Pocahontas Barbie and Malibu Barbie, with Southern California often portrayed as a particularly exotic, lush, and sexualized space. In her article "Native American Barbie: The Marketing of Euro-American Desires," Maureen Trudelle Schwarz details the ways that Barbie dolls, including Pocahontas Barbie, have been used to advance the ideologies of colonialist heteropatriarchy.

11. See Rayna Green's "The Pocahontas Perplex" and Andrea Smith's *Conquest* for more on the princess/squaw characterization of Native women.

12. For example, see Matthew Fletcher's *American Indian Education: Counternarratives in Racism, Struggle, and the Law*. Fletcher and others, especially in the field of Indigenous education, also counter that since assimilation programs and other colonialist agendas have been pursued most forcefully through educational settings (especially in government- and church-run Indian boarding schools), American Indian students especially need additional educational

support and community-based educational programs to combat that colonialism and rebuild cultural resources. In her letter to the editor, Mrs. Owen also joins the children's novelists that Donnarae MacCann discusses (in the article referenced at the start of this chapter) in implicitly referencing an interracial relationship in order to soften an arguably colonialist perspective, noting that "I even encouraged my own child to accompany her [referring to Georgia, and, by extension, Rain] to Native American events" to highlight her "highest respect for Native American culture" (33).

13. Rain also more subtly confronts dominant views of African Americans as she reflects in her journal about her curiosity as a young girl about Queenie's hair, and as she recalls a conversation with Galen in which she disagreed with people who told her she could be friends with, but not date black people (65, 28).

14. In *True Diary*, Junior similarly comes to see his complicity in colonialist heteropatriarchy, in part by confronting the possibility that his attraction to his white girlfriend Penelope might stem from his internalization of racist colonialist views (115).

15. This trend is evident in a range of texts, including Thomas King's *Truth and Bright Water*, Drew Hayden Taylor's *Motorcycles and Sweetgrass* and *The Night Wanderer*, and the majority of Alexie's and Bruchac's works featuring adolescent protagonists.

16. In focusing primarily on non-romantic relationships in the present world (even as they represent romances of the past), Power's stories and Smith's novel are like Lensey Namioka's young adult novel *Yang the Second and Her Secret Admirers*. Melinda de Jesús argues that this novel subverts the interracial romance triangle common in representations of Asian American romance, a triangle that usually results in an Asian American protagonist choosing a white partner, as it "seems to valorize female friendship over heterosexual romance" (Jesús 318–19).

17. An in-depth engagement with Indigenous masculinities is beyond the scope of this study. I hope that future scholarship will explore masculinity in Indigenous YA literature, a promising area of inquiry given the complex and varied portrayals of males (present Native males, absent Native males, and non-Native males) in the literature, and given the recent surge of scholarship in this area, epitomized in the 2015 collection *Indigenous Men and Masculinities*, edited by Robert Alexander Innes and Kim Anderson.

18. Craig Womack's novel *Drowning in Fire* relays a coming-of-age narrative of a gay Muscogee boy, and it is sometimes classified as YA in libraries, but it diverges

from many conventions of YA literature and is unlikely to be promoted as YA by teachers or librarians because of its explicit and extensive sexual content.

Chapter Four. That's One Story: Reworking Hybridity through Melissa Tantaquidgeon Zobel's and Drew Hayden Taylor's Speculative Fiction

1. In contrast to *The Night Wanderer* and other solidly YA texts that I examine in this volume, *Oracles* is a crossover text with appeal to both adults and young adults.
2. Distancing herself from this tendency, Cynthia Leitich Smith has avoided including any American Indian characters in her own vampire series and has said that when she does have Indian characters appear in the second book of a spinoff series, "they'll be regular (non-magical) human beings" (Message to the author).
3. In the introduction to the anthology *So Long Been Dreaming: Postcolonial Science Fiction and Fantasy*, Nalo Hopkinson writes, "one of the most familiar memes of science fiction is that of going to foreign countries and colonizing the natives." She continues, "for many of us that's not a thrilling adventure story; it's non-fiction, and we are on the wrong side of the strange looking ship that appears out of nowhere" (7). But, she contends, many postcolonial writers "take the meme of colonizing the natives and, from the experience of the colonized, critique it, pervert it, fuck with it, with irony, with anger, with humor, and also, with love and respect for the genre of science fiction that makes it possible to think about new ways of doing things" (9). While I would not classify *Oracles* or *The Night Wanderer* as science fiction, I do read them as extending this larger anti-colonial critique present across the growing body of Indigenous and postcolonial speculative fiction.
4. In her essay in *Science Fiction, Imperialism, and the Third World*, Judith Leggatt reads the 1997 science-fiction novel *The Moons of Palmares* by African American/Cherokee writer Zainab Amadahy as marshaling a similar critique of neocolonialism.
5. Womack argues that a "more astute model for tradition [than the one offered by hybridity critics] would acknowledge its meanings in a community rather than expending so much energy on its point of origin. It would acknowledge other possibilities than hybridity by recognizing traditions that are fluid yet still retain some kind of continuity with the community that claims them and perceives them as part of its own culture" (Weaver et al. 140). He concludes his chapter: "Embracing my hybridity is about as sexy as wrapping my legs around an H-bomb. While you might get a big tingle during the initial descent, it's the impact that will kill you" (174).

6. In this regard, *Oracles* and *The Night Wanderer* also part ways with the speculative Indigenous texts that Roslyn Weaver and the authors of *New World Orders* discuss, which, at least in the readings provided by Weaver's essay and *New World Orders*, are hopeful about Indigenous/non-Indigenous reconciliation (Weaver 102, 112; Bradford et al. 59–62). (In my view, Weaver too easily figures a mixed-race character as a positive agent of reconciliation without considering how colonial discourses of white privilege or practices of appropriation and romanticization affect both representations and readings of mixed-race subjects.)

7. The same pattern occurs in Joseph Bruchac's 2013 YA dystopian novel *Killer of Enemies*. The book is more cosmopolitan than Zobel's and Taylor's. Bruchac writes here, as in *Heart of a Chief* and many of his other books (a practice that has received some controversy), about a tribal nation other than his own, in this case the Chiricahua Apache. His Apache protagonist also engages in positive cross-cultural alliances as she struggles for her and her family's survival, and attempts to resist the oppressive rulers of her post-apocalyptic setting. (She has little choice in this matter given that most of her community has been wiped out.) Nevertheless, she homes in on specific Chiricahua landscapes and stories, and it is this homing in that enables her survival along with her broader contributions to her family and her larger intercultural society. For further discussion of Chiricahua Apache rootedness in *Killer of Enemies*, along with analysis of how Bruchac and other Indigenous writers marshal YA dystopia to challenge neoliberal notions of citizenship, see Zara Rix's *Speculating the Child Citizen* (101–41).

8. In contradicting her earlier analysis by concluding with a focus on Native protagonists' alleged attachment to the dominant society and position between cultures, Stewart may reflect the influence of freewheeling hybridity and stringent relativism in both Native and children's/YA literary studies (148). In the rest of the article, she draws on a variety of nationalist as well as cosmopolitan critics, and her reading of *Hidden Roots* enacts the culturally specific, community-oriented, politically conscious criticism called for by the literary nationalist school.

9. Critics and authors, including Clare Bradford and Louise Erdrich along with Zobel herself, highlight how colonialist perspectives affect the labeling of Indigenous and other minority-authored texts as "speculative," "magical," or "fantastic." They challenge mainstream critics who sometimes characterize textual elements as "unreal" just because they belong to what the critics perceive to be a "different" culture, even though members of that culture may well see the elements as realistic (Bradford, *Unsettling Narratives* 50, 56; Erdrich, "LaRose:

An Evening with Louise Erdrich"; Zobel, "Magical Futurism"). While readers will debate the "real" or "unreal" nature of some phenomena in *Oracles* and *The Night Wanderer*, in my view (and the view of Zobel and Taylor), both texts clearly fall under the speculative-fiction category because of *Oracles*'s futuristic setting and *The Night Wanderer*'s vampire character.

10. I draw heavily on Zobel's own scholarship regarding the significance of Mohegan Hill, as well as on other aspects of Mohegan history and culture, because she is the leading historian and one of the primary cultural caretakers for the small Mohegan nation.

11. In addition to the prevalence of magical mixed-race figures in speculative fiction, critics like Elvira Pulitano, Arnold Krupat, and Louis Owens have suggested that mixed-blood protagonists of Native literature—including in canonical texts by Leslie Marmon Silko, Navaree Scott Momaday, and Louise Erdrich—have special insights because of knowledge gleaned from two different cultures and experience in the spaces between those cultures.

12. In our 2015 interview, "The View from Crow Hill," Zobel similarly asserts, "*Oracles* is a cautionary tale for *anyone*, Indian people and non-Indian people. I wanted to bring attention to what I saw as some of the limits and dangers of New Age thinking: the consequences that can result when people meddle in spiritual practice that they don't really understand or when they water down Native cultural practices to the point where there isn't any integrity" (85).

13. This principle guides Tomuck, Winay, and Ashneon's interactions with the school children who visit their museum, as well as their medicine practice. As one busload of "pilgrims," as he calls them, climb the mountain, Tomuck thinks, "All who visited Yantuck Mountain got what they came for, whether they wanted it or not" (52). During his subsequent museum presentation, Tomuck illuminates his point through his interaction with a boy named John Mason, who he chooses as a helper after the boy belittles the Yantucks' attempt to preserve the natural environment: "All that nature is nice. But nobody needs it no more, Chief!" the boy says (53). The boy's scalp turns red and he feels sick after Tomuck has him touch a wampum bear club. But, we are told, the medicine in the club will cure the boy of his "spiritual infection," ultimately bringing him to a better place (55–56). By giving the boy the name "John Mason," the name of the English captain who, with the Mohegans' assistance, led the massacre of Pequots during the Pequot War, Zobel also subtly suggests that Mohegans as well as Euro-Americans need to face and find healing from difficult truths about their history.

14. See Lisa Brook's *The Common Pot* for a nuanced discussion of Zobel's and other Mohegan leaders' problematic celebratory stance toward Uncas (59–64). I focus on Zobel's positive interpretation of Uncas's actions representing a type of "cooperation without compromise"—despite there being plenty of room to read Uncas as significantly compromising his community's values—because that interpretation drives *Oracles*'s portrayal of Indigenous hybridity. That Zobel's portrayal stems from her positive interpretation of Uncas's legacy illuminates the fact that Indigenous approaches to hybridity, like Indigenous approaches to sovereignty, will always be open to critical analysis, debate, and revision.

15. In her discussion in *Reading Race* of picture books that offer revisionary histories from Indigenous perspectives, Clare Bradford argues that these texts "insist on how the past is present to Indigenous peoples and national cultures" (245). *The Night Wanderer* similarly insists that the past is present, and not just in the sense of historical colonialism continuing into the present—as I have been discussing here, and as Bradford focuses on in her analysis of the picture books—but also in the sense that the historical Anishinaabe community continues into the present.

16. Given the novel's suggestion that harm comes to those who date outside the community, Tiffany may be romantically doomed; she is related to most people her age on the reserve (12–13). Despite Ashneon's and Tashteh's deadly relationship in *Oracles*, Zobel's novel suggests more positive possibilities for intertribal and Native/non-Native romance, especially in its portrayal of the Irish/Native relationships among some of Ashneon's relatives.

17. As her homing-in leads Tiffany to connect more deeply with her land and her ancestors across time, the concept of home advanced by *The Night Wanderer* overlaps with other Canadian Aboriginal children's/YA texts that portray home in terms of "intergenerational connectedness" and "access to land" (Reimer xvi).

18. See Taylor's interview with Birgit Däwes, and his interview with John Moffatt and Sandy Tait where he talks about influences ranging from S. E. Hinton's *The Outsiders*, the nonfiction of Kurt Vonnegut and Isaac Asimov, and the fiction of Sherman Alexie, Leslie Marmon Silko, and Thomas King.

19. Taylor now has four collections of his own work that refer to him as a "Blue-Eyed Ojibway" in their title: *Funny, You Don't Look Like One: Observations of a Blue-Eyed Ojibway* (1996); *Further Adventures of a Blue-Eyed Ojibway: Funny, You Don't Look Like One, ~~Too~~ Two* (1999); *Furious Observations of a Blue-Eyed Ojibway: Funny, You Don't Look Like One, ~~Two~~ Three* (2002); and *Futile Observations of a Blue-Eyed Ojibway: Funny, You Don't Look Like One, Four* (2004).

20. See Taylor's interview with Birgit Däwes, and his interview with John Moffatt and Sandy Tait. The production of the graphic novel adaptation of *The Night Wanderer* further represents cross-cultural collaboration as a non-Native illustrator and non-Native adapter transformed Taylor's text in an attempt to reach additional Indigenous and non-Indigenous readers.

21. In addition to his interview with John Moffatt and Sandy Tait, Taylor also discusses cultural appropriation in his interview with Birgit Däwes and in many of his nonfiction essays, including those in the *Observations of a Blue-Eyed Ojibway* series. As he discusses in his interview with Moffat and Tait, he has represented multiple perspectives on the issue in his plays and short stories as well.

Coda. Alexie's *Flight*, Zobel's *Wabanaki Blues*, and the Future of Indigenous YA Literature

1. While the Penacooks do not actually possess federal recognition, as Bruchac explains in his author's note for *The Heart of a Chief*, he gives them recognized status and a reservation in his fictional world to protest the U.S. government's failure to acknowledge them. That move results in the novel avoiding attention to unique experiences faced by unrecognized Native nations.

2. *Flight* falls under broad rather than narrow definitions of YA literature as it appeals to a crossover readership of adults and adolescents. Alexie has strongly asserted that he does not see *Flight* as a YA text. Responding to Bill O'Driskill's observation in a 2007 interview that "Some critics have said *Flight* reminds them of young-adult fiction," Alexie said, "Go find me a young adult novel that has an 8-year-old Indian girl cutting off a Cavalry soldier's penis and stuffing it into his mouth. Unless the next Harry Potter is called *Harry Potter and the Gender-Mutilating 8-Year-Old Girl*. I worked really hard at making my 15-year-old sound and act like a 15-year-old. And because I was highly successful at doing that, people assume it's *for* teen-agers." Yet, *Flight* has appeal for teen readers and adheres to many YA conventions, not just a strong first-person adolescent voice. Alexie's reference to the Harry Potter series suggests a limited view of "young-adult fiction" that really only encompasses junior fiction and the younger end of the YA spectrum. Many mature teens can and have handled the graphic violence of *Flight*.

3. As Zits explains in *Flight*, "There's this law called the Indian Child Welfare Act that's supposed to protect half-breed orphans like me. I'm only supposed to be placed with Indian foster parents and families. But I'm not an official Indian. My Indian daddy gave me his looks, but he was never legally established as my father.

Since I'm not a legal Indian, the government can put me wherever they want. So they put me with anybody who will take me. Mostly they're white people" (9). In the United States, only children who are documented members of federally recognized tribes fall under the protection of the Indian Child Welfare Act (1978). Even then, many states have abused the clause in the law that allows children to be placed in non-Native homes under extreme circumstances, routinely placing Native children with white families even when there are Native guardians—often members of their own extended family—willing and able to care for them. In 2013, the tribes of South Dakota filed suit against the state for this practice, alleging that the number of children taken from Native homes has not significantly decreased since the passage of the Indian Child Welfare Act. In *Taking Back Our Spirits*, Jo-Ann Episkenew discusses the same phenomenon in Canada along with Mosionier's and others' literary representations of it. In the 1960s, Episkenew notes, "social-service agents apprehending children and placing them in foster care became the norm in many Indigenous communities." She continues, "This dark period in Indigenous history has come to be commonly termed the 'Sixties Scoop'; however, that label is truly a misnomer since the 'scooping up' of Aboriginal children did not end with the 1960s, in fact, and continues to this day" (65).

4. As he has in many other venues, in the speech Alexie explains that he did not read anything by an American Indian writer until he was twenty years old and his first creative-writing teacher, Alex Kou, gave him an anthology of Native American poetry called *Songs from This Earth on Turtle's Back*. Reading those poems changed Alexie's life, pushing him to become a writer and making him feel connected to other Native writers and artists like himself.

5. In their scholarship on *Flight*, Kerry Boland and Jan Johnson both interrogate the role of the white foster family in the novel, along with the text's broader emphasis on pain as something shared by whites and Indians alike.

Works Cited

Abercrombie-Donahue, Micki. *Educators' Perceptions of Indian Education for All: A Tribal Critical Race Theory Ethnography*. Diss. Bozeman: Montana State University, 2011.

Alba, Virginie. "Re-writing Cultures and Communities: Canadian Aboriginal Women and the Example of *Slash*." *Canadian Issues* 21 (1999): 190–207.

Alexie, Sherman. *The Absolutely True Diary of a Part-Time Indian*. Art by Ellen Forney. New York: Little, Brown, 2007.

——. "Alexie Discusses *Flight*, His First Novel in a Decade." Interview with Bill O'Driscoll. *Pittsburg City Paper: Book Reviews and Features*, 21 June 2007.

——. "Crossroads: A Conversation with Sherman Alexie." Interview with John Purdy. *Studies in American Indian Literatures* 9.4 (1997): 1–18.

——. *Flight*. New York: Grove, 2007.

——. Interview with David Miller. *Think Out Loud*. Live studio interview and discussion. Literary Arts. Portland, OR: Oregon Public Broadcasting. 24 Oct. 2012.

——. Interview with Enrique Cerna. *Conversations with Enrique Cerna*. KCTS, Seattle. 11 July 2008. https://kcts9.org/programs/conversations-enrique-cerna.

——. The National Book Award for Young People's Literature Acceptance Speech.

National Book Awards Ceremony. Marriott Marquis Hotel, New York, NY. 14 Nov. 2007. Online video clip. *YouTube.* https://www.youtube.com/watch?v=-6AbxJxDoI8.

——. Reading of *The Absolutely True Diary of a Part-Time Indian* and Discussion. Borders Books, Stamford, CT. 27 Nov. 2007.

——. "Sherman Alexie in Conversation with Williams Cole." *Brooklyn Rail: Books.* 1 Dec. 2003. http://www.brooklynrail.org.

——. "Sherman Alexie's *Iowa Review* Interview." Interview with Joelle Fraser. Reprinted in *Modern American Poetry.* Urbana-Champaign: University of Illinois, 2001. http://www.english.illinois.edu/maps/poets/a_f/alexie/fraser.htm.

——. "Tuxedo with Eagle Feathers." *Face.* New York: Hanging Loose Press, 2009. 79–82.

——. "Why the Best Books Are Written in Blood." *Wall Street Journal: Speakeasy*, 9 June 2011.

Alfred, Taiaiake. *Peace, Power, Righteousness: An Indigenous Manifesto.* Don Mills, ON: Oxford University Press, 1999.

——. "Sovereignty." *A Companion to American Indian History.* Malden, MA: Blackwell, 2002. 460–74.

American Library Association. Office for Intellectual Freedom. "Best of the Banned." *The 2012 State of America's Libraries.* Spec. issue of *American Libraries* (2012). http://www.ala.org.

Amnesty International. *Maze of Injustice: The Failure to Protect Indigenous Women from Sexual Violence in the USA.* Amnesty International, 2007. http://www.amnestyusa.org.

——. *Stolen Sisters: A Human Rights Response to Discrimination and Violence against Indigenous Women in Canada.* Amnesty International, Oct. 2004. https://www.amnesty.ca.

Armstrong, Jeannette. "The Body of Our People: Jeannette Armstrong." Interview with Victoria Freeman. *The Power to Bend Spoons: Interviews with Canadian Novelists.* Ed. Beverley Daurio. Toronto: Mercury, 1998. 10–19.

——. "Image, Music, Text: An Interview with Jeannette Armstrong." Interview with Karin Beeler. *Studies in Canadian Literature* 21.2 (1996): 143–54.

——. Interview with Hartmut Lutz. *Contemporary Challenges: Conversations with Canadian Native Authors.* Ed. Hartmut Lutz. Saskatoon, SK: Fifth House, 1991. 13–32.

——. "Jeannette Armstrong: 'What I Intended Was to Connect . . . and It's

Happened.'" Interview with Janice Williamson. *Tessera* 12 (1992): 111–29.

——— . "Land Speaking." *Speaking for Generations: Native Writers on Writing*. Ed. Simon J. Ortiz. Tucson: University of Arizona Press, 1998. 175–94.

——— . "Reclaiming Native Space in Literature/Breaking New Ground: An Interview with Jeannette Armstrong." Interview with Kim Anderson. *West Coast Line* 31.2 (1997): 49–65.

——— . *Slash*. 1985. Penticton, BC: Theytus, 2000.

Armstrong, Jeannette, Delphine Derickson, Lee Maracle, and Greg Young-Ing, eds. *We Get Our Living Like Milk from the Land*. Researched and compiled by the Okanagan Rights Committee and the Okanagan Indian Education Resource Society. Penticton, BC: Theytus, 1994.

Atteberry, Brian. *The Fantasy Tradition in American Literature*. Bloomington: Indiana University Press, 1980.

Blasingame, Jim. "From Wellpinit to Reardan: Sherman Alexie's Journey to the National Book Award." *ALAN Review* 35.2 (2008).

Boland, Kerry. "'We're All the Same People'? The (A)Politics of the Body in Sherman Alexie's *Flight*." *Studies in American Indian Literatures* 27.1 (2015): 70–95.

Bonilla-Silva, Eduardo, and David G. Embrick. "The (White) Color of Color Blindness in Twenty-First Century Amerika." *Race and Antiracism in Education*. Ed. E. Wayne Ross. Westport, CT: Praeger, 2006. 3–24.

Bradford, Clare. "Postcolonial Bildungsroman: Indigenous Subjects and Identity-Formation." *Waiguo Wenxue Yanjiu* 29.6 (2007): 10–18.

——— . *Reading Race: Aboriginality in Australian Children's Literature*. Melbourne: Melbourne University Publishing, 2001.

——— . *Unsettling Narratives: Postcolonial Readings of Children's Literature*. Waterloo, ON: Wilfrid Laurier University Press, 2007.

Bradford, Clare, Kerry Mallon, John Stephens, and Robyn McCallum. *New World Orders in Contemporary Children's Literature: Utopian Transformations*. New York: Palgrave, 2008.

Brayboy, Bryan McKinley Jones. "Toward a Tribal Critical Race Theory in Education." *Urban Review* 37.5 (2005): 425–46.

Brooks, Lisa. *The Common Pot: The Recovery of Native Space in the Northeast*. Minneapolis: University of Minnesota Press, 2008.

Bruce, Heather E., Anna E. Baldwin, and Christabel Umphrey. "*Flight* and *The Absolutely True Diary of a Part-Time Indian*: Post-9/11 Reconciliation." *Sherman Alexie in the Classroom: "This Is Not a Silent Movie. Our Voices Will Save Our Lives."*

Ed. Heather E. Bruce, Anna E. Baldwin, and Christabel Umphrey. Urbana, IL: National Council of Teachers of English, 2008. 111–31.

Bruchac, Joseph. *The Heart of a Chief*. New York: Penguin, 1998.

——. *Hidden Roots*. New York: Scholastic, 2004.

——. *Killer of Enemies*. New York: Lee & Low, 2013.

——. *Skeleton Man*. New York: HarperCollins, 2001.

Bruyneel, Kevin. *The Third Space of Sovereignty: The Postcolonial Politics of U.S.-Indigenous Relations*. Minneapolis: University of Minnesota Press, 2007.

Budde, Robert. "Codes of Canadian Racism: Anglocentric and Assimilationist Cultural Rhetoric." *Home-Work: Postcolonialism, Pedagogy, and Canadian Literature*. Ed. Cynthia Sugars. Ottawa, ON: University of Ottawa Press, 2004. 245–56.

Cadden, Mike. "The Irony of Narration in the Young Adult Novel." *Children's Literature Association Quarterly* 25.3 (2000): 146–54.

Campbell, Maria. *Halfbreed*. Toronto: McClelland and Stewart, 1973.

Canada. Indian and Northern Affairs. *Gathering Strength: Canada's Aboriginal Action Plan*. Minister of Indian Affairs and Northern Development, 1997. http://www.publications.gc.ca.

Canada. Indigenous and Northern Affairs. "National Inquiry into Missing and Murdered Indigenous Women and Girls." Government of Canada, 2016. http://www.canada.ca.

Canada. Justice. Canadian Multiculturalism Act (R.S.C. 1985, c.24, 4th Supp.; 1988, c.31, assented to 21 July 1988). *Government of Canada: Justice Laws Website*. Minister of Justice, 2011. http://laws.justice.gc.ca/eng.

Canada. Truth and Reconciliation Commission. *Final Report*. Truth and Reconciliation Commission of Canada, 2015. http://www.trc.ca.

Carpenter, Susan. "Misfit." Review of *The Absolutely True Diary of a Part-Time Indian*, by Sherman Alexie. *Los Angeles Times*, 16 Sept. 2007.

Clark, Beverly Lyon. *Regendering the School Story: Sassy Sissies and Tattling Tomboys*. New York: Garland, 1996.

Club Native. Dir. Tracey Deer. National Film Board of Canada, 2008.

Cook-Lynn, Elizabeth. "The American Indian Fiction Writers: Cosmopolitanism, Nationalism, the Third World, and First Nation Sovereignty." *Why I Can't Read Wallace Stegner and Other Essays: A Tribal Voice*. Madison: University of Wisconsin Press, 1996. 78–96.

Cormier, Robert. *The Chocolate War*. New York: Random House, 1974.

"Culture in the Classroom for School Success." *Native America Calling*. Podcast. 28 Mar.

2017. http://www.nativeamericacalling.com.

Currie, Noel Elizabeth. "Jeannette Armstrong and the Colonial Legacy." *Canadian Literature* 124–25 (1990): 138–52.

Deer, Sarah. *The Beginning and End of Rape: Confronting Sexual Violence in Native America*. Minneapolis: University of Minnesota Press, 2015.

Deloria, Philip. *Playing Indian*. New Haven: Yale University Press, 1998.

Deloria, Vine, Jr. *Custer Died for Your Sins*. New York: Macmillan, 1969.

———. *We Talk, You Listen: New Tribes, New Turf*. New York: Macmillan, 1970.

Deloria, Vine, Jr., and Clifford M. Lytle. *The Nations Within: The Past and Future of American Indian Sovereignty*. Austin: University of Texas Press, 1984.

Deloria, Vine, Jr., and Daniel R. Wildcat. *Power and Place: Indian Education in America*. Golden, CO: Fulcrum, 2001.

Dimaline, Cherie. *The Marrow Thieves*. Toronto: Dancing Cats Books, 2017.

Doerfler, Jill. *Those Who Belong: Identity, Family, Blood, and Citizenship among the White Earth Anishinaabeg*. East Lansing: Michigan State University Press, 2015.

Driskill, Qwo-Li, Chris Finley, Brian Joseph Gilley, and Scott Lauria Morgensen, eds. *Queer Indigenous Studies: Critical Interventions in Theory, Politics, and Literature*. Tucson: University of Arizona Press, 2011.

Eastman, Charles Alexander (Ohiyesa). *Indian Boyhood*. Boston: Little, Brown, 1902.

Elliott, David W. *Law and Aboriginal Peoples in Canada*. 5th ed. Concord, ON: Captus, 2005.

Emberley, Julia. "History Lies in Fiction's Making and Unmaking: Jeannette Armstrong's *Slash*." *Thresholds of Difference: Feminist Critique, Native Women's Writing, Postcolonial Theory*. Toronto: University of Toronto Press, 1993.

Enoch, Jessica. "Resisting the Script of Indian Education: Zitkala-Ša and the Carlisle Indian School." *College English* 65.2 (2002): 117–41.

Episkenew, Jo-Ann. *Taking Back Our Spirits: Indigenous Literature, Public Policy, and Healing*. Winnipeg: University of Manitoba Press, 2009.

Erdrich, Louise. *The Birchbark House*. New York: Hyperion, 1999.

———. *Chickadee*. HarperCollins, 2012.

———. *The Game of Silence*. HarperCollins, 2005.

———. "LaRose: An Evening with Louise Erdrich." Interview and discussion. Chicago Humanities Festival, Chicago, IL, 24 May 2016. *YouTube*. 24 June 2016. https://www.youtube.com/watch?v=gywvfuPsZtY.

———. *Makoons*. HarperCollins, 2016.

———. *The Porcupine Year*. HarperCollins, 2008.

———. *The Round House*. New York: Harper, 2012.

Fee, Margery. "Upsetting Fake Ideas: Jeannette Armstrong's *Slash* and Beatrice Culleton's *April Raintree*." *Canadian Literature* 124–25 (1990): 168–80.

Fletcher, Matthew L. M. *American Indian Education: Counternarratives in Racism, Struggle, and the Law*. New York: Routledge, 2008.

Flett, Donna Ellwood. "Deepening the Reading Experience of Drew Hayden Taylor's Canadian Vampire Novel for Adolescents." *Knowing Their Place? Identity and Space in Children's Literature*. Ed. Terri Doughty and Dawn Thompson. Newcastle upon Tyne, UK: Cambridge Scholars, 2011. 25–41.

Gansworth, Eric. *If I Ever Get Out of Here*. New York: Scholastic, 2013.

———. Reading of *If I Ever Get Out of Here* and Discussion. Native American Literature Symposium. Mystic Lake Casino Hotel, Prior Lake, MN. 28 Mar. 2014.

Gateward, Frances. "In Love and Trouble: Teenage Boys and Interracial Romance." *Where the Boys Are: Cinemas of Masculinity and Youth*. Ed. Murray Pomerance and Frances Gateward. Detroit: Wayne State University Press, 2005. 157–82.

Grauer, Lally. "Jeannette C. Armstrong: Translating a People and a Land." Osoyoos, BC: Osoyoos Museum, 2008. http://www.osoyoosmuseum.ca/ClassActs/women_armstrong.htm.

Green, Matthew. "A Hard Day's Knight: A Discursive Analysis of Jeannette Armstrong's *Slash*." *Canadian Journal of Native Studies* 19.1 (1999): 51–67.

Green, Rayna. "The Pocahontas Perplex: The Image of Indian Women in American Culture." *Massachusetts Review* 16.4 (1975): 698–714.

Gross, Lawrence William. "Cultural Sovereignty and Native American Hermeneutics in the Interpretation of the Sacred Stories of the Anishinaabe." *Wicazo Sa Review* 18.2 (2003): 127–34.

Hale, Janet Campbell. *The Owl's Song*. New York: Doubleday, 1974.

Harjo, Joy, and Gloria Bird, eds. *Reinventing the Enemy's Language: Contemporary Native Women's Writings of North America*. New York: Norton, 1997.

Haynes, Jeanette. "Unmasking, Exposing, and Confronting: Critical Race Theory, Tribal Critical Race Theory and Multicultural Education. *International Journal of Multicultural Education* 10.2 (2008): 1–15.

Highway, Tomson. *Kiss of the Fur Queen*. Toronto: Doubleday Canada, 1998.

Hodne, Barbara, and Helen Hoy. "Reading from the Inside Out: Jeannette Armstrong's *Slash*." *World Literature Written in English* 32.1 (1992): 66–87.

Hogan, Linda. *Solar Storms*. New York: Scribner, 1995.

Hopkinson, Nalo. Introduction. *So Long Been Dreaming: Postcolonial Science Fiction and Fantasy*. Ed. Nalo Hopkinson and Uppinder Mehan. Vancouver, BC: Arsenal, 2004.

Innes, Robert Alexander, and Kim Anderson, eds. *Indigenous Men and Masculinities: Legacies, Identities, Regeneration*. Winnipeg: University of Manitoba Press, 2015.

James, Kathryn. *Death, Gender, and Sexuality in Contemporary Adolescent Literature*. New York: Routledge, 2009.

Jasper, Inez. "Dancin' on the Run." Lets'emot Music, 2014.

Jesús, Melinda de. "'Two's Company, Three's a Crowd?': Reading Interracial Romance in Contemporary Asian American Young Adult Fiction." *Lit: Literature Interpretation Theory* 12.3 (2001): 313–34.

Johnson, Jan. "Healing the Soul Wound in *Flight* and *The Absolutely True Diary of a Part-Time Indian*. *Sherman Alexie: A Collection of Critical Essays*. Ed. Jeff Berglund and Jan Roush. Salt Lake City: University of Utah Press, 2011. 224–39.

Johnson, Naomi R. "Consuming Desires: Consumption, Romance, and Sexuality in Best-Selling Teen Romance Novels." *Women's Studies in Communication* 33.1 (2010): 54–73.

Johnston, Basil. *Indian School Days*. Norman: University of Oklahoma Press, 1988.

Jones, Manina. "Slash Marks the Spot: 'Critical Embarrassment' and Activist Aesthetics in Jeannette Armstrong's *Slash*." *West Coast Line* 33.3 (2000): 48–62.

Kamboureli, Smaro. *Scandalous Bodies: Diasporic Literature in English Canada*. Oxford: Oxford University Press, 2000.

Katanski, Amelia. *Learning to Write Indian: The Boarding School Experience and American Indian Literature*. Norman: University of Oklahoma Press, 2005.

Kelley, Robin D. G. *Yo' Mama's Disfunktional! Fighting the Culture Wars in Urban America*. Boston: Beacon, 1998.

Kertzer, Adrienne. "Not Exactly: Intertextual Identities and Risky Laughter in Sherman Alexie's *The Absolutely True Diary of a Part-Time Indian*." *Children's Literature* 40 (2012): 49–77.

King, Thomas. *Truth and Bright Water*. New York: Grove, 2001.

Krupat, Arnold. *The Turn to the Native: Studies in Criticism and Culture*. Lincoln: University of Nebraska Press, 1996.

Leggatt, Judith. "Critiquing Economic and Environmental Colonialism: Globalization and Science Fiction in *The Moons of Palmares*." *Science Fiction, Imperialism, and the Third World: Essays on Postcolonial Literature and Film*. Ed. Ericka Hoagland and Reema Sarwal. London: MacFarland, 2010. 127–40.

Leggatt, Judith, and Kristin Burnett. "Biting Bella: Treaty Negotiation, Quileute

History, and Why 'Team Jacob' Is Doomed to Lose." *Twilight and History*. Ed. Nancy R. Reagin. Hoboken, NJ: Wiley, 2010. 26–46.

Lipsitz, George. *The Possessive Investment in Whiteness: How White People Profit from Identity Politics*. Revised and expanded edition. Philadelphia: Temple University Press, 2006.

Lomawaima, K. Tsianina, and Teresa L. McCarty. *To Remain an Indian: Lessons in Democracy from a Century of Native American Education*. New York: Teachers College, 2006.

Lyons, Scott Richard. "Rhetorical Sovereignty: What Do American Indians Want from Writing?" *College Composition and Communication* 51.3 (2000): 447–68.

MacCann, Donnarae. "The Sturdy Fabric of Cultural Imperialism: Tracing Its Patterns in Contemporary Children's Novels." *Children's Literature* 33 (2005): 185–208.

Maracle, Lee. *Ravensong*. Vancouver, BC: Press Gang, 1993.

Marshall, Joseph, III. *In the Footsteps of Crazy Horse*. Illus. James Mark Yellowhawk. New York: Abrams, 2015.

McCallum, Robyn. *Ideologies of Identity in Adolescent Fiction: The Dialogic Construction of Subjectivity*. New York: Garland, 1999.

McKegney, Sam. *Magic Weapons: Aboriginal Writers Remaking Community after Residential School*. Winnipeg: University of Manitoba Press, 2007.

McNickle, D'Arcy. *Runner in the Sun*. Albuquerque: University of New Mexico Press, 1987.

Melamed, Jodi. *Represent and Destroy: Rationalizing Violence in the New Racial Capitalism*. Minneapolis: University of Minnesota Press, 2011.

Meyer, Stephenie. *Breaking Dawn*. New York: Little, Brown, 2008.

——. *Eclipse*. New York: Little, Brown, 2007.

——. *New Moon*. New York: Little, Brown, 2006.

——. *Twilight*. New York: Little, Brown, 2005.

Mohegan Tribe. "Our History: Uncas, Sachem and Statesman." Mohegan Tribe. https://www.mohegan.nsn.us/explore/heritage/our-history/sachem-uncas.

Molin, Paulette F. *American Indian Themes in Young Adult Literature*. Lanham, MD: Scarecrow, 2005.

Momaday, Natachee Scott. *Owl in the Cedar Tree*. 1965. Illus. Done Perceval. Lincoln: University of Nebraska Press, 1975.

Morton, Stephen. "First Nations Women's Writing and Anti-Racist Work in Institutional Locations: A Feminist Reading of Lee Maracle and Jeannette Armstrong." *Thamyris: Mythmaking from Past to Present* 6.1 (1999): 3–33.

Mosionier, Beatrice Culleton. *In Search of April Raintree*. 1983. Critical edition. Ed.
  Cheryl Suzack. Winnipeg, MB: Portage & Main, 1999.

National Council of Teachers of English. *English Companion*. Urbana, IL: NCTE, 2012.

Noodin, Margaret. *Bawaajimo: A Dialect of Dreams in Anishinaabe Language and
  Literature*. East Lansing: Michigan State University Press, 2014.

Ortiz, Simon. "Toward a National Indian Literature: Cultural Authenticity in
  Nationalism." Appendix. *American Indian Literary Nationalism*. Robert Warrior,
  Jace Weaver, and Craig S. Womack. Albuquerque: University of New Mexico
  Press, 2006. 253–60.

Owens, Louis. *Other Destinies: Understanding the American Indian Novel*. Norman:
  University of Oklahoma Press, 1992.

Parrish, Susan Scott. "The Female Opossum and the Nature of the New World." *William
  and Mary Quarterly* 54.3 (1997): 475–514.

Pattee, Amy S. *Reading the Adolescent Romance: Sweet Valley High and the Popular
  Young Adult Romance Novel*. New York: Routledge, 2011.

Petzold, Dieter. "Breaking the Colt: Socialization in Nineteenth-Century School
  Stories." *Children's Literature Association Quarterly* 15.1 (1990): 17–21.

Pocahontas. Dir. Mike Gabriel and Eric Goldberg. DVD. 1995. Disney, 2000.

Porzio, Allison. "Absolute Critical Literacy for Part-Time Critical Readers: Sherman
  Alexie's *The Absolutely True Diary of a Part-Time Indian* and Cultural Studies."
  English Record 58.1 (2008): 31–37.

Power, Susan. "Drum Kiss." *Moccasin Thunder: American Indian Stories for Today*. Ed.
  Lori Marie Carlson. New York: HarperCollins, 2005. 140–52.

———. "Reunion." *Roofwalker*. Minneapolis: Milkweed, 2002. 166–71.

Prashad, Vijay. *Everybody Was Kung Fu Fighting: Afro-Asian Connections and the Myth of
  Cultural Purity*. Boston: Beacon, 2001.

Publishers Weekly. Review of *The Absolutely True Diary of a Part-Time Indian*. Sept.
  2007. https://www.publishersweekly.com.

Pugh, Tison, and David L. Wallace. "Heteronormative Heroism and Queering the
  School Story in J. K. Rowling's Harry Potter Series." *Children's Literature
  Association Quarterly* 31.3 (2006): 260–81.

Pulitano, Elvira. *Toward a Native American Critical Theory*. Lincoln: University of
  Nebraska Press, 2003.

Ramirez, Renya K. *Native Hubs: Culture, Community, and Belonging in Silicon Valley and
  Beyond*. Durham, NC: Duke University Press, 2007.

Reder, Deanna. Preface. *Troubling Tricksters: Revisioning Critical Conversations*. Ed.

Deanna Reder and Linda M. Morra. Waterloo, ON: Wilfrid Laurier University Press, 2012. vii–ix.

Reese, Debbie. *American Indians in Children's Literature*. Blog. Debbie Reese, 2013. https://americanindiansinchildrensliterature.blogspot.com.

Reimer, Mavis. "Introduction: Discourses of Home in Canadian Children's Literature." *Home Words: Discourses of Children's Literature in Canada*. Ed. Mavis Reimer. Waterloo, ON: Wilfrid Laurier University Press, 2008. xi–xx.

"Rezpect Our Water: Sign Our Petition." Standing Rock Youth. *YouTube*. 15 Sept. 2016. https://www.youtube.com/watch?v=XL0aq05t7ds.

Rifkin, Mark. *The Erotics of Sovereignty: Queer Native Writing in the Era of Self-Determination*. Minneapolis: University of Minnesota Press, 2012.

Rinaldi, Ann. *The Second Bend in the River*. New York: Scholastic, 1997.

Rix, Zara. *Speculating the Child Citizen*. Diss. Storrs: University of Connecticut, 2016.

Robinson, Eden. *Monkey Beach*. New York: Houghton Mifflin, 2000.

Roediger, David R. *Colored White: Transcending the Racial Past*. Berkley: University of California Press, 2002.

Saldanha, Louise. "Bedtime Stories: Canadian Multiculturalism and Children's Literature." *Voices of the Other: Children's Literature in the Postcolonial Context*. Ed. Roderick McGillis. New York: Garland, 1999. 165–76.

Sarkowsky, Katja. "A Decolonial (Rite of) Passage: Decolonization, Migration and Gender Construction in Jeannette Armstrong's *Slash*." *Zeitschrift für Anglistik und Amerikanistik* 49.3 (2001): 233–43.

Schwarz, Maureen Trudelle. "Native American Barbie: The Marketing of Euro-American Desires." *American Studies* 46.3–4 (2005): 295–326.

Seale, Doris, and Beverly Slapin, eds. *A Broken Flute: The Native Experience in Books for Children*. Berkeley, CA: Oyate, 2005.

———, eds. *Through Indian Eyes: The Native Experience in Books for Children*. 5th ed. Berkeley, CA: Oyate, 2006.

"She Is Standing Up to the Dakota Access Pipeline for Herself and Her People." Upworthy, 24 Aug. 2016. *YouTube*. https://www.youtube.com/watch?v=s_sznbPUM0I.

Sheffer, Jolie A. *The Romance of Race: Incest, Miscegenation, and Multiculturalism in the United States, 1880–1930*. New Brunswick, NJ: Rutgers University Press, 2013.

Silko, Leslie Marmon. *Ceremony*. New York: Viking, 1977.

Simpson, Leanne. *Dancing on Our Turtle's Back: Stories of Nishnaabeg Re-creation, Resurgence and a New Emergence*. Winnipeg, MB: Arbeiter Ring, 2011.

Sinclair, Niigaanwewidam James. "Tending to Ourselves: Hybridity and Native Literary Criticism." *Across Cultures/Across Borders: Canadian Aboriginal and Native American Literatures*. Ed. Paul DePasquale, Renate Eigenbrod, and Emma LaRocque. Toronto: Broadview, 2010. 239–58.

Smith, Andrea. *Conquest: Sexual Violence and American Indian Genocide*. Cambridge, MA: South End, 2005.

Smith, Cynthia Leitich. E-mail message to the author. 19 Nov. 2012.

——. *Rain Is Not My Indian Name*. New York: HarperCollins, 2001.

——. "A Real-Live Blond Cherokee and His Equally Annoyed Soul Mate." *Moccasin Thunder: American Indian Stories for Today*. Ed. Lori Marie Carlson. New York: HarperCollins, 2005. 33–41.

Smith, Paul Chaat, and Robert Allen Warrior. *Like a Hurricane: The Indian Movement from Alcatraz to Wounded Knee*. New York: New Press, 1996.

Sneve, Virginia Driving Hawk. *When Thunders Spoke*. Illus. Oren Lyons. Lincoln: University of Nebraska Press, 1974.

Spack, Ruth. *America's Second Tongue: American Indian Education and the Ownership of English, 1860–1900*. Lincoln: University of Nebraska Press, 2002.

Standing Bear, Luther. *My Indian Boyhood*. 1931. Lincoln: University of Nebraska Press, 1988.

Sterling, Shirley. *My Name Is Seepeetza*. Toronto: House of Anansi Press, 1992.

Stewart, Michelle Pagni. "The 'Homing In' of Howard Camp: Hidden Roots in Joseph Bruchac's *Hidden Roots*." *Children's Literature* 39 (2011): 144–68.

TallBear, Kim. *Native American DNA: Tribal Belonging and the False Promise of Genetic Science*. Minneapolis: University of Minnesota Press, 2013.

Taylor, Drew Hayden. "Author Interview: Drew Hayden Taylor on *The Night Wanderer: A Native Gothic Novel*." Interview with Cynthia Leitich Smith. *Cynsations*. Blog. 13 Nov. 2008. http://cynthialeitichsmith.blogspot.com.

——. *Funny, You Don't Look Like One: Observations of a Blue-Eyed Ojibway*. Penticton, BC: Theytus Books, 1996.

——. *Further Adventures of a Blue-Eyed Ojibway: Funny, You Don't Look Like One, ~~Too~~ Two*. Penticton, BC: Theytus Books, 1999.

——. *Furious Observations of a Blue-Eyed Ojibway: Funny, You Don't Look Like One, ~~Two~~ Three*. Penticton, BC: Theytus Books, 2002.

——. *Futile Observations of a Blue-Eyed Ojibway: Funny, You Don't Look Like One, Four*. Penticton, BC: Theytus Books, 2004.

——. "I Just See Myself as an Old-Fashioned Storyteller: A Conversation with Drew

Hayden Taylor." Interview with John Moffat and Sandy Tait. *Canadian Literature* 183 (2004): 72–86.

——. "An Interview with Drew Hayden Taylor." Interview with Birgit Däwes. *Contemporary Literature* 44.1 (2003): 1–18.

——. *Motorcycles and Sweetgrass: A Novel.* Toronto: A. A. Knopf Canada, 2010.

——. *The Night Wanderer: A Graphic Novel.* Illus. Mike Wyatt. Adap. Alison Kooistra. Toronto: Annick, 2013.

——. *The Night Wanderer: A Native Gothic Novel.* Toronto: Annick, 2007.

Thompson, Melissa Kay. "A Sea of Good Intentions: Native Americans in Books for Children." *The Lion and the Unicorn* 25.3 (2001): 353–74.

Tillett, Rebecca. "'Your Story Reminds Me of Something': Spectacle and Speculation in Aaron Carr's *Eye Killers.*" *ARIEL* 33.1 (2002): 149–73.

Tilton, Robert S. *Pocahontas: The Evolution of an American Narrative.* Cambridge: Cambridge University Press, 1994.

Tingle, Tim. *How I Became a Ghost: A Choctaw Trail of Tears Story.* Oklahoma City: RoadRunner Press, 2013.

Treuer, Anton, et al. *Awesiinyensag: Dibaajimowinan Ji-Gikinoo'amaageng.* Minneapolis: Wiigwaas Press, 2010.

Trinoskey, C. Kelli. Review of *The Absolutely True Diary of a Part-Time Indian. Columbus Dispatch*, 22 Oct. 2007.

Trites, Roberta Seelinger. *Disturbing the Universe: Power and Repression in Adolescent Literature.* Iowa City: University of Iowa Press, 2000.

——. "Queer Discourse and the Young Adult Novel." *Children's Literature Association Quarterly* 23.3 (1998): 114–19.

——. "Theories and Possibilities of Adolescent Literature." Introduction. *Critical Theory and Adolescent Literature.* Spec. issue of *Children's Literature Association Quarterly* 21.1 (1996): 2–3.

——. *Twain, Alcott, and the Birth of the Adolescent Reform Novel.* Iowa City: University of Iowa Press, 2007.

TuSmith, Bonnie. *All My Relatives: Community in Contemporary Ethnic American Literatures.* Ann Arbor: University of Michigan Press, 1993.

Van Camp, Richard. *The Lesser Blessed.* Vancouver: Douglas & McIntyre, 1996.

Van Styvendale, Nancy. "The Trans/Historicity of Trauma in Jeannette Armstrong's *Slash* and Sherman Alexie's *Indian Killer.*" *Studies in the Novel* 40.1–2 (2008): 203–24.

Vizenor, Gerald. *Manifest Manners: Narratives on Postindian Survivance.* 1994. Lincoln:

University of Nebraska Press, 1999.

Wagamese, Richard. *Keeper'n Me*. Toronto: Doubleday, 1994.

Warrior, Robert. *Tribal Secrets: Recovering American Indian Intellectual Traditions*. Minneapolis: University of Minnesota Press, 1995.

Weaver, Jace, Craig S. Womack, and Robert Warrior. *American Indian Literary Nationalism*. Albuquerque: University of New Mexico Press, 2006.

Weaver, Roslyn. "Smudged, Distorted, and Hidden: Apocalypse as Protest in Indigenous Speculative Fiction." *Science Fiction, Imperialism, and the Third World: Essays on Postcolonial Literature and Film*. Ed. Ericka Hoagland and Reema Sarwal. London: MacFarland, 2010. 99–114.

Welch, James. *Winter in the Blood*. New York: Harper, 1974.

We Matter Campaign. "What Is We Matter?" We Matter. https://wemattercampaign. org/about/.

We Need Diverse Books. "About WNBD." https://diversebooks.org/about-wndb/.

Wilkins, David E., and K. Tsianina Lomawaima. *Uneven Ground: American Indian Sovereignty and Federal Law*. Norman: University of Oklahoma Press, 2001.

Williams, Sarah T. "Man of Many Tribes." *Star Tribune* [Minneapolis], 23 Mar. 2011.

Womack, Craig S. *Drowning in Fire*. Tucson: University of Arizona Press, 2001.

———. Personal conversation. 15 Nov. 2012.

———. "Theorizing American Indian Experience." *Reasoning Together*: *The Native Critics Collective*. Ed. Craig S. Womack, Daniel Heath Justice, and Christopher B. Teuton. Norman: University of Oklahoma Press, 2008. 353–410.

Wurth, Erika. *Crazy Horse's Girlfriend*. Chicago: Curbside Splendor, 2014.

Zitkala-Ša. "Impressions of an Indian Childhood." *Atlantic Monthly* 85 (1900): 37–47. Electronic Text Center, University of Virginia Library.

———. "An Indian Teacher among Indians." *Atlantic Monthly* 85 (1900): 381–86. Electronic Text Center, University of Virginia Library.

———. "The School Days of an Indian Girl." *Atlantic Monthly* 85 (1900): 185–94. Electronic Text Center, University of Virginia Library.

Zobel, Melissa Tantaquidgeon. Guest Lecture. Native American Literature. University of Connecticut, Storrs, CT. 16 Nov. 2011.

———. [Melissa Jayne Fawcett]. *The Lasting of the Mohegans: Part I, The Story of the Wolf People*. Uncasville, CT: The Mohegan Tribe, 1995.

———. "Magical Futurism: Raising the Undead in American Indian Literature." Panel presentation. University of Connecticut, Storrs, CT. 16 Nov. 2011.

———. [Melissa Jayne Fawcett]. *Medicine Trails: The Life and Lessons of Gladys*

Tantaquidgeon. Tucson: University of Arizona Press, 2000.

———. Mohegan History and Culture Presentation. University of Connecticut, Storrs, CT. 19 Nov. 2008.

———. *Oracles*. Albuquerque: University of New Mexico Press, 2004.

———. "The View from Crow Hill." Interview with Mandy Suhr-Sytsma. *Studies in American Indian Literatures* 27.2 (2015): 80–95.

———. *Wabanaki Blues*. Scottsdale, AZ: Poisoned Pencil, 2015.

Index